THE SHAAR PRESS

THE JUDAICA IMPRINT
FOR THOUGHTFUL PEOPLE

THE SHAAR PRESS

THE
PROTOCOLS

A NOVEL BY
YITZCHAK PARKER

TRANSLATED BY
LIBBY LAZEWNIK

Published by **SHAAR PRESS**

This is a work of fiction. Names, characters, places, and incidents are either the product of the
author's imagination or are used fictitiously. Any resemblance to actual persons, living or dead,
or locales is entirely coincidental.

Distributed by MESORAH PUBLICATIONS, LTD.
4401 Second Avenue / Brooklyn, N.Y 11232 / (718) 921-9000

Distributed in Israel by SIFRIATI / A. GITLER
6 Hayarkon Street / Bnei Brak 51127, Israel

Distributed in Europe by LEHMANNS
Unit E, Viking Business Park, Rolling Mill Road / Jarrow, Tyne and Wear, NE32 3DP/ England

Distributed in Australia and New Zealand by GOLDS WORLD OF JUDAICA
3-13 William Street / Balaclava, Melbourne 3183 / Victoria Australia

Distributed in South Africa by KOLLEL BOOKSHOP
Northfield Centre / 17 Northfield Avenue / Glenhazel 2192, Johannesburg, South Africa

ISBN 10: 1-42261-444-1 / ISBN 13: 978-1-42261-444-0

Custom bound by Sefercraft, Inc. / 4401 Second Avenue / Brooklyn N.Y. 11232

1

Marjayoun, Southern Lebanon, September 2008

ECHOES OF DISTANT EXPLOSIONS SHATTERED THE SILENCE of the dark night. The nine-man *Sayeret Matkal* team lay hidden among the boulders, watching what they had been told was the mouth of a cave. The Israeli Air Force pilots responsible for the explosions were performing a secondary function this night: distracting the enemy's attention. The real and crucial mission would be far quieter.

The intelligence they had received claimed with certainty that behind the bush they were reconnoitering lay a cave that served as forward Hezbollah headquarters on the Israeli front. For two hours now, they had been lying here without moving—waiting for positive proof that Salakh al Ovid was inside.

"Your mission is *not* to destroy the bunker," the company commander had stressed at their final briefing. "Leave that to the air force. What we need from you is Salakh al Ovid, a senior officer in Hezbollah's military arm, and a major strategist. If we can get our hands on him, we'll gain not only information, but also a sharp drop in the quality of Hezbollah's performance. Understood?"

The prevailing belief is that the lives of elite commandos are as intriguing as they're portrayed in novels. While it is true that such moments do exist, there are also long, monotonous hours of training exercises and surveillance. Major Ami Drori was second-in-command in the present action, answering only to Lieutenant Colonel Guy Ben-Dov. Ami Drori's role in the many successful missions in which he had participated had resulted in his unusually rapid rise through the ranks.

This was also the reason why, though he was due for a break, his leave had been postponed until after the current operation. The army's high command hung a great many hopes on Salakh's capture. His absence, it was reckoned, would shorten the war in a meaningful way. For this reason, the chief of staff had made sure that orders for this specific mission came directly from the "pit," the secure underground facility in the Rabin military base in Tel Aviv.

Both senior officers and men who had fought at his side claimed that Ami was the best soldier in the IDF. His wide-ranging ability, strong personality, and dedication to the mission had turned him into a precise and lethal weapon. A weapon you wanted to have at your side in a battle. The interesting thing was that, despite all of this, he was a modest man who didn't brag about his rank or accomplishments, claiming that he was simply lucky. Someone up there was watching over him.

Suddenly a voice brought the radio to life. "Abort! Abort! Return to the rendezvous point immediately!"

The figures among the boulders stirred slowly to life. "What happened?" Ben-Dov asked.

"The mission has been exposed! I repeat: the mission has been exposed! A large enemy contingent is on its way to you. Leave immediately!"

Ami seized the radio with a steady hand. "Does that mean that Salakh al Ovid *is* here?"

"Positive. But don't even think about it. Get out of there *now*!"

"You heard him, guys. Fold it up," Guy ordered.

Within thirty seconds, all their equipment was packed away and the unit was on the move. Guy Ben-Dov led the group for a few meters—and came to a sudden halt. "Where's Ami?" he asked sharply. He knew Ami Drori well enough to have an inkling of the answer.

"Ami! What do you think you're doing?" he hissed into his communications device. "That was an explicit order. You're putting the whole team at risk!"

Several long seconds of static were heard before the answer came. "Go on. I'll catch up with you."

Guy swore under his breath. As talented a soldier as Ami was, that did not excuse such insubordination. It was not the first time Ami had acted exactly as he pleased—but this time, he was endangering his friends. Guy personally planned to make sure Ami paid dearly for this. That was all he needed—for every soldier to do whatever he wanted.

He told headquarters what had happened. "How much time before we're intercepted?"

"Five minutes! Get him out of there now! We can't afford another soldier taken captive—and especially not a soldier of his caliber!"

Guy lifted his Tavor Assault Rifle and aimed it at Ami's retreating figure. Just as he had suspected: Ami was approaching the bush that concealed the cave mouth, and starting to slip inside.

"He's continuing the penetration. I have him in my rifle sights."

As commander of an elite unit, he could not afford to be overly emotional. His only consideration on the battlefield had to be the mission's success—at a reasonable cost. He watched Ami push aside the bush to expose the dark entrance. Only four minutes left before the enemy was upon them. Not enough time to go after Ami and force him to turn back. On the other hand, he could not endanger the rest of the unit.

"If you have a clear line of sight, you are authorized to take him down," came the dry order.

Guy had just been told to shoot his own man.

Tel Aviv's logic was cold and incisive. Another soldier must not be allowed to fall into Hezbollah's hands, to be used as a bargaining chip—especially not a soldier of such senior rank.

Guy hesitated. The fine line between a courageous call and an illegal order had never been more blurred. There had been operations in which he had sent soldiers to their deaths, but shooting one of his own men was another thing entirely.

No one would ever know whether he'd had a clean shot. "I lost him. He's gone inside."

"For G-d's sake, get out of there now!"

The soldiers stared at their commander in disbelief. Retreat from their position—and abandon Ami? This ran counter to all the values that had been instilled in them. But each and every one of them had undergone harsh survival training, and they were aware that being taken prisoner was always a possibility. They also knew that what Ami had done—disobeying a direct order at the height of an operation in enemy territory—was unforgivable. Not even his rank could excuse such conduct.

They turned rapidly and began moving toward the rendezvous point, weapons drawn. Muffled gunfire alerted them that something was happening back at the cave. They did not slacken their pace. Perhaps they would try to free Ami Drori from his Hezbollah captors in some future operation; for now—may Heaven protect him.

They reached the meeting point in three minutes. A Black Hawk helicopter was coming in for a landing, while two Apaches hovered above. The sound of distant fire from light weapons told them that Hezbollah fighters were moving their way. One of the helicopters turned in the direction of the fire, its mounted machine gun spraying the air. A division of over a hundred terrorists burst onto the scene and launched a mortal battle against the Israeli rescue force. RPG missiles flew at the choppers, missing them by inches.

"Let's go! Inside!" Guy shouted the moment the Black Hawk touched ground. He remained to the end, counting his men one by one. Seven soldiers and himself. One was missing. Ami.

He was poised to leap aboard and give the order for liftoff, when Ami's voice sounded suddenly in his earpiece. "I'll be there in thirty seconds!" he shouted, trying to make himself heard above the din of the powerful explosions.

"You madman! Where are you?" Guy didn't shout. He screamed.

"Coming at you from the north. I took a small detour."

Guy put his rifle's scope to his eye again—and stared incredulously. In the light of the exploding missiles he saw Ami dashing full speed toward them, a body draped over his shoulder in a fireman's hold. Amazing! The fool had gotten out of there alive.

He focused the scope on the wounded man and smiled for the first time that night. He recognized that face from all the briefings.

It was the face of Salakh al Ovid.

Tehran, Iran, 2012

Furious, the president of Iran kicked the leg of the expensive wooden desk in his office. He was sick and tired of the losers working on his nuclear program. It was always something: either a computer bug, or the disappearance of a top scientist, or else a simple equipment malfunction that held up the development of the long-awaited bomb.

The manufacture of a nuclear bomb using local resources was meant to be the jewel in the crown of his regime. He had gambled all his prestige on that burning ambition, yet the promised completion date had come and gone and the road ahead was still long. Had they really thought that the United States and Israel would not attempt to disrupt the process? He had explicitly warned that this was exactly what would happen, and still his people had not been able to prevent it. It was the second time this month that he had been informed that a scientist had mysteriously vanished. Heads would roll today. Someone wasn't taking this seriously enough.

American political commentators claimed that the Iranian president was a megalomaniac. Those close to him, however, knew that there was not a shred of truth to these claims. It was not for nothing that the Supreme Leader had chosen him to be president. His proven ability and his devotion to a goal were legendary. He knew exactly what was possible and what was not. With a cold, calculating assessment of the world, he had decided that if Iran wished to be a significant player on the world stage, she must become a nuclear power.

He also knew that the other world powers would not be happy about the addition of a new member to its exclusive nuclear club. But even here he was able to read the situation accurately, and to realize that—apart from some hurled snubs—they would fail to formulate a unified plan to prevent him from carrying out his threats. They were too divided to achieve any sweeping agreement.

Only the United States and Israel posed a real problem. The U.S., which for some reason regarded itself as the oldest child in the playground, issued a blistering denunciation here and imposed economic sanctions there. The U.S. would make trouble, but mostly the financial kind. In a practical sense, the Iranian president had nothing to fear from that country. It was to his benefit that America was preoccupied with the wars in Iraq and Afghanistan. Voices calling for the United States to stop interfering with the rest of the world—especially in the face of America's deteriorating economy—were growing stronger. And the American military, already spread thin on two fronts, did not relish the prospect of yet another one.

Taken altogether, these things added up to one prediction: the mighty US superpower would not do a thing.

But Israel... Israel was another story. A nation of madmen who acted more or less as they saw fit, come what may. He was well aware of Israel's attack on Iraq's nuclear reactor in Saddam Hussein's day and, later, on the reactor that Syria's Assad had attempted to build secretly. There was no reason for them not to do the same thing now—unless they were seriously deterred.

The president of Iran knew that Israel simply could not afford to allow his country to achieve nuclear capability. Those hypocrites, who had been concealing their own nuclear bombs for decades, were pleading with the world to stop him, as though they were the victims. Ever since the Holocaust, the Israelis had been playing on European guilt to obtain more and more power.

Meanwhile, he had been deploying his soldiers like a seasoned general. With Hezbollah planted to the north, Syrian and Iranian weaponry in Gaza to the south, and good relations between Iran and Egypt's new leadership, Israel would not be quick to attack.

The backlash would be very painful, especially in light of how weak and whimpering the Israeli public had become.

Nevertheless, he knew they *would* attack. The moment it became clear to them that Iran was nearing its goal, they would attack. He was preparing for that too, increasing his air power, installing a new early-warning radar system, adding to his stockpile of long-range missiles capable of targeting Tel Aviv. And, of course, a massive military weapons buildup—courtesy of the Russians.

As a seasoned politician, he knew how to identify conflicting interests in the world arena and how to turn them to his advantage. He had been watching with interest the developing friendship between Russia and China against the United States: an alliance between a superpower of the recent past and a superpower of the near future—pitted against the sole present-day superpower. This friendship was playing itself out in many areas, and he was adept at using it to maximum advantage when it came to U.N. votes on sanctions against Iran.

For the first time, the world was not submissively kowtowing to the United States. Russia and China stood proudly before her, preventing her from taking forceful action against Iran. In fine political double-speak, they said that Iran should certainly not be allowed to build a nuclear bomb—but that the world's response should be verbal rather than violent. Negotiations and financial responses, they urged, should be put into play. In other words, Iran should be free to do as she pleased.

Though the American sanctions were a bit hampering, an oil-rich regime such as Iran could survive a difficult period—as long as Russia continued purchasing oil from her, in exchange for weapons.

But the clock was ticking. The race to the nuclear prize was nearing the finish line. If the Iranian president succeeded in building a bomb before he was attacked, he would be the victor. No government would dare attack a nuclear power that had no hesitation about using its power—not even Israel. A minimal bombardment could set Israel back at least fifty years. True, Israel's reaction would be strong, and it would hurt. He also knew about the Israeli submarines bearing the "morning after" retaliation. Still, vast Iran would be capable of surviving what tiny Israel couldn't.

But now—there was yet another report of a missing scientist. How in the world did they lose people like screws that fell to the floor? That scientist was supposed to be under 24-hour surveillance! He'd have to put an end to this if he wanted his program to succeed.

Under normal circumstances, he would have pressed a buzzer summoning his personal secretary to his office. In his fury, he chose to stalk out himself and shout at the fellow to bring him the head of General Intelligence for questioning. He flung open his door, and paused in surprise at the sight of the man in the waiting room.

"What were you thinking, to leave my good friend waiting around like this?" he asked his secretary without missing a beat. He smiled at his honored visitor. "I came out the minute I heard you were here! Come in. I hope you haven't been waiting long."

General Karmiansky was unimpressed by the blatant flattery. "I've been here ten minutes, but that fool didn't let me in. I hope he had a good reason!"

"You told me not to let anyone in until you finished your phone call, sir," the secretary defended himself nervously. He realized that he had made a huge error in judgment.

"Idiot! General Karmiansky is not just anyone! He's the head of the cooperative team working with Russia. He gets to see me even before the king of Saudi Arabia. Understand?"

The secretary was still nodding his head rapidly as the Iranian president ushered his Russian friend into his office.

"I'll get rid of him this very day. I cannot believe he made you wait. He's going to pay for that!" the president vowed.

The Russian accepted the apology and took the chair he was offered. The president walked to his own chair and sat down. The last thing he needed now was to alienate the Russians, who were by and large his most important supporters.

"How can I help you, my friend?" he asked, all traces of his former anger gone.

"The correct question is not how *you* can help *me*," the other man replied, "but how *I* can help *you*." He leaned forward as though about to impart a secret, and lowered his voice even though he knew it was not at all necessary. The room was soundproofed and no one outside could hear a word.

"I heard about Dr. Hamiri's disappearance. And I also heard that he supplied valuable intelligence to the Israelis. Accurate information about the progress of Iran's nuclear program."

This time, the president was unable to conceal his anger. *He* had only just heard about the scientist's disappearance—and the Russians already knew where he was and with whom he had spoken. Somebody's head was surely going to roll!

"How do you know that?" he demanded—and immediately regretted the question. The Russian, he knew, would never reveal his sources.

"You know very well I can't tell you that," came the expected reply. "But I *can* tell you that the Israelis are very worried about your progress."

"So what else is new?" the president grinned. "It seems to me that apart from you people, the whole world thinks I'm trying to commit suicide."

"Yes. But here's something new: they've decided to attack."

The Iranian president jerked upright. "When?" he asked tensely. This information was worth millions. Billions.

"Within six months. Before you reach the critical mass in uranium enrichment."

The president stood up and began pacing around the room like a caged lion. The general watched him without a word. He'd been the head liaison man for years, and he knew when to squeeze and when to ease the pressure. He could guess at the thoughts that were whirling through the president's clever mind. He was thinking about the reactors' defense system, their dispersal in several locations in order to make an air strike more difficult, their proximity to population centers in order to delegitimize any attack on them, the depth at which several of the reactors had been built, and the air-defense system that Iran had just purchased from Russia at a staggering cost. Although the system was excellent, its Iranian operators would need a great deal more training before they reached the level of their Russian instructors.

"Do the Americans know?" the president asked suddenly.

"They have not authorized the strike, and they are certainly not prepared to participate in it. But they 'understand' Israel's need, and will not interfere."

"So it's us against Israel." Abruptly, the Iranian sat down. "It won't be easy for either side. The price they'll pay for the attack will be heavy, but so will the cost to us. How good is their intelligence?"

"Fairly good. Good enough to let them achieve their aim: delaying nuclear production."

The president chewed his lip as he always did when under pressure. The Supreme Leader of the Revolutionary Guard was liable to oust him after such a confrontation. A confrontation in which he would lose all hope of attaining the nuclear bomb.

He resumed his pacing as his mind worked on devising his next step. He must prepare the army and send word to Hezbollah and Hamas. Perhaps it would be best to strike first—though that would merely provide justification for an Israeli offensive against Iran.

The general watched him with interest, reading his thoughts and deliberations. The Iranian was no fool. The president fully grasped the ramifications of this valuable information. The general gave the man a few minutes to play out in his mind all the scenarios before he spoke.

"I have a proposal for you," he said at last. "A proposal that must not leave this room. If it leaks, we will of course deny all involvement."

"I'm listening," the Iranian snapped. He needed no reminders of the gaps in Iran's intelligence network.

"The idea is simple," the Russian continued, as if he hadn't noticed the president's irritation. "There is just one thing that would cause Israel to abandon her attack. The idea has received approval in the highest circles. Something must happen to surprise the Israeli intelligence bureaus, something that would cause Israel to doubt her ability to achieve her aim, and to become incapable of estimating the level of your reaction."

"Thank you very much," the president burst out. "A minute ago, you said that they have a very accurate idea of our abilities."

The general was undeterred. "All you have to do is carry out a 'secret' nuclear test. An exercise in which a tactical nuclear bomb is exploded in some remote location in Iran. Count on the Americans and the Israelis to see the explosion. The surprise will be total: 'How did they come to have such a bomb? Have we overlooked a secret nuclear reactor?' These will be questions without answers. In such a situation, Israel will not dare attack. They will not know *what* to attack—and, even more, they will be afraid of nuclear retaliation against their country. And here is where my idea comes in: *we will supply you with a tactical nuclear bomb.* Just one, of course. And you will use it for one purpose only—the nuclear test."

He sat back and gave the stunned Iranian time to digest what he had said.

"Our interests are simple," he continued, when he estimated that the Iranian had reached the point of wondering what was motivating him. "We've invested a great deal of money in you, and even now your financial situation is not dazzling… And if we can worry the Americans a bit so that they have no time to meddle in our local politics—all the better."

The president gazed at the other man through narrowed eyes. He didn't like when the Russian did this, when he made an offer that Iran couldn't refuse. The simple fact was that he had no way out other than this Russian handout. He didn't like feeling needy.

But the proposal made sense. And it was also apparently his only recourse. He must prevent the coming attack, and he was fresh out of better ideas. Still, it bothered him to feel that he was being toyed with.

"How do you suggest we do this?" the president asked.

"The operation must remain as contained as possible. You, me, a few trusted people whom you will handpick. Any intelligence leak would damage the plan and put both you and me in an unpleasant position."

"Who, at your end, will take responsibility for this?"

"I—and I alone. This has no connection with our president, and certainly not with the Duma (the Russian parliament). It is a secret operation that answers only to me."

Once again, the Iranian president stood up and began circling the room, taking care not to meet the Russian's eyes. He was liking the daring idea more and more. Unexpected twists like this made him feel young and focused. This was going to be exciting and suspenseful, the kind of action he savored.

"All right," he agreed. He especially liked the notion that, should the plan backfire, the man in front of him would be the scapegoat. As far as he himself was concerned, let the whole world deride the nuclear test. But if the plot were revealed, the general would pay not only with his career, but with his liberty. This plot would not pass muster with the Russian public. Should the story come to light, the general would be spending the best years of his life in some remote Siberian prison. The Iranian enjoyed this idea. It gave him an edge over the Russian.

"I will gather a small, select group to deal with the logistics of the plan at our end. They will take their orders directly from you. I must say that it is a brilliant and daring plan. I've always known that you were a true friend of Iran."

The general nodded and smiled. Were it up to him, nothing at all would have been done. But the order had come from very high up, and in Russia one did not ask questions. Now all he had to do was arrange for the bomb and let events unfold on their own.

2

Jerusalem, Juen 2010

E VENING FELL OVER JERUSALEM'S SHAAREI CHESED neighborhood. The daytime traffic jams typical of its narrow, winding streets were forgotten. A sighing wind drew the leaves from the trees as a slow sunset peeked from between the Wolfson Towers. Pedestrians made their way home, stepping from the sidewalk to the street and back again. Another day was over.

An old stone building constructed in the unique style of the city housed Shiras Yisrael, a yeshivah for outstanding students. The yeshivah's history was bound up with the building. The two had existed together for generations. Since the yeshivah had been founded in the new neighborhood outside the Old City walls many years earlier, the building's value had risen steadily—until it now competed only with the luxury residential dwellings of Rechavia.

A story was told in the yeshivah about a real-estate magnate who offered the rosh yeshivah a fortune for the old, cramped building. "You'll be able to move into a spacious, modern facility where the students can learn Torah without interruption," the businessman had cajoled, while pointing at a cat slipping through a hole in the broken gate. "After all, a pleasant living space expands a person's mind!" he added knowledgeably.

But Rav Rubinstein had refused. Under no circumstances would he leave Shaarei Chesed, a neighborhood that had gained renown through the Torah luminaries that had graced it. He was not willing to give up the special atmosphere that reigned in its old streets.

The big beis medrash was higher than it was wide. Dozens of boys between the ages of 13 and 17 sat almost shoulder-to-shoulder, learning with great diligence throughout most of the day and night. The standing joke was that if the students could only have been seated vertically instead of horizontally, the beis medrash could easily have doubled the number it held.

At this cool early-evening hour in Jerusalem, the regular *mussar seder* was taking place. At precisely 7:00 p.m., the boys closed the Gemaras they had been learning during second *seder*, and opened a volume of *mussar*—each according to his choice—to delve into character improvement for half an hour, until supper.

Yisrael Davis sat in his usual seat on the right side of the room, poring over the Ramchal's *Mesillas Yesharim*. He related to the simple yet profound words he read. Even more, he felt deeply satisfied to be nearing completion of the *sefer*. He flipped through the pages he had already learned, and then counted those that were left. Not many! What joy! The mashgiach would be proud of him.

"Yisrael...," someone whispered in his ear. He lifted his eyes from the *sefer* and looked at Yossi, seated beside him. Yossi Goldfarb, tall and broad-shouldered, was a charismatic boy. Although he was in *shiur aleph* and only 14½, he was the strongest guy in the yeshivah. Even the older *bachurim* in *shiur gimmel* hesitated to start up with him.

"What's the matter?" Yisrael asked.

"Feel like going out tonight?" Yossi asked with an inviting grin.

Yisrael wasn't interested. He looked back down at his *sefer*. "How can I? It'll interfere with my learning." He slanted a glance at Yossi and whispered, "Maybe you can go alone this time?"

"You know I'm worth nothing without you." Yossi was either sincere, or trying to inflate his ego. "You're the best basketball player I know!"

Yisrael blushed, but he knew that it was true. Last Friday, they had played in Liberty Bell Park, which was within walking distance of the yeshivah—and they had not lost a single game.

"The mashgiach will kill us!" Yisrael protested, in a vain effort to make Yossi abandon the plan.

"He'll never know…" Hastily, Yossi looked down at his *sefer*. The mashgiach, who had been circulating through the beis medrash, was heading in their direction. Yisrael dropped his eyes to his *Mesillas Yesharim*, and read, "for you will see that pride is more present in one who is more foolish…" The words might have been written expressly for him. *If I'm proud of my skill at basketball, I'm apparently a fool…*

The mashgiach paused beside Yossi. Yisrael stopped breathing.

"Why did you switch seats?" the mashgiach, Rav Aharon Grossman, asked kindly but firmly.

"I wanted to learn with Yisrael," Yossi lied without missing a beat.

Rav Aharon's soft eyes gazed evenly at Yossi. "In that case, it's a pity you forgot to bring your *Mesillas Yesharim* along…"

Yisrael stirred uneasily in his seat, as though it was he who had been caught in a lie.

But Yossi didn't bat an eyelash. "Now that he's agreed," he said, "I'm on my way to get it!" With a sly wink at Yisrael, he closed his Gemara, stood up, and went over to a bookcase on the other side of the room.

Rav Aharon took the empty seat beside Yisrael and riffled through the pages of his *sefer*. "Oh, I see that you're nearly ready to make a *siyum*!" he said encouragingly.

"Uh…yes," Yisrael whispered.

"You know that the Ramchal passed away at a very young age," the mashgiach continued. "He left this world at the age of only 39—and look how much he accomplished! If only we could do the same." He glanced into the *sefer* to see where Yisrael was up to, and read aloud, "'And our sages, may their memories be for a blessing, said that haughtiness is a sign of a paucity of Torah...' How true. Remember that, Yisrael," the mashgiach added as he stood up. "Try to stay away from haughty people. Haughtiness is a sign of a lack of Torah and *yiras Shamayim*."

Yossi, who'd remained at a safe distance until now, resumed his seat. "My father says that the mashgiach was a wild one when he was a boy. And he dares give me *mussar*!" He sat back in his seat and opened the *sefer* at random. "*Nu*, what do you say? Should we leave at 10? We can get to Liberty Bell Park by 10:15 and be back here by 11:15. An hour of play, and no one will notice a thing."

"And what if Yechiel notices that we're not here?" Yisrael asked, in a last, desperate attempt to wriggle out of the distressing invitation.

Yechiel Tzabar was the yeshivah's *av bayis*, dorm counselor. He was short, unpleasant looking, and still single at nearly 30. He was responsible for making sure that the boys got to bed at a reasonable hour and didn't wreck the dormitory. The boys didn't like him, both for his role and for his unyielding personality. He had no sense of humor at all. Very few of the *bachurim* treated him with respect, though he demanded it repeatedly. Like young boys everywhere, they gave him a hard time just for the fun of it. It was his good luck that the mashgiach relied on him completely; all he had to do was complain to the mashgiach about one of the boys, and that student would be quickly and severely punished.

Yisrael didn't care for Yechiel, but he tried to stay out of his way. Yossi, on the other hand, had turned bothering Yechiel into a national pastime. Not a night passed when Yossi did not make trouble for their dorm counselor.

"Believe me, Yechiel won't complain if I'm not around to drive him crazy one night," Yossi laughed. "He'd be happy if we left the dorm every night."

Yisrael returned his eyes to his *sefer*. "I don't think I'll go. I want to go to bed early tonight."

"Coward," Yossi hissed. "Scared that Yechiel the shrimp will tell on you. So *don't* come. I'll have fun without you." He glanced at his watch, which read 7:28 p.m., and slammed his *sefer* shut. "Gotta go—suppertime!"

Yisrael watched him head to the door, pausing to thump one or two *bachurim* on the shoulder on his way and to toss them a remark to make them laugh. Yossi was one of the lucky ones whom everyone wanted to please. Everyone wanted to be his friend; a compliment from him was considered a special thing. Yisrael felt a pang. He had disappointed Yossi. Yossi wanted them to go play basketball together, and he had refused.

He replaced the bookmark in his *sefer* and gently closed the book. Tomorrow, *b'ezras Hashem*, he'd continue.

On his way to supper, he wracked his brain for a way he could make up to Yossi for letting him down. But Yossi didn't seem to be suffering much from the disappointment. He sat at a table surrounded by a group of admirers and crowed, "Look at this *malawach*! More oil than dough! If the Maccabees had had this stuff, we'd never have had the miracle of Chanukah. Put a wick in it, and it'll burn for a month straight!" Not satisfied with words, he proceeded to demonstrate, squeezing the oil from the *malawach* into his plate. "Sammy's trying to kill us all! He's probably a mole, planted here by Hamas!"

Sammy Majdoul, the cook, emerged from the kitchen with a potful of eggs just in time to hear this announcement. He was a compact fellow in his 40's. Though shorter than Yossi, he was very strong and was one of the few in yeshivah who weren't afraid of him. He set his pot down on the central table and turned angrily to Yossi. "That's not funny! What do you think you're doing, making fun of food? What kind of behavior is that? Eh?"

"See for yourself!" Yossi said, pointing at his plate. "There must be a whole bottle of oil in each *malawach*. What happened—did someone donate a barrel of oil to the yeshivah?"

Sammy clenched his jaw in fury. He'd teach this kid a lesson if only he could. Someone had to educate him, and apparently his teachers weren't succeeding. If only someone would ask it of him, he'd be glad to put that insolent Yossi in his place. But no one had asked him, and he didn't want to lose his job. Without another word, he wheeled around and returned to the kitchen.

He could still hear the *yeshivah bachur* taunting him. "See?" he told his hilarious friends. "We caught him! Let him go back to his Arab friends in Gaza. He's trying to poison us!"

<hr />

Moscow, Russia, 1970

The Potgorsky family lived in a small apartment on the top floor of a tall residential building on Moscow's Chorozyo Street. The peeling old building contained many such flats, which were designated dwelling places for the middle or lower classes.

The Potgorsky family was not very different from most of their neighbors. Boris, the father, worked in the assembly line of a big steel factory for a minimal wage that barely managed to support his family. The mother was usually at home, though she occasionally took odd jobs to add a few kopeks to the household budget. But she, as opposed to her neighbors, did not allow poverty to rule her home. She used every spare minute to clean and organize the flat. Pretty pictures and curtains decorated the rooms in good taste. Dishes were never permitted to pile up in the sink, and the children were neatly dressed and well mannered.

Actually, not all the children. Mikhail, the youngest, was very different from his two older brothers. A contributing factor was the fact that they were tall and fair, while he was short and dark. They were handsome, while young Mikhail had been born with a face that looked perpetually embittered. A large nose in the middle of his face sealed his unprepossessing looks.

"*Zhid* (Jew)!" his big brothers teased him. "You must have been adopted!"

His bad nature and cruel and corrupt behavior sometimes made his parents wish that this were true, and that Mikhail was not their legal son. However, although Mikhail remained convinced that he had indeed been adopted, he was in reality the third and last scion of the Potgorsky family.

From his earliest days, he had always acted just as he pleased, with no thought for the consequences. Neither shouting, nor beating, nor pleading had the slightest effect; he continued doing what he wanted. He was not a stupid child; on the contrary, he'd been blessed with extraordinary abilities. He had a very quick grasp—another way in which he differed from his brothers—and his creativity was astounding. The different methods he used to hurt small animals or children weaker than he were original and brilliant. "Like the devil himself," the family priest once remarked.

Mikhail felt no connection to or affection for anyone or anything. Neither for his brothers, who had never refrained from subjecting him to a beating whenever he bothered them, nor for his parents, who were at their wits' end over him. The only thing that "helped" was a murderous thrashing that calmed him for a short time—or until he was out of his stern father's sight.

With time, even his mother, that gentle woman who so loved her other sons, and who accepted people almost without reservation, began to hate her youngest child. After all the things he had done, the priest —whose whispered prayers had no effect—told her that, for her own good, she'd be better off cutting such a satanic child out of her life. Though communism had rendered a large portion of the Russian population irreligious, Mrs. Potgorsky was a devout Catholic. And, "if the priest said so, the priest knew."

Mikhail posed a practical puzzle for all the educators to whom his parents appealed. He chose to be the "black sheep" of the family in every sense, and not just in his hair color. Instead of trying to compensate for his repugnant appearance, the exact opposite happened. He did everything in his power to justify the epithet that everyone had learned from his brothers: "Zhid!"

The negativity he experienced from his parents, his brothers, and the neighborhood children—who likewise delighted in taunting the strange boy—only encouraged him to hurt them again and again, no matter what happened to him as a result. Mikhail committed atrocious crimes. He teased animals, set fire to trash cans, and started up with anyone who came near. The severe beatings he suffered led him to stop being afraid of anything. What more could they do to him? He'd become inured to the pain. They all hated and despised him anyway. Let them all die!

Even before his 10th birthday, he was apprehended twice for damaging public property. Each time, he was treated to another sound thrashing from his father—to no effect. He skipped school regularly, though his teachers claimed that, with his sharp mind, he could be an excellent student. His problem was never a lack of ability. It was the fact that people hated him, and he hated them in return.

There was only one person in the world that Mikhail treated nicely. His name was Alex Kotorov.

Alex was Mikhail's age and sat next to him in school. The differences between the two were glaring. Where Mikhail was short and dark, Alex was tall and blond; where Mikhail was despised and rejected, Alex had friends wherever he went. He had a natural charm. Though not particularly intelligent or talented, he was a genius at human relations. Alex was the only child of Victor and Nadia Kotorov, who invested all of their hopes and efforts in him. Indeed, their son was pleasant and refined, and at the same time active, athletic, and accepted by his peers. He was possessed of a singularly attractive smile. His parents' friends envied them, not only for their money and influence, but also for the wonderful son they were raising.

No one knew why Alex liked the troublesome Mikhail, but it was a fact. Of all the children in the class who wanted his company, Alex chose wild Mikhail. Despite his classmates' disapproval, Alex treated Mikhail respectfully and sometimes invited him home so they could study together. Alex also tried his best to introduce Mikhail into the larger social circle—but failed. Mikhail wasn't interested. Alex alone was enough for him.

The Potgorsky family knew very well why Mikhail wanted Alex as a friend. It was not out of pure intentions as Alex believed. Mikhail had chosen him in a spirit of cold calculation. Victor Kotorov, Alex's father, was manager of the big steel factory in which Mikhail's father worked. Whenever Alex was around, Boris didn't dare beat his son, no matter what the provocation. The only times his family treated him nicely were when Alex came to visit. All at once, the Potgorskys became a model family. Mikhail's mother would offer their guest home-baked cookies and milk, his father would shake Alex's hand warmly, and Mikhail's brothers included him in their games. When Alex was in his house, Mikhail suddenly became the beloved son and the recipient of fond pinches on the cheek. Everyone would smile at him. For a short time, they were a genuine family. A loving family.

The moment Alex left, everything quickly reverted to normal. On one memorable occasion, not three seconds had passed after Alex left, before Mikhail's mother slapped him for bringing his friend home on the precise day that his father had chosen to bring home a set of silverware he'd "lifted" from the steel plant. "Your father's going to be fired because of you!" she shouted, with another smack for good measure.

Heaven knew, this had been Mikhail's plan. But, to his father's good fortune, Alex was not sharp-eyed. He scarcely knew what his father's factory produced. Though friendly and pleasant, he was not especially smart. Mikhail, who had ten times his intelligence, knew how to use him exactly as he wished. He invited Alex to his house at frequent intervals, and visited the Kotorov house just as often—if "house" was the right word to describe the mansion in which they lived.

Alex's parents welcomed Mikhail gladly. At first, it had troubled Mr. Kotorov that his son had chosen a friend from the lower classes—a friend whose father held a minor position on his factory's assembly line. While it was true that in the Soviet Union such class distinctions were not supposed to matter, and all citizens were considered equal…there was more equal and there was less equal. He'd have preferred to have his son make friends with someone on their own economic level—someone who lived in the luxury Rublyovka neighborhood in western Moscow that the Kotorovs did.

But in the end, he gave in gracefully. One could not choose another person's friends for him. He was not a parent who dictated what his child could or could not do. He loved his only son too much for that.

It was not surprising, then, that Mikhail was in the Kotorov house when the tragedy occurred.

It was a Thursday, at the height of the summer. It was a pleasant time of year in Moscow, and the temperature was a balmy 73 degrees. Mikhail played with Alex all day. His parents didn't mind that he wasn't home; in fact, they preferred for him to spend his time elsewhere. Alex's parents, in contrast, liked their son to stay close to home.

Evening fell. After enjoying a sumptuous dinner with Alex and his parents, Mikhail was ready to go home. Generally, Alex's mother would urge her husband to drive the boy home so that he would not have to make the long way on foot. Lately, however, Mikhail had been declining the offer. They didn't know it, but the last time his father had seen his boss driving his young son home, he'd flown into a rage. He had seized Mikhail and beaten him soundly. This filthy child of his irritated him to no end.

"Don't you ever bring him here again!" he'd shouted. "Do you think I'm stupid? Do you think I don't know that you wanted him to see that I left work a little early today? I could lose my job, and then where would you get food to eat? This is not a game!"

Mikhail didn't answer. Whenever he was beaten, he would withdraw into a remote part of himself that no one could access. He would enter his private world—a world that no one could approach, least of all his parents. But he learned that day not to let his father's boss drive him home anymore. He was always careful not to step too far out of bounds. It just might end in murder.

Tonight, Nadia Kotorov thought it would be nice if Mikhail slept over at his friend's house. The hour was late, and there was no school the next day. She didn't really like it when her son went into the poorer section of town to play at the Potgorskys. She preferred to keep him close to home. If Mikhail slept here, Alex would not have to go to him the following day.

The invitation made Mikhail very happy. It seemed he'd been hoping for it, for the minute the words were out of her mouth the boys began capering joyfully around the house. Smiling to see her son so happy, Mrs. Kotorov called Mrs. Potgorsky for permission.

Naturally, Mikhail's mother did not object. The two boys stayed up late, playing in Alex's room until Alex's mother came in and insisted that they go to bed.

The next morning, everything proceeded as usual. They ate breakfast, which included some foods and fruits that Mikhail had never tasted before. Then Victor Kotorov went to work, leaving the boys playing and his wife going about her various chores.

The moment Nadia saw her husband return home, she knew that something dreadful had happened. Victor never came home this early. He was a responsible and dedicated man who maintained a full calendar of inspections and appointments every day. She couldn't remember a single other time that he had returned before noon. His sober face confirmed that something had happened.

He signaled for his wife to leave the flower arranging she so adored and follow him into his study. After checking to make sure that the boys were out of earshot, he closed the door and told Nadia, "A big fire broke out in the Potgorsky's house last night. The rescue workers say that it must have been caused by a tipped-over candle or some such thing. Anyway, it spread rapidly, and… the whole place was destroyed."

Nadia sank into a nearby chair, her knees shaking. She hadn't expected this. "And…the family? The parents?"

He shook his head.

"The…children?" Her voice was nearly inaudible. She knew the answer even before her husband shook his head sadly again.

Mikhail was all alone in the world, without his brothers and with no mother or father to take care of him. And if she hadn't invited him to sleep here last night…he too would have been burned to death in the fire. The thought made a shiver pass through her body. He was her responsibility now. She was responsible for the fact that he was alive. It was up to her to give him the love and warmth that had been so cruelly and so unexpectedly snatched from him…

The sound of the childish voices, raised in their game, roused her from her shock. "He'll have to be told," she said quietly. "I think it's best that I do it. You take Alex out for a walk and tell him what happened. He's going to need help too… What a tragedy! The mother sounded so pleasant on the phone… I spoke to her just yesterday! It's hard to believe she's not here anymore. Unbelievable! He'll stay here for now, until some relatives can be found who are willing to take him in… What a terrible tragedy!"

<hr>

Jerusalem, June 2010

Ten o'clock. Night *seder* was over, and most of the *bachurim* had dispersed to their rooms. Yisrael, who would normally have lingered to learn a little longer, closed his Gemara and went to his room as well. He saw no point in dragging out his time over the Gemara. As it was, he hadn't been able to concentrate all night. His eyes had kept following Yossi, waiting to see him escape from the *beis medrash*.

But Yossi had apparently changed his plans. He had sat and learned with Mendy Markowitz, his *chavrusa*, as though he had no intention of going anywhere.

Perhaps the most impressive thing about Yossi was the fact that learning Gemara seemed not to pose any difficulty for him at all. It seemed as if he had inherited his quick grasp from his father, a serious *talmid chacham*. He would pick up the salient points in mere minutes, and asked good questions that often appeared in the various commentaries. The yeshivah's *ramim* (*roshei mesivta*) very much enjoyed discussing learning with him, and appreciated his knowledge and logical reasoning. They enjoyed his behavior and his arrogance a little less.

Yisrael was climbing the stairs at the exact moment Yossi came down, a black bag in his hand. "Last chance," he said with a smile, pausing for a moment.

Yisrael smiled too, feeling like a partner in crime. "You enjoy yourself. I'm dying of tiredness. Tell me all about it tomorrow…"

"See you!" Yossi continued down toward the gate. "If Yechiel asks, I wasn't feeling well."

Yisrael went to his room and lay down on his bed. He wanted to go! He loved playing basketball! But he also wanted to be a good *yeshivah bachur*…and good *yeshivah bachurim* didn't go out to play basketball at night—especially not in Liberty Bell Park, where there were plenty of secular boys whose speech was not especially refined… If there were a better alternative, a place to play with his fellow students, his indecision would have been worse. He remembered once asking his father if he could rent a lot so that Yisrael and his friends could play ball… How angry his father had been. "I didn't come to the Holy Land so that my son can be a basketball player!" He spoke Hebrew with a heavy American accent. "If you have time on your hands, you can sit and learn so that you'll succeed in yeshivah and become a *talmid chacham!*"

His father was a good man, but a very strict one. Maybe too strict. Yisrael had never been a troublemaker, but now and then he felt the need to rebel and do what he wanted instead of what his father wanted. Since his parents couldn't rent a lot or a gym, Yisrael and his friends went to play in Sacher Park, where there was a public playing field.

Yisrael's parents had made *aliyah* shortly after Yisrael was born. He remembered nothing of Monsey, New York, where they had lived before. From his mother he learned a little about his birthplace, but his father hardly ever talked about what had been before they had moved to the Givat Shaul neighborhood in Jerusalem.

Once, when he was small, he had heard something about a big quarrel between Tatty and his brother, Uncle Jeffrey. A fight that had made his father leave everything behind and move to Eretz Yisrael within a matter of weeks. What had they quarreled about? Yisrael didn't have a clue. He was forbidden to speak the name of Tatty's brother in the house, and Mommy tried to limit her stories about his rich uncle in America. To the best of Yisrael's knowledge, the brothers had had no contact at all in the past fourteen years. He wondered at the reason for such a serious break. But no answers were forthcoming.

Yisrael had two younger sisters: Bracha, 10, and the baby of the family, Tamar, who was 3. Sometimes, when he was younger, they used to pretend that Yisrael was their rich uncle from America who sent them presents on their birthdays. As they didn't even have a picture of him, they had to imagine how he looked.

It wasn't easy being the child of American parents. His friends would make fun of his mother's American accent when she called to him in Hebrew to come home. He'd laugh along with them, but inside he squirmed with mortification. If only his parents weren't different from everyone else's! He was able to recognize his father a mile off by the dented hat he wore. "*Hakadosh Baruch Hu* is not looking at my hat!" Rabbi Davis would declare whenever Yisrael brought up the subject. "He only cares about what's inside the hat."

His father's parents—Zaidy Moshe and Bubby Bracha—had died years ago. Zaidy, *a"h*, had owned a chain of luxury hotels in the United States, a chain that had apparently been divided on his death between his two sons, Tatty and Jeffrey. Maybe the quarrel had been about that...

Yisrael knew that his parents had money. He knew it by the large donations his father made, and the frequent visitors who came knocking on their door each night in search of *tzedakah*. Most of these supplicants would sit with Yisrael's father at the dining-room table and tell him the purpose of their visit. Each one left with a smile on his face.

They did not live like wealthy people. They lived in a three-bedroom apartment in Givat Shaul, an apartment that Yisrael's mother often claimed was too crowded. But his father would reply that there was plenty of room when people lived in harmony and peace. The kitchen was small and in need of a face-lift, the big table was old and a bit shaky, and the chairs had also seen better days. But the family never moved out, and never made improvements. Yisrael also could not remember when he had ever received money from his father for no reason. He always had to explain exactly why he needed the cash. Only after prolonged negotiations did he receive a little spending money. Yisrael wasn't a big spender; in general, he tried to follow the dictum often quoted by his father: "Who is rich? He who is content with his lot."

Right now, though, as he lay on his hard bed, he was not very happy with his lot. How he longed to play basketball! Yossi was having fun in Liberty Bell Park. And he? He would read a few pages in the boring book he'd borrowed from the yeshivah library, and go to sleep. And tomorrow it would be the same thing all over again. Much as he liked the dormitory, once in a while he would love to run about freely.

He pulled the thin blanket over him against the chill of the Jerusalem spring night. Without even bothering to take off his shoes, he fell into a troubled and frustrated sleep.

3

"YISRAEL, WAKE UP!"

Drowsily, he tried to open his eyes. "What's the matter? Is it morning already?"

"Yisrael, get up!" Yossi stood over his bed, shaking Yisrael's shoulder. "Get up! I need you!"

"What time is it?" Yisrael mumbled. "Is it 7 already?"

"No!" Yossi said. "It's the middle of the night. But you've got to help me. I'm in a little trouble."

All at once, Yisrael was fully awake. He sat up. What had happened? What kind of trouble?

"What time is it?" he asked again, as he searched for his yarmulke, which had fallen down the side of his bed.

"It's 2:30. I was playing basketball with some guys, and I got into a mess…"

"In Liberty Bell Park? I thought the lights go off much earlier there."

"True." Yossi was clearly laboring under a great deal of stress. "But I was playing with some guys, and when the lights went out they suggested that I go with them to a different basketball court. A court in Rechavia that I've never played in before. Apparently, it belongs to a secular high school or university..."

"*Nu*? So how'd you get in trouble?"

"Well... I played really well tonight. And there was one guy who thought *he* could play. So I made a bet with him..."

"You made a bet? About what? And how could you do that, anyway? We learned that you're not allowed to bet!" The questions burst out of Yisrael.

"Don't give me *mussar* in the middle of the night!" Yossi hissed angrily. "Don't you get it? I'm in trouble! I bet him a hundred shekels that I'd win the game. Where am I supposed to get a hundred shekels to pay him? You have to help me!"

Yisrael stared at him incredulously. "Are you trying to tell me that he's here now, waiting for his money?"

Yossi nodded slowly. "They're waiting outside."

"*They*? How many guys are you talking about?"

"There are four of them, and they're at least 18 years old. And if I don't give them the money, I won't only be in hot water with the yeshivah—they'll also beat me to a pulp."

Yisrael had never seen the confident Yossi so terrified and at a loss. He liked to boast that he could "polish off" ten guys at one time. Apparently, he'd been exaggerating a bit...But what to do? He tried to think about how much money he had. No, he didn't have a hundred. All he had left was about 20 shekels. He dug in his wallet and pulled out the crumpled bill. "I'm sorry. This is all I have."

"What?" Yossi snapped. "They'll never be satisfied with 20! What am I supposed to do with 20 shekels? They'll beat me up just for daring to offer it!"

"You don't have too many other options," Yisrael pointed out. "This is all I have. And if you start waking up the other *bachurim*, by tomorrow morning the whole yeshivah will know that you went out to play basketball tonight."

"What do I care about the yeshivah? Don't you understand that they're going to kill me?"

Yisrael looked around. Menashe and Ariel, his two roommates, had slumbered soundly throughout this interchange. Menashe had no money…and Ariel? He might have some. But if they woke up there was no chance that "loose lips" Menashe wouldn't spread the story to the rest of the yeshivah tomorrow.

"Do you know where they keep their wallets?" Yossi whispered, following his gaze…

"Are you crazy?" Yisrael was shaken by the very thought. "You want to steal their money?"

Yossi rose to his full height. Though he wasn't that much taller than Yisrael, he was strongly built and broader through the shoulders. "Don't interfere! You don't seem to get the fact that I have no choice!"

"Don't do it!" Yisrael whispered furiously back. "I'll go out with you and explain to them that you don't have the money now, and that you'll get it to them later."

Yossi didn't even bother answering. He went directly to Ariel's pants, which were hanging over a chair. It was the work of a second to pull out a wallet. He smiled when he saw a 100-shekel bill inside.

"No!" Yisrael came closer and grabbed his arm. "We'll find some other solution!"

"There *is* no other solution!" Yossi shook him off and went to the door. "I'll pay it back to him, *b'ezras Hashem*."

He left the room—and then poked his head back inside. "You'll be sorry if you tell anyone that I took the money. I'm counting on you to keep this quiet!"

Yisrael sat down heavily on his bed. What was he supposed to do now? Wake Ariel? Menashe? Yossi would be expelled from yeshivah in a heartbeat for something like this. And what should he say tomorrow, when asked who took the money? Lie? Tell the truth? Either way, he'd be in a mess. What was the right thing to do?

He noticed that he was still holding the 20-shekel note he had taken from his wallet. The first thing he should do was put the money into Ariel's wallet. Then he'd think about the rest.

He went over to Ariel's pants and took the wallet from its pocket. There was a little more cash inside. Maybe Ariel wouldn't even notice that the money was gone. Later on, Yisrael could make sure he got the rest of it back.

"What are you doing there?"

Yisrael froze, the wallet in his hand. Menashe picked up his head and turned on his night-light. "What are you doing with Ariel's wallet?"

Yisrael turned to him, pale as a sheet. "It's...not what you think," he stammered. "I'm not..."

Ariel, who'd been sleeping until now, woke up and tried to figure out what all the commotion was about. "What's going on?" he asked.

"It looks like we finally found the thief—*that's* what's going on!" Menashe said sharply, sitting up in his bed.

In recent months, the yeshivah had experienced several acts of thievery. Twenty shekels here, fifty there, and a number of coins that had mysteriously disappeared. The boys suspected the Russian janitor, but were unable to prove it. Yossi claimed that Sammy was the thief. "He's an Arab. What do you expect? It's in his blood!" No one had suspected that the culprit was one of the *bachurim*.

But now, as Menashe and Ariel gazed at their roommate holding a wallet that was not his own in the middle of the night, they believed that they'd solved the mystery.

"No! I'm not a thief! Ariel, you've got to believe me!" Yisrael pleaded. He'd never really gotten along with Menashe; he despised the slander that flowed unendingly from that boy's lips. But Ariel was his good friend. He *had* to believe him!

Ariel groped for his glasses in the dark, put them on and looked at Yisrael, holding his wallet. "How much do you need?" he asked. "You know I'd gladly lend you money."

"You don't understand," Yisrael said. "I have my own money, see? This 20 is mine. I'm putting it in your wallet because someone stole from you!"

"Someone? Who? And how much did he take?"

"What an unbelievable cover-up," scoffed Menashe. "Someone stole, and you're putting it back... How do you know anyone stole from Ariel anyway, huh?"

Yisrael didn't answer. He didn't want to tell them that Yossi had been the thief. And who would believe him? Yossi was the last person that anyone would suspect of stealing. He came from an important and well-respected family.

Ariel reached out and took his wallet from Yisrael. He looked inside. "I'm missing 100 shekels! And maybe also a few coins…"

"No, no—only 100 shekels," Yisrael blurted. Immediately, he realized his mistake.

"'Only 100 shekels,'" Menashe mimicked. "He knows exactly how much was taken. How strange!"

"Where's the money?" Ariel asked. "Give the money back, and I won't tell anyone, if you promise it won't happen again."

Menashe liked this idea. "Yes, give it back and we won't tell."

Yisrael knew that this would never happen. Even if, by some miracle, he had 100 shekels to give back, Menashe would never be able to keep this thing a secret. He'd explode with the scoop of the year: Yisrael—the yeshivah's thief! He was probably already trying to figure out who to tell first. "Yisrael the thief"—what an incredible topic of conversation.

But even if he'd wanted to, he didn't have the money. "Look," he told Ariel. "You know me better than anyone. Do you think I'm capable of stealing? You have to believe me when I say that someone else took the money, but I can't say who it was. All right? I'm begging you!" Ariel was torn. On the one hand, who could it be but Yisrael, caught red-handed in the middle of the night? On the other hand, he really wasn't the type to steal, and he was also not one of the boys who always needed money… But wait a minute! Maybe the reason he always had money was because he stole it?

What was the truth?

"It's not our job to judge," Menashe declared. "What do we know? The yeshivah will decide what to do with the thief!"

4

Cricova, Moldova, 1895

Y URI MARINOV WAS 15 YEARS OLD THE FIRST TIME HE LEFT
Cricova. He'd been born and raised in that little town in
Moldova, a modest country that borders on Romania and the
Ukraine.

The Marinov family was among the oldest in the town, and had
begun to make a name for itself in the wine-making industry. Yuri's
father, Sergei Marinov, worked hard to expand his small business,
which included a vineyard of fine grapes and a family winery that
improved with the years. He was an ardent admirer of the Russian
czar, who had turned Moldova into a piece of the Russian Empire's
giant puzzle. When, in 1894, Czar Alexander III died, Sergei had
cried.

"The terrorists are responsible for his death!" he claimed. Though
the czar had succumbed to an infection that was the result of a train
accident he'd suffered six years earlier, many in Russia believed
that the accident had been a deliberate act. They based their suspicions on the fact that the czar's father, Alexander II, had been

assassinated by a gang of revolutionaries who called themselves the Narodnaya Volya ("the will of the people"). "Anarchists who want to destroy the empire! May they all die a miserable death!" Sergei cursed the revolutionaries, who continued to grow and gain strength. Yuri listened to his father, and swore to hate them forever.

Like his father, Yuri loved the spacious vineyards that graciously accepted the rays of the benevolent Moldovan sun. He spent long hours among the vines, studying them and charting their growth. His family was one of the few that were involved in every stage of making wine from its very inception, starting with planting the seeds in the brown earth and on until the end of the long, slow process in the family's dim wine cellars.

At first, his father tried sending Yuri to school to further his education. But clever Yuri found the village school simple and boring, far more boring than the fascinating wine business. In truth, Sergei was not all that opposed. Who else would inherit his empire when he was no longer capable of running it? Who else, if not his only son?

So he taught his son everything he knew about making wine, from harvest to fermentation, and how to distinguish between the different grapes: Cabernet Sauvignon, Merlot, Pinot noir, and more, and what kind of handling each required in order to bring out its best.

On that Friday morning, Sergei was preparing to travel to the nearby city of Kishinev to tend to a business-related matter. At the last minute, he encountered Yuri, who had skipped school again and wanted to join him on his trip.

"But Father... What about the Jews in Kishinev?" Yuri asked in apprehension.

Sergei laughed coarsely. "That's all right. If you behave properly, they won't be able to harm you."

Yuri climbed aboard the wagon, not completely satisfied. When he'd been young, his mother would tell him stories before bed. Sometimes she spun tales about dwarves or giants, but most of the stories were about Jews. The most frightening story of all revolved around their holiday—Passover.

"Once, many years ago, the Jewish holiday of Passover was approaching and the rabbi of Kishinev was very angry. Why was he angry? Because the Jews have a special commandment on that holiday. Every year, they must bake a special cake, out of flour and… the blood of a Christian child!

"But that year, they hadn't been able to find a little boy or girl who had not behaved well. It's important to know that the Jews cannot do a thing to a good child who listens to his mother and father. They can only catch children who are insolent and do not behave properly…"

"But Mother," Yuri would always ask fearfully. "How do they know who is good and who isn't?"

"The Jews can smell it!" was the terrifying answer. "That's why they have such long noses. Anyway, that year all the children in Kishinev were good, and the Jews didn't know what to do. So the rabbi decided to send a messenger to the nearby town of Cricova, with instructions to find a bad child—and slaughter him for their holiday!"

At this stage of the story, little Yuri would burrow under the covers and wait for the rest.

"Well, on the day the messenger came, there was one little boy in Cricova who did not listen to his parents. That boy's name was… Yuri! Yuri refused to eat up all the cereal that his mother had made him. The messenger sniffed him out with his long nose, and crept close to the house with a long knife in his hand. He knocked on the door. 'Knock, knock!' In another minute, he would go inside and…

"But at that very moment, the clever father came home. He decided to save Yuri, even though Yuri had not been a good boy. The father gave the Jew a bottle of thick, red wine and told him that it was the blood of a Christian child.

"The Jew sniffed the bottle with his long nose, once, then twice, and said, 'This is not blood. It's wine!'

"But Yuri's father was not fazed. 'It's the blood of a boy who did not behave properly—mixed in with wine,' he lied.

"Finally, the Jew agreed to take the wine—this time. However, he said, the next time he would not accept blood mixed with wine, but only pure blood. But Yuri's father was not afraid, because he knew that Yuri would never be a bad boy again. Right, Yuri?"

"Right!" little Yuri would promise. His mother didn't know that, under the covers, he always kept a bottle of wine. Just in case that Jew came back. Maybe he'd agree to be flexible again…

And now, he was about to go to Kishinev! That stronghold of the Jews! True, he was older than when he had heard those stories. But his fear of the Jews was still planted deep. He couldn't understand how Christian children could not be afraid of living in Kishinev. Had his parents lived there, he would have forced them to move. There were a few Jewish families in Cricova, but Yuri's family had nothing to do with them, and he'd certainly never played with their children.

All the way to Kishinev, he sat lost in his thoughts, planning what he would do if a Jew tried to snatch him. Now that he was 15, he would not give in easily. He'd fight back with all his might. His father would undoubtedly help him, and his father was a strong and clever man.

The wagon slowly traversed the 20 kilometers to Kishinev. Within a short time, they were in the city square. Yuri gazed around, enchanted; he had never seen such tall, grand buildings. The big city was truly big! How many people there were, walking about in the middle of the day!

Every now and then he caught sight of a Jew dressed in black, and shivered. Why weren't the people running away? It took a while for him to realize that the Jews were a normal part of the cityscape.

The wagon stopped in front of a tall, ornate building. Yuri and his father climbed down and went inside.

"The man we're about to see is from France," his father prepared him. "He's a great expert in winemaking, and he has a few ideas for me."

Yuri had never seen a Frenchman before. The man was clean-shaven and dressed in an embroidered vest that was clearly custom made. His skin was pale and his hair was black.

"Pierre Barkozy," he introduced himself. Yuri liked him at first sight. Monsieur Barkozy was a cheerful and entertaining soul. But when the time came to discuss business, his laughter and enthusi-asm were replaced by a serious mien.

"I love wine," he announced. "Only a man who loves wine can properly create it." As if to demonstrate the truth of his words, he took large sips from the bottles that Sergei Marinov had brought with him.

"Excellent!" he declared. "But let me guess... This Pinot noir was nourished with Romanian fertilizer, was it not?"

Sergei was incredulous. Indeed, a large shipment of fertilizer had arrived from Romania at a bargain price. He had used it to fertilize most of his vines this year.

"Garbage!" the Frenchman pronounced. "Those Romanians mix in too much straw. Use only Russian fertilizer. It will improve the quality tenfold."

Next, Pierre suggested that Sergei try to produce champagne. "It's the next big thing!" he predicted. "The market for champagne will keep on growing, and anyone involved will make a great deal of money. But it's not simple," he declared. "In order to produce quality champagne, one must know what he's doing. Otherwise, it's no more than a bubbly drink.

"If you wish, I have a proposal for you," Pierre offered. "Send one of your workers to my factory. He'll work for me for a few years, and I will teach him the secrets of the craft. Then he will return to you and teach you. You could make a fortune out of that alone!"

"And what do you want in return?" Sergei asked.

"Twenty percent."

"Five!"

"Fifteen!"

"Ten percent, or nothing," said Yuri's father. Yuri was very impressed with his father's negotiating ability. With a handshake, the deal was concluded.

"What do you think of the boy?" Sergei asked the Frenchman.

Pierre pursed his lips doubtfully. "What does he know about wine so far?"

Yuri didn't understand why they were suddenly talking about him—but he was insulted. "What do you mean, what do I know about wine? I know everything about wine! I love wine just as much as you do!" He seized a full cup and took a delicate sip.

Pierre chuckled with pleasure. "That's enough for me," he said. "The boy amuses me. It's a deal!"

"I'm not a boy," Yuri admonished.

"And do *you* agree to this?" his father asked him. "Are you prepared to travel to France with Pierre for a year or two, to learn how to make champagne?"

Yuri's heart sank. So that's what they had been talking about! He was to go to far-off France. Far from his mother, from his father, from his beloved Cricova. He wanted to stamp his foot and cry, to scream that he did not wish to leave home. But he was embarrassed. He had just announced that he was no longer a boy. How could he start behaving like a baby?

"Certainly," he said bravely. "And I'll teach him a bit about wine!"

Pierre laughed, and mussed Yuri's hair. He had taken to the boy at first sight. He would treat Yuri as if he were his own son, the son he'd never had.

Tel Aviv, Israel, 2008

The happy ending did not make Lieutenant Colonel Guy Ben-Dov swerve from his decision. He could not lead operations where his men did whatever they wanted. Such a blatant act of insubordination must incur a severe punishment, to deter the rest of the group from nurturing dreams of being a hero too. If there was one thing a commander needed from his troops, it was trust—their trust in him, to take care of them in every situation, and his trust in them, to carry out his orders without question. Ami had damaged that trust a number of times already, but he'd always gotten away with it because of his personality and because of the fact that he was the best soldier Guy had ever met.

This time, he had crossed every limit. Guy saw his men thumping Ami on the shoulder and gazing at him with mingled envy and admiration, and he knew that he must do something—and quickly. Otherwise, he would lose long years of tedious, hard work. His choice was between a single soldier and an entire unit. It didn't matter how good that one soldier was; the unit had priority. Ami Drori would have to leave.

The Mossad was thrilled to get their hands on Salakh al Ovid. The intelligence that could be extracted from a leader of his caliber could significantly shorten the fighting. From their perspective, the mission had been crowned with success. From Ben-Dov's, it had been a failure—and Ami Drori knew it. He was not surprised to receive an urgent summons to headquarters. He knew he would have to pay for what he had done. But he didn't guess how high the price would be.

"Demote me to private," he yelled, "but leave me here! I've given my life to the army! Give me just one more chance. How many years have you known me—seven? Don't do this to me!"

"It's not only in my hands," his commander replied. "And even if it were, I'm not changing my mind. I can't lead missions when you act just as you please. You've been here long enough to know that, Ami. Believe me, if I thought the situation would change, I'd leave you. But both you and I know that won't happen. You'll always do what you think is right, no matter what I say."

Ami was silent. He knew that the subject was closed. Nothing he could say would change Ben-Dov's decision. In all honesty, he understood it. He, no less than Guy, understood the consequences of disobedience in battle. But what could he do? He'd had to get even with the terrorist who had planned the ambush that killed his only brother, a member of the Golani Brigade. He didn't regret what he had done for an instant. What would happen next? Only Heaven knew.

"You are demoted to the rank of captain and discharged summarily from the service." Guy did not meet Ami's eyes as he spoke. "You know this isn't personal. I owe you my life, as does the rest of the unit, more than once. But the good of the group must come before personal considerations. It has been a great honor to serve with you, Ami. I'm sure you'll succeed in your future life."

"And that's it? That's how my career in the IDF ends? What am I supposed to do now?" Drori asked his commander, his friend.

"You have several options. You can become a civilian and start making money, perhaps in some security firm in Israel or abroad. I know several people who'd be happy to have you. Or there's another proposal that you might want to consider… The choice is yours. No one else's."

"Well?"

"Yifat," Guy called his secretary, "is our guest here yet?"

"Yes. Shall I bring him in?"

"Please." Guy stood up. "You know Nachum Levi. I believe the two of you have met in the past."

Ami smiled. The army intelligence chief owed him a favor for an operation he had saved. Guy Ben-Dov shook the newcomer's hand warmly. "I think the two of you will get on fine on your own," he said, and turned to go. "Good luck, Ami. You'll always have free access to me. *L'hitraot.*"

The head of Israeli army intelligence wasted no time. He sat down in Guy's chair and began reading from a paper in his hand: "Major Ami Drori, age 31, born to his parents late in life. Mother dead, father suffering from Alzheimer's in the Misgav L'Zahav nursing home…"

"Where are you going with this?" Ami asked impatiently.

Nachum was unmoved. "Brother an army casualty… Married two years, divorced when his wife could not handle his demanding work schedule… Medals for heroism, etc., etc."

"I asked where you're going with this." Ami's voice was harder than before.

The intelligence chief set the file on the desk and looked at him directly. "I'm going to the fact that there won't be too many people to mourn you when you die," he said coolly. "Apart from your friends, of course."

"Are you threatening me?" Ami stood up to his full height. "Tell your people that it won't be easy to get rid of me. You can ask anyone around here."

"That doesn't fit your profile," Nachum said without blinking an eye. "It says here that you're an intelligent fellow. Explain to me, please, why I'd want to kill you—and, if I did want to, why I'd be meeting with you now?"

Ami was stymied. Put that way, it did not sound very logical. The situation in which he found himself had shaken his equilibrium. He sat back down and waited to hear more.

"I have a proposal for you, Drori: I need men like you. Men who are capable of acting alone and can take care of themselves. Add your family situation, and we've got a perfect setup. Tomorrow, we're going to 'kill' you in Lebanon. We'll have a funeral and the whole works, then change your face a little…and we have a perfect soldier who's registered nowhere. Simply ideal!"

"Forget it. I have to take care of my father."

"I'll take care of him. You know very well that there's nothing you can do to help him now. He's receiving the best possible treatment in the nursing home. We'll handle the finances and keep an eye on him."

"And why should I do this?" Ami asked. "I can make some money and be done with the army's nonsense and politics, once and for all. Why do you think I'd agree to join you?"

The intelligence chief did not answer. He stood up with a big smile and turned to the door. "How do I know that you won't go back to civilian life?" he asked. "How do I know that you're going to continue carrying out daring secret missions on behalf of the Israeli people?"

He paused in the doorway. Only his smiling face could still be seen. "Why do you think they pay me?" he asked—and vanished, leaving behind a bewildered new recruit.

5

Washington, D.C., 2012

BOB WALTERS, PRESIDENT OF THE UNITED STATES, WAS A tall, powerful man with black hair beginning to turn silver at the sides. He was not the typical smooth, smiling character who usually occupied the White House. He'd begun his career as a lieutenant in the U.S. Army infantry and fought in Vietnam, where he had won many medals for outstanding valor under fire, clear thinking, and extraordinary leadership.

When the war was over and he returned to civilian life, it never occurred to him to enter politics. Like many army veterans, he was disgusted with the timorous leadership in Washington that had refused to issue the authorizations necessary for the army to emerge victorious on the battlefield. The infighting, the delayed orders that caused the deaths of scores of soldiers, the evasion of responsibility for the lives of the cream of American youth fighting in Vietnam—all these things had led him to hate politics in general, and politicians in particular.

The reality he found in America after the Paris Peace Accords destroyed his belief in the system. Henry Kissinger, head of the American delegation, signed a peace treaty with the North Vietnamese—a treaty that sent the soldiers home. But instead of greeting the troops with flowers, as befit those who had risked their lives for their country, they were welcomed with shouts, with people spitting in their faces, with cries of "baby killer!" The anti-war movement claimed that the United States had attacked distant Vietnam without cause, massacred its helpless citizens, and sent armed troops in to slaughter innocent people. This degrading attitude, along with the army's flawed treatment of soldiers suffering from post-traumatic stress disorder as a result of their experiences in the enemy jungles, led to many of those soldiers never returning to themselves in America. A significant number even lost their sanity and ended up roaming the streets as homeless beggars.

Bob Walters was made of sterner stuff. He returned to his parents' home and joined his father in running the family shoe store. He left his war stories back in Vietnam, along with the bodies of many of his friends. No one ever heard him speak of the battles or missions in which he had participated. He concentrated on serving the few customers who visited the store, and hardly ever went outside after work hours. By nature a quiet man, the experiences he had undergone only deepened his silence.

The media, on the other hand, were not silent at all. The post-war years were given over to a postmortem of the war, including a great deal of criticism, but also the unearthing of those soldiers who had behaved with courage and heroism on the field of battle. Bob was undisputedly among their number. Tales of his heroic acts and self-sacrifice began to surface. On the recommendation of many men who owed him their lives, Bob was invited to a festive White House ceremony where he was presented with the Medal of Honor—the highest possible honor given an American soldier.

But Bob remained unmoved. He tossed the medal into his sock drawer to keep his Silver Star company. But his father, John Walters, rescued the medals from their hiding place and hung them on display in his store. "Even if *you* don't care, America is your native land!" he scolded his son. "Your parents deserve a little payback for their sacrifice. Do you think you were the only one who had it hard? Do you have any idea how a parent feels, waiting each day to see if his child will come home in a coffin? Do you know how many such parents I know? You're a hero now—a live hero, unlike others. It's time you got used to it!"

Bob protested, but he didn't argue. He lacked the energy to quarrel over this. To his surprise, the medals brought in a rising stream of customers. People felt a sense of national pride when they bought shoes chosen for them by a Vietnam war hero. Though there were still, here and there, isolated voices raised against the Americans' actions in the war, the majority simply enjoyed the aura that the medals exuded. The man who measured them for shoes had used those same hands to kill dozens of enemy combatants.

The change came when Stuart Hardy, the Republican candidate for the Senate, walked into the store one day. He sat down on the bench designated for trying on shoes and watched Bob, who was serving a particularly rotund customer.

John Walters came over and asked Hardy what kind of shoes he was looking for. Stuart smiled. "Do you know who I am?"

"Stuart Hardy, sir. But what difference does it make who you are? If you come to my shoe store, it can be for only one reason. Shoes!"

"This may surprise you, but I didn't come here to buy anything. I just want to have a little chat with your son."

John grinned. "So do I—but the boy doesn't like talking much, and that's a fact. What do you want to talk to him about, anyway?"

"About elections and such nonsense…"

"Good luck!" Now John laughed out loud. "You've hit on just the right person to discuss politics with! Well, if you're not interested in shoes, excuse me while I help this lady." He went over to offer his assistance to an elderly woman who had just entered the store. Stuart Hardy waited until Bob finished with his customer, and then approached him.

"Hi, Bob. I got your name from Tom Riker. He told me about the long nights the two of you fought together, about what a great leader you are, and about how you saved his life."

Bob was surprised. He hadn't expected this. This man had done his homework.

"How's Tommy-gun doing?" he asked.

"Tommy-gun" had been Tom's nickname in the unit. He was a soldier who preferred the Thompson submachine gun over the regulation M16, and the gun's nickname had stuck. In the course of one of their encounters with the Vietcong, a hand grenade had been hurled at him, destroying the lower half of Tom's body. His comrades had been ready to give him up for dead; the enormous flow of blood and his severed legs held out very little hope for survival. He would surely die long before he could be brought to any sort of hospital. But Bob had not given up. He had tied off the bleeding blood vessels, poured antibiotic powder into the wounds, and thrown Tommy-gun over his shoulder—all while returning enemy fire. He carried Tommy to one of the rescue helicopters and sent him on his way. That had been the last time the two had met. From what he had heard, Tommy had been saved but his legs had been lost.

"Tommy lives not far from city hall," Stuart said. "Do you know the big square? Right there, next to a newspaper stand, is where he lives. Your friend Tommy is homeless, Bob."

Bob's jaw locked as anger flared up inside. *What does this guy think he's doing? Is he looking to get beaten up?*

"I spoke to him a few days ago, and he told me what an outstanding leader you are. He said that you were the best commander he knew in the army. Can you believe that? Such an illustrious commander, selling shoes…"

The shoe in Bob's hand was squashed to a pulp. Only with difficulty did he restrain himself from exploding in the man's face. A man who'd never known the battlefield, or the smell of fear mixed with jungle humidity. Who'd never seen a man die in his arms. Why was he doing this? What did he hope to accomplish?

Stuart didn't make him wait long for an answer. "I need you, Bob. I need someone exactly like you on my side. An American hero who cares about America. Someone who's given his all for his native land."

"Forget about it!"

"There are many other cases apart from Tommy, dedicated soldiers who've been betrayed by their country. Instead of thanking them, their country has sent them into the streets. I'm going to change that! I'm going to launch a massive campaign against it. But I need you with me. In order for my campaign to succeed, I need a hero that the public will identify with."

"Let's not play games. All you want is power. You're not interested in helping anyone. So leave me in peace and go bother someone else. Get out of this store!"

John and the old woman trying on shoes stared in amazement at quiet Bob, who grabbed the respected politician and began dragging him to the door.

"Just a minute!" Stuart yelled. "You're right! You're right! But what difference does it make? The important thing is to take care of your army friends, right? Why should you care if I'm doing it for my own ends, if you get what you want?"

"What I want is not to have any dealings with liars!" With that, Bob threw the candidate for the Senate into the street.

Let him be glad I didn't kick him, he thought. How dare he come here and start rubbing salt into fresh wounds? Bob was already furious about the treatment the veterans had received. He didn't need to be reminded. Poor Tommy had been such an active, lively kid. How many more were there like him? The cream of American youth had sacrificed their lives, their sanity, and parts of their bodies in that accursed war—and then they were tossed away like old shoes? Just thinking about it made him want to tear up the whole block.

Later that same day, he went to the central square. He had to see poor Tommy for himself. And there, on the sidewalk, not far from the newspaper stand, exactly where Stuart had said, lay a legless beggar wrapped in rags. Bob peered at the derelict lying in a pile of newspapers and food, trying to see the lively Tommy. It couldn't be. The beggar didn't look like him at all.

"Help a poor man! Help a soldier who lost his legs in Vietnam! Help me with a little cash for medicine!"

Bob froze. It was fascinating how a man learned to recognize his fellow soldiers in such an absolute way. After shared exercises and tours of duty, a seasoned soldier could recognize a friend by the way he stood, by the way he wore his helmet, even by the sound of a familiar cough. There was no doubt about it: the voice that was pleading for help belonged to Tommy-gun.

Bob took a half-dollar coin from his pocket and placed it in the tin can jangling in Tommy's hand.

"Thank you, sir. Thanks for helping a poor man. That was fifty cents, right?"

"Right," Bob said.

The hand holding the can stopped moving. Tommy's eyes, which had been riveted to the ground, lifted. They raked the man standing over him. "Sir? Is that you?"

"At ease, soldier!"

Tommy grinned. "I'd do it, sir. For you, I'd do anything. You saved my life!"

Bob was silent. He wondered if it would have been better if Tommy had not been saved. If he had been left to die there, at least his family would have received honor and a bit of money, and he'd have merited an honorable military funeral. That seemed preferable to living here, a crippled beggar on the street.

"I was just talking about you recently!" Tommy remembered. Bob could smell the alcohol on his breath. "Someone asked me about war heroes, and I told him about you. You are, without question, the biggest hero I know. Are you still in the service?"

Bob shook his head. "No. I'm a shoe salesman."

Nothing prepared him for the laughter that roared out of Tommy's drunken mouth. Passersby stared at the crazy beggar who was laughing as he chatted with a respectable-looking man as if the two were old friends. Women quickened their steps and hurried away with looks of revulsion.

"Who'd have believed it?" Tommy chuckled. "The lieutenant, selling shoes! Ha, ha! What a pity!"

Bob was ready to leave, but Tommy sobered at once. "Never mind, sir. I was just joking. Seriously, I was joking!" He laughed some more at his own wordplay, and then seized Bob's foot. "You have no idea what it's like, sir! I tried. Believe me, I tried to make something of myself. But who wants to hire a used-up cripple like me? Would you? There are days when I curse you for rescuing me. Why'd you do it, huh? But you know what? At the end of the day I'm glad. Those Vietnamese worms didn't manage to kill me! One day, when I'll want to die, it'll happen. In the meantime, I live and laugh.

"You know what?" Tom continued. "I forgive the Vietcong for taking away my legs; after all, it was wartime. But America? My despicable homeland, that tossed me out there for nothing? I cannot, and never will, forgive them. Do you know what kind of stipend a crippled soldier gets from the army? Pocket change! Barely enough for food. Half a year ago, I sent in a request for titanium legs—a brilliant invention. And you know what they answered? 'That is not covered by your insurance, but we wish you much luck!' Not just luck, but *much* luck! Let them rot!"

Bob had had enough. He wanted to go. But his friend's hand was still clamped around his ankle with surprising strength. He didn't want to detach himself by force. Not yet.

"Look, Tommy-gun. I'm sorry for you. But sitting here begging and drinking all day doesn't seem too heroic to me. If you want to work, you can come try my store, and—"

"Work in a shoe store? That's heroism? With all due respect, sir, you're talking rot! You think you're better than me? At least I'm not hiding from the world in some little shop! How is it that you, who led hundreds of men into battle, whom people trusted with their lives and who was never wrong—how is it that you're a miserable shoe salesman, huh?" Tom breathed deeply. "Big hero! Let's see you do something real! Let's see you get America to recognize its stepchildren, its thousands of veterans who were thrown back into civilian life, unprepared and unrecognized. Let's see you be a hero in *real* life!"

Bob stayed calm. He shook his foot to free it from the beggar's grip, and then started to walk away.

"Sir! I'm sorry, sir!"

Bob did not turn around. He'd heard enough. Tommy didn't know it, but he had touched a raw nerve. Although no one had ever heard him complain about the boring nature of his work, he simply wasn't cut out for it. He really was bigger than that. The wounded warrior had hit the truth right on the nose. His work was his escape. His escape from responsibility. As a military leader, it was impermissible for him to abandon his men—and that's exactly what he had done!

How was it possible that Tommy, who had lost his legs for America, should be where he was? How was it possible that the many soldiers who had served under him were roaming the streets without someone to care for them?

That "someone" was supposed to be him. But he had escaped to his father's shoe store.

How despicable.

Jerusalem, June 2010

ON THE MORNING AFTER THE ROBBERY, THE YESHIVAH was in turmoil. The news that Yisrael Davis was the thief spread like wildfire through a thorn field. Menashe did not skimp on his description as he related dramatically, over breakfast, how he had woken in the night and caught Yisrael red-handed.

"The wallet was in his hands! And he, without missing a beat, said that he wasn't taking money *out*—but putting some *in*! Did you ever hear such a lame excuse in your life? He should be kicked out of yeshivah!"

There were a few boys who were willing to give Yisrael the benefit of the doubt—Ariel at their head. He wished none of this had happened. He'd have far preferred to lose that 100 shekels several times over than to see Yisrael in this state. But even he found it hard to believe his friend. All the signs testified to his being the thief. After all, the most successful thief is the one that nobody suspects.

Yossi backed Yisrael vociferously. "I know Yisrael! He's never stolen money from anyone in his life! If he says he isn't the thief, then I believe him." He threw an arm around Yisrael's shoulders. "You know as well as I do that our Arab is the thief. For some reason, Yisrael doesn't want to give him away. He has a heart of gold… But Sammy's the thief for sure, right?" He winked at Yisrael, as though to say, *See? I've given you an honorable way out.*

Before Yisrael could answer, the mashgiach entered the room. Silence fell. Rav Aharon Grossman came into the dining hall only at very infrequent intervals. Dozens of pairs of eyes followed him as he made his way to the center of the room.

"The *issur* of *lashon hara* is one of the most serious there is!" he announced, scanning the *bachurim* with deep seriousness. "Spilling blood verbally is considered a form of murder. If there are any problems, you should go to whoever's in charge and let him take care of it. But under no circumstances does anyone have the right to slander and publicly embarrass someone else! Is that understood?"

Most of those in the room bowed under the mashgiach's stern gaze. Many of those who had been positive about Yisrael's guilt wondered now whether they had been wrong in their hasty judgment. Rav Aharon glanced at his watch and continued, "It's late. Please finish eating, *bentch*, and go up to your *shiur*."

Activity resumed in the big room as the boys hurried to do as they had been bidden. The mashgiach went over to Yisrael and whispered in his ear, "Come to me before *shiur*."

Yisrael flushed and nodded. He had already decided that he would not betray Yossi under any circumstances. Though he was angry at his friend for putting him in this position, no one deserved the humiliation of being labeled a thief. He was already under suspicion; a few days would pass, and it would all be forgotten. The difficult morning he had just lived through would not disappear so quickly, but with Hashem's help within a few days everything would be all right.

He had eaten nothing that morning; he had no appetite. So there was no need to *bentch*. He left the dining hall on the mashgiach's heels, with every eye in the place fixed on him. A moment before he left, he caught a loud whisper from his roommate, Menashe: "Watch; our thief's going to get kicked out of yeshivah!"

He hadn't thought of that until now. They could expel him from yeshivah because of this incident.

No. There was no chance that the mashgiach would believe he would steal. But how could he prove it? Should he tell the truth? Give Yossi away? After all, Yossi really had stolen. Who said it was permissible to protect a thief? It was very possible that Yossi was also the one who had stolen all those other times... Was he being righteous in taking the blame upon himself—or wicked? He couldn't decide.

"Yisrael!"

Yossi caught up with him from behind, and tugged at his hand. "Listen. All you have to do is say that you think Sammy stole the money. I'll say that I saw him walking around the dorm late at night. And the whole thing will be over."

Yisrael stood still and yanked his hand angrily away. "But he's *not* the thief!" he almost shouted.

"Sssh..." Yossi hissed. "What do you care what the truth is? He's just a disgusting Arab who makes trouble for us. You don't have to say that you *know* he's the thief. Just say that you *think* he is. I'll do the rest!"

Yisrael said nothing. He was furious now. Not only had Yossi dragged him into this mess, but now he was trying to get him to lie for him. And he hadn't even said he was sorry!

He turned and continued climbing the stairs in the direction of the mashgiach's office. Yossi flew after him. "Don't you dare tell! You hear me? Don't you dare!"

What a mistake he had made. Until now, Yisrael had really been thinking about not telling. Now he changed his mind. After everything he'd done, Yossi had the nerve to threaten him?

He reached the office door and knocked.

"Come in, Yisrael." The mashgiach sat at his desk, wearing an expression that was frighteningly solemn. "Sit down."

Yisrael sat down facing Rav Aharon. He felt very small under the mashgiach's scrutiny.

"What happened last night?" Rav Aharon asked abruptly.

"I didn't steal the money! That's what happened!" Yisrael said without thinking.

The mashgiach looked at him long and hard. "I didn't ask what *didn't* happen yesterday, Yisrael. I asked what did happen."

"I don't want to speak *lashon hara*…"

The mashgiach did not allow him to hide behind this justification. "You know very well that it's not *lashon hara*," he said. "Stealing is not a joke, and it must be dealt with before it's too late. Now, I'm asking you again. Who took the money last night?"

Yisrael looked at him, defeated. "Yossi… He owed money and I didn't have enough to lend him."

"Owed money? To whom?"

"Maybe the mashgiach should ask him," Yisrael suggested evasively. "It has nothing to do with me."

Rav Aharon Grossman was silent. He gripped the end of his beard. "And what if he says that he didn't take the money?"

"Then he'd be a liar!"

"You know it's not that simple. Two boys saw you. Two kosher witnesses who testify that you're the thief."

Yisrael sank lower in his chair. If even the mashgiach didn't believe him, then the situation really wasn't simple. He'd only just realized that it was possible that people would really believe he was the thief! Until he had been told how it appeared from the outside, it had been clear to him that anyone who knew him would know it was nonsense. But now he wondered what he would have believed if he hadn't known the truth.

Yisrael hung his head in dejection. "He got involved with some guys… He owed them money… You can ask him…"

"Me?" Yossi opened his eyes wide, as though the idea that he'd steal was one that had never entered his mind. He turned to Yisrael, who sat to one side, watching. "How dare you!" He shook his head in disbelief. "After I defended you in front of everyone—you dare accuse *me* of being a thief? The truth is, I also believe that you took the money, and I defended you anyway! How ungrateful can you be?"

"Where were you last night?" the mashgiach asked curtly.

"What is that supposed to mean? In yeshivah!" Yossi exclaimed in surprise.

"You didn't go out to play basketball?"

"Me? The *rav* can ask Yechiel. I spoke to him after 11 last night!"

"Liar!" Yisrael burst out. "You came back at 2:30!"

"At 2:30, I was sleeping like a baby," Yossi said. "If there's a thief and a liar here, it's you, not me!"

"Enough!" the mashgiach ordered. "Shouting and quarreling will get us nowhere. Go to *shiur* now, and I'll think about what to do with the two of you. In the meantime, not one negative word will be acceptable to me. I will punish it severely!"

They left the room, two bitter enemies. Yisrael was so angry he couldn't even look at Yossi. What a creep! Did he think he could do whatever he wanted without getting caught?

"Idiot!" Yossi hissed before they entered the *shiur* room. "You thought you could go head-to-head with me? Now you've declared war. Let's see how you cope with that!"

They walked into the *shiur* room, where Rav Marcus was delivering an *iyun shiur*. Yossi sat in his place and immediately whispered something in the ear of Dovid Glazer, who was seated next to him. Yisrael could guess the topic of their conversation. Distractedly, he took his seat and noticed that most of his classmates were looking at him with disdain. Judgment had been passed. He was the thief.

There was no chance that he'd be able to concentrate on the Gemara. Rav Marcus' enthusiastic lecture hardly reached his ears. Something about a vow, and the handle of a vow... How could they suspect him like that? Even the mashgiach didn't believe him! Why was he even trying, when all the evidence was against him? Yossi had closed the net over him very well...

But wait a minute! There *was* a way out! When the mashgiach asked the dorm counselor if Yossi had been in yeshivah last night, the truth would come out. There was no doubt that he had been in Liberty Bell Park at that time. The minute the mashgiach knew that he'd lied about that, he'd realize that Yisrael was right!

In his excitement, Yisrael slammed his hand down on the table.

"Yes, Yisrael?" Rav Marcus said. "You have something to say on the topic?"

Yisrael turned red. He was clueless as to what the *ram* had been talking about until now, let alone being in a position to add anything.

"N-no... I'm sorry...," he stammered. "I was just thinking about something..."

His classmates laughed out loud at this. "He's thinking about what to do with the money," someone quipped cruelly. The laughter grew louder.

"Quiet!" The *maggid shiur* banged on his *shtender*. Under his stern gaze, the laughter died as quickly as it had appeared. "If there's one thing you need to learn from *Maseches Nedarim*, it's the power of speech! What a terrible thing when a person uses that power without discernment. Now, back to our *shiur*..."

As attention reverted from Yisrael to the Gemara, he breathed a sigh of relief. He felt as though he were in mortal danger. He tried to ignore the angry looks that Yossi was shooting at him, and also tried to focus on what the rebbi was saying.

The truth would come out. Everything was going to be all right.

7

B UT EVERYTHING WAS NOT ALL RIGHT.
Before lunch, the mashgiach called him back into his office. He looked into Yisrael's eyes for a long moment before he spoke, as though trying to read his soul. Yisrael felt uncomfortable. Why did this have to be so complicated? Didn't the mashgiach understand that he was telling the truth?

"I spoke with Yechiel Tzabar," he said at last.

"Well?" Yisrael asked expectantly.

"He claims that Yossi was in the dorm and didn't go out at all."

The air burst out of Yisrael's lungs. He hadn't anticipated this. How could it be? Yossi had gone to play basketball! He, Yisrael, had seen him go! And... Yossi himself had told him that he'd gone out to play until 2:30. And...

He no longer knew what to think. Was it possible he'd dreamed the whole thing? Could he still be dreaming? He knew that this was wishful thinking. But what was the answer? *How could it be*?

"Is there something you'd like to tell me?" the mashgiach asked. During the silence, he had taken a seat facing Yisrael.

Slowly, Yisrael shook his head. Tears swam up and filled his eyes, and he could not stop them. What was he supposed to say now? That he didn't know how this was possible? That he knew with 100 percent certainty that Yossi was the thief, and not he? Sobs rose into his throat. He hid his face in his hands.

"Did you take Ariel's money?" he heard dimly, through his tears.

His shoulders shook uncontrollably. He shook his head, sobbing harder. He felt like a small child who wants his father to help him. But he was old enough to know that that wouldn't happen now.

Rav Aharon allowed him to express his distress in a prolonged bout of tears. He sat facing the weeping boy and tried to figure out the right step to take. His long experience in educating youngsters had taught him to recognize the truth when he heard it. It was hard for him to believe that Yisrael was lying. And, privately, he thought it far more likely that Yossi Goldfarb would steal than Yisrael.

Yossi Goldfarb… He'd been long debating with himself what do to with that boy. He knew that Yossi's father, R' Menachem Goldfarb, was one of the more famous *chareidi* politicians, and he was slightly acquainted with him as well. R' Goldfarb was a talented *talmid chacham*, though also haughty and sharp tongued. His son had inherited both the talent and the haughtiness. If a way could be found to guide him properly, something special could emerge from him. But it wouldn't be easy.

On the other hand—Yisrael Davis. His father was an American Jew apparently living off an inheritance. Young Yisrael was also talented, relative to his classmates, but he lacked Yossi's sharpness. In good *middos*, however, he stood miles above the other boy.

But who knew? All the evidence pointed to Yisrael as the thief who had troubled Rav Aharon's sleep in recent weeks. He couldn't remember when there had last been a *bachur* in the yeshivah who had stolen. Thievery was a sign not only of a corrupt character and a lack of caring for one's fellow man, but also a lack of *yiras Shamayim*. A thief who thought that no one saw him steal, and who was not afraid of the Creator's all-seeing eye, was a heretic. Was it possible that this applied to Yisrael? Hard to believe.

The mashgiach sighed. This was not going to be easy. He rose to his feet and went to stand behind Yisrael, who was struggling to control his crying. He placed an encouraging hand on the boy's shoulder and said, "The truth can be recognized. I hope that, at least, you've learned one lesson from all of this—and that's to choose your friends carefully. Now go rest, and return to your learning with energy this afternoon."

Yisrael raised his tear-stained eyes to the mashgiach. He tried to subdue his tears—without notable success. Rav Aharon didn't push him. "I'm going to the *beis medrash*," he said. "Stay here as long as you need, and then go rest."

Yisrael tried to smile in gratitude, but produced only a pathetic grimace. He sat there, as dejected as he had ever been in his life. The mashgiach believed him—but who else would? Yossi had a perfect alibi: Yechiel Tzabar. No doubt he had threatened Yechiel, or promised him something. And he? He had been caught holding a wallet that was not his own. The facts spoke for themselves.

He took a tissue from his pocket and wiped his eyes. No one must see that he had been crying, or they'd add babyishness to their other accusations. They'd say that he had cried until the mashgiach was forced to give in. He must get a grip on himself, like a man, or he didn't stand a chance.

A series of deep, long breaths helped him feel a little calmer. He straightened, clenched his jaw, and started for the dorm, ready to confront Yossi, the thief, face-to-face.

The halls were empty at this hour. Yisrael remembered that he'd missed lunch. Well, that didn't matter; he had no appetite anyway. Most of the *bachurim* were already enjoying their afternoon rest, gathering strength for the remainder of the day. A small number went to the *beis medrash* of the shul next door, to continue learning even during the break. Not that they couldn't have learned in the yeshivah, but the change of location provided a sense of freedom and calm that renewed their energies. Every now and then, Yisrael went there, too. Today, he felt the need to rest. He had to relax, and perhaps make up some of the sleep he had lost the night before. He felt as though years had passed since Yossi had woken him to ask for a loan.

In the doorway of his room, he bumped into Menashe, who was trying to fit his mattress through the door.

"What's going on?" Yisrael asked.

Menashe didn't answer. He managed to haul the mattress through the opening, and let it fall to the floor with a loud thump. Then he went back into the room and dragged a red suitcase over to join the mattress.

"What's going on?" Yisrael repeated, raising his voice. Though he and Menashe had never been good friends, they'd also never quarreled or bothered one another.

"I'm not going to sleep in the same room as a thief!" Menashe spoke as if to himself. He didn't look at Yisrael. "I'd rather sleep in the hall!"

Yisrael couldn't believe his ears. What did this kid think—that he could do whatever he wanted? Suddenly he was a big *tzaddik* who couldn't tolerate it if others weren't perfect?

The anger that had been building up in Yisrael all morning exploded. He moved close to Menashe. "Put that mattress back in the room right now!"

"Or else—what?" Menashe taunted. "You'll beat me up?"

Yisrael felt his control slipping away. He grabbed the mattress and began dragging it back inside. He'd show them! They were treating him like garbage. Menashe tugged the mattress in the other direction.

"Leave it alone!" he yelled. "You crook!"

Yisrael breathed hard in his fury and gave the mattress a powerful yank. Menashe, who was smaller than he was, was pulled forcefully along and flew into the door frame. With a crow of triumph, Yisrael pushed the mattress into the room. That would teach him!

His happiness dissipated when he saw Menashe lying on the floor, his face covered with blood.

What have I done? He roused himself with brutal suddenness. Turning as pale as the doorway, he hurried over to Menashe.

Menashe was lying on his back. He brought a hand to his face.

"My nose! You broke my nose!" Tears poured down his cheeks, mixing with the blood gushing from his nose. Boys began popping out of rooms up and down the hall. They stared tensely at the battleground.

"He punched him!" someone cried, pointing at Yisrael, who was still crouched over Menashe. Yossi Goldfarb appeared out of nowhere and shoved Yisrael away from Menashe. "Thief and murderer!" he screamed. "One crime on top of another!"

"I didn't hit him!" Yisrael shouted. "He banged against the door frame!"

"He did too!" Menashe's bloodstained hand pointed at Yisrael. "He pushed me into the door!"

Several of the boys—with Yossi at their head—surrounded Yisrael and began shoving him. "Get out of our yeshivah," they growled. "If you won't leave voluntarily, we'll throw you out!"

Yisrael felt like a trapped animal. Many pairs of baleful eyes stared at him from every side. Where were his friends? Where was Ariel?

Ariel was learning in the nearby shul. But even if he had been there, it was doubtful whether he would have been able—or willing—to help. The mashgiach burst on the scene. "Everyone to your rooms!" he ordered.

The boys obeyed, disappearing into their rooms and peeking out at Yisrael, Menashe, and the mashgiach, who remained behind in the hall.

"Go wash your face," Rav Aharon told Menashe. "Then go down to Nechemia, in the office, and ask him to take care of you. He may have to drive you to the emergency room. But don't worry, it doesn't look serious. In a day or two you'll be as good as new.

"As for you," he turned to Yisrael. "Nothing justifies hitting another boy! You go down to the office too, and tell him to call your parents and ask them to take you home. We'll talk again in two days."

Downcast, Yisrael went into his room and packed some clothes. He couldn't believe this was happening to him. Kicked out of yeshivah! There had been boys who hadn't behaved properly and had been sent home—most of them, incidentally, had later returned—but they'd been the kind of boys who didn't learn well and who had discipline problems. He had never belonged to that group—but he was being kicked out all the same.

He would not let the other boys see him downtrodden. He would walk out with his head held high. He finished packing and made his way toward the stairs. Most of the *bachurim* were still awake, and they watched him go.

"*Baruch she'pitranu!*" Yossi Goldfarb sang out. Mocking laughter accompanied Yisrael out of the dorm.

He decided not to go to the office. He was not a small child who needed to be picked up. He'd find his own way home. The buses passed through this area fairly often; anyway, he needed some time to think about what to tell them at home. His father would be angry. Oh, how angry he'd be! Maybe his mother would cry… Until today, he'd given them so much *nachas*.

But what about *his* feelings? He'd done nothing wrong, but had been made to suffer anyway. Tears misted his eyes again. A car, traveling too fast and too close to the curb, honked and its driver cursed. Yisrael pulled himself together. No more self-pity! He'd behaved perfectly all right. He had nothing to be ashamed of.

Paris, France, 1897

Paris at the end of the 19th century was filled with life. The taste of liberty, bought so dearly in the French Revolution, was still fresh. Young people and opinionated people filled the cafés that sprouted like mushrooms after a rain, discussing a host of exalted subjects.

It was into this world that Yuri, a young and innocent boy, landed. Pierre took him under his wing and introduced him to the city. The many colors and endless debates made him dizzy. The freedom with which these people spoke of everything in the world, without fear, intoxicated him. If his father could have heard half of what was said here, he'd have exploded!

"A spirit of freedom is blowing in the world!" the people declaimed. "The season of the dictators, when a few individuals do just as they please—is over. And it started here!" They were proud. "Various despots have fallen. America also symbolizes liberty—but she takes second place to Paris, birthplace of democracy. The Russian czar will fall too. And after him there will no dictatorships left except in the Middle East, where the rules of the game are different."

The upbringing he had received led him to protest these ideas. Is a place where everybody does exactly as he pleases a good place? It seemed to him a prime recipe for anarchy and chaos. However, as time went on his opinions grew less rigid. The exuberant environment around him softened his opposition to democracy, though it did not erase it entirely.

A motley crowd of every nationality surrounded him on the Paris streets. Young people from many countries were drawn to Paris, where they could speak out unhindered—or so they believed. Various liberation movements held meetings that were not hidden from the eyes of their governments, who called them "terror organizations" and sent their best agents to look into any and every attempt at revolution or incitement.

Yuri met a few young men who were not afraid to tell him that they belonged to the Narodnaya Volya group that had assassinated Czar Alexander II. From them he also learned that Russia's internal security police, the Okhrana, had also established a branch in Paris, whose job it was to keep an eye on these revolutionaries, to stop them and even to hurt them. "Remember the name Pyotr Rachkovsky," he was told. "He's the head of the Okhrana—a rat with ties to all the senior politicians. If he decides to hunt you down, you're finished!"

But Yuri had nothing to be afraid of. He was not involved in politics and was not organizing any revolutions. He was too busy learning the secrets of making champagne.

"France is the cradle of champagne!" Pierre said with pride. "And our wines are also peerless. Just say the names Bordeaux, Burgundy, and others, and you'll see how closely France and wine are bound together."

Yuri listened and learned. Pierre made sure he was educated in other areas as well. He hired a tutor to teach the boy French and

English, mathematics and history. Repeatedly, he told Yuri—a reluctant student—"The more you know, the more good ideas you'll have, to help you in all areas of life. Even in making wine!"

But Pierre also wanted the boy to enjoy life. After Yuri completed his lessons at the end of an exhausting day in the winery, his mentor would see to it that he got out a bit.

In this way, three years passed. Yuri was hardly homesick any more. The new world he had discovered was like one long dream. But the day was fast approaching when he would have to return to Cricova, his birthplace. He already knew all there was to know about champagne, fine wine, and every kind of drink that can be made from grapes. He had also garnered a great deal of other invaluable information. He felt like a person who had completed a successful mission.

He spent the last month of his stay trying to soak up the life of the big city. His young soul wanted to enjoy everything before he returned to quiet Cricova. There was not a single night when he wasn't to be found in a café with the many friends he'd made, and the other young folk gathered there.

One night, after a great deal of drinking, his good friend Matvei Golovinski whispered to him that he had decided to confess. "Do you know what kind of work I do?" he asked, his eyes sparkling with his secret.

"You're a journalist," Yuri said, and burst out laughing. "That's not such a big secret!"

"Sssh… But you don't know what I *really* do," Matvei whispered. "I'm employed by the Okhrana to print pieces favorable to the czar in the newspapers. But no one must know!"

"What?" Yuri was genuinely astonished. "You work for the secret police?"

Golovinski nodded his head. "After I finished studying law in Russia, I worked there in the same field, before moving here. Rachkovsky approached me and asked me to continue providing my help, and I agreed. It's not a bad way to make a living."

Yuri tried to absorb this. His friend—a secret agent! Well, maybe not actually an agent, but someone who worked with agents. With all the revolutionaries wandering the streets of Paris in those days, Yuri was no longer sure who was on the right side.

A loud bang on a nearby table distracted him from the subject. A group of Jewish youths had gathered around the table and were loudly discussing something. Yuri felt the same distaste that he always experienced when he saw a Jew. While these men did not resemble the Jews he had seen in Kishinev, and looked just like everybody else here, a Jew was still a Jew. All of them were foul murderers.

"That's the gang from the Bund," Matvei said. "Who would've believed that Jews would be able to go about so freely? In my days in the Holy Brotherhood, I warned that the desire for equal rights would also enter the Jews' heads. What insolence! They want the right to vote—those worms!"

"I'd slaughter them, one and all," Yuri added. "A nation of miserable traitors!"

"Want me to tell you a secret?" the newspaperman whispered. "Pyotr Rachkovsky himself came to me. You've heard of the Dreyfus case?"

Yuri nodded. "The Jewish spy?"

"Right. But the Jews and some others claim that he's not a spy, that he was framed because he's a Jew. Anti-Semitism, they call it. Civil rights aren't enough for them; now they're starting to work on Frenchmen whose wits have been addled by the spirit of freedom. Even my colleague, Emile Zola, who's the most talented writer I know, went mad and published a letter in the Republican newspaper L'Aurore, titled 'J'accuse.' In it, he accuses the heads of the army of protecting the true spy, and of anti-Semitism against Dreyfus. Do you believe it?

"Anyway, Rachkovsky approached me and asked me to write something about the Jews, something that would show their true face. Something that could be sent home to Russia so that the Jews who had begun lifting their heads would scurry back into their caves in fear."

"But what could you write?" Yuri asked. "Even if you tell the truth about their killings and plotting, you'll have to show proof.

Otherwise, they'll simply accuse you of also being an anti-Semite! These days, you have to bring proof for the simplest things, even though everyone knows they're true. Look at what happened in the Dreyfus case, with the whole world criticizing France on his behalf. The Jews have influence everywhere. They'd have you in court before you could blink an eye."

"I know," Matvei sighed. "I have to find a solution…"

They lapsed into a long silence. The vociferously arguing Jews fell silent as a young Jew with light hair delivered a passionate oration. Yuri listened, and trembled.

"…the Basel Plan is just the first stage! Now that we've agreed to the establishment of a state in Palestine, we must continue working for it. Enough talk! We need practical action! There is no safe haven in the world for the Jews—not even France! Just look at what they did to Dreyfus, who was more French than most Frenchmen. We must look after ourselves!"

"Do you have any idea what the Basel Plan is?" Yuri whispered to Matvei Golovinski.

"All the Jewish leaders got together in Basel, to reach a decision about their future," came the answer.

Something about this sounded familiar to Yuri. When had he heard about a meeting of Jewish leaders? He didn't think it was about the conference in Basel, Switzerland. It had been in a different city… Perhaps Warsaw, in Poland?

"Hey!" Yuri remembered, and shot eagerly out of his seat. His friend gaped at him, as silence descended on the café in the aftermath of Yuri's shout. Even the Jews quieted down and studied him in surprise.

Yuri blushed uncomfortably. "Come on!" He dropped a tip on the table and tugged at his Russian friend's sleeve. "We need to talk privately."

He led Matvei back to Pierre's spacious home, where Yuri had a suite of rooms for his own use. He sat his friend down on a red sofa and selected a book from the bookcase.

"This is a German book, written by someone named John Retcliffe. In it, he describes a meeting of Jewish elders that takes place in the Prague cemetery, near the grave of a famous rabbi of theirs who lived in Prague. There are twelve representatives at this meeting, one from each of the Jewish tribes, and together they plan how to advance toward their goal of world domination. I didn't know that it was true. Do you happen to know how many Jewish representatives there were in Basel? Were there twelve?"

Matvei's eyes lit up. "I don't know—but we can find out. But even if there weren't…what difference does it make? The important point is that the Jews are trying to take over the world. I can write a whole article saying that they're planning revolutions and terror! It'll be huge. Enormous. But…how will we get around the fact that they'll label me an anti-Semite?"

"I have a brilliant idea," exclaimed Yuri. "Listen… Don't write an article *about* the Jews. Write the piece as though they wrote it themselves."

"I don't understand," Matvei said, baffled. "What do you mean?"

"The Jewish elders get together periodically and weave their wicked plots. So write a summary or protocol, as if it were written by one of those present—one of the Jews attending the meeting. That way, it will sound authentic. They won't be able to accuse anyone, because no one wrote it. It's just a genuine protocol."

"You're a genius," Matvei said, and he broke into a gleeful jig. The protocols of a secret Jewish meeting in which they plan to dominate the world through the use of terror—who would dream that it was fabricated? Brilliant!

He pulled a pen from his jacket pocket and began scribbling. "What else does it say in the book?"

"It says that the head of the tribe of Levi informs the group that their plan for world domination is progressing nicely, that everyone present must be responsible for his portion of the plan… You can write that one Jew is responsible for spreading communism and anarchy; another tends to the financial aspect—for instance, dominating the gold and diamond markets; and another is in charge of the media. And one Jew handles the bombings and other acts of terror… I could go on for hours."

"You're really articulate tonight," Matvei complimented him as he wrote everything down. "Maybe you should write a book your-self one day."

Yuri smiled proudly. Beautiful. In a single evening, he had helped a friend, organized a plan for getting rid of the hated Jews, and discovered that he could be creative when the need arose. He had really learned a lot in Paris. It had been well worth his while coming here. Maybe he would even sit down tonight and write down his plan for the future. After all, his idea for the tunnels in Cricova was tremendous. The potential was enormous. Why, under his leadership, little Cricova could turn into an international wine empire.

He parted from his friend, who hurried away to copy his rough draft into a notebook. Too bad he couldn't get credit for the piece… It would have brought him instant fame.

8

MATVEI GOLOVINSKI LABORED OVER HIS CREATION ALL
night long. The brilliant idea grew skin and sinews under
his expert hand. The fact that there probably wasn't a smidgen of
truth in what he was writing did not disturb him in the least. He'd
been doing the same sort of thing for years—writing commissioned
nonsense. Only this time, he would not be signing his name. No
one must know that he was the man behind this article. It must
appear authentic.

The secret organization needed a symbol, some sort of terrifying
beast, like a tiger, or a lion. His meager knowledge of the Bible led
him, at length, to settle on the snake. Moses, son of Amram, had
performed some sort of miracle with a snake. And the snake was a
frightening and crafty creature, just like the Jews.

He wrote, erased, and polished all night long, and by morning
he held a finished piece that he was satisfied with. His Protocols
rendered a faithful account of a meeting of the Elders of Zion, which
took place once every one hundred years. It described their most
recent meeting, at the end of the current century, in which they wove
an orderly plan for world dominion. They were the ones behind the

revolutions and the rise of democracy, which made the rabble easier to control through artful and clever use of envy and hate.

He decided not to go to bed at all, but instead to take his piece to the head of Okhrana at once. He was eager to hear the man's opinion. Besides, Rachkovsky's request for an article slandering the Jews had sounded urgent. Who knew? Perhaps Matvei would even get a nice bonus for this night's work.

Pyotr Rachkovsky was a man with a strong work ethic. He appeared at his office before 7 in the morning, a pile of newspapers under his arm. It was astounding how much incriminating material could be found in the newspaper. While many of Paris' freedom fighters were enthusiastic and aflame with idealism, few of them were professional enough to protect themselves from unwanted publicity. Many of his unit's arrests and "special treatment" cases had been made possible thanks to heedless information regarding suspicious gatherings and parties.

Matvei, knowing his employer's habits, decided to conclude his business first thing in the morning. He hurried to the building that housed the Okhrana's headquarters, trying to remember when he had last been up this early. Usually, his nights were long and his mornings devoted to deep slumber. He loved the nighttime; that was when he obtained his most useful information. Industrious folk who sleep at night and are up during the day are not revolutionaries. They have no time for such things. The kind of people who hanker after rebellions are those whose own lives are upside down. Dark plots are best woven in the night hours.

The twittering of waking birds seemed very loud to him. He wondered if they were this way every morning, or if it was only his happiness over his finished article that was making everything around him sound clearer and more beautiful. Within minutes, he was seated in Rachkovsky's tiny office, trying to make himself comfortable in a hard wooden chair and watching his boss skim the handwritten pages. It was impossible not to admire the man's quick grasp. A question here, a brief comment there—and in half an hour, he'd finished reading the material from beginning to end. Rachkovsky wore a smile.

"Perfect," he said. "A brilliant idea. A self-accusatory piece of writing... Simply wonderful."

The head of the Okhrana sank back in his easy chair, a dreamy look in his eye. He must think about his next step. The simplest way to move on with this beautiful plan would be, first of all, to get rid of the evidence. This young writer seated opposite him right now must disappear so that he wouldn't talk. The Protocols' success hinged on nobody's knowing who had written them. There must be no thread linking it to a Russian conspiracy.

On the other hand, it would be a pity to lose such a talented agent. He was already short on manpower. The head office in Moscow had not been generous lately, and he had been forced to rely more on his political skill than on secret operations to achieve results. The loss of another agent could damage his capability.

"Who else knows about these protocols?" he asked Matvei.

Matvei turned pale. Could Rachkovsky know that he wasn't the plan's creator? No—it couldn't be. There'd been no one there apart from himself and Yuri.

But what if he *did* know? What if Matvei were caught lying? He could find himself at the bottom of the nearest river.

"Only my friend Yuri Marinov. He helped me close up a few gaps. But there's no need to worry about him. He's a Russian who's very loyal to the czar. He very much supports the plan and would never do anything to undermine it."

Pyotr decided with lightning swiftness: the writer would live, and his friend would die. That would take care of two birds with one stone. It would eliminate the possibility that Yuri Marinov might be persuaded to talk about the Protocols—and it would help Matvei Golovinski understand what would happen if he opened his own mouth. There was nothing to lose.

"Excellent!" Pyotr said, a satanic smile playing on his lips. "This wonderful plan is sure to succeed. The czar will be pleased. As for Yuri, your friend, you are right. He will never do anything to hurt the plan."

Moscow, Russia, 1977

Seven years had passed since the tragedy. Seven years in which the Kotorov family showered Mikhail Potgorsky with love and warmth, years in which Mikhail became a member of the family in every way.

The terrible trauma he had undergone had transformed him completely. The disruptive child who never listened and never participated in class turned into the classic well-behaved youth. People who knew the boy could not believe the drastic change in him. If he had formerly been stubborn and disobedient, now there was nothing his adoptive parents asked of him that he did not carry out to the best of his ability. The undisciplined, rebellious behavior he had exhibited within his own family vanished as if it had never been. As if it had gone up in flames along with Mikhail's parents and brothers. Within a short time, he was the best student in the entire school.

Mikhail's meteoric rise to success did not affect his friendship with Alex in the least. On the contrary, Alex was by nature a warm-hearted boy who rejoiced in Mikhail's happiness when his friend shattered educational records and took the school's chess team to new heights.

Mikhail didn't just play chess; he understood the game in an extraordinary way. He did not see a series of black and white pieces, but a set of complex equations leading to different outcomes and possibilities. In this way, he was able to predict his opponent's moves, prepare for them and then respond with a winning attack.

Alex, on the other hand, didn't care for "the game of kings." He preferred sports, and enjoyed a good measure of success in soccer and other games. Above all, he was the most popular and admired boy in their grade. The undisputed class leader, Alex had earned the unstinting appreciation of all his schoolmates, bar none.

With their outstanding achievements—along with the Kotorov family's money and connections—both boys were accepted by Lomonosov University in Moscow with no trouble at all.

This university, named for scientist Mikhail Lomonosov, was the largest and most renowned in all of Russia. Tens of thousands of talented young people from the four corners of that giant country gathered in this institution to receive a higher education in the various sciences. It was not for naught that Victor and Nadia Kotorov chose to send the boys there. It was the best place in Russia for anyone who wished to advance in life.

The large number of students in the university fazed neither Mikhail nor Alex. Within a short time they began to stand out. Mikhail was the best chess player on campus and a genius in the fields of psychology, sociology, and a host of social sciences. Alex, meanwhile, was quickly recognized as a natural leader who soon took his place at the head of those students who were demanding changes in the government's priorities. Though his opinions and the stands he took led to his arrest for treason, he was quickly released through use of his father's connections. His detainment only added to his aura and laid the foundation for his reputation as a rising political star.

The political changes taking place in Russia during those years were slow but steady. The general secretary of the Communist Party, Leonid Brezhnev, managed to turn himself into the primary leader of the Soviet Union, pushing aside Alexei Kosygin, who had tried to save the Russian economy. Brezhnev was more interested in arming the Russian empire and burnishing its military than in economic developments aimed at rescuing the Russian people from lives of constant want. He succeeded in promoting his cohorts to strategic positions and turning his job into one of vast influence. Brezhnev was even more influential than the prime minister.

The Russian people, inured to their difficult lives, were quiescent at first. But the spirit of liberty that began to penetrate the people's hearts, and their desire to improve the quality of their lives, began to cloud their sense of national pride and their former desire to trumpet the virtues of communism to the world. Dating from Stalin's death, both the atmosphere of fear and the communist ideal were not as they had been before. Though the communists still ruled with an iron hand, voices calling for reforms and far-reaching changes in leadership were beginning to be heard—in whispers and secrecy at first, but gathering strength with each passing year.

The bond between the two young men grew more powerful with the passage of time. While Mikhail was not very interested in politics, Alex made use of his friend's ideas and cleverness more than once, and turned Mikhail into his confidant and shadow adviser. He did nothing that did not first gain Mikhail's approval. Mikhail was a genius at reading the field, and made a real science out of studying human behavior and cognitive processes. He could predict with almost 100 percent accuracy the consequences of any move, just as he had done with his chess pieces.

It was no secret that Mikhail and Alex were not brothers. Mikhail had never taken his adoptive family's name. He did not hide the fact that he was an orphan. On the contrary, he enjoyed the special status that society reserves for those who had been stricken by fate.

Within a relatively short period, he had outstripped his teachers. Even the best of the university lecturers could not keep up with his rapid pace and brilliant, penetrating questions. He became known as a rising star in the relatively new sciences of the human psyche and human society—psychology and sociology, respectively. Mikhail's level of precision was uncanny. He was graced with a powerful grasp of the human mind, and with the ability to sense another's feelings, especially the human weaknesses that are part of the human genome.

His many talents led to an outcome natural to such individuals: he disregarded his teachers' pleading that he focus on just one discipline. He did not want to limit himself to psychology or sociology. He wanted to know everything, and as thoroughly as possible.

"Become a clinical psychologist!" begged Professor Migrov, head of the psychology department. "You are adept at understanding emotional illness. You can do so much good for so many people. You can help cure people who suffer from a variety of psychological ailments. The satisfaction would be endless."

"Wouldn't it be better if I focused on research? That way, I'd be able to help a much wider base. Instead of treating a limited number of patients here in Moscow, I could make groundbreaking discoveries that would change the face of psychology around the world. After all, wasn't it you who told me that this science is still in its infancy, that there is still so much left to learn and to investigate? Why shouldn't I be the one to do it?"

The professor didn't argue. He knew that Mikhail was right. But he also knew that Mikhail wasn't serious about what he was saying. He didn't really want to submerge himself in research. As usual, he was just saying what the other person wanted to hear. Years ago, the professor had noted this ability of Mikhail's and had been careful not to fall into his trap. Mikhail had told him that he wished to do research because he understood the professor's dream of seeing the science become more and more precise. Mikhail's problem was always that he was too smart to accept advice... In the final analysis, the professor knew, Mikhail would do exactly as he pleased.

Meanwhile, Mikhail continued to add to his accomplishments. He earned his Ph.D. with bewildering ease, and continued his studies while writing articles to worldwide acclaim. His most famous work was his research on the roots of anti-Semitism. His conclusion was that every human group requires a sense of superiority in order to move forward. This sense comes to a person thanks to those groups he deems inferior to the one to which he belongs. Thus, anti-Semitism is born—from a need to feel stronger than the inferior group. And who is more inferior than the most exiled nation in history?

Not all of Mikhail's colleagues agreed with his theories. Many took issue with his conclusions and argued their cases in learned articles. But there was no psychologist of note who had not heard of Dr. Mikhail Potgorsky, the brilliant "Jewish" psychologist in Moscow. He was the next big thing in the field.

The only one who wondered why Mikhail did not deny the rumor that he was Jewish was Alex. He, after all, had known Mikhail's gentile parents. But he didn't let the question trouble him overmuch. He knew his friend well enough to realize that Mikhail did not do anything without good reason. Surely he had a reasonable explanation. In the meantime, Mikhail's "Jewish" nose had become his trademark and the subject of racial jokes. At the end of the day, the world's most well-known psychologists did tend to be Jews. This could only help his career.

What even Alex did not know was how much Mikhail himself was influenced by these rumors. His research into the roots of anti-Semitism had seized a disproportionate claim on his overall work on racism. The fate of the Jewish people fascinated him. In contrast to so many other minority groups, they had survived everything. Crusades, inquisitions, Arab massacres, and Hitler's most recent efforts—all these provided a fruitful field for in-depth study. He was taken aback by how deeply anti-Semitism had penetrated even the modern world, how even intellectuals believed in the wickedness and inferiority of the Jewish people.

Unwittingly, his research into anti-Semitism became his life's work. His professor's fear that Mikhail would not find one thing to focus on was proved groundless. He began to lecture on Jew hatred in universities, wrote long articles on the subject, and even opened a research facility called the Worldwide Institute for the Eradication of Anti-Semitism. An arrogant name, to be sure—but if there was anyone who could succeed in doing just that, it was Mikhail Potgorsky.

9

South Vietnam, 1967

TODAY'S MISSION WAS SUPPOSED TO BE SIMPLE. LIEUTEN-ant Bob Walters brought a company of soldiers to the area where an American Huey UH-1D helicopter had crashed. The crew had been rescued some time before, and Bob's job was to gather routine information. The army wanted to know what had caused the crash. Bob and his men would collect evidence and helicopter fragments to help solve the riddle.

America's air-power advantage was crucial. The light copters, introduced for the first time in this war, gave her a significant edge over the enemy. If there was anything to the rumors of a new Soviet missile in Vietnam's hands, forays by the army would prove impossible.

They advanced in a double line, with Bob at its head, their rifles loaded and expressions tense as their narrowed eyes tried to pierce the dense foliage around them. Every tree might be concealing an armed soldier. Every cluster of thick growth might contain enemies, waiting for their chance to leap from their ambush and dole out pain and death. The rain, which had been falling continuously for a week, no longer bothered the fighters. They'd grown accustomed to the weird weather of Vietnam. Wet feet became a feature of every operation; only in camp could they enjoy a pair of dry socks.

The swampy terrain made the going slow, the fat drops made it hard to see, and the noise of the rain thudding onto the ground made it difficult for their ears to catch the sound of undergrowth breaking under a hostile Vietcong heel.

Their destination was still a kilometer and a half away, when Bob sensed something amiss. He tried to put his finger on the problem, but could not. No hostile troops were visible in the area, there was no change in the landscape, and he heard no sound of distant gunfire. He continued walking as his tension mounted, but slowed the pace. Something didn't smell right. Something bad was going to happen.

The quiet. Something in the deep silence troubled him. Apart from the steady drumming of the rain, not a creature stirred around them. Not a snake or a monkey—only the irritating rain and the noises his men were making as they progressed through the swamp. He halted the line again, and listened. Not a sound. Had he become paranoid?

His men looked at him in surprise. Did he hear something they didn't? For a long moment they stood in absolute silence, before Bob decided to go on. He was not about to abort a mission simply because it was too quiet. They were too close to their goal.

A few meters on, he suddenly halted again. The seasoned soldiers behind him stopped too, their rifles pointed toward the foliage.

"What's the matter, sir?" Mitt Phillips asked from behind him. "Is everything all right?"

Bob didn't answer. He motioned for his soldiers to go into hiding at the sides of the trail, and they obeyed with alacrity. After spending some time in the field, every soldier knew how to melt into his surroundings and conceal himself in seconds. Bob held out a finger, pointed to his eyes and then at the distant trail. Following his pointing finger, the men spotted a Vietnamese soldier sitting in the middle of the trail, his gun on his knees. What in the world was he doing there? And why was he just sitting?

"Ambush!" Bob signaled his troops. In one respect, the Vietnamese were better than the Americans. They knew how to blend perfectly into the landscape. A Vietnamese soldier was capable of sitting in a hole no larger than his body for days—until the moment of attack, when the Vietnamese would begin shooting at the Americans from all sides. The clear bait that awaited them on the trail worried Bob. Where were the man's friends? How many guns were pointed at them this very minute?

Bob gestured for his men to remain alert. He pointed at Mitt Phillips and Tom Riker, ordering them with hand motions to join him.

They crawled in a broad triangular formation up the hill to the right of the trail. Bob wanted to establish an advantage of height over the enemy. If they had prepared an ambush for him a few hundred yards further on, that meant that they were arrayed on both sides of the trail and waiting for the Americans to pass below. Well, that wasn't going to happen.

They crawled quickly yet silently, their rifles in front of their eyes as they sank into the damp, swampy earth, until they'd made a wide circle to a spot overlooking the lone soldier. Their eyes were so close to the ground that they could absorb no visual information; in this situation they had to rely on their ears to pinpoint a possible ambush. Theoretically, the Vietnamese could be on the other side of the very tree they were passing right now.

When they had reached the rise above the soldier, Bob stopped crawling. Mitt and Tommy-gun stopped too, and rose up slightly, hands on their rifles, ready to fire if necessary. Bob raked the foliage with his eyes, but saw nothing. Again, he listened to the surrounding silence. Still nothing out of the ordinary. Could the soldier really be alone?

Whispering into his radio, he ordered his men to move cautiously forward on the trail. Bob, Mitt, and Tommy-gun scattered to either side. Mitt was carrying an M67, Bob had his American M16, and Tommy-gun held his ever-present Thompson submachine gun. They were tense. If this was really an ambush, their positioning could be crucial.

Michigan Childers led the group, which walked in tight formation. Bob was proud of his men as they moved with textbook precision. Every soldier played his assigned role. Some pointed their weapons to the right, others to the left. None of them looked back. They trusted one another totally.

Again, Bob scanned the area. No movement. Either the Vietcong had infinite patience, or there was no one here. If they were preparing to attack, they should already be starting to move forward.

Michigan approached their objective. He pointed the barrel of his M16 at the lone Vietnamese soldier and screamed, "Hands up! Let me see your hands!"

Bob watched them, his finger on the trigger. Why was no one moving? Where were the soldier's companions?

The seated soldier slowly lifted his eyes to Michigan, and smiled. This drove the Americans crazy. "*Gio tay!*" Michigan yelled, using the only Vietnamese words he knew. "Hands up!"

The soldier didn't move a muscle. He continued smiling. Bob could see him mumbling something under his breath. His smile was strange. It was not a smile of happiness or even of acceptance. It was a kind of smile that Bob had never seen before in his life. He moved his rifle around the area once again, and then made up his mind: there was no one else here. He motioned to Mitt and Tommy-gun to follow him as they crossed the distance to the rest of the group.

Michigan moved closer to the soldier, his itchy trigger finger almost letting a bullet fly. An alarm began clanging in Bob's head. This wasn't right! The smile on the man's face was the smile of a dead man. The words he was mumbling were some sort of prayer…

"Retreat! Retreat!" Bob began running toward his men, shouting at the top of his lungs. "Go back! Back!"

Michigan's finger pulled the trigger, and the soldier on the trail died on the spot. Bewildered, the soldiers began running in the direction from which they had come. Where was the enemy?

A deafening explosion lifted Bob into the air and flung him face-down onto the ground. It was a trap! That accursed soldier had been sitting on a bomb.

Bob's ears rang and his head felt heavy. He ran his hands down his body and ascertained that he was in one piece. His men. What had happened to his men?

He picked himself up off the ground, and saw Mitt and Tommy-gun scanning the surrounding area for a sign of the enemy. This was the correct move. They must not approach the wounded men before ascertaining that there was no immediate danger. He looked down at the trail and saw four soldiers sprawled out on the ground. The rest had been outside the bomb's range when it had exploded.

"Help!" Daryl White was one of the soldiers lying on the ground. "I can't feel my feet!"

"Medic!" screamed Hickson. "Medic!"

"The area is clear," Mitt shouted. Bob and the others ran toward their wounded comrades.

"Michigan is dead!" the medic announced sorrowfully. "He was too close to the bomb."

Bob Walters reported the incident over his radio. One soldier dead and three wounded, one of them gravely. Should they proceed with their mission?

"Aborted. There's no need to go on. It appears that the helicopter crashed through pilot error. You may return to base."

Bob and his men collected their wounded. Michigan would not be going on any more missions with them. The injured men would probably be sent home. Bob didn't know who he was angrier at, the Vietnamese soldier who had been blown up in front of his men, or the military authorities who had endangered his company in an unnecessary mission. But he was sure of one thing: He would never forget the look of that Vietnamese. A dead man's smile—on a live man's face.

10

Jerusalem, June 2010

"I'M CALLING THE MASHGIACH RIGHT NOW," SHOUTED Yerachmiel Davis. "What does he mean by throwing a boy out just like that? What chutzpah! And what do they want him to do at home? Mop the floors? A *yeshivah bachur* should be learning Torah—not mopping floors!"

"Tatty, enough!" Yisrael pleaded. Yerachmiel, who loved the Yiddish language, insisted that his children call him that.

"Why did they kick you out of yeshivah?" his father demanded.

"Ummm…they think I stole money. But I didn't take a single shekel. Someone else did."

Yisrael tried to explain recent events at length, but his father didn't understand. "If Yossi is the thief, why did they throw you out of yeshivah, and not him?"

He looked suddenly at his son, standing before him in frustration, and asked, "*Did you steal that money?*"

Yisrael couldn't believe his ears. Did his own father suspect him? "No," he answered firmly.

Yerachmiel didn't believe him. If Rav Aharon had sent Yisrael away, and not someone else, it meant that Yisrael was the thief. He was slightly acquainted with the mashgiach and knew him to be a *talmid chacham*. It was impossible that he would make such a mistake. If he had kicked Yisrael out, it was a sign that he knew something Yerachmiel didn't. The father moved closer to his son and shook him, hard. "Why did you take the money? Do you want to be a thief, like your uncle?"

Hurt as he was, Yisrael was also stunned. He had never before heard his father mention his brother in the United States before. So that was the story! His uncle had stolen money, and that was why they had quarreled. His father must be pretty upset if he had actually seen fit to speak of Uncle Jeffrey.

"Tell me!" The grip on Yisrael's shoulder tightened. "Where is the money?"

"I burned it, okay? Leave me alone!" Yisrael was furious. But he didn't anticipate the painful reaction to his insolence. His father, crimson with rage, smacked him across the face.

Yisrael fell back, a red mark stamped on his left cheek. He nearly lost his balance. When he'd been a little boy, his father had sometimes hit him for especially naughty behavior. But for at least the past five years—since Yisrael had reached the age of 9—Tatty had not lifted a hand to him.

He turned quickly toward the door, opened it wide and ran outside.

"Where are you going? Come here right now!" He heard his father, but he didn't look back. He was no longer a little kid, and he would not be treated this way. He could manage on his own.

He took the two flights of stairs from his parents' apartment to the street in mere seconds. Only then did he slow down and look around. Where to now? All his friends were in yeshivah, he had no money on him, and his growling stomach was reminding him that it had been a long time since he had eaten a bite. He didn't want to go back home. He'd show them! There was no point standing around on the sidewalk in front of his house. Tatty might come looking for him, and Yisrael lacked the strength for him now. His father was a naive American who had no idea how things worked here. He thought that whatever the yeshivah did was holy... They wouldn't kick Yossi Goldfarb out; his father was too well connected. A word from him, and a number of the biggest and most famous yeshivos in Yerushalayim would close their doors to students from Yeshivas Shiras Yisrael...

He turned toward Jerusalem's String Bridge being built across Herzl Boulevard, not far from his home. The bridge was supposed to have been finished long ago, but everything in this place always took so much time. The slow-moving traffic was a direct outcome of the delayed construction. The afternoon sun beat down mercilessly as he passed under the bridge, not far from the Central Bus Station. Should he board a bus to some distant city? Go to the beach in Ashdod or Tel Aviv? The idea excited him, but he knew he wouldn't do it. First of all, today was women's day at the separate beach, and anyway—he smiled bitterly to himself—he didn't have as much as a shekel on him. He'd given Ariel his last 20, in the worst deal of his life...

Sacher Park! He made up his mind. Sacher Park was less than ten minutes away on foot. He'd go play a little basketball to distract his mind from the predicament he was in. Surely there'd be some good players there at this time of day. What a great idea!

He quickened his pace and within minutes was entering the big park in central Jerusalem, not far from the Supreme Court. A few more minutes and he'd be back in Shaarei Chesed and his yeshivah. But what place did he have there, now that they had thrown him out?

He approached the spacious green fields, each filled with different groups of people. Some of them stood beside barbeques that sent heavenly aromas into the air—making Yisrael's stomach clench and his mouth water. Finally, he reached the playing areas. As he had expected, the basketball court was very active. Both sides of the court were hosting games of three-on-three.

With a single glance, he noted that the game on the right side was much more interesting than the one on the left, where the players were young and inexperienced. He turned to the right and approached a lone boy sitting on the fence, watching the game with an alert expression and throwing out an occasional comment.

"Can anyone play?"

The international law of the urban basketball court said that anyone interested in playing could sit on the side and wait. When the game was over, the losing team walked off the court and those who'd been waiting walked on. If there were not enough potential players waiting, some members of the losing team could make up the numbers and try to take revenge on the team that had just beaten them.

"I'm waiting." The boy eyed Yisrael from head to toe. "What, you want to join?"

Yisrael blushed uncomfortably. How hadn't he thought of that? He was dressed as a *yeshivah bachur*: his weekday suit pants, dress shoes, and a white shirt. Normally, he'd have changed into sports clothes for a game. Still, there had been other times when he'd played like this. It hadn't slowed him down much...

"Yes," he answered. "Okay?"

The other boy pursed his mouth doubtfully. He was about 18, secular, tall and thin. "Okay," he said. "Let's see what you're worth... By the way, I'm Gadi."

"Nice to meet you. I'm Yisrael." Yisrael sat down beside him to watch the game, which was being conducted energetically and with a great deal of arguing. "What's the score?"

"Six-one, for the one in the red." He pointed at a muscular boy wearing a red T-shirt with torn sleeves. "That guy does whatever he wants on the court."

Yisrael watched the boy in the red T-shirt, who at that moment received a pass from his teammate, a guy in sparkling white shorts. He dribbled the ball rapidly, feinted to the right and left and then easily outmaneuvered the guy from the opposing team who'd been designated to guard him. Within a second, he was under the hoop and tossing in the winning shot.

"Oof!" Another quarrel broke out among the losing team. "Why'd you let him in?"

"Who let him?" the losing guard said. "As if *you* could guard Yoram any better... He got two points off of you!"

Gadi and Yisrael stood up and walked onto the court. "Come on, take your shots," Gadi told the losers. The way to determine which of the three would join the newcomers was for each of them to try to sink a ball into the hoop from the white line drawn at a distance of about three meters away. Whoever got the shot while the others missed would remain on the court.

"I have to leave anyway," one of them said. "I have no more strength to keep losing."

"I'm going too," announced a guy that Yisrael had privately dubbed "Baldie"—the one who hadn't managed to guard Yoram. "I've got to get to work."

"All right, then you're with us," Gadi told the third boy in the group. "I'm Gadi, and this is Yisrael… Let's show them, guys!"

"I'm Shimon," the boy said. "And it won't be easy. They're a great group."

Shimon was short and plump. He wore a big black yarmulke and a white T-shirt. The black cotton socks that peeked out of his white sneakers testified that he too was a *yeshivah bachur*. He grabbed the ball and passed it to the other team. "All right! Let's play!"

"Just a second." Gadi wanted to impose order on the court. "I'll guard Yoram. You"—he pointed at Shimon—"guard Manny, the guy in the navy pants. And Yisrael will take Jay."

Yisrael studied the player he was supposed to guard. There was no doubt in his mind that the guy was American. He wore a Yankees baseball cap, wide athletic shorts, and red Nikes. Yisrael shook his opponent's hand politely, despite the scornful grin that told him Jay did not perceive him as a real threat.

Yoram received the ball from Gadi and passed it to Jay, who returned it to him at once. Without skipping a beat, he lifted his arms and threw the ball right over Gadi's raised hands.

"One-nothing!" he crowed.

"Help me with him," Gadi said. "I can't do it alone."

Yoram began a new attack. This time he chose to dribble the ball at dizzying speed, confusing Gadi, who didn't know which direction he was headed for. When Gadi turned left, Yoram cut quickly to the right, bypassed him, and dropped the ball neatly into the hoop.

"Let's switch," Yisrael suggested. "I'll guard him."

Gadi didn't like having doubt cast on his guarding ability, but the facts on the ground spoke for themselves. "You think you can stop him?" he scoffed.

"We'll see," Yisrael answered, and tossed the ball to Yoram.

Yoram too did not see Yisrael posing any genuine threat. He bounced the ball blithely, trying to surprise Yisrael with a lightning attack. Yisrael stood tensely facing him, then shot suddenly toward the ball as it bounced off the ground. Yoram tried to throw out his arm and grab it, but Yisrael was quicker. He shoved the ball forward, ran after it—and caught it.

"Nice," Shimon yelled. "Pass it to me."

Yisrael saw him vying with Manny for position under the hoop. He passed Shimon a fast ball that went straight into his outstretched hand. Shimon used his large body to prevent Manny from blocking him, then raised his arm and tossed the ball into the basket above him.

"Two-one!" Gadi clapped. "Let's show them what's what!"

He caught the ball and began a new round. Now Jay was guarding him, while Yoram guarded Yisrael. Jay put pressure on Gadi with a very close guard, not giving him room to advance toward the hoop. Yisrael struck out to the three-point line, and Gadi passed him the ball. In a pickup game, an ordinary basket is worth one point; a basket from the three-point line is worth two.

Yisrael loved shooting from a distance, and he was very good at it. He received the ball from Gadi and let off a quick throw, before Yoram even reached him.

"Yes!" Gadi screamed. "Three-two, us!"

"A fluke," Manny declared.

All the spectators seemed to agree with his assessment. Gadi began a new attack, passing the ball to Shimon, who passed it to Yisrael, who was still standing a good way from the hoop. He aimed the ball and threw it at the basket from nearly the same spot as before. Once again, the ball arced gracefully through the air and sailed straight into the basket—without causing a ripple.

Gadi jumped for joy. "Five-two! Let's go, guys! We're wasting time!"

Their opponents were taken aback. They had no idea how they'd suddenly found themselves lagging so far behind.

"Stick close to him," Jay told Yoram, who needed no encouragement. Yoram was a very competitive player, and a confident one. Until now, he'd let Yisrael off easy. He hadn't taken him seriously. But now, he would guard him with all his might. Yisrael wouldn't budge a centimeter without Yoram as his shadow.

This time, Shimon launched the attack. He sought a way to pass the ball to Yisrael, but Yoram was constantly in the way. Gadi darted to the right, and Manny, who was focused on helping Yoram guard Yisrael, was late in reaching him. Gadi hesitated a moment, and then decided to try his luck from the three-point line. He threw the ball, which described a high arc before dropping through the hoop.

"We won!" Gadi crowed. He was a boy who took the game very seriously. He was angry when he lost, and exhilarated when he won.

Shimon and Yisrael exchanged high fives with a big smile, while the other team accused one another of failing in their guard duties.

"A rematch?" Yoram suggested. He wanted his revenge.

"Sorry, I'm outta here," Manny said. "Gotta go."

"No! Without you, we're not three-on-three," Yoram said.

"I'm going too," Jay said. "I'm wiped out. We played and won lots of times. Now we lost. Get over it."

He gathered his belongings and parted from the other players. Manny and Shimon left soon afterward, leaving only Gadi, Yoram, and Yisrael on the court.

Yoram looked over at the boys playing on the other half of the court. "What can we do with them? We might as well just practice, or play one-on-one." He seized the ball, threw it, and scored a point.

Yisrael took the ball next, ran over to the three-point line, and once again sent the ball sailing smoothly through the hoop. Yoram was impressed. "You have some arm!" he said. "Let's practice some three-point shots. You first." He handed the ball to Yisrael. "So far, you've got one shot out of one. Let's see how many you can get inside in ten tries."

Gadi and Yoram stood near the hoop, passing the balls back

to Yisrael as he threw them. Their admiration grew by leaps and bounds. "I've never seen someone with such a good arm!" Gadi declared. "He's going to get ten out of ten!"

And that's exactly what Yisrael did. He smiled bashfully at his new friends' appreciative cries. With a last throw, he walked over to join them. "Okay," he said. "Who's next?"

"What do you mean?" Yoram asked. "Let's see how many you can get inside in a row. Keep throwing! It's a new record!"

Yisrael returned to the three-point line, throwing now from the right side and now from the left. The sixteenth throw bounced off the hoop and fell outside.

"Fifteen baskets in a row! Wow! You're a professional!" Yoram exclaimed in shock. "How old are you, anyway?"

"Fourteen...and a half."

"Do you play with some sort of team?"

"No, just sometimes with my friends." He remembered a certain turncoat friend—Yossi. "I played a little in school, and now only sometimes on a Friday. I've never spent a lot of time on it."

"What a waste. You should join my team," Yoram decided. "I play in HaPoel Yerushalayim's Youth team. I'm sure they'd love to have you."

"What's 'HaPoel'?"

Gadi guffawed.

"HaPoel Yerushalayim is one of the best teams in the country. And also in Europe," Yoram said with pride. "And its youth team has young talent that'll develop into professional players. With us, you could become a lethal player."

"I don't think so..." Yisrael could just imagine his father's reaction to such a proposal. "Do you want to turn into an animal?" Tatty would shout. "Someone who's only interested in his muscles? Don't you remember that you say in *Shacharis* every day: 'He does not favor the strength of a man's legs'? What about the things that are really important—Torah and *yiras Shamayim*? When will you invest yourself in those things? When you're old and can't run anymore?"

In truth, as much as he loved playing basketball, he also loved to learn. It wasn't hard for him to understand the Gemara, and the knowledge that he was doing the right thing, the thing that Hashem wanted him to do, was worth no less than the sense of triumph at the end of a good basketball game.

But right now, he was angry at his father. Tatty thought him a thief. After that, could he still tell him what to do? He didn't trust his son, but he wanted his son to trust him?

"Mmm... I don't think so," he told Yoram. "There's no chance that my yeshivah will let me play basketball. I'm not even supposed to be here today."

"Forget all that nonsense!" Gadi interjected. "You could become a great basketball star. Do you have any idea how much money you could make? Millions."

Yisrael was at a loss. How had he come to be in this situation? Playing basketball with a couple of secular kids, instead of learning *mussar* with his friends in yeshivah. He looked at his watch, and started. It was already 7:30. *Mussar seder* was over. They'd be going down to supper now. Supper! How hungry he was.

"Look," Yoram said. "Give me your number and let's play again. It was really fun meeting you."

"I...I don't have a cell phone," Yisrael said.

"What? You must be the first person I've ever met who doesn't have one." Gadi was stunned. "How do people reach you?"

"There's a public telephone in yeshivah," Yisrael replied. "Yeshivas Shiras Yisrael. Ask for Yisrael Davis."

"Okay," Yoram said. "Take my number... Do you have a pen?"

"No..."

"So how will you write it down? No cell phone, no pen..."

"Tell me the number. I'll remember it."

"Are you kidding me?" Yoram asked suspiciously. "You'll remember? All right, here's the number. Zero five four..." He rattled off his cell phone number. "But call me. Okay?"

"Okay..." Yisrael didn't really plan to call, but he didn't want to say so. The late hour and his empty stomach were clamoring loudly for his attention.

Perspiring from his exertions on the court, Yisrael weighed his next move. He couldn't go back to yeshivah. He didn't want to go back home. He was angry at Tatty. He'd manage on his own.

But what was he going to do now? He had to eat, and he didn't have any money. Not even enough for a stick of gum.

For a moment, he thought of an original solution. He'd go to a nearby wedding hall, sit down at the table like an invited guest, and eat dinner. There were a number of such halls in Givat Shaul, not far from his parents' house.

But what if someone recognized him? And besides…he wasn't dressed for a wedding. He had no tie, and his jacket and hat were at home. He hadn't taken them with him when he'd run out of the house.

"Where do you live?" Gadi asked as he collected his things. There was a Mazda key on his key ring. "I'm going to Kiryat Menachem. Need a lift in that direction?"

"Uh…Kiryat Menachem?" The Kiryat Menachem neighborhood was far away, across Mount Herzl, in the direction of Hadassah Ein Kerem. He had nothing there, but he could always return home if he chose—though he didn't think that would happen. "Thanks." Yisrael didn't know what he'd do there, but he had no better ideas at the moment.

"I'm parked right up here." They climbed in the direction of the Supreme Court, and Gadi opened the door of a battered white Mazda. "Wait'll you hear my sound system," Gadi boasted. Indeed, the music that began blasting out of the expensive system could be heard far and wide. Drivers in passing cars threw them sour glances. Apparently, the bass guitar that shook the whole car and gave Gadi such pleasure was far less pleasing to those motorists. Yisrael felt extremely uncomfortable. There he sat, in his white shirt and black yarmulke, in a car blasting secular music for the whole street to hear.

"Could you lower it a little?" he shouted at Gadi, trying to be heard above the noise.

"What?" Gadi yelled back, wildly cutting off a black Mercedes that was moving too slowly for his taste. He made a rapid left onto Herzl Boulevard. Yisrael thought it might be a good idea for him to get out of the car right now. If he wanted, he could go home from here; his house was just five minutes away.

"Look at that guy!" Gadi fumed. "Who taught him how to drive?"

The black Mercedes was approaching them at high speed. Its driver honked angrily, and flashed his brights over and over. Gadi slammed his foot on the gas pedal and yelled, "I'll show him what's what!" He leaned forward, concentrating on the road, and tried to slip into the next intersection before the Mercedes.

Yisrael stopped breathing. The deafening music was giving him a headache. The high speed at which they were moving seemed very dangerous to him. As good a driver as Gadi was, what would he be able to do if some parked car decided to pull out in front of him? There was no chance in the world he'd be able to brake in time...

The Mercedes pulled up on their left. Yisrael couldn't see inside the car because of the tinted windows, but it seemed to him that there was more than one figure inside. The vehicle's powerful engine roared, and the Mercedes shot forward to overtake Gadi's Mazda. Then, suddenly, it slowed down, forcing Gadi to do the same. Gadi cursed out loud and slammed on the brakes. The car let out a screech that could be heard even over the music. After a long slide, stretching a good few meters, the car finally came to a full stop not far from the traffic light where the road turned into Mordechai Ish Shalom Street.

Yisrael let out his breath in a gasp. That was close! What was going on here?

Gadi's face was twisted with fury. Yisrael couldn't believe the way the pleasant boy he'd known until then had turned into a raging monster.

"I'll show him!" Gadi screamed. The song on the CD ended at that moment, and his scream echoed a long way. Cars came up behind them and honked for them to clear the road, but Gadi saw nothing. He pulled a bat from somewhere and stepped out of the car. He began walking toward the Mercedes, yelling and waving the bat.

It happened so fast that Yisrael almost didn't see it. All four doors of the Mercedes swung open at once, and four overgrown young men came out and jumped Gadi. The bat flew out of his hand. The four pummeled him repeatedly until he lay on the ground, unmoving.

Yisrael watched in terror. He wanted to help Gadi, but he knew he didn't stand a chance. Cursing and spitting at the figure lying prone on the ground, the four turned back to their car. Suddenly, one of them noticed Yisrael in the Mazda. He called out to his friends. Yisrael felt suffocated as they raced toward him and flung open his door. It never occurred to him to try to lock it. One of them grabbed him by the throat and dragged him out of the car.

"I'm just hitching a ride!" Yisrael didn't know where the words came from. "I don't even know him!"

The youths exchanged questioning looks. "Let's get out of here," one of them said to the rest, "before the police come."

Yisrael's legs buckled when the thug who was holding him let go. He fell limply to the ground. The youths ran back to their car, tumbled inside, and left in a squeal of rubber.

Only then did the drivers of the cars behind them come out to investigate. One older man ran over to Gadi, sprawled on the ground, and yelled, "They killed him!" Yisrael couldn't shake off his shock. In the same daze, he heard another man shout, "He's not dead—just unconscious!"

Someone came over to Yisrael. "Are you all right?"

Slowly, Yisrael shook his head. No, he was not all right. He heard the distant wail of sirens, and then flashing red and blue lights told him that the police had arrived. He wanted to stand up, but his body refused to obey him.

"The ambulance is on its way," he heard someone say. "It'll be here in a minute."

"Are there any eyewitnesses?"

"Yes. That boy—the one on the ground—was in the car. These two men also saw what happened. They were in the cars directly behind this one."

Heavy footsteps sounded, and then someone sat down beside

Yisrael. He looked up with glazed eyes. He didn't know much about the ranks of police officers, but the many symbols on this one's uniform told Yisrael that this was no ordinary patrolman.

"Hello," the officer said. "Are you okay?"

This time, Yisrael nodded. He tried to rid himself of the fog that seemed to have encased his brain.

"Take a deep breath through your nose," the officer advised. "And then breathe out through your mouth."

Yisrael did as he was told. Once, and then a second time, he inhaled the clear night air. His heart, which had been beating frantically as though it wanted to escape his chest, gradually calmed down.

"I'm Dan," the officer introduced himself. "I heard that you saw something unpleasant here."

Only now did Yisrael dare to look over at Gadi. He was still lying on the road, with three paramedics from Magen David Adom and Hatzolah clustered around him. Two officers also stood there. One of them picked up the bat from the ground.

"What's this boy's name?" asked Sergeant Dan Cohen.

"Gadi," answered Yisrael. "Is he okay?"

"I don't know yet," the officer said. "But I don't think it's critical. Now, tell me—where do you know Gadi from? Is he a friend of yours?"

"No...um...we played basketball together, and...he gave me a ride...and then..." The tears burst uncontrollably from his eyes. This was the second time he'd cried today, he thought with a bitter inward smile. And until today, he'd thought himself impervious...

Dan placed a hand on Yisrael's shoulder. "And then what happened?"

"They fought over the road...and Gadi went out...and they beat him up...and they almost beat me..."

"Do you know what kind of car they were driving?"

"Yes. A black Mercedes."

"Do you know the model? The number?" The sergeant pulled out his radio.

Yisrael shook his head.

"Look for a black Mercedes," Dan said into his radio. "With... uh... How many were they?" he asked Yisrael.

"Four."

"And you'd be able to identify them, right?"

He'd never forget the menacing face of the hoodlum who'd yanked him out of the car. He'd thought it would be the last thing he ever saw in his lifetime. He wasn't sure if he could identify the others, but he most likely could.

Gadi was loaded into the ambulance, and one of the officers drove his car to the side, to free the road for the long line of vehicles waiting impatiently behind. "I want you to come to the police station with me and press charges. All right?" The officer looked at Yisrael. "How old are you?"

"Fourteen and a half."

"Then we'll need one of your parents to come to the station with you. Where do you live?"

"No!" Yisrael recoiled. "My parents can't know about this!"

"There's nothing to worry about. You didn't do anything wrong. It's that gang we're looking for—they're the problem. You have to press charges so we can punish them."

Yisrael was adamant. Under no circumstances was he prepared to tell his parents that he had hitched a ride with a basketball buddy and become embroiled in a fight. How had it happened? Just yesterday, he'd been sitting and learning peacefully, and suddenly he was involved in all kinds of trouble. It was all that Yossi Goldfarb's fault. What a rotten kid.

"Come with me," the officer said. He took Yisrael to a gray Ford that was parked in the center of the road. The only thing that betrayed the fact that it was a police vehicle was the flashing blue light in the front window. "Come. I'll take you home."

Yisrael got into the car and tried to picture his neighbors' reaction on seeing him emerge from a police vehicle. That mustn't happen. His fears were allayed when Dan slipped into the driver's seat and removed the flashing light from the window. Now no one would know.

The radio came to life. "Gadi Rebibo was arrested in 2008 for assault and battery. He broke someone's jaw. Apart from that, he's clean."

"The medical team says that he's regained consciousness and can be questioned in the hospital. His condition is stable," someone else reported.

"Did you hear that?" Dan asked. "Your friend's going to be all right."

"He's not my friend. I hardly know him."

"Okay, okay. Now tell me something. Did you see who started the fight?"

Yisrael closed his eyes and nodded. "Gadi got out of the car with a bat. Then they jumped on him and beat him up. But they blocked the road in front of us. They're the guilty ones. Look what they did to him!"

"If there's one thing you can learn from what you saw today, it's that your friend Gadi is a violent guy. He once got into a fight that needed to be broken up by the police. There'll always be someone stronger than you are. People who deal in violence sometimes get hurt themselves. I was wondering why they left the bat on the road. The real problem is that they can plead self-defense."

"Self-defense? They practically lynched him. They didn't even stop when he was lying on the ground."

"Yes, but they didn't hurt you, and he went out to them. They could get something for that, but with a good lawyer they'll be acquitted."

Yisrael leaned his head back. He didn't comprehend such legal niceties, and he didn't understand how someone who did something so awful could go free. "So why do I have to go to the police station?" he asked. "It won't even help."

"As a matter of fact, at this stage I don't think we'll need you," Dan said, as he turned onto Najara Street. "Just show me where you live, in case that changes. I'll come to you if necessary. From what I understand, Gadi himself can testify against them. That's enough for now."

It was 10 o'clock at night when Yisrael got out of the police car in front of his parents' house.

"Take care of yourself. I don't want to see you getting mixed up in such things again," the officer warned him.

The officer drove away, thinking about the confused young boy he'd just dropped off. In his long experience as a detective in Jerusalem's central precinct, he'd encountered various naive individuals who'd become embroiled in one kind of incident or another. But this boy was a pure soul, a true innocent who had become exposed for the first time to the cruel world with which Dan was so familiar.

He sighed and drove on to join a patrol car that had stopped a black Mercedes on the Ein Kerem road that fit Yisrael's description. Just another day on the job.

11

Paris, France, 1897

UNLIKE MATVEI GOLOVINSKI, YURI SLEPT VERY WELL THAT morning. It wasn't until 11:30, when the sun had nearly reached its zenith, that he opened his eyes and sat up in bed. Generally he was in the winery at this hour, but lately he'd begun to permit himself a little indulgence. He had worked hard enough these past three long years. Now he could afford to loosen the harness from time to time.

He ate a cold breakfast that the maid had left for him earlier. When he was done, he debated whether to go to work or to keep avoiding it. Finally, he opted to take the day off. First of all, because he could. And second, because he knew it would be a good idea for him to write a final letter to his parents before his return home. This was an obligation he had neglected somewhat during his stay in Paris. His mother would have his head for it when he came home. Perhaps one more letter would appease her somewhat.

The events of the previous night were fresh in his memory, and he wanted to share them with his father, who would be very happy to hear the story. He sat down at the ornate desk in his workroom and began writing in a neat, rapid script:

Hello Father and Mother,

It's been a while since I last wrote. Forgive me, Mother... I was simply overwhelmed with organizing my trip home with all the valuable equipment.

I learned an enormous amount here, and I've thought a great deal about how we can propel the family business into the new century that's about to begin. The world is changing and the markets are growing. Whoever wants to succeed will have to think ahead, and think big.

Father, I am enclosing some technical papers that will be necessary in producing champagne. Apart from that, I wanted to tell you about something that I thought of. A wonderful idea that can turn our little Cricova from another small town that produces wine to a worldwide center of wine production and storage, no less.

Do you remember how you used to shout at me when I was a little boy and went down into the mines? Yes, the endless mines that are near and underneath Cricova. You told me that the tunnels stretch for dozens of miles, the result of quarrying for stones to build the city of Kishinev and its environs. You also told me that they held demons and the spirits of miners who died there. Today I understand that you were only trying to prevent me from wandering there. But from my disobedience came a tremendous idea.

The temperature of those underground tunnels should be approximately a steady 12 degrees Celsius all year round. The temperature outside should not have any effect at all because of the tunnels' great depth. Also, the level of humidity should be maximal there. I remember how damp my clothes would always get when I wandered about down there.

Now, imagine a maze of underground streets, sprawling for kilometers, used for producing and storing wine at the perfect temperature. Cellars filled with old bottles that will turn the remote village north of big Kishinev into a genuine wine empire. Hundreds of thousands of bottles and barrels of wine filling the tunnels. A giant storehouse with optimal conditions for wine. I don't think there would be any place in the world to equal it. And the most amazing thing of all is that it's all prepared already. All we'd have to do is step in and use it. Amazing!

By the way, I haven't told anyone about this—not even Pierre. He's been wonderful to me all this time, but he's also a hardheaded businessman and he might want to appropriate the idea for himself... Anyway, perhaps you could find out how we might take legal possession of the tunnels. The authorities don't have to know why you need them. No one has been interested in them for years, so there's no reason for anyone to begin now. When I come home we can launch the fabulous project at once. Brilliant, don't you think? (I can see Mother smiling with pride. Here's a hug...).

And while we're on the subject of fabulous projects, listen to this: Yesterday, I advised the Okhrana about how to get rid of Russia's Jews once and for all. They're going to publish a so-called protocol of a secret Jewish meeting in which the Jews plan for world dominion. It's bound to work—one doesn't need to try too hard to persuade people that the Jews control the world. I saw so many Jews here that it was frightening. You have no idea of the kind of power and influence they have. Unbelievable. Now they're pressuring the French authorities to free a Jewish spy, and I wouldn't be surprised if they succeeded.

I also wouldn't be surprised if this imaginary meeting actually took place. I'm ready to believe anything of the Jews. They're sly and they're dangerous. Who knows—perhaps in the new century we won't need to be afraid of them anymore. Maybe His Majesty the czar will finally succeed where others have failed.

All right, my hand's getting tired... I'm looking for-
ward to seeing you soon.
    Yours with love,
    Yuri

He decided to send the letter at once. All he needed now was to get lazy again and forget; then his mother really would have his head. He grabbed his coat from its hanger and hurried to the post office before they broke for lunch. One less thing on his mind... To his good fortune, he was the last customer.

"Five minutes later, and I wouldn't have been here anymore, monsieur," the clerk said as he accepted the envelope. "You're lucky. I nearly left early today."

Yuri turned back in the direction of Pierre's house. He had a few other things to arrange today.

The sound of heavy footsteps behind him did not cause him to turn his head. It was the middle of the day and there was nothing strange about people walking about outside. He veered into a nearby side street, and still he heard the steps. Now they were beginning to trouble him.

Someone was approaching him from behind—too close. He was about to turn his head to see who it was, when a cord was stretched over his head and tightened on his throat. Yuri couldn't believe it. What was going on? His hands went instinctively to the cord in an attempt to free his throat and draw in some air. But the stranger did not let go. He was horrifically strong.

The mysterious stranger dragged Yuri into a nearby doorway to conceal him from the eyes of possible passersby. Panicked, Yuri kicked and scratched, but he didn't have a chance. The cord stopped his breathing and began to pierce his skin. He couldn't even scream. Who could it be? Whom had he harmed that would want to do this? The Jews! They must have discovered the plan somehow. The Jews were trying to hurt him before he revealed their secret plans.

He struggled to breathe—in vain. The cord prevented any air from entering his windpipe. Finally, his body grew limp. Everything began to turn black around him, and his consciousness clouded.

Yuri's brain, starved for oxygen, could hardly process information anymore. Nevertheless, when he heard a voice through the darkness, whispering in Russian, *"Spokoyinoy nochi* (Good night)," he realized with surprise that his murderer was a Russian after all.

The collapse of the Soviet Union in the year 1991 created once-in-a-lifetime opportunities. Alex Kotorov, who had been a low-ranking member of the ruling party, advanced at meteoric speed and within a short time became a central figure in the party. There was no doubt in anyone's mind that once Boris Yeltsin and a few other old-timers disappeared from the map, Alex would be a shoo-in for the new Russian presidency.

The changes in the Soviet Union happened fast. States like the Ukraine and Lithuania detached themselves from Mother Russia and declared full independence. The ruling echelon changed with lightning swiftness, so that someone who had been standing on top of the world one day could find himself standing trial and facing severe punishment the next. Many wealthy families lost everything they had, while many others made a fortune by taking advantage of the rare opportunities the revolution had left behind.

The Kotorov family was one of the latter. Though they had been among the richest families in Moscow even before, in two quick moves Victor Kotorov attained dominance over the steel firm he managed, and then over two other steel companies that had gone bankrupt. Within days, he became the largest steel manufacturer in Russia, and perhaps in the world.

Rumor had it that the only reason the Kotorov empire hadn't collapsed was because Alex was a rising force in Russian politics. This had protected his father from accusations of being on the wrong side of the map. Very few people were aware that the person advising both Alex and his father all along had been none other than Mikhail Potgorsky, the family's adopted son and brother.

Meanwhile, Mikhail had established himself at the apex of worldwide research—and this was despite the fact that his area of interest was an unusual one. His professor's fears proved to be groundless when Mikhail decided to pursue his doctoral research in depth.

He gathered vast quantities of material on the topic of anti-Semi-tism and researched the various incarnations of the Jewish people among the nations of the world. He was fascinated by the fact that wherever this talented people went, they were subjected to over-whelming suffering in comparison to any other group or nation.

It defied logic—the way that time after time, countries that had thrived with the help of the Jews could decide to shoot themselves in the foot and decimate their Jewish populations. Take ancient Babylon, for example, which fell apart at around the same time that the center of Judaism moved to Europe near the end of the first century. Or Spain, which banished its Jews at the height of its power in the year 1492—only to see the curtain rise on the Ottoman Empire, which had gladly welcomed the ousted Jews. This constant pattern of blossoming that occurred in every place the Jews came ought to have had the opposite effect. The various nations of the world should have been fighting for the privilege of hosting them. Instead, history proved that the Jews suffered and were exiled from every place where they tried to take root.

The suffering had reached appalling new heights during Hitler's regime. There was no question that had Hitler not diverted so many of his resources to ridding the territory he had conquered of its Jews and had instead focused exclusively on expanding his world dominion, he would have been unstoppable.

All of these examples, and all the resources that had been devoted to harming the Jews, seemed to prove Mikhail's claim: every nation needs a sense of superiority, which it attains through oppressing a power inferior to it—in most cases, the Jewish people.

In the end, after much coaxing by Alex, Dr. Mikhail Potgorsky also joined the Russian ruling party. But his motives were differ-ent from Alex's. He had no desire to rule. It was Alex who was made of the stuff of leaders, not he. He only wanted to do what he knew best: to counsel his friend as to the wisest steps to take. And this he did with consummate professionalism, time after time. It was no coincidence that Alex had risen so speedily to the level he'd attained. He owed his rocketing political career to Mikhail.

But all of Mikhail's dabbling in politics did not come about at the expense of his true love. He did not pause in his research for a moment. Right now, he was deeply involved in studying the most famous anti-Semitic document in the world: *The Protocols of the Elders of Zion*.

This riveting document, which apparently describes a secret gathering in which Jewish wise men—the Elders of Zion—meet to plan their domination of the world, fascinated Mikhail. Its development and true origins would provide material for many research papers in the coming years. What he knew right now was that *The Protocols* had its source in a fictional passage in a book by French author Eugène Sue, written some time in the middle of the 19th century. The relevant portion of his book described a group of men in a certain Christian sect who met secretly in the graveyard to weave a plot for world dominion. Later on, the idea was copied by others, including the renowned writer Alexander Dumas, who made it the Freemasons who were plotting to take over the world.

The first person to turn the dangerous plotters into Jews was an anti-Semitic German author by the name of Goedsche, writing under the pen name John Retcliffe. In his novel *Biarritz* he describes a meeting of representatives of the twelve Jewish tribes in the Jewish cemetery of Prague—adjacent, in fact, to the grave of the Maharal of Prague. The tribal leaders plan for Jewish hegemony in the world at large.

If it hadn't been so sad, it would have been laughable. How could such a proven pack of nonsense be believed? Any researcher with half a brain could expose the fraudulent nature of the narrative. Nevertheless, this false document became a fount of tragedy for the Jewish nation.

Mikhail was at the point in his research where he was trying to understand how the document had made its way from Europe to Russia. What was clear was that, at some point near the latter end of the 19th century, the document had reached Russia and was used by the czar to channel the masses' anger away from his regime and toward the Jews.

In a series of pogroms, thousands of Jews were killed in different towns and cities across czarist Russia. The wave began in the city of Kishinev, where the Jews were accused of murdering a Christian child in order to use his blood. Approximately fifty Jews were killed, and thousands wounded and tortured, while the local police aided and abetted the marauders.

That was only the beginning. Numerous towns jumped onto the bandwagon, blaming the Jews for a variety of crimes. The Jews, no longer feeling safe in Russia, launched a great migration away from that country—mostly to the United States. It was estimated that about a million and a half Jews left Russia during this period at the start of the 20th century.

The continuation of *The Protocols'* journey was better known. In the year 1905, a priest by the name of Sergei Neilus—a University of Moscow law graduate and a man close to the czar—printed *The Protocols* in the version extant today, and confirmed with certainty that the document was authentic. He declared that this was precisely what the Jews had done in their conference in Basel: planned how to conquer the world.

This declaration caused *The Protocols* to become even more widespread, ostensibly as a true document describing the wickedness of the Jews.

Later on, even the venerable *London Times* published *The Protocols* as true, and only afterward retracted its claim. In America, millionaire Henry Ford disseminated *The Protocols* by the thousands. The next major player to take advantage of the fraudulent document was none other than Adolf Hitler, who used it to support the righteousness of his path. He too disseminated *The Protocols* as though they had actually taken place.

To Mikhail's surprise, he found that *The Protocols* did not belong in the past. He was astonished to find that, despite all the indisputable proofs that the thing was false, there were still nations that encouraged, and even took a hand in publicizing *The Protocols of the Elders of Zion*. Prominent among these were Arab countries such as Egypt and Syria, in addition to the Palestinian Authority, who pointed to the State of Israel as the present center of Judaism, a state that wished to sow destruction in the world as part of its ultimate plan for world dominion.

All of this was already known. What Mikhail was seeking was the path by which the document had made its way to Russia. Alex didn't know it, but there was a reason why Mikhail had advised Alex to hold the party celebrating his friend's election as speaker of the Duma in the Moldovan wine center of Cricova. Something in his research had led him to believe that he might find the answer to his question there.

The people of the small town were flattered by the important visit. The local council cleaned the streets leading to the endless wine tunnels until they gleamed, and the largest and most lavish hall, used only for the most important visitors and boasting the flags of Moldova and Russia ranged side by side, was pressed into service for this official event. The VIP delegation was treated with the highest honor that Cricova could produce: a comprehensive tour of the various wine cellars—including, of course, a taste of all the finest and most expensive wines they held.

Alex, a wine afficionado, complimented Mikhail on his choice of location. They arrived in Cricova along with their families early in the afternoon and would be leaving the next day. The program had been planned to prevent the delegation members from leaving town with their heads still heavy from all that fine wine...

Alex had been married close to ten years. Marina, his wife, had given him two daughters, Irina and Yalena. It was no coincidence that he had chosen names for them that sounded similar to his wife's. He had done so on the advice of his best friend, to compensate her in part for the work that took him away from home for the better part of the week. It was a rare occasion that took the entire family on an outing together, even one lasting just a few days.

Apart from Mikhail in attendance as a friend of the family, Dadushka and Babushka (Grandpa and Grandma) Kotorov also came, as well as a few close aides. Mikhail had arranged for his friend to have a brief respite in his heavy workload. He knew how important it was for Alex to invest in his family life. A divorce would look very bad on his resumé. It might affect his chances of becoming president one day.

Mikhail himself had never married. He claimed that he did not believe in the institution of marriage. He rejected Alex and Marina's oft-repeated arguments on the subject.

Even Victor Kotorov, who was very well versed in wine lore, was moved by what he witnessed in this little town. Whole underground streets were used to store a multitude of wine at the perfect temperature. The locals had acted wisely when they had given the long subterranean streets the names of different grapes. It was a unique experience, for example, to travel down Cabernet Sauvignon Street and see the barrels of wine that had been made from those vines filling the well-lit streets.

"How much wine do these tunnels hold?" Alex asked, enchanted.

The manager, who had chosen to switch places with the usual tour guide because of the importance of these special guests, produced the statistics from memory: "We are spread over more than 120 kilometers of streets, half of which are used for wine storage. At last count, we had over nine million bottles. About a million and a quarter of them are stored in our reserves here—under optimal conditions."

"Is all this wine produced locally?" Victor asked. "I can't believe this is the first time I've visited this place."

"Not exclusively," the manager replied with a proud smile. "We have a unique collection of wine that has arrived from a wide variety of locations. That will be our next stop, before we reach the main event: tasting our special wines."

They continued the tour, finding it hard to believe that they were riding comfortably along in vehicles about a hundred meters below ground. They passed Merlot Street and turned left at Pinot Noir Street. Under the special lighting, the barrels of wine blended naturally with the underground earth. After several minutes' travel, the driver stopped the car and his guests stepped out into the humid air that was so important for the wine peacefully resting all around them.

"Right this way," the manager said as he took his honored visitors into a white tunnel shaped like a wine goblet. "Here we have a very special collection, of which any collector in the world would want to have at least a portion. Stored here are 158 kinds of very rare wine. The jewel in the crown is..." He advanced a step and pointed at a bottle of vintage wine that was covered with a glass globe. "This! Does anyone want to guess what this wine is?"

The visitors pressed forward curiously. Each of them would have given a great deal to be able to state the source of the special wine regarding which the manager was waxing so lyrical. They approached the dusty bottle with caution, trying to read what it said. Mikhail spoiled the fun when he pointed to a small label attached to the bottle's other side: "Jerusalem, 1902? Is this Jewish wine?"

"Indeed. This is the only bottle in the world left of this rare wine. It also bears the special status of being the oldest bottle of wine in the world. There is no price for a bottle this rare, despite the fact that we've received estimates of more than a million dollars, no less. Nearby, you can see Jon Becker liquor from the same year. Together, they form a world record that you won't see anywhere else."

"Both of these are more than a century old," Alex marveled. "Though it's hard for me to believe they'd still be drinkable..."

"This wine is a collector's item," the manager said. "Come. Our guide here will show us the rest of the collection."

He stepped aside in favor of the tour guide, who was able to tell them something about every single bottle—what it was, and where it came from. "This, for instance, is an Italian wine from the year 1936, known as Marsala Superior..."

Mikhail was troubled. Something was disturbing him. He pulled the manager gently aside and whispered, "How did these Jewish bottles get here?"

The manager bit his lips nervously. It was clear that he was not happy about giving out this information. After a short hesitation, he said, "Have you ever heard of Hermann Goering?"

"The Nazi war criminal?"

"Yes." The manager nodded.

Hermann Goering had been one of the heads of Hitler's police and commander of the Luftwaffe—the Nazi air force. He'd established the Gestapo and was considered the most senior Nazi to be judged and condemned at the famous Nuremburg trials. Just hours before his sentence was to be carried out—death by hanging—he committed suicide in his cell with the help of a poison pill.

"Well, that well-known Nazi had expensive tastes. He systematically looted many works of art all across occupied Europe, and he acquired a most impressive collection of famous paintings and *objects d'art*. Among the things he amassed was a notable collection of rare wines. This collection was seized by Russia's Red Army when Berlin fell. And that's how the wine came to be here."

"So it is possible that this specific bottle was kept by some Jewish family for decades, until that murderer came along and took it?"

The manager bowed his head. "Indeed, it is sad..."

Mikhail did not buy into the man's sorrowful expression, but he didn't pursue the topic further. "I understand that these tunnels were created when stones were quarried from the mountain in order to build the city of Kishinev hundreds of years ago. How and when did they become storage tunnels for wine?"

The smile returned to the manager's lips. "In the middle of the previous century, the tunnels were put to the use you see now. Most people don't know who the genius was who came up with this successful idea. But if you will come to me later, I'll show you something interesting. Meanwhile, let's return to the tour, shall we?"

Mikhail smiled and rejoined his colleagues, who were listening to an account of a wine called Henry Meer from the year 1947. The tour was fascinating, and even Alex's young daughters enjoyed running along the long tunnels. As promised, the tour ended in a pleasant, air-conditioned reception hall where they had a chance to taste a variety of fine wines.

Alex sat in the comfortable armchair he was offered and tried in vain to compete with his father at guessing the type and year of each of the old wines they were given to taste. Before long, cries of triumph or joy filled the big room as father and son were found to be right or wrong in their guesses. Mikhail did not know much about wine and did not take part. He was knowledgeable about much more important things. Right now he was interested in hearing what the manager of this unique winery had to tell him.

He watched the Kotorov family and smiled. It had been a long while since they had spent time together. The pressures of work were continuous, the meetings and conferences numerous, and the intrigues and alliances that had to be forged took up every spare minute of Alex's day. How good it was that he, Mikhail, had managed to take him away from all that for a brief time. These beautiful moments would strengthen his family for the rest of the busy year to come.

Presently, the manager returned to the room. With a benevolent eye he watched the little girls racing happily about and playing with empty wine bottles and corks of various sizes. Alex, his wife, and his father were all laughing together as they sipped more wine.

Finally, his eyes fell on Mikhail, who was looking through a folder of documents. Dr. Potgorsky evinced an unusual sophistication. The manager had also heard that he might be Jewish. All he needed was for the Jews to claim ownership of his bottle of rare wine—the crown jewel of his collection. It would be a pity for them to try. The wine would remain here at any price.

He approached Mikhail and whispered, "Do you want to join me?" Mikhail roused himself from the research papers he'd been reading. For him, a vacation was time to spend on his hobby. He never needed extra time for games. He was above that.

He stood up and followed the manager to a spacious office. Alex and the others, busy with the pleasures of drink, didn't even notice that he was gone. The manager took out an exquisite box of old wood, seated Mikhail in an armchair, and gave him an old paper to read. The Russian letters were clear, though the page on which they were written testified to the passage of a great length of time since the words had been set down in ink.

"This is the handwriting of the originator of the idea to use the underground tunnels for storing wine," the manager said proudly. "A local boy who lived at the end of the 1800's. The letter was kept in the family for a long time. It wasn't until the 50's—about fifty years after it had been written—that someone in the family actually implemented the great idea. Read for yourself."

Mikhail sat up and read the letter with interest. He was a veteran researcher; handwritten letters were his bread and butter. It wasn't difficult to see from the writing and the various expressions it contained that the letter writer had not been an ignorant villager, as might be expected of a local boy from that era. The lines he read testified that he had been an intelligent person of vision.

There were signs that pointed to the fact that the letter had been mailed from Paris. Interesting how a simple Moldovan family had managed to send off a son to be educated in Paris… Let's see… The letter opened with an apology for not having written in some time… He had studied there for several years… And then the writer presented his plan:

I wanted to tell you about something that I thought of. A wonderful idea that can turn our little Cricova from another small town that produces wine to a worldwide center of wine production and storage, no less.

After this introduction, he outlined his idea—the results of which Mikhail was experiencing at that very moment. So his plan had come to fruition. Hats off to him.

But the rest of the letter interested Mikhail more:

By the way, I haven't told anyone about this—not even Pierre. He's been wonderful to me all this time, but he's also a hardheaded businessman and he might want to appropriate the idea for himself… Anyway, perhaps you could find out how we might take legal possession of the tunnels. The authorities don't have to know why you need them. No one has been interested in them for years, so there's no reason for anyone to begin now. When I come home we can launch the fabulous project at once. Brilliant, don't you think? (I can see Mother smiling with pride. Here's a hug…).

The letter ended abruptly. Mikhail turned the sheet of paper over, expecting to see the continuation, but he was disappointed. Something about the end of the letter bothered him. There was no logical conclusion to it. Someone had cut off the rest of the letter. From his vast experience, he was prepared to wager that there had been a continuation to what had been written. But he couldn't find another word.

"Well, what do you say?" his host asked. "Brilliant, no? To think how many years he was before his time."

"Where's the rest of the letter?" Mikhail asked.

"The rest? There is no rest! That's the whole letter! It's been passed from manager to manager for years. That's all it says." He stuck out his hand to take back the historical letter.

Mikhail was in no hurry to return it. He lifted the page closer to his face and scanned it carefully. His trained eyes realized in a second that the bottom of the letter had been cut with a knife or some other sharp object. This letter definitely had a continuation. The question was, what had happened to it?

Very possibly, after all these years, it had either disappeared or been destroyed. But it was interesting to speculate why someone would have cut it this way, as though to conceal something secret. As though something had been written there that someone hadn't wanted the world to see. What could it have been?

The manager's hand was still held out. Mikhail gave him the letter, which was quickly restored to its box.

"What was the name of the person who wrote the letter?" Mikhail asked.

"Yuri Marinov! Descendants of the Marinov family still live in Cricova and receive nice royalties."

"And you know nothing about the rest of the letter?"

"This is the first time I've heard such an idea."

Mikhail didn't press him. It was clear that the man was speaking the truth. If there was more to the letter, it wasn't here. From experience, he found it hard to believe the missing segment would ever be located. But his spirit of research was already at work, weaving a plan of action. Even if his search proved fruitless, he had to try.

He rose from the armchair and thanked his host, taking care to erase every vestige of the strained atmosphere that had reigned in the room when he'd practically accused the manager of concealing the rest of the letter. He thumped the man's shoulder and complimented him on the wonderful work he was doing. The manager was quickly placated and warmed up tremendously when he heard that the head of the Duma had not enjoyed himself so much in a long time.

They returned to the honored delegation, each of whose members seemed on the verge of a hangover. Mikhail gave himself a pat on the back for anticipating this situation and arranging for them to spend the night. Traveling in this state would have been a nightmare. He gave their hosts a hefty tip and made sure the members of his group reached their rented rooms, where they could properly sleep off their wine.

He had other plans.

After checking to see that everyone was in his or her allotted room, that all the Kotorovs and their attendants were satisfied, and that the girls' nanny had put them to bed, he turned to a few curious local lads who had come to gape at the famous personalities and asked them a simple question. Two minutes later, he set off on foot in the direction of a farm not too far away, where he stopped and knocked on the door.

The old woman who opened the door studied him suspiciously. His clothing made it obvious that he was not from those parts, probably one of the winery guests. She didn't like the guests, who were generally loud and drunk and always viewed themselves as superior to the simple village folk.

"What do you want?" she said, scowling.

"Good evening to you, babushka!" Mikhail answered with a smile. He could read the old woman easily, and knew that a bit of flattery would soon win her over. "What a beautiful garden!" he said as he pointed to the flourishing flower beds near the house.

"You didn't come here to talk about the garden." The old woman spoke gruffly, but her manner had softened somewhat. "What do you want?"

"This evening I heard about the local boy who first raised the idea of turning the tunnels into a winery. I would love to hear more stories about him. I wanted to know if you could tell me where his family lives. I think their name is Marinov."

The old woman spat out a curse. "An accursed family! Their money destroyed the family. Curses on Yuri Marinov for doing that to his family."

Mikhail was curious. What had happened to the Marinovs? "It

seems you know everything that goes on around here."

The woman smiled. "Here I was raised, and here I'll die. Cricova is my home, and everyone knows what's going on in their home. I even remember the first bottle of wine that came out of the winery. If you have time, you can come in and I'll tell you about the Marinovs."

Mikhail didn't hesitate. He followed her into the house. She poured boiling water from an ancient pot that stood on the fire and prepared him some sort of unidentifiable hot drink. Despite his revulsion, he accepted the cup willingly. He had a hunch the story would be worth it.

"Yuri died before I was born," the old woman began, "but the legends about him were still alive and well. I remember how, when I was a girl, my mother told me with pride that a local boy had thought up an idea for getting rid of the Jews who had taken over every good part of Moldova. It wasn't like today, when you aren't allowed to tell the truth. Back then, everyone knew that the Jews were like poison. There were no rich Jews in America then, telling everyone what to do. They knew how to deal with them properly."

She breathed hard, with excitement and exertion, and continued. "Yuri sent the czar some sort of idea for getting rid of them, and you know what the Jews did?" She paused dramatically, to stretch out the suspense for her rare guest. Years had passed since she had had such an attentive listener who actually cared to hear what she had to say. "They murdered him."

Mikhail made a mental note to check into Yuri Marinov's death. Not every grandmother's tale was necessarily true, though it was always possible there was a kernel of truth in her words.

"But what they didn't know was that they were too late. Not only had Yuri had time to send the czar his plan, but he had also managed to send a copy to his family, who boasted all through the village that the czar was taking advice from their son. Their pride didn't last long, though, because the Jews murdered him. But they avenged his death and participated in cleansing Kishinov of its Jews. You could say that it's largely in the merit of Yuri Marinov that Moldova today is freer of Jews than it ever was."

Mikhail caught his breath. Her story reinforced what he'd been thinking. Was it possible that this same Yuri was the original source of *The Protocols of the Elders of Zion*? That could be a revelation on a global scale—and it was up to him to prove it. From her story, he understood that all of this had been written in a letter that Yuri had sent. The letter he had held not long before. But how could he get his hands on the missing portion—if that were possible at all?

"You said that something happened to the Marinov family," he reminded her.

"Yes, that's right. Yuri had no children, because he was killed before he married. But his only sister had ten—and every one of them died, except for the youngest, Nikolai, named after the czar."

"Nikolai grew up a wild man who inherited the Marinov wine empire and drove it into the ground with lightning speed. He had everything he needed to succeed, and instead spent his days drinking himself into a stupor.

"In his 40's, when I was a young girl, a passing visitor accidentally entered Nikolai's house. That drunkard sold the visitor all the family heirlooms, in return for a paltry sum and a tiny royalty from the winery. To this day, the Marinov family is very poor and lives off a small stipend from the winery. And all because that stranger read the cursed letter and realized he had a fortune on his hands."

It had been that stranger, Mikhail grasped, who'd undoubtedly cut off the part about *The Protocols*. The stranger had understood that anti-Semitism was no longer in favor and would destroy the winery's reputation. Therefore, he'd gotten rid of the proof.

How much he, Mikhail, would give to read that missing portion. It was only a small part of a letter, but it had changed Jewish history. What a pity he would never see it.

He stood up and handed the old woman back her empty dirty glass. When she hadn't been looking, he'd poured its contents into a nearby plant. There was a limit to the amount one must sacrifice for information. He thanked her profusely and on his way out complimented her again on her flourishing garden. The old woman thanked him too. He'd made her year by listening to her so attentively.

"Good-bye, you nice man," she said as he walked down the path. "How sad that the only one left from that genius is a grandson of his sister's—the son of the fool who sold everything. And he's just as foolish and drunken as his father was. All he has in life is a bit of money and wine from the winery, and half of some old letter."

12

Jerusalem, June 2010

YISRAEL STAYED HOME TWO MORE DAYS BEFORE THE mashgiach allowed him to return to yeshivah. They were never-ending days, when he felt imprisoned in his house while his relationship with his father swiftly went down the drain. Tatty was so angry at him. How could Yisrael hit a fellow student? He was not prepared to listen to explanations about how and why it had happened. One wasn't allowed to hit, period.

Yisrael remembered his father hitting *him* from time to time, when he would do something wrong. He had never thought twice about it, but now it bubbled inside him like a poison. Everyone was against him. It was also the first time he felt resentful about learning, because Tatty forced him to go to shul every day and study the material that the others boys were learning in yeshivah.

Mommy, on the other hand, did listen to him, and she understood him. That was the sole point of light in those dark days, two long days that ended with him standing, furious and betrayed, in front of the mashgiach.

The mashgiach tried to talk to him, but Yisrael hardly listened. All he cared about was his upcoming reunion with his friends. What kind of reception would they give him? Yossi must hate him—but that was okay, because Yisrael hated *him* too. And Menashe… Well, he was another miserable character. But Ariel? What would his best friend think of him? Did Ariel still believe in his innocence?

He finished his interview with the mashgiach, put his things in his empty dorm room, and went to the classroom where Rav Marcus was delivering his *iyun shiur*. He placed his hand on the doorknob, took a deep breath, and opened the door with what he hoped was a nonchalant expression. As though nothing had happened.

His plan fell apart when sudden silence descended on the room. His classmates, who'd been vigorously debating some point with the *maggid shiur*, all stopped talking at once. Only Rav Marcus' voice, arguing with Efraim, the class *masmid*, could still be heard.

Rav Marcus had clearly not noticed the newcomer's entrance. But he did notice the sudden silence. All the boys were staring at the doorway, where Yisrael stood, pale as snow and shaky in the knees.

Rav Marcus quickly took charge of the situation by greeting his student joyfully. "Yisrael! We missed you. We happen to be right in the middle of discussing the classification of a *nazir*. Does it fall into the category of an *issur gavra*, or is it something else? Come, listen to what Efraim has to say…" He asked Efraim to repeat his argument, while Yisrael gratefully took his seat, wishing he could simply disappear.

Gradually he got into the spirit of things. The *sugya* was one that was familiar to him, and he participated as the *shiur* went on—much to his teacher's relief. Rav Marcus was aware of recent events, but chose to act as if he didn't have a clue. He trusted the mashgiach implicitly in these areas. Rav Aharon understood people; over the years, Rav Marcus had witnessed that clearly. *B'ezras Hashem*, Yisrael Davis, who was one of his best students, would get back into the swing of things and this whole sad episode would be forgotten.

If Yisrael thought the *shiur* went well, the following *seder* showed him just how things really stood. The other *bachurim* steered clear of him. His friends chose not to sit near him. And, apart from one or two students who did not take part in the *cherem*, no one exchanged a single word with him. Even those who felt sorry for Yisrael, or believed him innocent, were afraid to violate the clear prohibition imposed by Yossi Goldfarb.

Yanky Sherman, one of the less popular boys in the class, did come over to Yisrael to tell him about the *cherem* resolution. "But I didn't agree. I won't be a part of it," he declared.

This did not exactly encourage Yisrael. He'd never had anything to do with Yanky. Actually, no one in his class had anything to do with Yanky, who was—how to put it?—a bit odd. His clothes were always in disarray, his hands were dirty, and he always said whatever he thought, without censoring himself.

"It's not that I don't think you stole," Yanky continued. "But I believe that you've repented and won't do it again." He beamed at Yisrael. Yisrael felt like kicking him.

The situation worsened as the day went on. When he took a seat in the dining room at lunchtime, all the boys sitting around the table pointedly stood up and moved to other tables. Yisrael would have preferred insults and curses. If someone fights with you, at least you're communicating. Here, he was alone on the battlefield. Yanky didn't count.

But Ariel was the one who broke his heart completely. At the afternoon break, he didn't show up in their room. This was nothing new, as he often spent the break learning in the nearby shul. But Yisrael thought it would have been more fitting for him to take the trouble to come up and talk to his suffering friend. Menashe had already moved to a different room and no one had come to take his place. Thus, Yisrael rested alone that afternoon. His solitude lasted into the following *seder* and to the end of the long day.

After night *seder*, he returned to his room. This time, Ariel was there. He was arranging the already neat covers on his bed, clearly uncertain about what was the right thing to do. This angered Yisrael.

"Well?" he demanded. "Are *you* against me too? Like everyone else?"

Full of anger and hurt, Yisrael didn't try to find favor in anyone. What he didn't understand was that some of the boys were willing to give him a chance, but his animosity pushed them away. As far as Yisrael was concerned, anyone who even considered the possibility of him stealing wasn't worthy of being called a friend.

Ariel was in no rush to answer. He smoothed his sheet again and paid close attention to the precise positioning of his pillow. Finally, he replied in a low voice, not looking at his friend.

"Look, I don't know who's responsible for everything that's been happening here lately, but something bad has gotten into you. Even if I don't believe that you stole, you broke Menashe's nose. I have to be open with you. You were my best friend…but today, I'm not so sure about that anymore. I don't hate you, like some of the kids here, but it's not the way it was. Who knows? Maybe, with time…"

"But I don't have time!" Yisrael burst out. "I don't have time to wait and see if I have even one friend in this whole annoying place. Decide now: are you with me or against me?"

He breathed hard, furious with Ariel. After all the time they'd spent together, the talks they'd shared long into the night—this was how Ariel behaved? Yisrael hated the yeshivah now. He hated his friends, hated Ariel and even the mashgiach, who hadn't stopped Yossi from maligning him. If he'd had any place to go, he'd get up and leave right now.

Ariel didn't answer. He quietly got ready for bed and made no further attempt to talk. Yisrael did not try to talk anymore either. He didn't need false friends. He'd get along fine on his own.

The following days were horrible. He went from being a popular and accepted boy to an utterly rejected one. Yisrael withdrew into himself. He learned alone, ate alone, and hardly exchanged a word with anyone. Rav Aharon, seeing the boy wither before his eyes, tried his best. He spoke with Yisrael again and again, trying to encourage him. Yisrael didn't listen. He also tried to change the hostility toward Yisrael by praising him publicly, and by having personal talks with some key *bachurim* in Yisrael's *shiur*. Nothing helped.

Yisrael, for his part, did not help matters with his withdrawn and aloof attitude. The whispers of "thief!" that he heard from time to time reminded everyone what this was all about. Finally, the mashgiach had no choice but to call Yisrael's father in for a serious and urgent talk.

Exactly what they talked about, Yisrael never knew. But the message that came through was clear: For Yisrael's own good, he must find a new yeshivah. A yeshivah where no one knew what had happened, where he had no enemies, where he could start fresh and on the right foot. It would be a pity for him to spend two more years like this, an outcast from yeshivah life. The two years before his passage to *yeshivah gedolah* were critical in a growing boy's development. Here, his emerging character would suffer terribly, and who knew if it would even be possible to correct the situation later on?

Tatty categorically disagreed with the mashgiach. He thought that time would do its healing trick and then everything would be fine again. He pressured the yeshivah to keep Yisrael, but the mashgiach insisted, and Tatty was left with no choice. He made the rounds of the various other yeshivos that Rav Aharon had recommended, dragging Yisrael along with him. In one of them, he hoped, there would be an educator who would know how to set his son back on track.

But Yisrael wouldn't cooperate. He was wounded to the depths of his soul and decided that, if *his* yeshivah didn't want him, he would not attend *any* yeshivah. He could learn alone, like his father, or even go out and get a job. At this point, he no longer cared. The important thing was to be rid of Yossi, his torturer, and all the others who had turned their backs on him in his hour of need. When taking the entrance test for the various yeshivos, he played dumb. He told one mashgiach that he wanted to kill himself—anything so as not to be accepted.

He laughed when his father told him that the mashgiach had urged him to take Yisrael to see a psychologist. Tatty did not find it funny. More and more people had been suggesting that he do that very thing. Did they think his son had emotional problems? They knew nothing. He came to the conclusion that the *chareidi* educational system did not understand the situation. They were making a mountain out of a molehill. A child simply hadn't found his place in yeshivah, and they were ready to send him off to a psychologist. Nonsense. If the situation had been handled correctly, none of this would have happened.

Yerachmiel Davis was at his wits' end. He lost faith in everyone and decided that only he could save his beloved son from the quicksand in which he was mired. Flying in the face of the mashgiach's advice to shower Yisrael with love and warmth, he dragged his son out of bed at 7 every morning and sent him out of the house. "Go to shul for *Shacharis*. After that, you'll get some breakfast." Only strong-arm tactics would teach the boy his place. A boy needed to know how to obey his elders.

Yisrael fought him every morning—and lost. But there was not a single morning that he returned for breakfast. He'd rather go hungry than humiliate himself and beg for food. He didn't go to shul. Instead, he would sit on a bench in a nearby park and wait for time to pass. At exactly 9, when his father went out to learn, he would go back home—and into bed.

His mother didn't bother him too much. Though she continually cried about him, he found he could no longer care. He was sick and tired of all of them. He was sick and tired of life.

In the end, Tatty gave up on him, too. He ignored his son, who spent most of the day huddled in bed. Or that, at any rate, was what Yisrael thought. His father no longer forced him to go to shul.

In truth, Yerachmiel Davis refused to give up on his only son. He shed copious tears over Yisrael in his prayers, raced from one educator to another pleading for advice, and spoke regularly on the phone with Rav Aharon, the mashgiach, to update him and ask for his help. But no one had the magical formula to solve the problem. They were unanimous in urging that Yisrael see a professional. Yerachmiel was disappointed in them. What did they know? His son was perfectly all right. It was only the *yetzer hara* that had slightly overpowered him.

One day followed another in idleness and inaction. Nothing interested Yisrael anymore. Neither the Torah, nor his family, nor even his little sisters, who had tried at first to include him in their games, before they realized that Yisrael was very angry. That he was no longer as nice to them as he'd been before. Or as big of a *tzaddik* as he'd once been. He never davened anymore.

Day and night blurred together for him. At times, he was awake all night and made up for lost sleep throughout the day. He discovered that the quiet night was a good friend to his bad feelings. He put earbuds in his ears and listened to slow, quiet music as he roamed restlessly around a chilly Jerusalem. More than once, he played with the fantasy of a car hitting him and sending him to the hospital. How everyone would be sorry then for what they'd done to him.

They would beg his forgiveness. But he wouldn't forgive them until they had a taste of what they had done to him. Yossi, the mashgiach, Tatty—everyone. He hated them all. Maybe he would even die in the accident, and they would finally all cry over him. They would realize that it was they who had actually killed him. He was such a good boy. And they were the ones who had destroyed him.

The height of the summer was behind him when the call from Yoram came. Yisrael was alone at home at 10:30 in the morning. His mother had taken his sisters to the beach, Tatty was most likely deep in his learning, and only Yisrael was home. Asleep.

The phone rang and rang, finally rousing him. Someone was being very persistent. Irritably, Yisrael dragged himself out of bed and went to see who was calling.

"Hello?" he barked.

"Yisrael? It's Yoram. I've been looking for you for two weeks. What happened to you?"

"Yoram? From the basketball court? What do you want?" A worry crept into Yisrael's mind: *Was the incident with Gadi coming back to haunt him?* "How did you get my number?"

"You lied to me," Yoram shot back. "You promised you'd call, and you didn't."

"Look… A few things have happened since then, and I've been really busy," he apologized. "But how did you get my number?"

"I called your yeshivah a few times. It took hours till someone picked up. And then they finally told me that you weren't even learning there. I thought you'd lied to me. But I called them again, and a different boy answered, and told me that you'd left the yeshivah and were home now. Do you know how many Davis families there are in the Givat Shaul area? It took me five tries before I found you."

"But what do you want?" Yisrael asked in surprise. "Why did you try so hard to find me?"

"Listen," Yoram ordered. "My trainer is forming a special basketball camp. He's going to teach us how to play the game, and he's looking for players to join the group. I told him about you, and he didn't believe me. You have to come play with us. It'll be great!"

Yisrael stared at the phone with eyes that were pink with too much sleep. He wasn't interested in playing. He wasn't interested in anything. He just wanted to go back to bed and sleep. But how could he get rid of Yoram?

"Look…I can't really come. I have a lot of stuff to do. And anyway, my parents would never let me go."

"They don't have to know," Yoram said. "I'll come get you at 10 tomorrow morning, and bring you back at 4. Tell them that you went to yeshivah or something."

Yisrael smiled sadly to himself. As if they would believe him if he told them he'd gone to yeshivah. How amusing…

On the other hand, what did he have to lose? It wasn't as if he was doing anything at home.

"I don't know," he said evasively. "I don't feel so well…"

"Stop running around in circles," Yoram said, annoyed. "I'll be waiting outside your house at exactly 10 a.m. tomorrow. If you don't come down, I'll come up to pay you a visit. Bye."

Yisrael stood in his living room openmouthed, receiver in hand, for several long minutes after Yoram hung up.

13

MOMMY COULD NOT BELIEVE HER EYES WHEN SHE SAW Yisrael the next morning, dressed and ready to leave the house before 10 o'clock. She couldn't remember the last time he'd rolled out of bed before 1 in the afternoon.

"Where are you going, Yisrael?" she asked in surprise.

"Nowhere special. Just to meet a friend…" He went down to the street.

Yoram was already waiting. "Hey, get in. You're in luck—I planned to go inside to fetch you."

Yisrael got into the car and looked around in interest. He wasn't familiar with this model, but it was obvious that it was a very expensive vehicle. The good smell and pristine condition it was in testified that its owners took very good care of it.

"What do you think of the car?" Yoram asked with a proud smile.

"Beautiful! What kind is it? A Mitsubishi?"

"Yes, but do you know which model? This is not a standard car. Ever heard of the Mitsubishi Revolution?"

"Revolution? As in rebellion?"

"Right! You have no idea what an amazing sports car this is. It can compete with the best sports cars there are. And don't ask what it costs."

"How much?" Yisrael asked.

"I told you not to ask." Yoram laughed. "But don't worry—my father's the one who paid."

Yisrael looked at the car with respect. Everything was handsome and clearly high-quality: the seats, the steering wheel, the dashboard… Apparently, Yoram's family had money. "By the way, what's your last name? You already know mine…"

"Yoram Harel. Nice to meet you," Yoram said in a formal voice. "Ever heard of CDF?"

Yisrael shook his head. In his surprise, Yoram almost lost control of the car.

"Really? You never heard of CDF? It's a top Israeli company—trades on the stock market, second only to Teva."

"How should I know that? Do I work in the stock market?" Yisrael never liked being ignorant of something, especially not something that everyone knew but him.

"Okay, okay. I forgot that you're just a kid," Yoram said, insulting him unwittingly. "CDF is a private company that manufactures a special part for fuel engines. All the big companies in the world buy from us—General Electric, Rolls Royce. And any firm that can afford it."

"Well, what does that have to do with anything?"

"My father founded the firm." Yoram beamed as he imparted this stunning piece of information. "My father is the big boss."

That explained the costly car, and perhaps also its driver's self-confidence. Yisrael found nothing to say. Yoram turned on the radio to listen to some music, but it was precisely 10:00—time for the news broadcast.

"Enough about that murder," Yoram said irritably. "Don't they have anything else to talk about?"

"What murder?"

Yoram stared. "Where are you living? Do you mean to tell me that you didn't hear about the murder of the science minister? Is there anything you *do* know?"

Yisrael flushed. How could he explain to Yoram that nothing interested him these days? That, in recent weeks, he'd hardly spoken to a soul?

"Who killed him?"

"Some Arab sniper. A single shot, right on target. He was driving on the Tunnel Road and an Arab sniper from the village of al-Khader got him. The news people are saying that it was an impossible shot. That the sniper was a real professional."

"Didn't they build a protective fence there?"

"They did. But there are holes in between, simply because a solid fence isn't needed. The fencing is enough to foil any possible attack."

"And now we see that, if Hashem wants, anything is possible..."

"Enough already! What is all this? Are you trying to turn me into a *baal teshuvah*? No lectures, please. Okay?"

Yisrael didn't answer. This Yoram could be annoying. Who said anything about becoming a *baal teshuvah*?

They made the rest of the trip in an uncomfortable silence. It was only as they neared the Malcha shopping mall that Yoram spoke again. "We're going to play in the official court of HaPoel Yerushalayim in Malcha."

They parked in a lot that Yoram claimed belonged to the professional athletes who came here to play. Yisrael picked up the bag that held his clothes and stepped out of the sparkling car. Yoram hurriedly stopped him. "That's okay. You'll get everything free here—clothes, and even shoes. Everything's on the Baron's tab."

They entered a playing area more spacious than Yisrael had ever seen. Hundreds and even thousands of empty seats surrounded the court. "You have to see this place when it's full," Yoram crowed. "Amazing!"

About twenty boys, Yisrael's age or older, ran about aiming basketballs at the hoops on either end of the court. They all wore matching red uniforms and new white sneakers. Yisrael noticed that only one of them wore a yarmulke on his head, and it was a knitted one. Definitely not his style.

Several men in gray passed among the players, issuing orders accompanied by shrill blasts on a whistle. One of them, in his 60's by the looks of him, white-haired, very tall, and perpetually smiling, came up to them and scolded Yoram. "What's this? Late again!"

"Let it go, Chico." Yoram was unshaken by the rebuke. He placed a hand on the man's shoulders, as though they were friends and peers. "Wait until you see what I've brought you."

Yisrael felt uncomfortable under their scrutiny. Also, Yoram's manner with the older man was strange to him. In Yisrael's circles, respect for one's elders was a strict principle. Not, apparently, in Yoram's.

Chico looked Yisrael up and down. It was obvious that he was very skeptical about this new player. But he didn't say a word, except, "Go get dressed, and quickly. We're about to start a practice game."

Yoram led Yisrael to the changing area. "Do you know who that was?" he asked, and then continued without waiting for a reply. "That was Chico Kleiner. He was a top player for Israel and HaPoel Yerushalayim in the 70's. The man's a living legend. He was offered a transfer to Maccabee and refused out of loyalty. There's nothing like that today."

Yisrael had once heard something about Maccabee Tel Aviv, Israel's leading team for many years now. Only later did he learn about the bitter rivalry between the Jerusalem and Tel Aviv teams. He and Yoram reached a well-appointed locker room, where they rapidly changed into red uniforms and returned to the court.

"It looks good on you," Yoram complimented him. "You almost don't look like a *doss* in that uniform. If you'd only take off your yarmulke, no one would even know."

Yisrael ignored Yoram's tone—when someone called a religious person a *doss* he was not paying a compliment—and instead instinctively raised his hand to protect his head. "What are you talking about?" he retorted. "There's no way I'd take off my yarmulke!"

"Relax," Yoram laughed. "Didn't you see that there's another *doss* in the group? I'm sure he'll have an extra bobby pin or two for you."

"I don't need them." Yisrael always carried a few bobby pins in his wallet. He'd learned that trick from Yossi, who'd said, "You never know when you'll want to play!" The mere memory of Yossi infuriated him.

"You two are on the red team," Chico Kleiner said when they came closer. "We'll have a warm-up game and go on from there. Let's go—one, two!"

Yoram signaled for Yisrael to follow him to the left side of the court, where three tall boys were waiting for them. One of them was very thin but of exceptional height. Yisrael didn't think he'd ever met a young person that tall. In fact, he didn't think he'd ever met anyone, at any age, that tall.

"Okay. Let's show them what it's all about!" Yoram said. On either side of the court stood five players, also in red shorts. But their shirts were white.

"We'll start with zone defense. You!" He pointed at the skinny giant. "You're in charge of the colored zone. Ron closes in on the right side, and Jabbar takes the left side. The *doss* and I will take the top. Understand? Any questions?"

Yisrael didn't understand a thing. What was a zone defense? And what were they guarding on top? But he didn't want to expose his ignorance in front of the others. He decided to go with the flow and figure it out alone.

"Where are you going?" Yoram yelled as he moved toward the basket. "We're guarding the top!" He pointed at the area farthest from the hoop, near the halfway point on the court. "I'll guard the right side and you take the left. Get it?"

Yisrael blushed and nodded. "Top" was far from the hoop, and "bottom" was near it. Simple.

"Okay, that's the defense," Yoram continued. "In offense, I'm point guard, the tall guys move inward and you, Yisrael, wait on the three-point line for passed balls. Understand?"

The four other players nodded. The power structure was clear. Yoram was the team's unquestioned leader. Yisrael noted that the trainer himself, Chico Kleiner, was issuing orders on the other side of the court. Apparently, Yoram's status was not simply that of a mere player.

A member of the white team went to free throw line and threw a basket. Chico blew a long blast on his whistle and announced, "Whites open! Come on, let's see what you're worth!"

Yisrael was tense. He'd never played with professionals before. The opposing team scattered over their half of the court and raced around with blinding speed.

Yisrael tried to see who he was supposed to guard, and failed. There were two players near him; he didn't know which of them to go after. Finally, he decided to latch onto a dark boy running past him who was moving toward the basket, calling out to a player on his team to pass him the ball. This was a mistake. The opposing team's point guard noticed the redheaded player standing near the three-point line on the left—Yisrael's side—and hastily passed him the ball. The redheaded player didn't waste a second. He hooked the ball, took a deep breath, aimed, and threw it at the hoop. It landed neatly inside, with a sibilant rustle.

"Three-zero!" cried a bald man standing near Chico. Later, Yisrael would learn that his name was Dani and he was Chico's assistant.

"What was that supposed to be?" Yoram yelled at Yisrael. "He was supposed to be yours!"

The other players also muttered angrily, but the trainer didn't allow them to be idle. "Hey! What are you waiting for? Go on the offense!" The tall, thin one—Nachi—ran over to the outside edge and passed the ball to Yoram. Yoram began dribbling it rapidly, as his team members ran ahead to the other side of the court. Yisrael ran to the hoop area, feeling like a dwarf among giants. All the other players were at least a head taller than he was.

"What are you doing?" Yoram shouted again. Furiously, he motioned for Yisrael to move away. Yisrael remembered that he was supposed to wait for the ball on the three-point line. He hurried over there, but meanwhile Yoram had passed the ball to Yaron, who raced toward the basket and shot the ball while running. From out of nowhere, a tall player from the other team rose up and blocked the ball as it made its way through the air toward the basket. The ball was thrown in Yisrael's direction. He tried to catch it, but a different player from the other side was there first. He grabbed the ball and ran for his team's basket. Yisrael raced after him, but he was too late.

"Five-zero," Dani announced.

"Time-out!" Yoram called angrily.

Chico whistled and nodded his consent. "One minute time-out. Yoram and red team—to me, now!"

The members of the white team exchanged high fives and smiles. Even this early in the game, it was clear that they had the upper hand.

The red team clustered around Chico, who demanded an explanation from Yoram. "I thought you said he could play." He talked about Yisrael as though he wasn't there. Yoram was breathing hard, from exertion and anger. He remembered that, if blame was to be apportioned, it was he who had brought Yisrael here. No one else.

"Just give me a minute with him," he requested, and dragged Yisrael far from Chico and the others. "You're messing up, big time," he hissed at Yisrael. "I thought you knew how to play."

"I do know how!" Yisrael was red with mortification. "But I don't understand half of what you guys are saying. I never played with rules before!"

All the breath left Yoram. He began laughing wildly. Every player turned to watch him, astonished. At last, he regained control over himself and whispered to Yisrael, "You're right. I completely forgot... All right, all I want you to do is stand on the three-point line and wait for a pass from me. And, in defense...try at least to bother the one with the ball, okay?"

Yisrael nodded uncertainly.

"All right! Back to the court," Dani called. Yoram got the ball from Nachi and darted forward on the offense. Yisrael ran to the three-point line and waited for a pass, but a player from the rival team stuck close and prevented Yoram from passing to him. Tall Nachi shoved his way inside to the hoop and Yoram threw him the ball. He caught it and threw it at the hoop—but missed. The other team hurried to carry out an offense of its own.

Yoram made life hard for the white-team player who was dribbling the ball. He guarded him very closely and from time to time thrust a hand out toward the ball. After a number of tries, he succeeded, and the ball flew off the court toward the reserve bench, where alternate players were sitting and watching the game. Chico blew his whistle and called, "Red ball!"

Yoram hurried over to Yisrael. "Come on, get rid of your guard! Don't stand in one place. Get away from your guard so I can pass to you." He grabbed the ball, which had been passed to him from the other side of the court.

Yisrael did as he had been told. He ran to the right side of the opponents' court, and the minute a player came to guard him he changed direction and ran over to the left. The player designated to guard that side came one second too late to intercept Yoram's well-aimed throw. One second in which Yisrael managed to catch the ball and toss it cleanly into the basket.

"Five-three!" Dani announced, while Yoram jumped and yelled like an Indian. Yisrael noticed Chico look at him and jot something down in his notebook.

The other team did not manage to get a basket in the next offensive, and Yoram led with a wild attack of his own that ended at the hoop itself, leaving the score tied at five. Now it was the other team that asked for a time-out. Yisrael saw Chico call Yoram over and give him instructions, pointing at Yisrael. Yoram nodded, and in each of the next two offensives he arranged again for Yisrael to get the ball. Yisrael added six more points to the red side. They were leading now, eleven to seven.

"Thirty seconds left!" Dani called. The white team was galvanized. They managed to get another basket, which moved them up to two points from a tie and three from victory.

"Don't give them three!" Yoram called out, and redoubled his guard on his opposing player. Yisrael was charged; he wanted to show them that he was a good player. He decided to trick the white team's player who was running with the ball. He ran back toward the basket as though he didn't notice the redhead standing at the three-point line on his side. The white point guard swallowed the bait and passed the ball from a distance to the freed-up redhead. This was exactly what Yisrael had been waiting for.

He shot right into the ball's path and managed to slap it with his hand. Within a second, he was near the white team's hoop, where he delicately fed the ball to the basket. Such a throw was the heart's desire of every basketball player: no one had enough time to run over and guard him, and at such proximity the ball had a 99 percent chance of landing inside. Yisrael was already celebrating his victory—when the ball spun twice on the rim and fell outside.

Stunned, Yisrael didn't react quickly enough. The white point guard, who'd raced after him in an attempt to stop him, grabbed the ball as it fell and threw a long pass to the redhead in the center of the court. The redhead, freed of any guard, ran forward and threw a three-pointer from the exact same spot as he'd done at the start of the game. The ball made its way in a high arc. Yisrael tracked it with his eyes as it moved as though in slow motion, rising higher and higher and then slowly falling…right into the hoop.

"Time's up!" Dani announced, throwing the white team into a frenzy of celebration. Yoram was boiling, though he tried to control himself. He went over to Yisrael and said, "It could have happened to anyone." But the other players on their team were furious. "Why'd you throw at all? We were leading by two points! All you had to do was babysit the ball until the end of the game!"

Yisrael didn't know then that in professional basketball this was the wisest course. His spirit of competitiveness hadn't even allowed him to think about not trying to take a shot that seemed so easy. But the sad outcome taught him that lesson—the hard way. Better a victory in hand than an extra point on the hoop.

14

Russia, 2010

THE WORLD DIDN'T APPROVE OF RUSSIA'S WEAPONS SALES to Iran. The new defense system that Russia had sold Iran lowered the world's ability to operate against her when necessary, and inestimably increased the losses that might be incurred in such an operation. The mockery the Iranian president made of the UN inspectors who tried to ascertain that he had no nuclear program infuriated the United States. For years, the two nations had been in a state of quiet hostility—ever since the revolution and the kidnaping in the American Embassy. The Americans didn't even have a diplomatic presence in Tehran anymore, and they worked strenuously against the state, which stood at the center of the "Axis of Evil."

Had it been up to the United States, economic sanctions would have crippled Iran years ago. But the days of total hegemony were over. Though the United States of America was still considered the strongest power in the world, both China, which was developing rapidly, and Russia, always a serious rival, were slowly eating away at America's authority as the world's policeman. They were not afraid to halt or minimize the condemnatory UN proposals against Iran, and demanded that the United Nations not interfere with the sovereignty of any nation.

Like all nations, China and Russia acted according to the dictates of their own self-interest—and only theirs. From the perspective of the elected president in Moscow, Russia must preserve her status as a power equal to the United States, and not one that would simply do as she was bid. Also, she was interested in retaining her complete dominion over her territories, making sure that no other government interfered with Russia's internal affairs. What took place in Russia stayed in Russia. Therefore, Alex Kotorov chose to work methodically against the United States' policy of interference in every conflict in the world. Iraq, Afghanistan—and now, Iran.

In addition to all of this, he also, of course, had an overwhelming economic interest in the matter. The export of arms was an important source of income in the Russian economy, and the Islamic nations paid good money for weapons.

The Chinese too dreamed of playing a larger role on the international stage. To that end, they continually thrust spokes into the wheels of the American wagon—which was dependent on the Chinese economy no less than China's was dependent on that of the United States.

Because of all these factors, nothing succeeded in halting the selling of arms. The second part of the deal went into effect with a convoy of enormous armored trucks making its way from Russia to Iran.

Beneath the radar of all the world's intelligence networks, the trucks were transferred to the Iranian Army, where a crew of Russian experts began to help assembling the system and training the Iranians in its operation.

The denunciations from the United States and Europe did not move President Kotorov overmuch. Nor did the criticism of his political opposition and the various news media disturb him. The Russian people, by and large, loved a strong leadership that refused to submit. With his unwavering foreign policy, Alex Kotorov had restored national pride to Russia. The people loved him and voted for him—and the people got exactly what they wanted: a strong leader who did not bow to American demands.

The only thing the newspapers didn't understand was how it was that his Jew-loving friend did not manage to influence him. It was no secret that one of the president's closest advisers was none other than the famous researcher Mikhail Potgorsky, rumors about whose supposedly Jewish antecedents reared their heads from time to time. Dr. Potgorsky was known as a fervent admirer of the Jewish nation in general, and of the State of Israel in particular. And despite his open opposition to the Iranian deal, the president had signed the contract.

Word in the Kremlin had it that relations between the two had cooled since that deal. Not even a formal denial convinced the rumormongers otherwise. A long article that appeared shortly afterward claimed that a black cat had crossed between the two old friends. That cat was named Vladimir Solosenko.

Solosenko, who served as the Russian prime minister—a largely formal position—was a self-declared Jew hater. As part of his political platform, he'd claimed that the Russians lost to the Germans in World War II because of "subversives from within." In closed-door conferences, he'd been heard to state more than once that it was the rich Jews of America who had won the Cold War.

In personality, Vladimir Solosenko very much resembled President Kotorov. He too was an eloquent politician, an athlete, and a wealthy man in his own right. He was ambitious and lucky and had reached the apex of Russian government with startling ease. His connections and a natural charisma had sent him rocketing up to the head of the Russian influence ladder. The president's and prime minister's similar lifestyles and hobbies brought them very close. Both of them came from prosperous homes; both were articulate and charismatic. And both had made their way to their leadership roles with relative speed.

In Russia, the president is the one who, in the final analysis, leads the nation. In this, Vladimir was subservient to Alex. But no one believed that Vladimir was content with his position. Everyone

knew that he would not stop at prime minister. One day, he would
want to try for the presidency.

In the meantime, Solosenko developed an excellent working
relationship with his president. He supported Alex publicly, calling him the most successful leader since the revolution. He kept
his cards close to his chest and did not try to undermine Alex. His
political instincts told him that Alex's position was too secure to
challenge. Therefore, he made the strategic decision to fold his
hands and use Alex's political success to further his own.

The problem was Mikhail Potgorsky. He was smart and well
able to read Vladimir's intentions. Though Mikhail tried to warn
his friend about the prime minister, Vladimir managed to overcome this obstacle. In contrast to Mikhail, he—like Alex—was very
fond of sports. Their similar interests were the basis for a marvelous means of connection. Vladimir organized hunting trips, soccer
matches, and many other events of this kind. Events at which Alex
Kotorov was the guest of honor, of course.

It was natural for their shared leisure time to bring the two men
close. Though Mikhail tried, at first, to disrupt the growing friendship, he failed utterly. Alex needed these activities to free himself
of the stresses of his high office, and Vladimir was the right man in
the right place. He knew how to arrange high-quality affairs. Alex
Kotorov hardly missed a single party that Vladimir Solosenko threw.

In the natural course of things, Mikhail attended some of these
parties as well. After a brief time, he stopped. This was not for him.
To the best of his understanding, he would not be successful in separating the two.

In the international arena, this gave Russia a huge edge. It was
rare for heads of government to see eye-to-eye. This unity of power
led to a stable coalition that steered the Russian ship through secure
waters. The Russian economy grew steadily, Russian science was
almost restored to its former glory, and the general quality of life in
the country improved steadily. The Russian papers praised the pair
at every opportunity. "The Russian twins," they were called in the
global press, which was wary of the lack of competition in Russian
politics.

Very few people were privy to Vladimir's ambitions. One of them was Alex. Vladimir was open with him and didn't hide a thing. While Mikhail warned his friend against subversion, Vladimir promised Alex that he would never act against him. "I will not challenge your position, my friend. True, when you finish your second term and have to step down, I will want to run. But why should you care about that? Either way, you won't be able to be president forever." He grinned. "Perhaps you'd like to be prime minister…"

Alex liked this idea. The alliance between the two was proving profitable to both sides. Thus, for the first time in years, Alex pushed his friend Mikhail aside and brought Vladimir Solosenko close.

Vladimir, for his part, didn't forget to repay Mikhail what he owed him. The moment he acquired Alex's trust, he began acting to limit Mikhail's influence.

"That Jew will lead you to lose everything!" he told Alex one day, when Mikhail tried forcefully to promote Israeli interests. "All Jews think about the State of Israel first, and only afterward about the country that gave birth to them. I know he's your good friend, but you have to look out for Russia's interests. Not his."

This venomous dripping did its job. Mikhail began to find less and less favor in Alex's eyes. For the first time since they'd met, there were occasions when Alex refused to see Mikhail. It was reasonable to suppose that the numerous hours that the president and prime minister spent together were to blame. If, until then, his closest friend had been a Jew—or at least someone who wished he were a Jew—under the prime minister's influence the president cooled off their relationship. Mikhail Potgorsky was no longer welcome in the Kotorov home. The only times they met were in the corridors of the Kremlin and at social events.

This was also the first time that the media heard a word of criticism from the doctor about his friend, the president. In an interview that appeared in *Argumenty i Fakty* (*AiF*), the most highly circulated newspaper in Russia, he came out strongly against the weapons deal that, in his opinion, threatened the delicate balance of power in the Middle East. "A nuclear Iran poses a danger to Russia as well," he was quoted as saying. "Not just to Israel. My old friend is making a fateful mistake when he helps arm the Iranians."

The president did not react officially to his friend's criticism. In times past, the doctor would have been arrested and sent to Siberia, but even now the president did not restrain himself entirely. Shortly after the piece was published, Dr. Potgorsky was sent on a "diplomatic mission" to the United States. He was appointed coordinator of policy between the Russian and American governments. For many politicians, such a position would have been considered a prize. In Mikhail's case, the intention was to oust him from the center of Russian power.

Mikhail wasn't broken. His diplomatic talents shone in his new position. The network of contacts he built up in Washington was among the best in the Russian embassy. He was a sought-after guest at the White House, not only because he represented giant Russia, but also because of his excellent ties to local politicians.

Years before, on his first visit to Washington, he had been invited to speak before AIPRO—the American Israel Peaceful Relations Organization, which acts on Israel's behalf in Congress—on the topic of the history of anti-Semitism. That talk was his first introduction to the influential Jewish lobby. They loved his speech, which was delivered in fluent English, and interrupted him dozens of times to applaud.

That talk opened many doors for him. Jewish senators shook his hand warmly and invited him to various parties, a number of politicians sent him questions about ways to fight anti-Semitism in the modern world, and his speech was published in its entirety in the Washington News-Time, the local arm of the huge "News-Time" chain.

Only later did he learn that Jeff Davis, owner of the news chain, had been present in person at the conference and had also enjoyed the scholarly talk. They met at a tea party arranged by Republican Senator Russel Rosenbaum to celebrate his victory over a talented young lawyer who had tried to take away his seat.

Jeffrey Davis approached him with a wide smile and introduced himself. "I thought you Russians invented anti-Semitism!" he joked.

"I never thought I'd hear some Russian tell me that Americans also consider me inferior... Seems to me that most Americans would die to be in my place, don't you agree? I'm the embodiment of the American dream. Doesn't that shatter your theory about Jewish inferiority?"

"Throughout history, Jews have always made more money than the average gentile," Mikhail answered, unflustered. "The Jewish mind works overtime... But that does not cause a Jew hater to think that Jews are better than him. On the contrary—he accuses the Jew of acquiring money in underhanded ways. By succeeding, you're actually encouraging anti-Semitism, not fighting it."

For the first time in a long time, Jeffrey was stymied. He shook the Russian's hand warmly and expressed his admiration. "You have quite a head on your shoulders," he said enthusiastically. "Are you sure you don't happen to be Jewish?" He burst into an infectious laugh that drew in those around them. Out of politeness, even the usually restrained Mikhail joined in the laughter.

Thus began a special relationship between the Russian doctor of psychology and sociology, and the wealthy tycoon from New York who happened to be the most influential millionaire not only in AIPRO, but also in the general political scene. It was a friendship that opened all doors to Mikhail in Washington.

⁓⊱⊱⊰⊰⁓

Iran, 2012

General Karmiansky rubbed his hands together with pleasure. This had been one of the simplest and yet one of the most brilliant operations he had ever led. Right under the noses and eyes of the best intelligence bureaus in the world, he'd transferred a small tactical nuclear weapon to the most hated nation in the world. Or maybe not the most hated nation, but certainly the most feared one. He had employed the open door tactic, which postulated that the best place to hide something is exactly where everyone is looking. A place where no one would dream he'd dare hide the treasure.

The fifteen trucks were now parked in a large army base at the outskirts of the Iranian capital, where soldiers were unloading them, one by one. They didn't know that just meters away, in a truck that had been marked as already unloaded, lay a bomb that could have caused them, and anything found within a radius of several hundred yards, to vaporize in seconds.

The most complicated part of the operation had actually taken place in Russia: moving the bomb from the sealed city of Novouralsk and tacking it onto the big arms delivery. But with the right orders, anything was possible in Russia. Because of "technical difficulties"—in other words, the difficulty in hiding an ordinary, registered nuclear bomb from the Americans' discerning eyes — the Iranians had been given a bomb known as a "nuclear suitcase."

Many years had passed since the arms race between the United States and Russia, when both sides had tried to develop weapons that would destroy the balance of power and provide an additional deterrent to a possible attack. Both in the United States and Russia, horrifying nuclear bombs had been developed—bombs whose advantage lay in their mobility. A bomb installed inside a suitcase, accompanied by a simple code to set it off. This would make it possible to smuggle several such bombs into the enemy's backyard and attack him from a point of ambush.

Although both sides had agreed to get rid of such bombs in the arms treaty they had signed, a small number of nuclear suitcases still remained in storehouses in Novouralsk. The fact that they'd never been registered made it easier to let one of them drop off the Americans' radar screen now.

True, it was a relatively small bomb. But it was enough for the plan. Now came the last stage: seeing to it that the bomb passed into the correct hands without leaving any traces of its origins.

The plan had been a simple one. Every truck would be parked in a bunker on the base, far from the eyes of the curious satellites circling the earth. In the middle of the night, a special unit sent by the Iranian president would transfer the bomb to a more secure location. From that moment on, the general would be divested of responsibility. Then the ball would be in the Iranian president's hands. He didn't like the idea of that madman playing with the nuclear bomb, but it was not he who made these decisions. And, in truth, a trial bomb exploding somewhere in the Iranian desert would hurt no one.

He made sure that all the technical details were in place, and entered the limousine that would take him to the president's official residence. In a broadcast that would be transmitted live to the nation, the president would thank him for his contribution to Iran's security and for his assistance in protecting the state from hostile enemies. After the public encounter, they would meet privately, and the general would give the Iranian the codes to arm the bomb. The orders he had received had been very explicit: he must ascertain that immediately afterward, the president transferred the final payment for the arms delivery.

The Iranian had been dragging out his payment for a long time now, and Moscow was seriously displeased.

15

ALI HAMID HAD GROWN UP IN THE REVOLUTIONARY GUARD. His father, Abu Ali Hamid, was an officer in the Al-Quds Force, the guard's elite secretive unit. He had trained his son virtually from infancy to a life of strict obedience and to the use of a wide array of weapons and guerilla warfare.

The long training had turned Ali Hamid into a pitiless warrior. He was an assassin who feared nothing and was prepared to sacrifice his life for the goal. Not for naught had his superiors used him to carry out the most complex assignments. He never disappointed them.

The Al-Quds Force comprises approximately 15,000 elite fighters, carefully chosen from among the 120,000 in the Revolutionary Guard. The unit is responsible for special commando operations in Iran, and across the border. A significant part of its job is to supply arms and money to terrorist organizations such as Hezbollah, Hamas, and the like throughout the Arab world. They are also in charge of training fighters in these organizations and advancing their fighting capabilities.

Ali Hamid had an additional advantage over his comrades. He was fair-skinned and could easily pass for a Westerner. This fact had caused him to be sent on numerous secret missions across the Atlantic. Missions so secret that he couldn't even share them with his fellow soldiers. He'd studied English, German, and French and was reasonably fluent in all three. He could manage anywhere in Europe and America.

With all this, he was still surprised when he received an urgent summons to the office of the president himself. There would be no other soldiers present, and no officers. Just the president and him. This must be something very serious.

He'd have been happier if he could have told his father about the secret summons. Who knew? It might be a trap, a means to finish him off for some mistake he had made or some information he had uncovered that somebody wanted to keep hidden. He tried to think what the reason could be for having him escorted, within five minutes of receiving the summons, to the president's personal secretary waiting outside for him in a black car with no identifying license plates. But orders were orders. He packed his personal equipment into a large knapsack and slipped into the car's backseat. He preferred sitting behind the driver; this gave him an extra edge of control. Very odd that the secretary instead of a chauffeur was driving.

"What's the story?" he asked with feigned nonchalance.

The secretary threw him a quick glance in the rearview mirror, and returned his eyes to the road. He didn't bother answering. In truth, he had no clue why he had been sent so suddenly to fetch this soldier—but he'd never admit as much to the man seated behind him.

Ali's political instincts were screaming that something big was happening, something that the president was preparing to do in a hurry. But no one told him anything. He hoped it didn't mean he was suspected of spying or anything like that. He might yet find himself swaying at the end of a rope in the central square...

He did not repeat his question. He held his bag on his lap, his hand resting casually inside. Something suspicious was going on here, and he wasn't feeling calm. Inside the knapsack he gripped his favorite gun, the Israeli Desert Eagle that he had obtained on one of his missions abroad. He loved the weapon's size, and, even more, he loved the fact that it was his first battle trophy. While forced to use less noticeable weapons in his secret operations, this was still his gun of choice. If anyone thought they could knock him off quickly and quietly, they could think again. He would not go down without a fight.

The car moved rapidly through the city streets, disregarding the traffic signals. No one would dare trouble an unmarked car. It made its way confidently to the president's residence without being stopped for inspection. Ali relaxed his grip on the gun. If they'd wanted to kill him, they would not have bothered to bring him here. It must be something else. Something big.

He stepped out of the car and followed the secretary to a nearby elevator. He didn't take his knapsack; there was no way they would let him come in here with a weapon. Indeed, at the building's entrance he was subjected to a careful body search. What did surprise him was the fact that the secretary underwent the same thing. Apparently, no one was trusted here.

A minute later, he found himself alone with the president in the latter's ornate office. The president didn't invite him to sit. Instead, he stood up and shook the soldier's hand. Ali had everything he was looking for. He came from a good family, and loved his family. This was always vital, in case there was a need to make use of it at some future date. Ali was talented and clever enough, and, most important of all, he believed in the goal.

The president had spent long hours debating how much to reveal to the young man facing him. By nature, he preferred sharing as little as possible. He'd never enjoyed showing his hand. This time, however, he decided to hide only what was necessary. After all, he was putting all his eggs in one basket—a basket by the name of Ali Hamid.

"I've heard good things about you," he said, opening with a compliment. He knew what an impact a personal meeting with such a senior personality could have for a simple soldier. One good word, and the boy would do whatever he wished. "What I want you to do is the biggest thing you've ever done in your life. To be more accurate, it's the biggest thing that any Iranian could do in his lifetime. I understand that you've already been to the United States."

Ali nodded. Just this year, he'd supplied arms to a special group of Islamic freedom fighters in California. It had been a top-secret operation that had succeeded on his side, but failed after he'd departed and left the weapons in the fighters' hands. One of them had boasted to his friends when drunk and exposed the whole plan.

"I'm going to be frank with you. I'm about to tell you something that no one in Iran knows. Needless to say, this is all most highly classified."

Ali nodded again, and the president continued. "Israel is preparing to attack us. Yes, it's true. We have an exact date for the attack and we'll be ready to meet it. But I am not interested in embarking on a general war with the heretics yet. We will do that at the right place and at a time that suits *us*, not them. Therefore, here is the plan. Israel will not dare attack if America does not permit it. And we are going to cause the Americans to veto an Israeli attack on Iran."

Ali listened in silence. Why was the president telling him all of this? Why was he revealing diplomatic plans of which he had no notion? This was a matter for politicians and strategists, who knew how to take advantage of alliances and treaties in order to get what they wanted. Not for soldiers. Unless the president was planning some sort of ground operation... Yes. That must be it. That was what the president wanted. He was preparing a secret operation. Ali was flattered that, of all the soldiers in Iran, he'd been chosen to carry out the mission.

"The idea is very simple. We're going to convince the Americans that if they authorize an Israeli offense they will pay a high price. We will explain to them that we have planted dozens of bombs on the streets of the United States. Bombs that will be activated against them in the event that Israel attacks Iran."

Ali listened intently. Was the president serious? Did he have any idea of the size of the operation he was talking about? Dozens of soldiers! Soldiers prepared to die for their mission, but still good enough to carry it out. And all of this in the United States...which, since the attack on the Twin Towers, had been tracking every suspicious face. It was an impossible mission. There was no way to carry out something of this magnitude without exposure. One or two soldiers, perhaps, could get away with this—but no more than that. With so many soldiers involved, the Americans would discover one of the conspirators, and from there the road would be very short until exposure for them all.

"What you're about to do," the president continued, "is save Iran, your homeland, and buy us the necessary time to achieve a nuclear bomb. A bomb that will protect our nation from the Zionists and their minions. I chose you, and you alone, because you're the best and I cannot allow myself to take any risks. I need you to be responsible for taking a package that will be delivered to you, and planting it in America. In Washington, to be exact, at the next AIPRO conference. That's the Zionist organization that leads the American president around by the nose.

"You will be responsible for making sure the bomb goes off as the president is delivering a speech to them—selling his soul to the devil for a bit of cash. At the right moment, you will activate the bomb and disappear. But not before you make certain that it's gone off. Understand?"

"Just a minute. The goal is to harm the president? Because that's impossible. It's impossible to get close enough to him to hurt him. Certainly not with a bomb—no matter what its size."

The president smiled. "No, my friend. The goal is not to harm the president. I've already explained that. The goal is to make them *believe* that we could explode a dozen such bombs.

"For my part, you can set it off outside the building. All I want is for him to hear the explosion, feel the earth trembling, and hear the screams of the injured calling for help. That will shake him up. It will bring the fear closer. It will lead the president to understand that it's not worth his while to stand on the wrong side of the conflict."

Ali absorbed the message. The goal of the operation was to inflict terror, not death. Not that it really mattered; it simply made his mission easier. To activate a bomb in Washington was one thing. To assassinate the president of the United States was another thing entirely.

He was surprised that the Iranian president was issuing his instructions in person. Ali had never heard of anyone who'd received his orders directly from the president. Apparently, he was truly afraid of a leak.

The president took out a number of maps and lists and outlined the plan, step by step. Ali followed in some astonishment. The man knew his stuff. It was obvious that he hadn't forgotten his own years in the Islamic Revolutionary Guard. They said he had been an outstanding soldier. Who knows? Ali thought with an inward smile. Perhaps one day *I'll* be president...

The president issued his instructions to the young soldier. He liked what he saw. Ali seemed intelligent and focused. All the recommendations had said that he was the best man for the job. A pity he would not return from it alive...

The president enjoyed the word game he had unwittingly played: "You will activate the bomb and disappear." "Disappear" was a good word... What he hadn't bothered telling the dedicated soldier standing before him was that the bomb he'd be taking with him to Washington was no ordinary one. There was no need to explode it inside the auditorium where the president would be delivering his speech, because even at a distance of dozens of meters, this particular bomb would decimate everyone in the auditorium—including the president of the United States himself.

The nuclear bomb he now possessed gave him the feeling of power he adored. The Russians' plan was a good one. If the bomb were to go off in some remote desert, the Israelis and Americans would be afraid to attack. But just imagine how they'd tremble if they thought that a number of such bombs were already circulating throughout their countries... How they would hesitate before daring to start up with him then!

He had a choice of sending the bomb to either Israel or America. Though his heart urged him to harm Israel—where carrying out the mission would also be simpler—his mind told him that it would be more effective in America. Should Israel be attacked, the Americans would not yet have cause to feel afraid. They would think that the distant United States was safe from such bombs. And then they would attack Iran in turn.

But if the bomb went off in America… True, there would be a high level of anger, and the desire to turn Iran into another Iraq could drive the Americans to rash behavior. But the secret threat that would reach the new and alarmed administration would announce that should Iran be attacked, this would be only the beginning. The American government would be told that dozens of nuclear suitcases were already scattered throughout the United States. The prospect of a wave of nuclear explosions would frighten America. She would be forced to yield. The administration would find a way to save face—such as blaming al-Qaeda for the bomb and venturing on an insane rampage in Afghanistan. They would tell the foolish American people that the guilty party was some sheikh, who would be slain to satisfy the people's desire for revenge.

Bottom line: they would not dare attack Iran. Not after the living example. And they would absolutely forbid the Israelis to endanger them with an attack of their own.

The idea was simply brilliant. The only drawback was the Russian angle. The Russians would not like the scenario. But because they had no official knowledge of the bomb, they would be unable to say a word. Perhaps they would circumscribe their arms sales to Iran a bit, but that was all. Russia needed Iran no less than Iran needed her.

All that remained now was to make sure the bomb actually worked. The conditions that the Russians had set would play out in the president's favor. They'd sent him a relatively small bomb— a portable one apparently left over from the Cold War, when those in power had tried to send nuclear packages through the borders. At this very moment, one of his scientists was working on inserting the bomb into the smallest possible suitcase. A special suitcase, developed in Iran, that prevented any radiation from leaking. It would be impossible to introduce the bomb into the United States while it was hot. Radiation detectors all over America would sniff it out in seconds. This suitcase would solve the problem. Obviously they'd have to kill the scientist who was working on it…

The president was sacrificing a great deal of quality manpower for the sake of the mission's secrecy. That was why it *had* to succeed.

This one bomb was going to buy him all the time he needed.

16

Washington, D.C.

BOB WALTERS' TRAJECTORY TO THE WHITE HOUSE WAS not a planned one. He was not ambitious and had never dreamed of sitting in the president's chair. All he wanted to do was improve conditions for army veterans and, if possible, change government policy regarding military activity abroad.

As someone who had personally been burned in the Vietnam War by the conflicting interests of the decision makers, he had reached the firm conclusion that America must concentrate on America. The rest of the world could take care of itself. The United States lost hundreds of soldiers each year in battles far away from home. Bob wanted to change that.

His years in politics softened this stance a bit. He learned that, at times, national interest resided thousands of miles from his country's borders, and there was no escaping the need to send troops out to protect those interests. However, it was a long road from there to becoming involved in every skirmish across the globe.

He was the right man at the right time. He began his career at the side of a local politician who wanted a war hero for his campaign, but quickly found his own place in the conservative Republican Party leadership, although his opinions about foreign policy weren't traditionally Republican. His forceful personality, uncompromising integrity, and natural leadership qualities quickly turned him into a well-known Republican icon. But still, no one thought that he'd be president. He lacked the ruthless ambition necessary to run for the most influential position in the world. He was not prepared to use slander or defamation or other weapons and so was not considered a real threat.

He finally entered the presidential race because there were no other serious contenders within the party. The media wondered whether the reason no dirt had been found on him to date was simply because no one had dug deeply enough so far. Or could it be because he was truly an honest man? Most of the reporters believed the first reason to be the correct one.

But their research came up empty. They burrowed through dusty archives and interrogated elderly soldiers who had fought with him in Vietnam. The only stories that emerged were new tales of heroism that had not yet been told, and which only burnished the halo of the American hero-leader that the country needed now. Though the Democratic president who ran against him was fairly popular, the heavy losses in Iraq, Afghanistan, and other world arenas troubled an American public already trying to cope with deep economic crisis. They didn't like billions of dollars being wasted on wars throughout the world.

The Republican Party knew how to spot an opportunity, and Bob Walters was summoned to step up to the plate. The polls, which promised any other candidate a painful defeat to the incumbent, brought a rare unity to the party, which accepted Bob as almost the only contender. In local primaries, he won such a stunning majority that the media began to believe, for the first time, that the coming election would go to the Republicans. This time—for a change—they were right. Winning by a tight but secure margin, Bob Walters found himself standing at the helm of the world's superpower.

Like all presidents before him, Bob found that ideology does not always walk hand in hand with reality. It was impossible to bring all the soldiers home immediately, and impossible to abandon America's allies. Nevertheless, he instituted a more restrained policy than in the past with regard to the country's foreign affairs, and began working to limit American forces scattered across the globe. The Iraqis, Saudis, Israelis, and a long list of other nations did not like him for this reason, but they hadn't elected him and he was not obligated to them. He was responsible, first and foremost, to every American citizen, and only afterward to the citizens of the world.

The world's economic situation, which had moved from crisis to crisis in recent years, also robbed a hefty portion of his time. Bob was not the kind of man who let his advisers do whatever they pleased. He wanted to understand exactly what was taking place: what the economic challenges were, the nature of the problems, and how they might be solved. Although, until then, he had not been especially adept at understanding numbers, he'd always been a diligent student. He did not spend the days of his presidency in idleness.

It would be impossible to say that Bob Walters loved his job. The opposite was true. He suddenly discovered that he owed something to many different interest groups, even if they opposed his worldview. Take, for example, his upcoming meeting with the Israeli prime minister. The fact that they did not like each other was an open secret. Though the Israeli leader had also moved from a military background to a political one, their philosophies were worlds apart. The Israeli prime minister viewed military operations as the solution to almost every problem. He had no compunctions about sending his soldiers to fight anywhere he wished—even, as far as he was concerned, Iran.

Even small things about the prime minister bothered him. The man couldn't even speak English properly! What kind of Israeli leader didn't bother working on his English, when the sole power protecting that tiny, war-torn country from the United Nations and the world was America? Without America's almost automatic support, many economic sanctions would long ago have been leveled against Israel.

But what could he do when they practically owned Congress? There were limits to what even the president of the United States could achieve. The Jewish lobby dominated Congress and nearly always succeeded in torpedoing any effort on his part to cut back on aid to Israel.

Not that he had anything personal against the Jewish state. For his part, let the entire Middle East belong to the Jews. After all, they were much closer to Western culture than the Arabs who lived in the region. The world would be a lot more peaceful and secure with the Israelis in control of the region. Nevertheless, the fact remained that the Arabs were in the majority. And the Israelis refused to understand the simple math, which proved that they didn't belong in the Middle East. They were like a bone stuck in the Arabs' throat. A bone that was causing the price of gas to skyrocket, and the whole world to slowly sink into an economic quagmire.

While it was true that Israel was a fact that could not be denied, she was certainly capable of limiting her provocations. Here was where politics stepped in. The militant Israeli government refused all negotiations. While it was true that the security of her citizens took precedence over all other considerations, that was a long way from refusing to compromise on the issue of borders with international guarantees. The Palestinians, too, annoyed him with their unwillingness to give up terror as a means of achieving their goals. But what could you expect from them? This was the only way that worked for them until now.

One of the hardest things about being president of the United States was the knowledge of how easy it could be to bring historic differences to an end, if only both sides were interested in doing so—and knowing that they were not. For each, it was easier to dig in their heels and paint themselves as the strong ones that refused to yield to the enemy's demands.

But the freeze in negotiations was not going to be the main topic this week. The Iranians had succeeded in putting themselves center-stage with their ambitions for the nuclear bomb. Bad enough that North Korea had unexpectedly achieved nuclear capability; the world needed no more madmen with light trigger-fingers who had possession of nuclear arms. This frightened Israel, for obvious reasons, and would therefore be the centerpiece of their discussions this week. The question was only if he could use their fear to advance the peace process. Something like: "Give me an agreement, and I'll provide you with protection from Iran."

Actually, Iran was not only an Israeli problem. Nearly the whole world was afraid of a nuclear Iran: the Iraqis, of course; the Saudis; the Turks—essentially, everyone except a few particularly radical Islamic republics. Even the Arabs themselves did not want the Iranians to reign supreme over them through nuclear capability.

And this raised another problem. If Iran produced the nuclear bomb, all those countries would be forced to participate in an arms race—and who knew where that would end? Although that did not necessarily mean that this issue should not be used as an opportunity to put a little pressure on Israel.

With emphasis on the words "a little," so that Congress wouldn't be too angry…

Milan, Italy, 2011

The train from Milan to Venice left typically late. As opposed to the other lines, most of the passengers going to Venice were not dependent on a timetable and didn't press the rail employees too much. They waited in Milan for half an hour before the train was finally given the green light to leave. The Italians, well versed in the "efficiency" of their country's railroad system, did not become overly excited, and they did their best to soothe the anxious tourists. There was nothing to worry about, they said. This was Italy.

Actually, this specific train had been delayed for reasons that were not standard at all. It had come about as the result of an urgent call from Interpol to the security chief in Milan. Intelligence information pointed to the possibility that one of the most wanted men in the world was on this train.

Ami Drori, seated in a car near the front of the train, sensed the unusual activity on the part of the security forces. He did not become flustered. His cover could stand intense scrutiny. His weapon was in the car behind this one, in a suitcase in the luggage compartment, and there was nothing to identify it as belonging to him. The briefcase resting on the small table in front of him held only the most standard objects, ordinary belongings of a business-man with very clear objectives in Venice. According to his papers, he was a representative of a Czech glass company on his way to Venice to close a deal.

Apart from all of this, he knew that he wasn't the man they were looking for. Had anyone asked him, he could have pointed out the old man sitting three cars back, hunched over a cup of hot tea. It was the old man they were seeking, not him.

Upward of half a year of surveillance and investigation had cul-minated in this train ride. He hoped that the Europeans would not get in his way. His orders had not specified "at any cost." He was counting on Jon Perrera—or whatever his real name was—to handle them. He would not meet his end here in some random train check. It was not for nothing that there was a half-million-euro bounty on the man's head. Perrera was one of the most professional hired kill-ers on the continent. Ami had seen him at work and knew what he was worth. He would not be taken down so fast.

Three policemen appeared in the car's entrance, scanning the passengers slowly. Ami decided to look back. He didn't want to appear afraid of an inspection. One of the officers met Ami's gaze, and waited for Ami to look aside. Ami smiled, but didn't turn away. Uneasy, the young police officer pointed him out to his older col-league, who leveled his gaze on Ami and checked something in the paper he held. Ami knew that he was checking to see if Ami resembled the picture in his hand. The officer lifted his eyes again and studied Ami, who met his scrutiny with an innocent expres-sion. After a moment, the policeman shook his head and moved on to the next car.

His young companion did not follow suit. He approached Ami and asked for his identity papers. Ami opened his briefcase, asking, "What's the matter, sir? Is there any special reason for this delay?"

The police officer riffled through the papers he'd been given and didn't answer. Ami didn't press him; too much confidence could also raise suspicion.

"A business trip, eh?"

"Yes," Ami replied. His Italian was nothing to write home about. He tried to inject a Czech accent into it. "I'll be the only visitor to Venice who's not there to have a good time. You Italians are touchy negotiators."

The shadow of a smile crossed the serious young policeman's lips. Quickly, he tightened his jaw and returned Ami's papers. "Good luck, Mr. Ojenik." He hurried away to join his colleague.

"Ciao," Ami said with a smile. He put the papers back into his briefcase.

No, there was no way in the world that they'd catch the man here. Jon Perrera, who resembled a very old man at the moment, was actually in his 30's. His resumé boasted scores, if not more, of murder cases that had never been solved. He was a master of disguise and a talented sniper. There was a good reason why they'd sent Ami after him. It was nearly impossible to track him down. If a prize of half a million euros had not succeeded in bringing him in, he must be very skilled at what he did.

Indeed, less than five minutes later the train started its journey. Someone in Interpol had no doubt been reprimanded for his faulty intelligence and life had returned to normal.

Ami stretched out in his seat. He had no urge to see if Jon was still aboard the train. That would have been an amateur's mistake. Beyond a doubt, the murderer had stayed. After all, he had a murder to commit tonight.

A judge on Italy's criminal court was about to join his family on vacation in Venice that evening. He was planning to stay until tomorrow morning, when he had to return to court. For the honored judge, it would be a rare escape from the exhausting marathon under extensive coverage in the media—the case of Italy versus the Griacco family.

The Griacco family had ruled Italy's underworld for years. Threats, extortion, and murder were just a few of the charges brought against them. The family's head, already in jail for the past two months, would be spending the rest of his life there if even just a portion of the charges could be proved. The police and the prosecutors were under tremendous pressure. Throughout the trial, there had been dozens of problematic episodes associated with the case: threats to potential witnesses and assassinations. Threats had been made against anyone who became involved in the case and their families—to the point where the prosecution had begun to encounter difficulties in proving its charges. If the Griacco family emerged from this trial without a conviction, it would be a particularly harsh blow to the Italian judicial system.

For many months, His Honor, Judge Alfredo Bernioni, had been too busy to find time for his family. He spent his days locked away in the courthouse, which was heavily protected against an attempted attack, and only left the fortress at infrequent intervals. Today, spontaneously, he had decided to take a short break and join his family, who were on vacation in Venice under tight security. An attack on the judge's family could serve as a deterrent and an example to anyone who chose to testify against the crime family—but it could also arouse media and legal outrage against them. Therefore, the judge was not overly worried. Besides, the security really was good. Wherever his wife and daughter went, they were accompanied by at least three armed police officers. Nevertheless, the judge had felt the need to spend a little time with them, to try in some small measure to make up for the fact that they hardly ever saw him anymore.

What the judge didn't know was that word of his secret trip had been leaked. The contract on his head had brought one of the most dangerous assassins in the world to Venice. The same assassin that was now sitting in the fifth train car from Milan to Venice.

And the same train that Ami Drori had chosen for this trip. The State of Israel had an account to settle with Jon Perrera—an account that had led it to send one of its own best assassins after him.

An intensive intelligence effort had produced the information that Perrera was the sniper who had killed the Israeli science minister. Contrary to what they had believed, it had not been an Arab sniper acting from ideological motives. The killer was none other than an Italian hired gun who had received $5 million for the job. The money had come from a Saudi tycoon who wanted to do something on behalf of the Palestinian cause. He chose the science minister, who was known for his right-wing views, and paid cash for the assassination.

It was not only a desire to avenge the minister's death that had prompted Israel to send Ami after the murderer. The death that he had perpetrated on Israeli soil could open the door to a flood of invitations to European assassins who were much harder to track and to neutralize than local Arab terrorists. Israel wished to nip this trend in the bud and send a clear message to the underworld: any killer who, blinded by Arab money, agreed to carry out an assassination or bombing would find the full force of Israel's secret services coming after him.

The order that Ami received had been clear: Jon Perrera was to be destroyed. Not injured, not handed over to the authorities. He must serve as an example of the long reach of Israel's arm.

Ami had to confess that so far this had been his most difficult mission in the service of his country. He had never been faced with so talented and so dangerous an enemy. To himself he admitted that, except for the element of surprise that he had over Jon, who was unaware that his identity had been exposed by the Israelis, Ami didn't know if he'd have had a chance of bringing him down.

Just a minute, Ami stopped himself. *You haven't brought him down yet. Though it seems like a done deal—never underestimate him.* From experience, he knew that complacency is the biggest killer of all.

He knew about the contract that had been put out on the judge, and about the intelligence leak, and he knew that Jon had set out for Venice. Ami had selected this train by process of elimination. An airline flight required too many documents that would be hard to obtain at the last minute. A car could attract too much attention. A train was a classic choice; the large number of passengers was a great help in preventing a person from standing out. Armed with this knowledge, locating the murderer had been simple.

He could go over to him right now and shoot him, but escaping from a moving train was problematic. There was no reason to endanger himself any more than necessary on this job. He'd be able to operate with greater freedom in Venice itself.

"Next stop—Santa Lucia. This is the last stop. Please take your luggage with you. On behalf of Train Italia, we would like to thank you for choosing us and to wish you a pleasant stay." The measured tones brought most of the passengers to their feet, seeking their bags. Ami glanced at his watch and hastily sought his own suitcase. A quarter to four. A 45-minute delay was not that terrible.

He was one of the first to leave the train and approach the terminal's exit—and the entrance to the colorful city of Venice.

He paused at the head of the broad stairs leading down to the street. Ahead of him, water flowed peacefully through the Grand Canal, the foremost and largest of the canals that bisected Venice into two islands. Many excited tourists milled about in the plaza fronting the train station, snapping pictures and trying to board the bus-boats that departed from there and continued along the length of the river.

Pulling his suitcase behind him, Ami headed down the stairs. The best way to tail somebody was to stay in front of him, not behind. Jon was a top-tier professional, and Ami could not permit himself to make a mistake. One error, and long months of work would go down the drain. He made a guess about where the assassin would be headed. If he were in Jon's place, he would choose a hotel close to the station to enable a quick escape. Such a hotel, with a window facing the Grand Canal, would allow him to watch the people moving along the water. The easiest way to carry out the killing would be through a precise shot at the judge as he passed down the canal to join his family. Long-distance sniper shots were Jon's specialty. This one would be child's play for him.

Ami checked his watch again. From the corner of his eye, he spotted the assassin appearing at the head of the stairs. Ami lowered his hand and continued down the stairs, turned left to the street leading along the length of the canal, and stopped to read the sign that bore the street name: Rio Tera Lista de Spanga. He waited until he was sure that Jon had indeed turned in this direction, and then continued strolling slowly along, studying the various shop windows he passed.

Every glittering display was calculated to entice tourists inside to buy a souvenir. Restaurants and ice cream parlors teemed with customers. There didn't seem to be a single local person, only entranced tourists from a vast number of countries. Not for naught was Venice considered one of the top tourist spots in the world. She was a special and ancient city built on a series of small, linked islands, and offered the unique experience of a city built on water. New studies claimed that Venice was slowly sinking, but this only increased the stream of visitors eager to gaze on the spectacle before it disappeared.

The primary means of transportation in the city was by private boat, gondola, taxi-boat, or bus-boat. Cars were not permitted to enter the city—and had they been, they would not have been able to get far. At fairly close intervals, bridges stretched over the moving water, with stairs going up and down to enable pedestrians to reach the other side. The many staircases made it hard for bicycle riders as well as for people in wheelchairs. The best way to get around Venice was on foot.

Ami came to a portion of the street that boasted several hotels. One of them, he knew, would serve as the sniper's hideaway. He entered an adjacent shop and inspected the merchandise offered inside. Jon Perrera passed the store and entered the Hotel Principe with a confident stride. Ami waited a second before he followed. He was under no illusion that Jon had not scanned the street very well before he had gone inside. He was a professional and would have done so in his sleep. Ami had no doubt that the killer had seen everyone who'd been standing in the street, from the train station to here. Including him. If he saw one of them again, he would check out that person very well.

But Ami didn't need any more information. He wouldn't dream of walking into the hotel to see which room the assassin was given. Jon Perrera would recognize him at once, and remember that he'd seen him on the train. That would only cause difficulties.

Instead, Ami left the shop—gently pushing aside the shopkeeper, who was coaxing him to buy something—and retraced his steps down the street. He knew which hotel the assassin was in.

Now he needed to cross to the other side of the canal and find a hotel facing the Principe. That should not be a problem, as dozens of hotels stood all along the canal, offering visitors ancient rooms or rooms sparkling with newness, to give them a pleasant stay in the city that floated on water.

A five-minute walk brought him to the perfect place. A three-and-a-half-star hotel that had taken its name from the canal that flowed past it: the Grand Canal. How original.

He entered the hotel and stepped up to the reception desk. "Hey, may I have a room, please?" he asked in American English. It was easiest for him to sound authentic in English. An additional advantage was that, as an American, everyone would expect him to be sure of himself and to do whatever he pleased—in his own language.

The Italian reception clerk flashed a professional smile. "Sure. That's 100 euros for a regular room."

Ami took out his wallet. A hundred Euros for a regular room was not cheap, but it was also not outrageous. He could try to bargain, but he preferred not to do so. Instead, he asked the clerk how much a room facing the canal would cost. From his experience, he knew that those were the most desirable rooms and the hotels took advantage of this in order to charge even more.

"We have a room for 200 euros. It is beautiful," the clerk praised the room at twice the price. He studied the guest, ready to go down if asked. But Ami didn't haggle. "Okay. I'll take it."

The reception clerk's smile grew even wider. He motioned for a crisply uniformed bellboy to come closer. "I'll need to copy your passport. And…uh…with your permission, I'll need a credit card for security. Hotel policy."

Ami pulled out his American passport, which gave his name as Donald Brock, and handed it to the clerk. From his wallet he withdrew an American Express platinum credit card and placed it on the counter. The clerk worked with professional efficiency, photocopying the passport and card and returning them to Ami. This American stranger was rich enough to possess a platinum card; there'd be no money problems here. It was just strange that he hadn't chosen to check into a more expensive hotel.

The bellboy offered to carry Ami's bags and show him to his room. Ami declined, politely but firmly. His bag was a bit heavier than an ordinary suitcase and he didn't want the bellboy to notice. He thanked him and trailed him to the elevator. The bellboy stepped inside and pressed the button for the second floor, where they got out and walked to the second door on the left. Room 213.

The bellboy opened the door for Ami and, with a broad smile, bowed and allowed the guest to precede him into the room. The bellboy followed him inside and hastened to throw open the curtains, revealing the canal flowing directly below. He showed Ami how to use the various amenities, and bowed again. Ami got the hint and handed him a 10-euro tip.

The bellboy thanked him profusely and left the room, still smiling.

The first thing Ami did was close the curtains. He did not want the assassin to sense any movement. There were still a few good hours before the judge was due to arrive in Venice. In the meantime, he had to prepare for action. Jon would not expose himself before it was necessary to do so. He was no doubt studying the canal at this very minute through a crack in the curtains—just as Ami was doing. When night fell, he would darken the room, draw the curtain, open the window and sit in the dark room with his sniper rifle at the ready. That would be the best time to attack him.

Ami was well armed, and with his night scope he would locate Jon with ease. How ironic that the sniper who had ended so many lives with a long-distance shot was about to have his own life ended in the same way.

But he mustn't count his chickens before they hatched. Ami knew that very few plans of operation were carried out exactly as planned. Jon had several advantages. First of all, he was located in a room closer to the exit from the city, so his escape route was shorter. Also, both his sniping abilities and his power to survive had become legendary. If Ami's first shot missed its target, he could forget about a second chance. And then he too would become a target.

He placed his suitcase on the bed and began scanning the room, section by section. He was not afraid that someone was looking for him, but the habit of years had taught him not to feel secure anywhere before he checked for bugs and hidden cameras.

The many times he'd planted such "toys" in various rooms helped him ascertain within minutes that the place was clean. Only now did he allow himself to open his suitcase and lift the lid of the secret compartment to expose the dismantled rifle hidden there. He took it out and assembled it with an expertise born of endless training.

He placed the rifle on the bed, picked up a gun that had also been in his bag and thrust it into his belt. A sniper had to be ready with short-range weapons as well in the event that someone tried to take him by surprise from behind.

Now all that was left for him to do was to stand by the window and try to locate the assassin's room in the hotel opposite. This wasn't too complicated. The Hotel Principe's outer wall was painted dark pink and dull orange. The many years that had passed since the paint had been applied were obvious. The salty sea air had wreaked havoc on many of the old buildings, and this hotel was no exception.

Forty-two windows were facing the canal. A quick count broke them down into about twenty rooms. He moved his binoculars from window to window until he'd narrowed down the possibilities to five rooms. The sniper was in one of them. The others held guests or else were thrown wide open. It was early. There were still more than three hours left before things would start happening. He'd continue standing here and narrowing down the possibilities until he found the assassin.

In his profession, patience was the highest virtue. He had had occasion to spend whole days in an ambush position—an ambush that had not always produced results. If people only knew about the long hours when one had to lie in the rain or the scorching heat, waiting—sometimes in vain—for the end of a thread that would lead to the proper destination…

About 10 percent of the time, the work was exciting and adrenalin producing; in the other 90 percent, you were counting the seconds and asking yourself why you hadn't chosen a different line of work—such as tailoring perhaps, or making shoes…

He would stand here and watch, until the right moment.

Jerusalem, July 2010

WITHIN TWO DAYS, YISRAEL FORGOT ALL ABOUT THE unpleasant start of basketball camp. Chico was very excited by his near-perfect aim and said that he'd never seen such natural basketball ability in his life. Such a compliment was precious, in view of the fact that the legendary Chico Kleiner had given it.

"You have a lot to learn and to work on," he told Yisrael. "But being able to get the ball into the basket like that is not something one can learn. It's an inborn talent. We'll work on your dribbling and other skills, but you have enormous potential. Maybe the most I've ever come across. You could be an international player."

The praise was like cool water on a parched soul. For such a long time now, he'd done nothing but suffer and hear himself criticized. Now, all at once, everything had changed. He'd gone from being a suspected thief, ostracized by his peers, to a boy who was popular and well-liked—maybe, for the first time in his life, even admired.

The smile that was restored to his face after all this time prevented him from seeing that not everyone shared his happiness. Many of his new friends envied the dizzying success of "Yoram's *doss*," as they called him. Interestingly, even Yoram had begun to be jealous of his protégé. He'd been playing for Chico Kleiner for years, ever since he'd been a young boy, but he had never had such fulsome praise directed at *him*. Yoram, who'd dreamed of playing in the NBA for as long as he could remember, was not so thrilled that Yisrael was outstripping him. But he tried not to show it. He continued to encourage Yisrael and to treat him favorably, so that only a sharp ear would pick up the note of envy in his voice when he praised Yisrael's feats on the court.

At home, the change in Yisrael was quickly noticed. While his mother was happy to see the color return to her only son's cheeks, she shared her husband's worry. What was the source of the sudden improvement? Yisrael refused to say a word about what he was doing and where he disappeared to each day. His behavior was perplexing, to say the least. Something was happening to him. Something secret. And anything secret could only hint at further trouble. Neither questions nor threats were effective. He was careful not to give himself away.

On the Thursday of the last week of basketball camp, Tatty forbade Yisrael from leaving the house until he revealed the identity of his new group of friends. But Yisrael slipped out when the time came, ignoring his father's threats and accepting a ride from Yoram. Basketball gave him a feeling of satisfaction and happiness that had been sorely lacking in recent months, and he had made up his mind that no one was going to stop him.

He didn't notice how much his spirituality had deteriorated over the past few weeks. When Chico announced that they'd be playing a friendly game against a team from Haifa that Shabbos—"A game with official league rules. A game with referees and a twenty-four second clock, what we've been training for"—Yisrael was surprised to find that he was seriously considering attending.

"Is there anyone who can't make it?" Chico asked, looking around at his excited campers.

Yisrael gazed down at the floor. How could he play on Shabbos?

To publicly desecrate the Shabbos—had he sunk so low? True, he hardly ever davened anymore. And it had been weeks since he'd opened a Gemara. But it was a long way from there to transgressing a prohibition that carried with it the Torah punishment of *sekilah*.

On the other hand, playing basketball was not forbidden in the Torah. It wasn't like lighting an actual fire, for example. If he wanted to get ahead in the sport, he'd have to sometimes play on Shabbos. Surely there was a rav somewhere who would give him a *heter* to play...or maybe not. But did he really care anymore? After everything that had been done to him in yeshivah and at home? He'd tried with all his might to be a good Jew. He'd tried to be a *yeshivah bachur* who sat and learned, trying to make strides in his Torah study and in *yiras Shamayim*. And they'd rejected him. Did he owe them anything in return?

"Um...I can't come." It was the confident voice of Yoni, the more modern kid. Everyone, players and trainers alike, turned to the proud religious youth who announced, "I don't play on Shabbat! Sorry, but I won't be able to be in the game."

A few disparaging comments that his teammates threw at him were quickly silenced by the trainer. "Good for you," he said warmly. "Listen and learn," he told the other boys. "Here's a person who sacrifices for what he believes in. That's deserving of respect, not insults. As you go on in life, you'll learn that the most important thing is a person who stands by his principles, even though there are less and less people like that today... What about you?" he asked suddenly, turning to Yisrael. "Will you be coming?"

Yisrael blushed a fiery red. Why couldn't he have said earlier that he wouldn't play on Shabbos?

"I'll drive you there, so you won't have to break the Shabbos," Yoram offered. "I drive on Shabbos anyway, so it doesn't matter if I pick you up."

"I don't think that's allowed..." Yisrael whispered.

"All right. I want a decision by tomorrow morning," Chico Kleiner said. "This could be a special opportunity to show yourself to the world of professional basketball. But it's your decision... Anyone who wants to can bring family members to the game. This time, we'll have an audience. Encouragement is one of the most influential factors in a basketball game."

The group's excitement was infectious. This could be amazing! And what would he have to do already? It might not even be blatant *chillul Shabbos*… All the way home, he struggled with the terrible dilemma. For some reason, Yoram was silent as he drove and didn't try to influence him. Yisrael had expected a slew of arguments and plenty of cajoling, but Yoram said nothing.

Deep in his heart, Yoram hoped that Yisrael would not show up at the game. Yisrael would steal the show, as he'd been doing consistently for the past two weeks. Yoram too was eaten up by conflicting desires. On the one hand, he liked Yisrael and felt responsible for him. After all, he was the one who had discovered him. But, on the other hand, Yoram too had dreams of becoming a professional basketball player, and Yisrael seemed poised to threaten his standing as the team's most talented member.

Meanwhile, Yisrael had reached a conclusion: He would leave the decision to his parents. Now it was up to them. If Tatty started fighting with him again, he'd go to the game. He'd show them… But if they didn't yell at him…then he wouldn't go.

To be honest, he was terrified of what awaited him at home. He had never disobeyed a direct order by his father before. Maybe Tatty would even decide to beat him, as he used to do… But he was no longer a small child. If Tatty hit him, he would leave home for good. He'd find someplace to go. Yoram would probably be happy to host him. It would even be preferable to sleep in the streets. Lost in his thoughts, he didn't notice that Yoram had parked near the bus stop opposite Angel's bakery, their usual meeting place.

"Let me know what you decide," Yoram said shortly. "If you want to come to the game, we'll meet on Herzl Boulevard, under the bridge. I have no desire to have your friends throw stones at my car."

Yisrael didn't say a word. He knew that cars passing here on Shabbos were not pelted with stones. But he also didn't want to climb into a car on Shabbos so close to home. A shiver ran through him as he pictured it… Was he really thinking of traveling on Shabbos, like a secular person?

He made his way home slowly. The closer he came to his building, the heavier his heart felt. What was waiting for him at home? He had a premonition that something big was about to happen. Something bad.

"What can happen already?" he tried to calm himself. "They'll throw me out of the house? So let them." His bitterness grew. He climbed the stairs and opened the door wide. Let them just try to do something to him.

His heart sank like a stone as he took in the scene in the living room. Tatty was sitting at one side of the table instead of in his usual place at its head. Mommy was bustling about the kitchen, clearly trying to put together some sort of refreshments for the important visitor who sat at the head of the table. Yisrael turned pale. His legs trembled as he recognized the rosh yeshivah, Rav Rubinstein, sitting in his house and awaiting his return.

Rav Yosef Rubinstein was a man with a special radiance. His thick white beard lent weight and wisdom to his appearance. Even in his late 60's, his bearing was erect. He looked regal. From the stories that had circulated at yeshivah, Yisrael knew about the rosh yeshivah's extraordinary intelligence and his breadth of knowledge in every branch of Torah.

Though Yisrael had spent nearly a year at the yeshivah, he had never spoken to him personally. When Rav Rubenstein delivered a general *shiur* to the entire yeshivah every Thursday, there had been few who had ventured a query or comment, or attempted to answer one of the rosh yeshivah's questions. The depth and clarity of his delivery had left little room for debate. And even if someone did argue, it was usually one of the older and more experienced *bachurim*. Certainly not a kid from *shiur aleph*.

And now, the rosh yeshivah was sitting in his house and waiting for him. What was he supposed to do?

Yisrael had no idea that were it not for an explicit warning from the rosh yeshivah, Tatty would have come over and slapped him on the face. He'd been so angry at his son for disobeying a direct order that he hadn't known what to do. If Yisrael had stopped listening to words, then perhaps a few smacks would help him understand that he'd better get his act together. Just imagine—the honored rosh yeshivah came to visit, and he hadn't even known where his dear son was. What mortification! As though his son were a wild boy who roamed the streets.

But the rosh yeshivah had sat with him for a long while, soothing him. He'd said all sorts of things about how this generation needed to be treated with love. Of course he loved Yisrael. Otherwise, why would he care that the boy didn't learn anymore and hardly ever davened?

The rosh yeshivah had added that it was forbidden to smack young people nowadays. Tatty wasn't so sure that he agreed. In his personal experience, he had learned that one good smack can make the nonsense fly out of one's head. Who knew that better than he? As a boy, he'd been thrashed by his father plenty of times, and he'd turned out all right. Jeffrey had been the baby of the family and handled with silk gloves, and look how he'd turned out… Why, he was hardly even a Jew.

The rosh yeshivah was the first to break the thundering silence. "Hello, Yisrael!" he said. He stood up and walked over to Yisrael, one hand outstretched to shake his. "How are you feeling?"

Yisrael looked nervously at the radiant, smiling face. Did the rosh yeshivah know where he had been till now? Did he know that his former student had been debating with himself just a few minutes earlier about whether or not to desecrate the Shabbos? If not, why was he here? Yisrael had never heard of such a house visit before. What did the rosh yeshivah want from him?

He shook the hand that was extended to him, and tried in vain to produce a coherent answer.

"Answer the rosh yeshivah!" Tatty barked. "Tell him where you've been wandering."

Rav Rubinstein placed a warm hand on the boy's shoulder. "It's all right," he said. "Will you take a little walk with me?"

Yisrael nodded mutely. He was eager to get out. Yisrael's father was wearing a look that Yisrael hadn't seen for years; he seemed on the verge of exploding. The rosh yeshivah thanked his mother politely for her hospitality, then shook his father's hand and parted from him with a brief whisper. Within a minute, Yisrael found himself walking at the rosh yeshivah's side down the street near his house.

Although rabbis were not an unusual sight in this neighborhood, Rav Rubinstein attracted more than a few stares. Walking with him, Yisrael felt very important. Everyone was doubtless wondering who it was walking with the rav like that. The rosh yeshivah himself paid no attention to the stares. He strolled slowly, eyes down, not saying a word.

They walked in silence for several minutes until Yisrael thought that maybe it was he who was supposed to start talking. But something stopped him. The reverence that lingered in his heart did not allow him to trouble the rosh yeshivah with chatter. So he walked at the rav's side and waited tensely for him to say something.

After several minutes, the rosh yeshivah took a seat on a bench, and motioned for Yisrael to sit beside him.

"I was very upset to hear what happened to you in yeshivah," he began. "I know that you went through some difficult moments, and I'm sorry about that."

He paused, and then continued, "I am sure you're familiar with the story in *Maseches Berachos* about Rabbi Akiva, who was forced to sleep in a field outside the city with only a rooster, a donkey, and a candle to dispel the darkness and loneliness. Right? It's a well-known story. Before long, the wind put out the candle, a cat gobbled up the rooster, and a lion trampled the donkey. But Rabbi Akiva, who had lost even the little that he had and was left all alone in the dark, did not lose faith. He declared, 'Whatever *Hakadosh Baruch Hu* does is for the good.' And indeed, because of the darkness and the fact that he had no noisy creatures with him, Rabbi Akiva was saved from a troop of soldiers who passed through that night and attacked the city.

"Now when you read that Gemara, you knew that Rabbi Akiva had been correct. But I ask you: What would have happened if those soldiers *hadn't* come that night? What if he had really been left with nothing, and never discovered why Heaven had decreed that he remain in darkness? Would we have still understood that everything Hashem does is for the good? I'm not so sure... After all, there was no happy ending.

"But I want to stress a point of truth here. It's important that we remember that Rabbi Akiva did not wait for morning and the miracle to say that all is for the good. It was right then, in the midst of the darkness, seemingly without hope, that he stood up and announced, 'Everything is for the good.' And how did he know that? Because Rabbi Akiva, that great *tanna*, knew that nothing in this world just happens. This world has a Conductor, and He brings everything about. And if you understand that, then there are no more questions. Because if *Hakadosh Baruch Hu* does everything, then of course it's for the good."

The rosh yeshivah broke off. Yisrael, who'd been listening to every word, was astonished at the simplicity of the rav's speech. Of course he knew the story, but somehow, now he really understood it. He could picture Rabbi Akiva with nothing going right for him and still accepting the decree with resignation.

No, not with resignation—with happiness. As if everything that had happened to him was exactly what he had wanted to happen. What greatness!

"Now, I want you to know that I was very upset about the fact that the yeshivah became a place that was no longer good for you. I was saddened by what happened, and sad that you had to go through it. We do not understand everything... But it's important to understand one simple thing: There is a reason for everything we go through in life. *Hakadosh Baruch Hu* confronts us with challenges, and we have to try to rise to them. If it has been decreed that you must experience an ordeal, it is your obligation and your privilege to do so with dignity. I know that you could blame many people for what happened...whether they are *bachurim* from the yeshivah or someone else. But, in the final analysis, you have a choice. Do you allow the episode to destroy your life, or do you forge onward with your head held high? That is the question, and only you can answer it."

"But what if I don't have the strength?" Yisrael said. "What if I'm tired of trying to succeed? To start all over in a new yeshivah... Why did it have to be me? Maybe the rav will throw Yossi out of yeshivah and I can go back. He's a thief and a liar. He's..." Yisrael couldn't finish his sentence. Even he knew that it wouldn't help. Everyone in yeshivah thought that he was the thief. Nothing would change that.

"I know that you're angry at him, and rightly so," the rosh yeshivah said. "But I have a feeling that one day you'll learn to see that there's no such thing as an evil person who has no hope. Everyone can do *teshuvah* and correct his ways. Who knows? Maybe one day he'll be in a position to help you."

Yisrael almost laughed out loud. Yossi—help him? That didn't sound too logical. He'd rather die than accept help from that traitor.

Abruptly, the rav changed the subject. "What do you know about Switzerland?"

"Switzerland? Um...nothing. Chocolate? Watches?"

The rosh yeshivah smiled. "Yes, and snow... I have a close friend who has a yeshivah there, and he plans to open it up to Israeli boys next year. He'd be glad to accept you. What do you think about trying to make a fresh start out there? The Swiss air is known to work wonders for people."

Yisrael was thunderstruck. He, who had barely even set foot out of Yerushalayim, fly abroad? To Switzerland?

A current of excitement passed through him. It could be amazing. But also scary... He didn't know a soul in Switzerland. What if he didn't like it there? How would he return home?

"Uh... is that for a lifetime?" he asked.

The rosh yeshivah smiled. "Not for your whole life. In two years, you'll be taking your tests for *yeshivah gedolah*! I, personally, will want to know where you choose to go."

"My father will never agree," Yisrael suddenly remembered. There was disappointment in his voice. Tatty had not left the country since they had moved here. He claimed that it was forbidden for a Jew to leave the Holy Land.

The rosh yeshivah was unperturbed. "It's all right. I've already spoken to him. In any case, my friend, Rav Yaakov Schwartz, will be in touch with you in the next few days. I want to hear good things from him about you in the coming year."

In his imagination, Yisrael had already floated away to Switzerland. Snow-capped mountains and enchanting vistas that he'd never seen before. This could be fun. Who in the neighborhood would believe that he, Yisrael Davis, was going to live abroad?

Yow-ee! Soon he'd be flying away!

18

Zurich, Switzerland, August 2010

RAV SCHWARTZ LOOKED APPREHENSIVELY AT HIS WATCH. It was so late. He'd never get to the airport in time. He crouched beside his beat-up Ford Transit, struggling to get his spare tire into place. Ordinarily, he would have called a tow truck or perhaps asked one of his many friends to help him. But he was in a rush now. Four boys were due in on the 7:30 flight—and he'd just had a flat tire.

His old car stood out in stark contrast to the shiny new cars that sped past him. In Switzerland, even old cars looked as if they'd just come off the production line. Not that there were many of those on the roads. Most of the passing vehicles whose drivers were throwing scornful looks at the bearded Jew crouched beside his stalled vehicle were at least a decade younger than his poor car. But what to do? He preferred spending his money on things that were more important than cars. His yeshivah—Yeshivas Birkas Aharon, named after his father, Aharon Schwartz, *z"l*—did not suffer from a surplus of funds. Although those parents who were able to pay did so happily, many of them couldn't. What was really sad was that even more of them didn't want to.

Rav Schwartz had been born in Switzerland, but he'd done most of his learning in Eretz Yisrael. His father was Swiss, but his mother, as she often declared, was and always would be a native of Bnei Brak. While they spent most of the year in Zurich, they moved to Bnei Brak during the winter months in order to escape the Swiss cold for a bit.

Rav Schwartz knew that his mother hated living abroad. She didn't like being a stranger. The cold that they fled was not the physical chill that attacked Zurich each year with the predictability of a well-oiled Swiss watch, but the cold radiated by the people. The cold that now prevented those people from stepping out of their cars to offer their help to a stranded driver.

A screech told him that his jack was about to crack beneath its load. That wasn't supposed to happen. Apparently, he hadn't put it in the right place. One day he'd have to ask someone to teach him the right way to change a tire. He looked again, and whispered a quiet prayer. Although El Al flights often landed late, there was a limit to how much time four Israeli *bachurim*, ignorant of the local language, could wait around in a foreign airport. This was simply irresponsible on his part. If he did not succeed now, he would abandon the car and take a taxi, come what may.

He stood up and shoved the tire in with all the strength of his foot. He was so surprised when the wheel slid neatly into place that he didn't notice the jack waver and then clatter to the ground. Fortunately, the car landed gently on the spare tire instead of on his foot. With a murmured prayer of thanksgiving, he hastily twisted in the screws. Later, he would ask someone to check to see if everything was in its proper place. Right now, he had to hurry to the airport.

He moved back into traffic, weaving among the lanes with Israeli expertise. "I'm half Swiss and completely Israeli," he would respond to those who asked where he was from. Now he was driving like a real Israeli.

The huge culture gaps were almost indescribable. In Switzerland, everyone drove in his own lane and did not pass another vehicle except with good reason. Even when a driver did pass, the maneuver was executed with patience and with every signal mandated by law. In Israel, people treated lane markings as mere suggestions. Drivers cut right and left as they pleased. There was no signaling and not much checking in rearview mirrors. There was a sense that every Israeli was certain the highway had been built for his personal use, and let the other drivers beware.

He glanced at his watch again. It was 7:59. They were probably waiting at the airport exit now. He hoped with all his heart that they'd taken his advice and packed coats in their hand luggage. While winter had not yet begun in Israel, it was already very cold in Switzerland, especially for young native Israelis who barely knew what snow looked like.

He had learned their names and looked at their passport pictures so that he would know how to find them. Not that that would pose any real problem. Anyone could pick out a *yeshivah bachur*, especially among the gentile faces all around.

Yanky Glazer, 17, from Bnei Brak. Thrown out of yeshivah because of discipline issues. Rav Schwartz's gut feeling was that Yanky would be the hardest nut to crack this year. Every year there was at least one like that.

Next...Baruch Mishkowski. The son of a Jerusalem rosh yeshivah. A genius who had real social problems. Rav Schwartz knew the type well: boys who were too gifted and didn't understand the first thing about human relations.

The next boy on the list also came from Yerushalayim. Yisrael Davis. How had Rav Rubenstein described him? "A good boy who got in trouble through no fault of his own." He had not gone into detail, and Rav Schwartz had known better than to ask. If the boy wanted to, he would share the story himself. If Rav Rubinstein had recommended him, there was no cause for concern.

A large part of the unique effectiveness of his special yeshivah was the fact that he took boys who'd been virtually given up on and offered them a chance to start afresh. All too often, he'd seen how a *bachur* who'd been thought of in his yeshivah as a clown or a loser flourished when given the opportunity to build a new image with no preconceptions, a new start in a whole new setting. It was no coincidence that most of his students came from countries other than Switzerland. This year, for example, eight boys were arriving from England, Belgium, and France. Another four were coming from the United States. This, together with the seven Israelis, brought the number up to nineteen. Add one local boy, and he had twenty altogether. Exactly the number he'd hoped for.

Tonight, the first four Israelis had flown in. Tomorrow, the rest would arrive. This was the first time he'd agreed to accept boys from Eretz Yisrael—a whole new challenge. The familiar nervousness that always came with the start of a new year tickled inside his stomach.

Rav Schwartz drove off the exit ramp leading to the airport. He was not as late as he'd feared. And anyway, they were Israelis; they didn't have any conception of being on time. As he scanned the parking lot for an empty space, his mind went over the facts about the fourth boy on today's list, Gilad Gil from Nahariya.

Gilad was the son of the famous *baal teshuvah* Shai Gil. Shai had been the world champion in middleweight boxing, and his return to his roots had stunned fans of the sport in Israel and throughout the world. Rav Schwartz had once seen him at a convention in Jerusalem and had been very impressed. Contrary to expectations, the legendary boxer was a clear-thinking and articulate intellectual. Not surprisingly, he'd become a sought-after speaker among the *chareidi* public, who were enchanted by his story. He titled his lecture "From the Boxing Ring to the Beis Medrash."

Gilad had been a small boy when his parents embraced an observant lifestyle. From the little that Rav Schwartz had heard, he'd always been drawn to the world of sports. Shai's only son had refused to believe his father's assertion that sports were empty and meaningless. Apparently, apart from a talent for boxing, Gilad had inherited his father's stubbornness and dedication to a goal. The same community activist who had directed Shai to Rav Schwartz had predicted that Gilad would not remain observant. "He's simply not interested," he had said. "He could easily have remained in his previous yeshivah. All he had to do was say he was willing to stay. But he wasn't willing. The only reason he agreed to come to your yeshivah is because it's outside of Israel, far away from his father's supervision. It's hard for me to believe that you'll be able to influence him."

Rav Schwartz had listened in silence. Had he agreed with the fellow's assessment, he would not have accepted the boy. He had neither the time nor the money to waste. But he believed that every Jew has a choice, for good or for ill. If he did his part, and if the boy was even slightly open to listening, then *Hakadosh Baruch Hu* could save him. Sometimes he failed with the very boys that he expected to succeed with—and the opposite was also true. When dealing with human souls, all bets were off.

He parked the car and hurried to the arrivals terminal. Small knots of people were waiting there, gazing expectantly at the door through which the various passengers were emerging. Here and there came restrained cries of welcome and brief hugs. How different from the clamor of Ben Gurion Airport...

He searched for his boys. They weren't hard to find. Not far from a coffee shop stood the four Israelis, talking in pairs and watching what was happening around them with interest, trying to pick up the new culture they had just entered. The mountain of luggage around them told observers that they'd arrived for more than just a quick visit. With Hashem's help, they would be spending the entire winter in Switzerland.

Rav Schwartz made a guess. The pair standing on the right were Gilad Gil and Yisrael Davis, and the two on the left were Yanky Glazer and Baruch Mishkowski. It wasn't too hard. The first two were tall and athletic looking, while the others were shorter and wearing glasses. He took a deep breath and approached them at his usual brisk pace.

"*Shalom aleichem!*" He shook their hands and introduced himself. A joke or two that he used every year thawed the atmosphere, and within a short time they found themselves crowded into the Ford Transit together with their luggage.

The good atmosphere lifted his spirits. With Hashem's help, this would be a year of success and growth. The most important thing in the kind of work he did was to establish a positive bond with the boys. If he wanted to be able to help them, he had to make sure that they felt comfortable talking to him about anything under the sun. The jokes and chuckles at his car's expense were worth a king's ransom.

The hardest part of his job was knowing how to set proper boundaries. The most important advice his rosh yeshivah had given him when he'd come seeking a blessing for his new yeshivah was simple but crystal clear: "Don't be your students' friend."

It had taken him time to understand how on the mark this advice really was. The first instinct of many who work in the field of *kiruv* is the notion that the ends justify the means. In order for these young people to feel comfortable in the adults' company, they believe, he must speak their language and go down to their level.

"How mistaken they are," the rosh yeshivah had asserted. "These boys don't come to you to be their friend. They have enough friends. They come to you to get something. To learn Torah and *derech eretz*. If you're just like them, what is there for them to learn from you? The opposite is true: they'll teach *you* a thing or two."

What Rav Schwartz had learned firsthand was the difficulty in pinpointing the narrow boundary between a rabbi who cares about you, and a friend who does everything for you. The beginnings were the hardest part, the stage at which such boundaries are learned. It would get easier for everyone as the year went on.

In the meantime, things were going well. Tomorrow he would come back to pick up the rest of the arriving Israelis. The Europeans and the Americans would join them two days later. In his heart, he composed a silent prayer from the depths of his being. A prayer that Hashem would help him bring these youngsters to the path of Torah and mitzvos, that *Hakadosh Baruch Hu* would make the harmony and happiness presently reigning in the backseat only stronger with time.

19

Venice, Italy, 2011

JON PERRERA WAS NOT PARANOID, BUT IN HIS LINE OF WORK it never hurt to be too careful. His true name, Antonio DeVita, was nearly forgotten as a result of the time that had elapsed since he'd last used it. He was an Italian by birth but had worked all over the world. In many countries, he topped the list of Most Wanted Men, a position he had earned through a great deal of hard work and daring operations carried out with consummate skill. The fact that he had not yet been caught was largely due to his caution and the careful measures he took to protect himself. He did not rely on luck, preferring to abort an operation planned amid much toil and sweat if he thought there was a danger he'd be exposed. There was always time to carry out the mission at a later date. And even if there wasn't—what use were the millions he received if he'd spend the rest of his life behind bars? If, that is, he stood trial in a country that did not have the death sentence…

Something was troubling him about the current mission. An inner sense of danger that he could not shake. Something he couldn't put his finger on. On the surface of things, it seemed like a simple operation, a precise shot at an easy target, followed by a quick escape on the first train out. Before anyone could act, he would already be many kilometers away.

But something bothered him. Maybe it was someone he'd seen in the past. A familiar face. He staged a mental review of all the passengers who'd sat in the train compartment with him, but no red flags were raised. He had a special memory for faces—actually, for every detail surrounding him. He could stroll down a bustling, crowded street and later tell you who had walked by and which vehicles had passed. Someone that he'd seen today was familiar from the past, but he couldn't pinpoint who.

For a brief moment, he considered aborting the mission. He dismissed the thought almost at once. It had surely been the search on the train that had aroused this feeling. It suggested some sort of leak, but not something serious enough to endanger the operation. No one knew about his plan. Even the parties that had hired him for the hit didn't know. The information they'd supplied about the judge's impending trip had been accurate. It had come from a court clerk who had proved himself in the past. The judge would come.

Apart from that, had they known more, they would have arrested him on board the train. The simple policemen who had conducted the search had shown that the information they'd received from Interpol had not been specific. Otherwise, they would have sent in a unit of experts. His name was worth bringing in the best they had.

It was probably nothing. Just normal stress.

Nevertheless, he decided not to waste time. Two hours remained until the judge's arrival, two hours in which he could soothe his suspicions through a final check. He hid his weapons in a suitcase in the closet and placed an almost invisible hair on the door. If someone opened it, the hair would fall and he would know. Now he would go out and take a little walk around the neighborhood, trying to see if something suspicious stood out to him.

In a high-tech world, it was hard to find people who knew how to shadow someone properly. Everyone relied on their technological tools: satellites, cell phones, sophisticated GPS navigation systems.

All these things served the law enforcement agencies. But if you knew how to guard against them, there were few threats to worry you.

Jon did not carry a cell phone on his person. Anyone who needed to reach him knew how to do so. In his pocket was a device that only received messages and did not reveal his precise location. If someone had a similar device, he could find his general location—within an approximately three-kilometer radius—but it was unlikely, since the device was not registered in his name, and in any case very few people could obtain one.

Even this did not satisfy him. Each week he switched his device, to make it even more difficult to trace him and prepare a successful trap. The satellites roving through outer space posed another problem that had a solution. These satellites are incapable of capturing a photo on the diagonal. If one does not turn his face upward, it is impossible to clearly identify him. There did exist professionals who were expert at reading satellite images, but even they could be tricked.

Every so often, he entered a place that was teeming with people—a hotel or mall—and changed his clothes, put some sort of hat on his head, and left together with a group of people through the main entrance. With the aid of a bent back or shuffling gait, he would lose any annoying shadowers and go on to the next operation. So far, the system had worked beautifully. There was no reason for anything to be different today.

He left the hotel and turned right into a street packed with tourists. In a fraction of a second, he ascertained that none of the people near him constituted a danger. For him, the street was a stage and everyone in it had a specific role. Some were hawking wares, others were tourists, and so on. In this street, everyone was playing his appropriate role. No one appeared out of place.

When he operated in Italy, he always felt confident in his reading of the situation. As an Italian, he could recognize who was local and who was a foreigner. In Venice, especially during the peak seasons, most of the people were tourists; but tourists too behave in a specific way. It was easy to home in on someone suspicious.

He walked quickly; there was no need to turn his head to see if anyone was following him. The store windows served as adequate mirrors. Apart from this, if he couldn't rely on his hearing, he was getting old. Hearing is just as important as vision, if not more so, when one is being followed. There are things that are impossible to see, but if you know how to listen you can hear them. The cocking of a gun, for example... The sounds around him told him to stay calm. They were all appropriate to the surroundings. Excited tourists babbled in a host of languages, an old beggar asked for donations from passersby, souvenir sellers tried to lure in customers. A gondola owner, dressed in the traditional trousers and hat, coaxed an elderly couple onto his boat. The sure stride of a pair of policemen...

He turned his head slightly to see them. The pair walked slowly, chatting to each other, until they reached the beggar. The law forbade begging in Venice. It was a jarring note in the pastoral atmosphere and could chase away tourists. Jon continued on his way as the officers ordered the beggar to depart the scene. From experience, he knew that the beggar would leave for a few minutes and then return to the same spot. It was impossible to be rid of them...

He decided to turn left after the bridge, near the Jewish restaurant. He would enter the Jewish ghetto. He'd sit down for a few minutes and decide once and for all whether or not he was being followed. There was no place to hide in the ghetto. The broad square did not provide comfortable hiding places.

He slowed his steps to see if anyone else changed the tempo of his walk to suit his. Nothing. A minute later, he was sitting on a bench in the Jewish ghetto, watching children running after a large flock of pigeons that had settled there. The usual guard sat in his booth overlooking the square. When the authorities had reached the conclusion that it was worth their while to invest in security in the Jewish tourist sites, they'd established this guard booth in the Jewish square.

Incredibly, after everything that had been done to them here, Jews still returned to visit the place. Thousands of Jews had been deported for destruction from this spot, and now they were thronging back to sightsee among the remnants of the past. A quick glance showed Jon Perrera that the guard was busy reading a newspaper and neglecting his duties.

When five more minutes had passed, Jon's fears abated entirely. No one was after him. He stood up and began to make his way back in the direction of the hotel. There was work to do.

A distant, vibrating sound reached his ear. It couldn't be the device in his pocket; the sound wasn't that close, and in any case he didn't feel the device's vibration. Just to make sure, he placed his hand in his pocket. No, it wasn't coming from there. It was probably some tourist's phone that was vibrating.

But why should a tourist leave his phone on the "vibrate" setting in the street? And why should that disturb him?

In the next shop window, he saw him.

He'd seen that man before! When had it been? It took him just two seconds to remember the man from the train. He'd walked behind the man briefly when they'd reached the city. But that still didn't necessarily mean anything. It was logical to see someone who'd been on the train with him. After all, Venice was not that big.

But something about the stranger disturbed him. He didn't know what it was. He had a feeling he'd seen him before...

Suddenly, he caught the sound of rapid footsteps. The stranger quickly closed the gap between them. Jon's hand moved automatically to his pocket and gripped his gun. He was moving now on the instinct of a killer who sensed danger. He whirled around, gun cocked and ready, but he didn't get the chance to use it. Ami was not surprised by the swift reaction. He hadn't expected anything less from the Italian assassin—and so, he was able to let off the first shot.

He fired three shots into Jon Perrera's chest, and watched the assassin fall to the ground with a crash, still gripping his gun.

Terrified screams rose from every side. People scattered and fled in panic. Some hid behind sales booths or trees, while others froze where they stood. A group of Chinese tourists went into hysterics, shrieking repeatedly.

Ami had always found the behavior of a crowd in such situations fascinating. Once in a very long while, there would be one individual who did not fall apart and who could later render an accurate account of what had occurred. In the Venice police station, one brave young Italian would be able to describe how the stranger sent three bullets into the chest of the man who held a gleaming gun, then lowered his arm and, with a maddeningly slow and confident gait, calmly walked away.

Ami didn't run. Running invited the pursuit of potential heroes. His steps were long but not rapid as he disappeared into the nearest building. He climbed one flight up and exited through a window facing the parallel street. His appearance did not cause a stir, as people on the street were too busy running either toward the source of the gunfire or away from it. No one knew exactly what had happened, and Ami took advantage of this to let himself be swallowed up in the crowd streaming vigorously toward the train station.

The message he'd received a few minutes earlier had changed the plan. He'd been summoned home. Something more important had cropped up. His orders had not said that he must finish his present mission. That's the way it was in the service: one minute, the mission at hand is top priority; the next, something new comes up that changes everything.

Ami climbed lightly up the stairs leading to the station and examined the schedule of departures. In a minute and a half, a train would be leaving for Arth-Goldau in Switzerland. The trip would take a little over six hours. From there, he could make his way easily to Zurich and the airport. This was his way out.

He hurried to Platform 5 and boarded the train. Half a minute later, the wheels began to turn and the train left the station, leaving the Italian island city. A brief visit to the lavatory was enough to let him lose his tailored suit and matching hat and put on a white T-shirt and black cap, both emblazoned with the word "Venice." His gun had long ago been hurled into the bottom of the canal. Now, wearing an outfit bought in one of the dozens of souvenir stands in Venice, he looked like any other tourist returning from a dream vacation in Italy.

It was a good thing that he was leaving Italy. He would find it much easier to board a plane in Zurich than in Milan. The search for him would not cross the border so quickly. By the time the Italians even realized what had happened he'd be back in Israel.

Sometime in the coming days, someone would make the connection between the dead man and the room in the Principe Hotel.

In searching his room, they would find his rifle and would understand that an assassination had been prevented. Perhaps someone in the police department would even make the connection between the judge's visit and the assassin's death.

Either way, no one would shed too many tears over Jon Perrera. Now all Ami had to worry about was having someone tie up the loose ends on his side. His own rifle needed to be picked up from his hotel room, and the bill paid. That would not present undue complications. He leaned back and his pulse, which still pounded with adrenalin, began to slow. One day, he would pay with his life for his tendency to finish a job at any price. In the meantime, only the bad guys were suffering.

There was no question about it: a world without Jon Perrera was a much nicer place to live in.

20

Zurich, Switzerland, Winter 2011

THE FIRST MONTHS OF THE NEW YEAR SURPASSED RAV Schwartz's expectations. The boys bonded beautifully, and their connection with the staff was established more quickly than he had hoped. Apart from Rav Schwartz, the yeshivah employed two *maggidei shiur*, along with five *kollel* men who learned with the *bachurim* during their learning *sedarim*. He maintained a policy of keeping the classes small—a maximum of seven boys to a *shiur*. The most important thing for his boys, he believed, was a personal relationship. No boy must be allowed to disappear into the crowd.

The month of Elul was long behind them, along with the elevation of the *Yamim Noraim*, which had been particularly moving this year. Several of the boys had approached him after Yom Kippur and said that this was the first time they'd actually felt a connection to that great day. The first time they'd understood its importance. Until now, it had been hardly more than a nightmare to them. Sad, how one could lose out on the best things in life when there was no guiding hand.

On Succos, the staff and students were officially on their *bein haze-manim* break. However, like every year, enough boys remained in the yeshivah that he needed to look out for them. While the majority of the Europeans went home for the holidays, most of the others stayed in Switzerland, either because family budgets prohibited flying them back, or because they simply didn't like being home.

R Schwartz took those who had stayed behind on an excursion through Switzerland. He took them along the Bahnofstrasse, the central street of Zurich replete with upscale shops and restaurants. At the end of the street, they took a boat ride across Lake Zurich and then continued on to Lucerne by bus. They visited the famous Lucerne Yeshivah as well as the railroad museum. Afterward, they climbed to the top of Mount Pilatus and took a strenuous hike that ended with the obstacle course in the rope park there.

They visited Swiss villages and crossed dense forests. Rav Schwartz did his utmost to make the trip a success—and it was. His aching back told him so for weeks afterward...but it was worth it! The experience had done wonders for the boys, and he'd deftly maneuvered their infectious enthusiasm into an appreciation of the Creation's beauty, with the exclamation, *"Mah rabbu ma'asechah Hashem!"*

When Succos was over, so was their vacation. The long, wearying winter *z'man* was poised to start. The *bachurim* who had traveled home returned to yeshivah—except for one American whose parents had reconsidered their decision to send him to Switzerland. For the nineteen optimistic boys, the new *z'man* at Yeshivas Birkas Aharon began.

The hours resembled those at other yeshivos, although their midday break was longer—from 1 to 4 in the afternoon—and the *shiurim* were shorter.

Rav Schwartz believed that what helped the boys progress the most were the shared hours of one-on-one study with the kollel men and the *ramim,* and the personal bond that grew between them. He placed special emphasis on learning the simple meaning of the various *sugyos* before plumbing their depths. "A house without foundations cannot stand," he liked to say.

He loved each boy as though he were his only son, tracking their progress and making sure to take each *bachur* out for a walk around the neighborhood so that they could speak privately. Rav Schwartz had been married for seventeen years, and these were the only children that Hashem had given him. He didn't know what he'd have done without them—just as they didn't know what they'd have done without him. He watched them grow right before his eyes. He saw friendships form, and boys who had been considered lost find their natural place in front of the *shtender*. It was not for naught that many in the *chinuch* world regarded him admiringly as something of a magician.

But there was no magic or enchantment involved. There was plenty of hard work and ceaseless caring. The yeshivah was the core of his life, and all his energy was directed toward helping "his" boys move forward. To his good fortune, his wife was a full and faithful partner in his important work. She happily baked and cooked the meals, and she remembered who liked to eat what. If R' Schwartz was the boys' second father, then she was their mother. For all his fine qualities, R' Schwartz was not very adept at financial and technical matters and barely knew how to change a lightbulb. All the logistics and bill paying fell under her aegis. There was good reason for R' Schwartz's oft-repeated declaration: "*Sheli v'shelachem— shelah.*" Everything that I have and you have—is due to her.

By the middle of November, the picture was clear. Everyone knew their place and role in the scheme of things. They knew their rebbeim and their friends. They knew where the small Jewish bakery was located, and the nearest kosher grocery.

"How expensive things are here!" laughed the boys from Jerusalem, citing the high prices. "For the price of a single apple, you could buy the entire Machane Yehudah *shuk*!"

Actually, the prices were not all that steep. Something that might cost 5 shekels in Israel cost 5 Swiss francs here. Except that the franc was worth approximately four times the shekel...

However, while prices in Switzerland were higher, so was the earned income. The Swiss received their salaries in francs, not shekels. This caused most of the Israelis to limit their purchase of food and make do with the nutritious meals that the rebbetzin prepared for them each day. Yisrael Davis was one of the few who could permit himself to go shopping. His father sent him a generous allowance each month.

This generosity on his father's part had surprised Yisrael at first, but he'd quickly grown accustomed to it. From the perspective of distance, things appeared a little different than they had looked before. When he had parted from his parents at the airport, Yisrael had been surprised to see tears in his father's eyes. He'd expected as much from his mother, but not Tatty. Lately he'd thought his father hated him. Now, as they said good-bye, for the first time in a long time he understood that Tatty loved him. This surprised Yisrael, and gave him pause. He would have to think about this... Okay, maybe he hadn't actually believed that his father hated him, but that's the way it had felt. It had been such a difficult and stressful time that he nearly wept with joy when it came to an end.

What he didn't know was that the physical distance was no less important to his father than it was to him. Now, with his son learning so far away from home, Yerachmiel Davis had plenty of time to think about what had happened.

How was it that the son who had been a steady source of unmitigated *nachas* had deteriorated so rapidly in the course of a few weeks' time? When Yisrael was at home, sitting about idly, his father had been busy thinking of ways to get him back on track. He'd been laboring under stress and trying to find ways to get Yisrael back to yeshivah—by force, if necessary. Now that his son was in a place of Torah, Yerachmiel sat down and made an accounting with himself. A long backward look, to see where *he'd* gone wrong.

R' Davis did not know exactly where his son had been spending his time when he left home, but he had no doubt it had not been in a place with *sifrei kodesh*. He'd grown up in the United States, and he knew many who had strayed from the correct path and wound up in the street. Now, in hindsight, he understood that his son had been out there too. What good fortune that the rosh yeshivah had intervened when he had. Otherwise, who knew where it might have ended? Certainly not in yeshivah.

One of the conclusions he came to was that he had erred in not supporting his son. When Yisrael came home, broken by what had happened in yeshivah, he should not have lectured him. He should have refrained from yelling and scolding. Yisrael had been in need of a shoulder to lean on, and a listening ear. Someone to hear him and help him through a hard time.

Even if, Heaven forbid, he *had* been the thief—the mere thought shook R' Davis—it was still a father's job to help. True, sometimes one has to scold and punish, but one has to know when it's better to support and embrace. Yerachmiel's inner integrity told him forcefully that he'd been wrong. He hadn't been there when his son needed him.

This realization brought about a noticeable change in his approach. If, until now, he'd given his son a small allowance, and then only after a clear and comprehensive explanation of what the money was needed for, now he sent Yisrael a respectable sum each month. Let him learn without having to worry about anything. He didn't overdo it, of course; giving a teenager too much money would also be a mistake. But he certainly sent a nice sum. A sum that showed Yisrael his father loved him and was proud of him.

Yisrael, for his part, did not hoard his treasure for himself. He bought nosh for his friends, and especially for Gilad Gil, his best friend. From the moment they'd met on the plane, they'd taken to one another. Both loved sports, and this common denominator provided fodder for long conversations far into the night.

They were not at all alike. If Yisrael had no doubts about what was right and wrong, Gilad struggled with many basic questions, such as the existence of a Creator. Yisrael had never questioned this; he'd only searched for a way to cope with the challenges that *Hakadosh Baruch Hu* had placed in his way. In their lengthy debates, he heatedly defended his burning faith and the fact that the world has a Leader.

The rosh yeshivah, Rav Schwartz, understood how important it was to discuss with the boys this vital topic. Once a week, he delivered a *shiur* in basic Jewish thought during which the boys could ask any questions they had. No question was considered unfit for discussion, as long as it was asked with respect and a sincere desire to receive an answer. Even Yisrael was surprised to see how little he had understood until now about the true nature of *emunah*.

The friendship between the two Israeli boys pleased the rosh yeshivah for a number of reasons. They seemed to complement one another. Yisrael gave Gilad the simple faith the other boy so sorely lacked. Until now, faith for Gilad had been a matter for the intellect, not the emotions—apparently, a perspective he had received from his father. From Yisrael, he learned that basic *emunah* is meant to touch the emotions.

Yisrael, for his part, gained from Gilad the self-confidence he'd been missing. The trauma he had undergone at his yeshivah had undermined his equilibrium. The appreciation he received from Gilad, and from all of his new friends, built him up again. The boy would go far.

Rav Schwartz knew that the two boys were teaching each other something else too. Yisrael taught Gilad to play basketball and Gilad taught Yisrael the finer points of hand-to-hand combat. Rav Schwartz didn't know much about these skills, but he believed that as long as they remained in the correct proportion, there was nothing to be lost in these pastimes. These boys needed a relaxing pastime after their hours of learning. Better that they busy themselves with this than wander around bored.

Yisrael and Gilad found a gym belonging to a school not far from the yeshivah. It was generally deserted at night, and they went there often. Sometimes they played basketball with local students who had stayed late. This was something Rav Schwartz liked less. He didn't want his *bachurim* befriending gentile boys. The locals admired Yisrael and called him "the Jewish champion." He became renowned in the school as an unbeatable basketball player, and the students flocked to the gym just to watch him play.

When things were quiet, they would train in Thai boxing, which Gilad had studied for years. Yisrael enjoyed it immensely, and within a few months became a worthy opponent for Gilad. He wondered if this skill would have come in handy when those hoodlums attacked Gadi on the road. He sensed that it probably would not have proven useful. Then again…

If, at the start, Gilad managed to get him on the floor within seconds, now they could go for hours on end without a conclusive defeat. In basketball, on the other hand, though Gilad improved greatly, he never reached Yisrael's precision at throwing the ball.

Gradually, the old yeshivah building turned into a warm home for all the boys. They made progress in their learning, and Rav Schwartz was pleasantly surprised at their development in other areas.

"This is going to be a good crop," he said with a satisfied chuckle, when his rebbetzin told him about Jay, the spoiled American, who'd lately been helping out in the kitchen. Jay had once not known what a frying pan looked like; now he knew how to fry eggs and chop a salad.

The long winter passed quickly. As the Pesach break approached, Rav Schwartz could announce with complete sincerity that he had not had such a successful year since the yeshivah began.

Nineteen contented boys made a satisfying *siyum* on *Maseches Makkos*. For most of them, this was the first tractate they had ever finished. For all of them, it had been a winter of hard but fulfilling work.

Yisrael couldn't believe how excited he was to go home. To see Mommy and Tatty, his little sisters—who had no doubt grown while he was away—and the only country in the world where he felt comfortable to speak Hebrew. If there was one thing that exhausted him about Switzerland, it was their annoying language.

He knew the English alphabet, thanks to his mother's insistence, but the signs in Switzerland were above his reading level. For some reason, the Swiss connected their words, putting several of them together into one long word so that, for example, the street on which the yeshivah stood was named Brandschenkestrasse. It took him a few minutes just to read the endless word. He counted nineteen letters. Nineteen! He couldn't think of a single word in Hebrew that was that long.

One of the local kollel men had explained to him that the name should be broken down into three words: *brand*—meaning burnt, *schenke*, a tavern or pub, and *strasse*, which means street, as in

Banhofstrasse, or "the street of the railroad station." He had translated the yeshivah's address as "Burnt Tavern Street" or some such
thing.

Yisrael had merely rubbed his eyes and muttered, "The Swiss are
just plain crazy! Didn't they ever hear of putting spaces between
words?" Actually, with time he had become better at unraveling
the street names using this method. But how good it would be to go
home and see clear signs in Hebrew. He was counting the minutes.

Every Friday, he would call home and speak with Mommy, and
then with little Bracha and Tamar. If Tatty were home, Yisrael would
speak to him too. That week, Tamar ruined the surprise when she
announced that they were all planning to go to the airport to meet
him. When she realized her mistake, she tried to pretend she'd been
confused, and that he'd see them at home. He played along and told
her that he'd manage fine on his own. But there was no question in
his mind: they were coming. He couldn't explain that he would
have preferred that they didn't come. He was embarrassed to have
everyone at the airport witness his emotion. But they wouldn't
have understood. They were coming, and that was that.

Now he sat in the plane, struggling to open the kosher meal that
refused to submit. They wrapped those meals up as though they
expected you to eat the wrapping too. Only after he used his pen to
tear the tough foil did he finally manage to reach the treasure hidden within. Some sort of ground beef dish, beans, and a dry roll.
He gazed at the food mournfully, and only cheered up when he
remembered the wonderful food his mother had certainly prepared
for him at home.

He offered his portion to Eliezer Berman, seated beside him, who
pounced on the meal as though he hadn't eaten in a month. Eliezer
was the only one in yeshivah who'd gained weight that winter.
There was plenty of food at yeshivah, as Eliezer's bursting shirt
testified, but the rebbetzin insisted that the boys eat healthily and
in the correct amounts—and respectfully, they obeyed. Eliezer had
tried his best, but Rav Schwartz himself had begged the rebbetzin
not to bother the boy on this subject. Eliezer had much more important personal battles than a diet to fight that winter. He couldn't

be asked to make war on all fronts. In general, this was the rabbi's method: advancing step by step. "Slowly but surely," he'd say. "If you jump too high, you usually end up falling down."

Yisrael slept through the rest of the flight, waking to the passengers' applause on landing at Ben Gurion. He hastened to collect his carry-on bag and joined the stream of eager passengers moving toward passport control and the baggage claim. He parted from his friends just before it was time to step outside in the arrivals area. He gestured for them to go ahead, letting them believe that he had to pay a visit to the restroom. He didn't want them to see his family. Not that he was ashamed of them. He was simply not a little boy anymore.

After a short delay, he took a deep breath and rolled his suitcase toward the exit. The waiting throng was crowded around the opening, confusing him. He searched for a familiar face, but didn't find one. Uneasy, he lowered his head and walked toward the right-hand exit. Maybe they'd decided not to come, after all.

"Sruli!" The sound of the nickname his father had used for him years before roused him. Before he knew it, he was surrounded by his family. Their excitement was contagious and he returned his father's powerful hug.

In the large taxi they had hired, they begged Yisrael to tell them all about his year and to describe snowy Switzerland. While spring was at its height here, back there winter seemed loathe to leave. He'd heard that summers were beautiful there too, but right now he was enjoying the warm sun, in such stark contrast to the snow that still lingered in Zurich. He tried to think of stories he hadn't told them on the phone, and ended up telling about his flight and the distasteful meal he'd received.

Amid the laughter and the joy that accompanied them home, he reached the same conclusion as before. It had been a good idea for him to go to Switzerland—if only for the family bonds that had been strengthened while he was gone. He studied his parents with fresh eyes.

When he was young, Tatty had been the big, strong father who knew everything. Then he turned into the tyrant who told him what to do and didn't care what Yisrael thought. Now he saw only what his father really was: a simple Jew who tried to guide his family toward a good Torah life. Sure, he'd made some mistakes, but who didn't? He had not done so from personal interest, but from love. A love that Yisrael hadn't known existed until recently. But better late than never.

To his surprise, he realized that he loved his father too. He loved him very much, despite everything. And one day, when he found the courage, he would even dare admit it out loud…

21

THE AMERICAN INTELLIGENCE COMMUNITY INCLUDES sixteen member agencies, each responsible for a different area of gathering, cataloging, and dealing with intelligence information vital to the defense of the nation. After the glaring oversight that culminated in 9/11, a committee was formed to investigate the tragedy. It was discovered that the various intelligence agencies had overlooked the bits and pieces of intelligence data that had pointed to the terrorist plot targeted at the Twin Towers. The committee decided to create a position whose occupant would unify all the various agencies. The person in this position would be responsible for ensuring that all incoming intelligence be passed to all agencies in real time.

Until that point, there had been cases where agencies had refrained from sharing information with other agencies out of concern for prestige or for other reasons. Had anyone put together all the pieces in time, the tragedy of 9/11 might have been averted. This resolution was implemented in 2005 with the creation of a new position, the Secretary of Homeland Security, whose job was to try to unify all the various powers that be.

Matthew Klinger had been serving in this position for two years and didn't remember when he'd last been this surprised. The phone conversation just concluded had caught him off guard for the first time in years. His Russian counterpart had been positive: a tactical nuclear weapon was on its way to the United States.

The first thing he did was place a quick call to the director of the FBI, Howard Simons, and to Mike Gray, assistant director of the CIA, summoning them to an urgent meeting. Ordinarily, he would not have bypassed the CIA director, who was presently in Egypt, looking after American interests in the post-Mubarak era. But this was not an ordinary situation. The director's assistant would update the director on events. Right now, he had no time to waste on transatlantic phone calls.

The head of homeland security was directly answerable to the president. He was responsible for advising the president and the National Security Council on every area of national security. Matthew decided not to bring this new intelligence to the president just yet. Not before he heard what the FBI and the CIA had to say on the matter. If what he'd just heard was true, heads were going to roll. How was it possible that the billions of dollars sunk into these agencies didn't produce results when they were needed? A crisis of the magnitude of 9/11 was taking place—on his watch.

He mentally raced through the protocols that had been written to address such an eventuality. A nuclear bomb could appear in the form of two possible threats: in the course of open warfare with another country, or in the case of a terrorist cell that managed to lay its hands on such a bomb and choose to detonate it on American soil. He was not yet sure what they were dealing with here. The Russian security officer had also been uncertain about the origins of the bomb—either Iran or a terrorist organization. What was certain was this: the bomb was on its way to American soil at this very minute.

In the fifteen minutes until the men he'd summoned appeared in his office, Matthew Klinger raised the preparedness level of each of the agencies under his purview, including the army, to High—the level used when there was a very high likelihood of a terror attack. The Coast Guard and airport authorities were ordered to organize for maximum alertness. If the bomb was not here yet, Matthew was determined to stop it on its way.

He reviewed the president's schedule. The most important upcoming items were his meeting with the Israeli prime minister—which was taking place at this very moment—and a speech to AIPRO. The wielders of the nuclear bomb might have chosen from among any number of targets: Times Square in New York, the White House in Washington, the Pentagon, or hundreds of other strategic locations. Readiness levels must be raised in all of them, and preparations made in the event that the bomb is actually set off. Scenarios for every possible eventuality were lying in his drawer. He fervently hoped he wouldn't have to use them.

By the time the FBI director walked in, he already knew that they were looking at something serious. "What's the quality of the intelligence?" he asked.

The assistant director of the CIA, following on his heels, announced, "I spoke to the director, and he's just as surprised as I am. We've had no indication of an immediate threat of this caliber. Where did it come from?"

"Igor." As Matthew revealed the name of his source, he could see the other men's hearts sinking. Igor Morkovski was a top-notch intelligence agent. Communications between the Russian intelligence agencies and those of the United States were firmly cemented once he had stepped into the job. Although he'd formerly belonged to the KGB, which had earned a reprehensible reputation during the Cold War era, a great deal had changed in the world since then. Today the primary challenge confronting the two powers, now that they no longer feared a war between them, was international terror. In the face of a terrorist community equipped with the best that technology had to offer, there was no escaping the need to cooperate against their mutual enemies. Though their interests often clashed, in general this cooperation was a productive one. If Igor Morkovski claimed that there was a nuclear bomb, it was a claim that could not be lightly dismissed.

"I'm going to set up a command post in the White House, and I want you two there," Matthew barked. "Talk to your people and your colleagues. I want full transparency. I want representatives from the NSA, the DIA...from everyone. If what I've been told is true, we're living on borrowed time. Now let's get to work!"

Their phones were out even before they'd left the room. The nightmare was starting.

Even if they managed to stop the bomb in time, this crisis would not be forgotten. How was it possible that a nonconventional weapon was making its way to America—in total silence?

Zurich, 2011

The summer semester at yeshivah picked up exactly where it had left off. The *bachurim* resumed their studies with vigor and, after the first few days of exchanging stories from their vacations, they were immersed in fruitful labor. They began learning *Maseches Shabbos*, a long tractate dealing primarily with the laws of Shabbos. They learned the thirty-nine forbidden *melachos* and their source in the work of the Mishkan, trying to classify each *melachah* in the order in which they learned it. This time, they didn't start at the beginning of the tractate, but at the twelfth *perek*, "Haboneh," which deals with the *melachah* of *boneh*—the act of building—that is prohibited on Shabbos.

If, until now, the boys had translated this *melachah* as the prohibition of erecting a building on Shabbos, they now learned to define it more exactly. Digging slightly in the ground could be considered *boneh* if one's intention is to store something there. It needn't be a tall or complete structure. Every prohibition had its specific guidelines and measures, and anyone who transgressed them violated the Biblical injunction to observe the laws of Shabbos.

Rav Schwartz had something new to share with them at his general *shiur* to the yeshivah: "Did you know that the Chazon Ish said that the prohibition of turning on electricity on Shabbos is because of the law of *boneh*? Here's his exact language: 'Because he is maintaining its nature of keeping the electrical current flow-ing continuously.' In other words, he classifies the *issur* of *boneh* as 'maintaining something in its operative state.' Therefore, it's for-bidden to turn on a light on Shabbos—and not because of the laws of *mav'ir*, because there's no fire involved."

Zelig Schiller jumped up. "That means if I walk into Manor on Shabbos—not to buy anything, of course," he added quickly, to laughter from his fellow students. Manor was the name of a large chain of stores, famous throughout Switzerland. The doors of the local store, like many others, opened automatically when a customer approached them. "So if I just pass near the door, and it opens, I've built something?" he ended disbelievingly.

"Very possibly," the rosh yeshivah answered with a smile. "We've already explained that the Torah did not forbid work because it doesn't want us to labor hard and perspire. If that were the case, one would be allowed to drive a car on Shabbos, and use electric-ity. Even using a lighter or matches on Shabbos would be permis-sible, because these days igniting a fire is not hard work. But that's not what the Torah prohibited. The Torah banned *meleches mach-sheves*, work that creates something—even if the work involved in that creation is minimal. *Hakadosh Baruch Hu* wants us to take a break from creating, just as He did on Shabbos, the seventh day of Creation."

"So why are we allowed to go to the Kosel?" asked Eliezer Berman with a shrug. The other boys laughed.

Nachum Maimon leaped into the fray. "You don't understand. Rebbi is saying that you *are* allowed to exert effort on Shabbos. You can walk somewhere and sweat a little. It wouldn't hurt you to drop a few ounces."

Eliezer blushed, but Rav Schwartz hastily intervened. "It seems to me that someone who doesn't understand the question shouldn't be in a rush to laugh at others," he told Nachum, who abruptly stopped laughing. The other boys enjoyed seeing him put in his place. Nachum insulted others very easily, and Rav Schwartz knew it.

"What Eliezer is asking is: How is it possible to walk to the Kosel, when everyone knows that there's a camera there that takes pictures and broadcasts them throughout the world. Is that it?" he asked Eliezer, who nodded gratefully.

"That's a good question," the rosh yeshivah complimented him. "And there may even be an additional prohibition here—the *issur* of writing. When a person moves in front of a camera or video cam, he changes the picture on the screen, which may be considered a forbidden *melachah*."

"It's not only the Kosel that has a camera like that!" exclaimed Shmulie Kahan, the sole local boy. "There's even a place that takes videos of happenings and can broadcast them all over the world. And there are cameras pointed at the railroad tracks in various locations, so that the managers can keep an eye on cargo that they're sending by train. My brother and I did an experiment—and he saw me standing near the tracks. He could even hear what I said there! I could show all of you the place. It's not far from the train station, but hardly anyone knows about it…"

"Calm down, please," the rosh yeshivah said with a smile. Shmulie tended to become overexcited. He was a hyperactive kid, and a curious one. It was typical of him to have discovered such a place.

Shmulie didn't get the hint. "But it's interesting, because it's not a live broadcast. It broadcasts every ten minutes. So you can even get into the picture there, and then run home and see yourself on the computer, standing and talking near the train tracks. Once, I even…"

"Enough!" Rav Schwartz frowned in mock anger. Actually, he was holding in his laughter.

The *bachurim* didn't hold in theirs. Their mirth took the wind out of Shmulie's sails. Still, he whispered to Yisrael, seated beside him, "After *shiur*, I'll show you the place. No one is ever there. I'm the only one who knows about it."

Rav Schwartz regained control of the *shiur*, and the group discussed the exact definition of *boneh* for a full hour. It was a *melachah* that would accompany them through their learning in the months to come.

22

THE SUMMER WAS NEARLY OVER WHEN IT HAPPENED.
Yisrael would never forget a single detail of that fateful day. He and Gilad were playing basketball along with a few of their fellow yeshivah students in the sports hall, as some local kids watched and cheered every move he made. "Pass the ball to the champ," they yelled in Swiss German to whoever had the ball. "*He'll* get it in the hoop!"

Yisrael smiled, and passed the ball to his teammate. Victory interested him less than the good atmosphere of the game. He tried very hard not to lord it over his friends, and to play as equals—though it was often extremely frustrating to watch someone fumble a shot at close quarters. A shot that he could have landed in the basket with his eyes closed.

Suddenly, Shmulie Kahan came into the court and raced over to Yisrael.

"Rebbi is looking for you. It's urgent!" he panted. "He's waiting for you in his office."

Yisrael was surprised. What could the rosh yeshivah want from him? Did he intend to scold him for taking some of the *bachurim* out to play basketball? But it was their break time, and he had understood from Rav Schwartz that it was okay to play now and then. Perhaps he wasn't happy with the results of Yisrael's weekly exam. Or had something bad happened?

"Do you know what Rebbi wants?" he asked Shmulie.

"No. But he looked really angry!"

Angry? What was he angry about? Yisrael gave the ball to his friends, hastily dressed, and started back to the yeshivah. What had he done wrong? Was it because he had been a little late to davening? Various possibilities ran through his head as he made his way toward the rosh yeshivah's office. He tried to formulate explanations for all the things that Rav Schwartz might want to berate him for. What was Rebbi so angry about?

He knocked on the door and was told to enter. The first thing he saw was that Rebbi was not angry. He looked the way he had when there had been a terrorist bombing in Eretz Yisrael and an old friend of his was killed. What had happened? Had someone died? Someone connected to *him*?

Rav Schwartz stood up and put his arm around Yisrael's shoulder to lead him to a chair. Something *had* happened! Yisrael felt a suffocating sense of danger as he sat down, suddenly weak. Everything around him appeared paler than usual. Was he about to faint?

Rav Schwartz bit his lip. What he was about to do was one of the hardest things he had ever done in his life. "I have something very sad to tell you," he whispered sorrowfully.

Yisrael couldn't take the suspense. "Who?" he asked, as though from the midst of a dream. For some reason, he was certain that someone had died. This could be nothing less than that. The only question was—who?

"A young driver lost control of his car. He plowed onto the sidewalk and hit your father..."

"Tatty...? *Tatty*?" It couldn't be. This must be some sort of mistake. He'd just seen his father, not long ago. It couldn't be that he... Tears welled up in his eyes and poured down his cheeks. He felt as if all the air had been sucked out of him. This wasn't really happening. It must be a bad dream. He spoke, the words hardly audible. "Was he... injured?"

The rosh yeshivah tightened his arm around Yisrael. Tears were streaming from his own eyes as well, wetting his beard. "He was killed instantly..."

Yisrael's shoulders shook. He made no attempt to control his sobs and raised his voice in heartrending weeping. "Tatty! It can't be... But I love him! He can't be... Not now!"

Rav Schwartz didn't say a word. There were no words that could help at this stage. Right now, all he could do was join in his beloved student's grief and be with him as his world collapsed. If *he* was finding it hard to accept the terrible news, he could only imagine how Yisrael must be feeling.

Even before Yisrael had reached his office, Rav Schwartz had made some urgent arrangements. He got the boy a seat on the next flight to Israel and asked one of his staff members to accompany him on the difficult flight home. He would have done so himself, but was prevented by yeshivah business: the next morning he had to be in Zurich for a meeting that could not be put off. Instead, he had made sure that Shimi Baranovich, a young but mature fellow who learned with Yisrael, would fly back with the boy and remain with him for several days. Rav Schwartz himself planned to come to pay a *shivah* call during the course of the week.

There were a few things that Yisrael had to know. According to halachah, he was now an *onein*, and prohibited from doing mitzvos or saying *berachos* until his father was buried.

But passing on this information would have to wait until they were en route to the airport. Right now, Yisrael had to pack a bag with the things he would need for the flight home, which was due to depart in a little over four hours. How mysterious were Hashem's ways... All that was left was to hope that Yisrael would survive this blow and overcome it. In the meantime, the entire yeshivah would participate in his mourning.

The week of mourning felt, to Yisrael, like one long, exhausting day. He knew that, someday, he would absorb the fact that this was real. One day, he would understand that Tatty would never come home. But for now, everything still seemed surreal to him.

He recalled very clearly the last time Tatty had said good-bye to him at the airport. On that occasion, Tatty hadn't cried. He'd smiled and hugged Yisrael warmly. He had expressed his satisfaction with what the yeshivah in Switzerland had done for his son. It had restored to Yisrael the joy in life that had been stolen from him.

Yisrael appreciated this. He had heard from more than one of his fellow students whose parents were not happy with the new yeshivah, one that had no reputation in the yeshivah world and was considered a weak place in terms of the level of the learning. He knew that there were parents who were too blind to see the good that the yeshivah was doing for their sons; they preferred to listen to their neighbors, who clucked their tongues over the boy who had disappointed his parents. The boy who hadn't made the grade in a regular yeshivah.

If only he had known that that would be the last time he would see his father, he would not have been in such a hurry to step back from Tatty's embrace. But he hadn't known, and he hadn't wanted to look like a little kid, so he had hastened to free himself of his father's arms and say good-bye. Though he had spoken to Tatty on the phone once or twice since then, that parting was the one that haunted his dreams.

Many people came to comfort him in his grief. Rebbeim from his former yeshivah—including the rosh yeshivah and mashgiach—as well as from his present one. But what was gone would never come back. He wasn't sure he could ever return to yeshivah. From now on, he was responsible for his mother and sisters. He and no one else.

It was only after the *shivah* was over that he reflected on the surprising fact that Tatty's only brother had not bothered to attend his funeral. The quarrel between them had apparently been extremely serious if he hadn't even called to express his condolences. His mother shrugged off Yisrael's questions. Throughout that terrible week, she demonstrated a strength that Yisrael hadn't known existed. The delicate woman he knew was coping bravely with her loss, and making sure that the house was orderly even during the week of mourning. Yisrael knew that she cried into her pillow at night, but in the daytime it was she who encouraged her children and gave them warmth and love.

She was also adamant in her refusal to hear of Yisrael's returning home. "You have nothing to do here," she said flatly. "You're going back to yeshivah to learn, exactly as Tatty would have wanted you to."

He didn't argue too much. She had logic on her side. But he felt incapable of leaving home this way. He felt as if he were betraying his family when he said good-bye to his little sisters and flew away. And nothing in yeshivah felt the same as before. He was an orphan now. He was pitiable. Though no one said so out loud, the sympathy on his friends' faces was clear. Not all of them knew how to behave naturally toward him, as the wise rosh yeshivah did. Rav Schwartz welcomed Yisrael back and treated him exactly the same as before. He didn't let him get away with things that he hadn't let him get away with before, and Yisrael appreciated that. The rosh yeshivah was also wise enough not to press him to return to basketball. Yisrael wasn't ready for that yet. He devoted the rest of the summer to learning for the elevation of his father's soul.

Rav Schwartz kept him under close observation. There were a few occasions when he forced Yisrael to leave the beis medrash and get some sleep, or invited him out for a walk. The boy mustn't burden himself excessively. That wasn't healthy for anyone.

The summer z'man ended, and most of the boys elected to stay in Switzerland to camp out and take nature hikes. Not Yisrael. He hurried home to his family. He had to make sure that all was well with them.

Whoever it was that had said troubles come in groups knew what he was talking about. The second Yisrael walked into his house, he sensed that something wasn't right. It took a little time for him to realize what was bothering him, but he finally got it. The house was neglected.

Or maybe "neglected" wasn't the right word. Mommy would

never allow her home to appear that way. But something was missing. It was only when he opened the fridge to get a cold drink that he
realized what had been troubling him. The refrigerator was empty.
Apart from a pitcher of water and a bit of white cheese, there was
no food at all in the fridge that had once been full to bursting. The
understanding that his mother's face was gaunt from hunger rather
than pain frightened him. Did his mother lack money for food?

He hurried to confront her, his face a mask of concern. She
pulled him into her bedroom. "I don't want the girls to hear!" she
exclaimed softly. "They have enough to worry about."

"What happened, Mommy? Tatty didn't leave you any money?
Why didn't you say anything?"

"Sit down," his mother ordered in a milder tone. "It's time you
heard the full story. You're not a little boy anymore."

She sat at the edge of her bed and held her son's hand. "You
know that your grandfather, Zaidy Moshe, was very wealthy. He
ran a famous hotel chain in America—dozens of hotels throughout
the United States. Despite his material success, Zaidy Moshe was
an uncompromising Jew. I've heard so many stories about his self-
sacrifice to keep mitzvos, and how he would give up a huge business deal if it interfered with Shabbos or any other mitzvah.

"Zaidy had two sons, Tatty and Jeffrey. He sent them both to
fine Jewish schools. But while Tatty did what his father wanted and
devoted himself to his learning, Jeffrey didn't want to continue on
in yeshivah. He wanted to get into the business world right away.

"At first, Zaidy refused. But when he realized that it was better for his son to work than to walk the streets, bored, Zaidy gave
Jeffrey a minor management position in one of his hotels. Jeffrey
proved that he was not lacking in talent. He grabbed the challenge
with both hands and, through a series of firings, quickly mounted
an efficiency campaign in that hotel. Zaidy didn't like the unfeeling way his son operated, but decided to let Jeffrey learn from his
mistakes. The problem was, Jeffrey's operation was a huge success.
The hotel he ran doubled its profits within a short time. Within that
same period he had raised both its quality and its revenues.

"From there, the path to success was short. He improved hotel after hotel, turning Zaidy's empire into the largest in the United States, with an income in the hundreds of millions of dollars. But this didn't satisfy him. He wanted more. He wanted to be famous and influential. He had always had a tendency to dominate others, and the way he chose to do it was by buying one of the largest media outlets in the country. Have you ever heard of the News-Time network? Jeffrey Davis is its sole owner.

"Anyway, while Tatty was sitting in yeshivah and learning, Jeffrey grew stronger and stronger, until he was the most influential person in Zaidy's chain. But there was no doubt in the mind of anyone who knew the family as to which son Zaidy loved more. He appreciated Torah study much more than material success, however great. Jeffrey knew this, and he came to hate Tatty because of it. The hatred of an *am ha'aretz* for a *talmid chacham*. Every encounter between them turned into a quarrel, and you know Tatty… That is, you *knew* Tatty. He wasn't one to give in easily. He would put his younger brother in his place and point out Jeffrey's spiritual deterioration. Which really annoyed Jeffrey…"

Mrs. Davis closed her eyes for a long moment and breathed deeply. She spoke about her husband as though he were still alive; she had to keep reminding herself that he was gone. Her departed husband had had his faults. He had been a bit stricter than need be, and perhaps he ought to have been more patient with his brother who had strayed from the path. Still, all in all he had been a very special man. He had been straight and honest and had tried always to joyously fulfill his Creator's will. There were so many good things he had done in his life that only his wife knew about. He had not been one to seek recognition for his righteousness. And there were many things, she knew, of which even she was unaware. That was the way he'd been, quiet and good.

She opened her eyes, stroked her beloved son's hand—her orphaned son who had had such a difficult year—and went on with her story.

"In his last years, Zaidy was very ill. He died at a relatively young age, before he was 60. And that's when Tatty learned that Jeffrey had not sat by idly all that time. He was too smart for that.

In his role as the business' operational director, he'd had both Zaidy and Tatty sign documents that transferred ownership of the chain to himself.

"Zaidy, who'd trusted him, had never thought to check what he was signing, and Tatty never dreamed that his brother would do something like this to him. He was often called upon to sign papers that he didn't understand, and just as he'd signed them when Zaidy had given them to him, he continued doing so for his brother. The judge deemed it the most despicable legal act he'd ever seen. Tatty could not claim that he hadn't known what he was signing, because the documents always explained what they were about. His excuse, that he'd never bothered reading the material, was considered unacceptable in the eyes of the law.

"Zaidy was gone, and from a legal standpoint there was no inheritance. It all belonged to Jeffrey. But the judge who presided over the case of Tatty versus Jeffrey ordered that Tatty be paid compensation. Zaidy's business, which was now Jeffrey's business, had to pay Jeffrey's brother $10,000 per month. Pocket money, the judge called it."

"Pocket money?" Yisrael burst out. "Ten thousand dollars is a lot of money. I don't know anyone who makes even half that amount each month."

"True," his mother smiled. "But don't forget that we're talking about an empire worth billions. What's $120,000 a year? Small change."

"So we were supposed to be billionaires?"

"Hashem gave us exactly what we were supposed to get. As you said, even so we didn't lack for anything."

"So what happened to all the money? Tatty wasn't a big spender. I never saw him waste money on anything we didn't need. We didn't even have a car."

"Your father spent a great deal of money," his mother said proudly. "You have no idea how many kollelim he supported, or how much *tzedakah* he gave."

"But didn't he leave anything over? It's not like him not to think of you, in case…something happened."

"The truth is, we didn't worry. Why save? We had a sure, steady income. And even if we suddenly needed a large sum, any bank would have been happy to lend it to us. 'How much should we set aside? And for what?' Tatty would ask. 'So that our children should fight over money? So that the same thing should happen to them that happened to my family? We're better off putting it in a sure place. In our *tzedakah* account in *Shamayim*.' Neither he nor I knew that when he...died...the money would stop coming. That's not what the judge said. The judge said explicitly that the income should continue as long as the business was viable. But for some reason, the minute he died the money stopped coming."

"Have you tried speaking to Uncle Jeffrey?" Yisrael asked. Until today, he had looked forward to meeting his rich uncle. Now he hated him with all his heart. To take advantage of poor Tatty's innocence like that!

"His secretary said that he doesn't want to speak to me. That I can go to court and see that that's what was written in the agreement. 'During his lifetime.'"

"But you just told me that the judge said otherwise!"

"I know. I remember the exact words. But count on Jeffrey to know how to turn things around. Don't forget, he has first-class lawyers in America. I'll never be able to win against him."

"And you and Tatty didn't save anything?"

His mother smiled at Yisrael, and smoothed his hair lovingly. "Tatty put $150,000 aside for each one of you children, for when you get married, *im yirtzeh Hashem*."

"I have that much money?"

Mommy smiled.

"Then use it! What were you thinking? You need to buy food... and clothes."

"Absolutely not," his mother said firmly. "You'll need that money one day. And anyway, the money is locked in an account until you are at least 18. Even if you wanted to, you couldn't take it out earlier."

Yisrael couldn't believe what he was hearing. He had returned home from yeshivah and found that his mother was starving, that she was poor, and that he was rich. What was he supposed to do now? If he could, he would have run to the bank, taken out the money, and given it to his mother. Even without her consent. But there were two more years to go before he could touch the money. What could be done in the meantime? Would they have to accept charity?

"Don't worry, Yisrael," Mommy comforted him. "I've spoken to several realtors and our apartment is worth a lot—nearly two million shekels. A few people have come to see it, and maybe one of them will want to buy it. Apart from that, the insurance from the accident is due to be paid soon. It'll be all right."

"But where will we live? Where will you live?"

"There are several possibilities. Either we can buy a small apartment; we don't need such a big one. Or else we can rent one. Either way, we'll have a little money put away and everything will be all right. The main thing is not to worry. You have to remember that *Hakadosh Baruch Hu* supports everyone. Not Jeffrey."

Yisrael almost exploded with fury. If Jeffrey had been with him at that moment...he'd have shown him what was what! But he could not remain unmoved by his mother's serenity. She didn't have a cent, but she didn't look particularly worried. She was counting on Hashem to help her. She wasn't harboring murderous thoughts about her husband's corrupt, thieving brother.

He wasn't on his mother's high level. If he could have, he'd have flown to America the next day to teach that creep a thing or two.

"Mommy? Yisrael?" A soft knock sounded on the door. Bracha had returned from the day camp for toddlers that she'd organized with her friend from the building next door, and she wanted to see her brother. "Can I come in?"

"The girls don't know anything about this, and I want it to stay that way. Okay?" Mommy whispered.

Yisrael nodded, and went on to amuse his younger sisters with stories from his time abroad. But his head was someplace else. He couldn't stop thinking about possible ways to help his mother in her hour of need.

23

YISRAEL TOSSED AND TURNED IN HIS BED, BUT HE COULDN'T fall asleep. Since Tatty had died, he'd passed any number of sleepless nights. But this was different. Now he wasn't thinking about his father, but about Jeffrey.

How could a person treat his own brother that way? He tried to imagine himself stealing Bracha and Tamar's inheritance, but failed. And it wasn't as if Jeffrey needed the money. Even 10 percent of the inheritance would have still left him a very wealthy man. And yet, he had decided that he wanted it all. What a despicable human being. And then, not to respond to his brother's widow when she needed a bit of cash? And not to attend the funeral? Who did he think he was?!

Yisrael punched his pillow viciously. He hadn't felt this angry in a long time. He ground his teeth, imagining what he'd like to do to the scoundrel he called his uncle. There was no chance he would manage to fall asleep tonight. He got out of bed and put on his clothes. He needed some air.

Very quietly, he slipped out of the house and locked the door behind him, trying his best not to wake anyone. All he needed now was to cause Mommy worry on top of everything else she had on her plate. His mother, a widow… Tears stole from his eyes as he thought of her. The only child of elderly Holocaust survivors. Yisrael had never met his grandparents on his mother's side; they had both died before she married. His mother was an orphan herself, and now she had to raise three more… And, on top of that, to be so short of money. He knew that Mommy had grown up in near-poverty. She had told him once that her parents had been poor. But after so many years in which money had not been a problem, it would be hard for her to return to that now.

But what could he do? Should he go out and find a job? Stop learning in yeshivah? That would kill his mother. She would never agree to it. But how could he concentrate on his studies knowing that his mother had an empty fridge?

His anger returned, full force, as his legs took him along Kanfei Nesharim Street. Despite the late hour, there were still a few people on the street, night owls who liked the peace and quiet to be found in the dark. A group of yeshivah boys on their summer break sat in a late-night inexpensive restaurant, laughing at some joke. Yisrael walked past. He could have been one of them. Most boys his age led worry-free lives and were enjoying their vacation. And what about him? He was suffering for them all…

A wave of self-pity engulfed him. *Why me? What did I do so wrong that this is how* Hakadosh Baruch Hu *is treating me?*

He breathed deeply, forcing himself to calm down. These feelings would pass. He knew well enough that this was incorrect thinking. Each person must undergo what has been decreed for him, and if it was decreed that he must suffer this, then he was capable of coping with it. As he mastered his thoughts, he marveled at how far he had come in his yeshivah in Zurich. Only now did he notice how much stronger he was than he'd once been. He didn't let himself wallow in his misery the way he used to. He fought back.

Yisrael took in another long draft of summer-night air and encouraged himself. He could do this. He would do whatever it took and, with Hashem's help, all would be well. The only question was: what was the right thing to do?

A daring idea popped into his head. He turned around and

began walking rapidly back in the direction of home. He would not give in to his corrupt uncle. His mother didn't deserve to suffer anymore. If his uncle thought he could cut off the monthly stipend with impunity, he was making a mistake. His brother, *a"h*, had a son—and that son was going to counterattack.

He went silently back inside and found the family phone book. Jeffrey's number must be in here, or how had Mommy called him? He turned the pages and struggled with the English script, difficult for him to read. Zero, zero, one, the country code for calling America. The number was here. Under the words, "Jeffrey— Office," he found his uncle's number.

He went to the phone, but suddenly hesitated. What was he thinking? Did he believe that he, a boy in his mid-teens, could challenge a sophisticated tycoon? That he could order Jeffrey to give his mother money, and his uncle would obey? His English had always been less than fluent when he spoke with someone he didn't know. His low self-confidence would make him stammer and forget his basic vocabulary. If only he could yell at him in Hebrew.

But he wouldn't give up. He would *not* chicken out. He was doing this not for himself, but for Mommy. He must not give up!

Mustering his courage, he dialed the number in the small telephone book. He took long breaths and tried to organize his thoughts. The sound of distant ringing reached his ears, along with the words he planned to say. "You're not okay. My mother is starving because of you! You should be ashamed of yourself."

But wait a minute… What time was it there, anyway? He nearly hung up when he saw his watch point to long after midnight— when a secretary answered in English, "Jeffrey Davis' office. How can I help you?"

The time difference. They're seven hours behind us. It must be afternoon there…

He couldn't think fast enough to figure out the exact time. He also hadn't planned what to say if a secretary answered. For some reason, he'd thought that Jeffrey himself would answer the phone. What an idiot. Would a man as rich as that answer his own phone?

"Hello?" The secretary was waiting for a sign of life.

"Um... Hi. I'm...um... Jeffrey is my uncle. I'd like to speak to him, please."

"Who are you, please, sir?"

"My name is Yisrael and I'm calling from Israel." He felt foolish. "I'd like to speak to Jeffrey."

"I'm sorry, sir. What would you like to speak with Davis about?"

"Um...my father died and he owes my mother money!"

"I'm sorry, sir. Mr. Davis cannot take your call. He is very busy..." The secretary was experienced at filtering out madmen with strange requests. For some reason, every Jew thought that Mr. Jeffrey Davis owed him something. She'd fielded scores of calls from institutions and private individuals, asking for donations. She didn't know how they found this number; it wasn't listed in the phone book. "If you'd like a donation, you'll have to send a request form to Mr. Davis' foundation. I'll give you a number where you can get all the details. Are you ready to write it down?"

"I don't want a donation!" Yisrael forced himself not to shout. He mustn't wake his mother. "I just want to talk to my uncle."

"I'm sorry, sir. Mr. Davis is very busy. Have a nice day."

"Don't hang up!" Yisrael lost his composure when the dial tone told him that she was no longer with him. What a frustrating lady! She didn't understand that he was not some beggar. Why, he could have been her boss if his uncle hadn't stolen the inheritance from them.

The sound of an opening door restored him to reality. Little Tamar had gotten out of bed and was approaching her brother, half asleep.

"Can't you fall asleep?"

Yisrael smiled at the drowsy words as he led her back to bed. "Everything's all right," he said soothingly. "Go back to sleep, Tamar. Tomorrow we'll play together, okay?"

The child nodded groggily, and smiled as he tucked her in. "It's so great that you're home," she said, and fell asleep in a second.

Yisrael left the room quietly. He'd have to be more careful. What luck that Mommy hadn't woken up. She'd have been very sad to see him so worried.

He returned to the phone and dialed an American number again, but not the one in his uncle's office. This time, he called his yeshivah friend, Yaakov Yosef Steinfeld.

Yaakov Yosef was the kind of kid who knew everything about everyone. He loved politics and politicians and knew every last detail about them. Yisrael's uncle was a famous and influential millionaire. No—billionaire. If there was anyone who'd be able to tell him a little about his uncle, it was Yaakov Yosef.

This time, there was no need to rehearse what he would say. Yaakov Yosef was thrilled to hear his friend's voice, and his stream of stories and questions infused Yisrael with new life. After he finished updating Yisrael about his experiences on his flight home, he finally addressed himself to Yisrael's query.

"Jeffrey Davis? The richest Jew in America, and the world? Of course I've heard of him. Just a minute—don't tell me he's connected to you somehow. Hey, *his* name's Davis, too! Is he a relative of yours?!"

Yisrael didn't want to answer this. His family's story was complicated, and he didn't really feel like sharing it with anyone. Certainly not an information agency like Yaakov Yosef Steinfeld.

"If we were related, would I be calling to ask you? Don't tell me you don't know that I'm actually his boss…" He laughed out loud, hoping that the joke would satisfy his friend. He didn't lie, only circumvented the truth. "I just heard that he's a well-connected man and thought you could tell me a little about him."

Apparently, Yaakov Yosef bought the story. After all, if they *were* family, why would Yisrael have to ask a stranger about him?

"Well, it's like this. He had some fifteen billion dollars, the last I read. Hotels, computer firms, and one of the biggest media networks — News-Time. What else do you want to know? He's interested in politics and contributed a lot of money to the current president's election campaign. He's involved in AIPRO, the Jewish-Zionist organization, and has given tons of money to the State of Israel and various institutions there. The Israeli prime minister is a personal friend of his. In short, he's a very wealthy man who's famous and has friends in high places. But why do you ask?"

"Is this Davis religiously observant?" Yisrael asked, evading the question.

"Religious? He hates religion—but he loves the State of Israel. He thinks he's a real Zionist. If I didn't happen to know that he's a close friend of R' Goldfarb in Eretz Yisrael, I'd suspect that he hates the ultra-Orthodox."

"R' Goldfarb? R' *Menachem* Goldfarb?"

"Yes...why? Do you know him? He's one of the most famous ultra-Orthodox politicians, and very close to the prime minister."

"I know. I used to go to yeshivah with his son," Yisrael said painfully. Incredibly, the mere sound of that name still had the power to hurt him.

"So you can ask him whatever you want to find out. He knows Davis better than most people."

Yisrael doubted he'd do it, but he thanked Yaakov Yosef anyway. He changed the subject and with difficulty managed to end the call. That guy sure loved to talk...

It was nearly 4 o'clock in the morning by the time he crawled into bed. He had three-and-a-half hours to sleep before the *minyan* he liked to attend. It had been a long time since he'd missed davening with a *minyan*, and he didn't want that to change. Not today.

24

THE ESCAPE PLAN FOR THE PRESIDENT IN THE EVENT OF A nuclear attack by a hostile power included a quick helicopter ride for the president, the secretary of defense, and the chairman of the Joint Chiefs of Staff to Andrews Air Force Base, not far from Washington. Standing by at the air base was an E-4C plane code-named Silver Dollar. This plane would lift off the moment its passengers were aboard.

From the outside, the plane resembled a standard Boeing 747, with a bulge on the upper section. Inside, however, it became abundantly clear that this was no ordinary passenger plane. Occupying the center of the space was a war room for the president and his staff. From this room the president could control the various components of the U.S. armed forces in the event of war.

A sophisticated communications center was the plane's primary war tool. With the help of an enormous number of antennae, the president was equipped with every possible form of communication. Frequencies attuned to satellites circling the globe or submarines prowling the depths of the oceans allowed for the relaying of orders in real time. The plane was capable of remaining in the air for three continuous days with the aid of air-to-air refueling, a period of time long enough to enable the plane to find a landing in a friendly and secure location.

One of the most famous secrets in the world is the "football." This is a suitcase containing America's nuclear codes, which allows the president, when necessary, to control his country's nuclear capability. With the help of this suitcase, the president can supervise the United States' nuclear arsenal. An arsenal that includes attack aircraft carrying nuclear bombs, submarines, and intercontinental missiles.

The innocent-looking suitcase, which serves as a sort of sophisticated communications device, is always within arm's reach of the president and allows him the ability to respond when necessary. It is carried by a special Secret Service agent who is handcuffed to the suitcase and who accompanies the president wherever he travels. In the event of nuclear war, the United States would do everything in her power to ensure that she retained her ability to respond to her attackers with the full force of her nuclear arsenal.

Since the end of the Cold War, the plan had become almost theoretical. Today, there existed no such threat to the United States. There was greater fear of a nuclear attack by some terrorist organization than by a hostile government. In the event of such a contingency, the plan outlined an additional recourse.

Beneath the White House's East Wing lay an underground bunker—the Presidential Emergency Operations Center, or PEOC for short—capable of withstanding a nuclear attack. The PEOC was meant to provide shelter for the president and the vice president in times of emergency. Here too a communications and control room had been built for the president's use. Its disadvantage, as compared to the mobile plane, was that it was located in the exact place where hostile forces would seek the president. Its great advantage was that it offered the president a safe haven just a two-minute walk from the Oval Office.

After the attacks on the World Trade Center, Vice President Dick

Cheney had been brought there, as President Bush was flown from place to place until the threat was clarified. The vice president had run the country from the bunker, with the help of National Security Adviser Condoleezza Rice and hand-picked members of the cabinet who joined him in the operations center.

Despite the uncertainty over the source of the bomb, Matthew Klinger chose the second option. To the best of his knowledge, the bomb could already be in the area; the president must not be exposed for a single additional moment. He directed the Secret Service crew responsible for the president's safety to transfer him to the secure bunker at once. By law, at a time of imminent danger he could order the president to do this even against his will.

Bob Walters evinced no opposition to the plan. The sudden threat had come at a bad time. He had just concluded a long, difficult meeting with the Israeli prime minister. They had intended to hold a joint press conference, but that wouldn't happen now.

How insufferable that Israeli was! The man thought he could fight, and beat, the whole world. He'd known many generals like that in the course of his life—men who thought only with their weapons… And anyway, what was the point of a private meeting when the man didn't even speak English? Thirty minutes had been wasted before he'd grasped that the prime minister was asking for a guarantee in the event of an Iranian attack. This was something they could have arranged through their staffs.

Iran, Iran—that was all they knew. Let them at least give something back in return. Let them somehow advance the endless talks with the Palestinians. Let them show him some results! Those two—the Israelis and the Palestinians—were causing him more problems than the rest of the world combined.

Nevertheless, he did his best to tamp down his feelings and address the present situation. John Rivers, guard shift supervisor of the Secret Service, did not offer much in explanation for this change in plan. There was some sort of advance warning about a nuclear bomb. Where? When? Who? He had no answers. What was going on? Was it possible that there was a nuclear bomb on U.S. soil and no details were known?

"Sir, you can ask Matthew Klinger yourself," John said. "He'll meet us there. Right now, we have to move."

"Where are my wife and children?" the president asked.

"The First Lady and the boys are already in the secure room, sir."

"And where's Barry? We'll have to rearrange our schedule for the next few days. I have several meetings…"

"Everything is under control, Mr. President," John replied. "The chief of staff is being taken to the PEOC as we speak. He's already working on the necessary changes and will be in full communication with Matthew. Let's continue to run things from there."

The president allowed himself to be persuaded. A nuclear bomb… Who would have believed it? And the Israeli prime minister here. All he needed was for something to happen to the Israeli while he was here in Washington. That could lead to an immediate war, if Iran was responsible.

Even now, Walters mused, it was very possible that he would have to act against Iran. If that government was really the one behind this bomb, he'd have no choice. He thought this over on his way to the bunker. They walked quickly—almost ran. As though a bomb could go off at any moment.

He had made this trip several times in the past. His staff insisted on conducting such drills from time to time. But things were different when the threat was real. No smiles in sight. No jokes to be heard. Only thoughts about what would happen if such a bomb really went off in Washington. He ran through his mind a list of the people he knew in the area. The list was long. Senators, politicians, security personnel, and ordinary citizens. What would happen to all of them if the threat materialized?

His military background did not permit him to sink into such thoughts for long. There was work to be done. But it was different now. Bob Walters was not accustomed to fleeing to bunkers when fired upon. He was used to returning fire.

This time, that wasn't his job. He must hide so that the United States could survive. He was too valuable to be placed at risk. He must go down to the bunker without protest.

"What's going on, Dad?" Steven, Walters' older son, asked.

At fifteen and a half, he very much resembled his father and was mature for his age. He came running toward Bob. "Are you all right?"

"Excellent," the president said with a smile. How typical of Steven to think of others first. His younger son was more like his wife, tall and quiet. He was sitting on his mother's lap. The First Lady looked pale. She'd never grown used to the pressures of her position. She didn't like the publicity or the fact that an entourage accompanied her everywhere she went. She was a woman who highly valued her privacy, a privacy that had dissipated long before her husband had won the election.

Bob went to her quickly. "Don't worry, everything's under control. I have to meet with Matthew now, but I'll join you a little later. Take care of your mother, Steven, okay?"

He stooped to tousle his younger son's hair. "Everything's okay, Dick. Dad's here."

The 6-year-old didn't even look at him. He was focused on a candy that one of the agents had given him. The president hastily parted from his family and went over to the battle station. Matthew was already waiting there. Numerous computer screens flashed their ever-changing displays.

"Tell me you have some inkling of what's going on," Bob said as he sat down by the table. "And where's the rest of the gang?"

"Mike and Howard are on their way," Matthew replied. "The CIA and the FBI are just as surprised as we are. They're coming here now with the latest update, but don't bank on it. The rest of the crew is being picked up by Secret Service agents right now. They'll be brought here with all possible speed."

The memorandum for this type of situation specified exactly which people were considered "essential for the defense of the United States." The individuals on this list were selected to join the president in the event of a nuclear attack. The rest of the country's citizens would have to take their chances, exposed to the bombs and to their no-less-terrifying fallout.

But each of these VIPs had friends, relatives, and acquaintances who would remain on the outside. Their phones were taken from them at once, to prevent undesirable communications. A public panic could cause more harm than a nuclear bomb.

If word got out of a genuine threat, the media would begin searching for the president. When they discovered he was not available, chaos would ensue. Questions would be asked, and within a short time it would be discovered that the high defensive brass had disappeared. The panic would reach a climax. People throughout the country would start fleeing. Accidents, violence, and plunder would only heighten the chaos. The news must not leak out. Not before the response crews were ready.

"Okay, Matthew—I want to hear the story. Every detail. No whitewashing!"

"I just got off the phone again with Igor Morkovski. He's the one who called me with the information."

"The head of Russian intelligence?"

"Yes. He claims that there was a transfer of Russian arms to hostile forces—Iran, apparently—and a nuclear bomb is now on its way to U.S. shores."

"In other words, the bomb isn't here yet?"

"He couldn't say for sure, Mr. President. The bomb left their radar when it went over to the Iranians."

"Bring me a phone immediately. I'll speak to Iran's president myself. He wouldn't dare do this."

"Yes, but it's a little more complicated. Igor says this isn't an Iranian operation. He claims there are Russian players behind it."

"Russians? One of theirs, or the Russian Mafia?"

"He says that it's not clear to him yet. All he knows is that one nuclear bomb is missing—and the man behind its disappearance is here in Washington."

"Here? Who?"

"Dr. Mikhail Potgorsky."

"The Jewish professor? I'm supposed to be meeting him tomorrow!"

"I know, sir. That meeting will not take place. Igor says it was Dr. Potgorsky's signature that released the bomb. He's the only link we have."

"Then arrest him. Seize him and interrogate him at once."

"It's a little more complicated than that, sir. First of all, he has diplomatic immunity. And besides, the Russians want him themselves."

"Let them want. Our top priority is that bomb. We can deal with them later."

"I understand, sir. But it might be a good idea to think about something else. It won't be easy extracting information from Potgorsky on American soil. Congress will crucify us if any torture is involved, and there's not much time. The Russians have promised to get all the information out of him through full cooperation with us. Everything they learn from him will come straight here. They are even prepared to give us a live hookup to the interrogation. But they're being stubborn on one point. They gave us the information, and they're demanding that this be done their way."

Bob Walters considered. His military instincts urged him not to surrender the only thing he had. But Matthew was right. They were no longer engaged in the Cold War. The Russians also had an interest in stopping the bomb in time, and perhaps their means were better. He knew about Russian interrogation methods. Things that would be considered extremely problematic from a legal standpoint in America happened on a daily basis in Russia.

"What does the CIA have to say about all this?"

"We don't think we have a choice, Mr. President," said Mike Gray, assistant director of the CIA, who'd just entered the room. "If they wanted to, they could simply make him disappear themselves. They have the infrastructure to make that happen. They chose to work with us, but this game belongs to the Russians. We don't have time to start bickering with them. If we don't cooperate fully, they may decide to conceal vital intelligence from us."

"This is no game, Mike!" the president burst out. He took a deep breath and sat back down in his seat. He was getting old. It wasn't like him to explode like this under pressure. Where was the man who'd made so many cool decisions under fire?

"Forgive me, Mike, but I'm not sure I agree with you. We are dealing with a threat of the highest degree in the United States of

America. I don't think the Russians can allow themselves not to be open with us. After all, this bomb came from them. This could be a catalyst for war! They wouldn't dare hide intelligence from us."

The director of the FBI walked in, flanked by the Speaker of the House and the chairman of the National Security Council. There was no time for handshakes or greetings. "Mr. President, they don't need to hide intelligence from us in order to hurt us. Right now, Mikhail Potgorsky is our only lead. But this can't be a one-man operation. Carrying out a terrorist attack of this caliber calls for a broad infrastructure. A large organization, and some sort of political engine. What happens when Potgorsky talks? It's a near certainty that his partners are Russians, living in Russia. We'd have to be 100 percent synchronized with them in order to succeed."

"So what are you saying? That we simply hand over our sole link to the bomb?"

"For now, sir. And we'll sit hard on their tails until we get something concrete from them. Don't forget, at this point all the information we have comes from the Russians. Our own intelligence bureaus are completely in the dark here."

Bob Walters retreated. He knew how to give in when they'd convinced him. "Make the call, Matthew. In the meantime, I want a report on what we have from our own sources. Can someone give me an estimate of possible casualties?"

"We still don't know what kind of bomb we're dealing with, sir. But we've made various estimates to cover every possible scenario. It must be remembered that, in our arms race with the Russians, it was they who staged the largest nuclear test. 'The czar's bomb,' they called it.

"On October 30, 1961, at a little after 11:30 in the morning, the Russians dropped a trial bomb from an airplane at a height of 10,500 meters. The bomb exploded about 4,000 meters over the testing ground in Novaya Zemlya. The force of that blast, which reached fifty megatons, set a record for a nuclear explosion that has not yet been broken.

"For comparison's sake, the bombs we exploded over Hiroshima and Nagasaki were between sixteen and twenty kilotons—and they caused the immediate deaths of approximately 140,000 people. In such a huge explosion, the heat from the blast would cause painful burns for people standing sixty miles away. If such a bomb were to explode in Washington, D.C., we'd wake up to find the city gone, electronic communications down, hundreds of thousands dead... and whoever didn't die would be exposed to radiation at levels dangerous to life. The injured and burned would crowd the hospitals that are still standing...and that's even before we start talking about the damage caused to the ground itself from radiation exposure. It would be years before it would be possible to return and try to rehabilitate the city. It's impossible to even guess at the damages such a tragedy would incur."

"But we're not talking about a bomb of the magnitude of 'the czar's bomb,' right?" the president said. "Such a bomb can't just disappear or be smuggled across the border. I'd like everyone to please do me a big favor and stop giving me irrelevant data. This is not the time to protect yourselves. I need concrete information about what kind of bomb this could be and what it might be capable of doing. Please—stick to the facts!"

Howard Simons reddened slightly, but quickly recovered. "You're right, sir. Apparently, we're not talking about that kind of bomb. I only mentioned it as an example of a possible scenario. My people have compressed the statistics into a few possibilities. Bottom line, logic dictates that we're dealing with a suitcase bomb.

"In 1997, A Russian general by the name of Alexander Lebed, who headed Russia's National Security Council, formed an investigative committee to track down the nuclear bombs that had been made in the Soviet Union. The committee discovered that, of the 132 suitcase bombs created during the Cold War, only forty-eight were still in Russian hands after the revolution. In other words, eighty-four of them had disappeared."

"What do you mean, disappeared? Where to?"

"We don't really know, Mr. President. In the year 2,000, a Russian colonel by the name of Loniev who had defected to the United States appeared before Congress. According to Colonel Loniev, there is a reasonable certainty that the Soviet Union, in its time, introduced such suitcases into various countries for use when needed. He claimed that these suitcases were apparently to be found even inside the United States, that they'd been smuggled here when we were not in a state of war, in order to be in place in time of crisis. He testified that he himself had been assigned to choose prime locations for planting those bombs."

"How reliable is this Loniev?"

"Russian sources, of course, denied his story. They even claimed that such suitcase bombs had never been made. Later, however, they unofficially admitted that the suitcases did exist—but what could we say, when we'd done the same thing? We called them SADMs — Special Atomic Demolition Munition—an acronym for small nuclear weaponry. Let's not forget that we were very close to a nuclear war at the time, and it was in the best interests of both sides to smuggle such mobile bombs into the enemy's territory."

"So you're telling me that what we're facing now is a nuclear bomb in a suitcase? A bomb that is already inside the United States, ready to blow up in our faces?"

The assistant director of the CIA intervened. "I don't think that's what will happen. Of course, it's a possibility—but then it would be a Russian operation, with no connection to Iran. If you ask me, I'm doubtful about the validity of Colonel Loniev's claims. It's hard for me to believe that a bomb like that could remain hidden inside the United States for such a long period of time. My guess is that there are no such bombs in our country. I think something completely different happened to them.

"In my opinion, the Russians hid in their own storehouses a quantity of those unregistered bombs, nuclear bombs that would not have to be dismantled by any arms treaty. After all, if they don't exist, how can you get rid of them? What I think is that one of those bombs was stolen from their hidden arsenal, and they're just as worried as we are."

"You *think*? Is there anyone here who actually *knows* something? I can't believe that we still don't know a thing! Well, what was agreed upon with the Russians, Matthew?"

Matthew Klinger had returned to the table after a lengthy phone conversation. "Our agents trapped the professor in his house and are now transferring him to the Russians. The Russians have promised us everything. Whatever we want. They feel guilty about the bomb."

"They *are* guilty! But we'll deal with that later. Right now, I want to hear more about this bomb. What is it capable of? What kind of damage can it cause if it explodes? Estimated casualties, the destruction radius, methods of coping and decontamination. Everything!"

Mike Gray pressed a button on his handheld device and the statistics appeared on the large computer monitor at the head of the table. "Our experts have built models based on our own SADMs and on the Russian's nuclear shells. In their opinion, we're talking about a package no bigger than twenty-four by sixteen inches—the size of an ordinary suitcase. The bomb should weigh in the area of sixty-five pounds, and the power of its explosion could reach a full kiloton. In other words, about 1,000 tons of TNT.

"We figure their scientists used a minimal quantity of plutonium to create a critical mass. They filled in the rest with substitute accelerants. These materials degrade with time, and that plays out to our benefit. The older the bomb, the smaller its power. If we're really lucky, perhaps it'll even be too old to blow up."

"Let's not rely on luck, okay?" The president scanned the group assembled in the control room. All of the people on the list were present in the room. Some of them had come from their government offices, while others had been dragged from their homes. The common denominator among them all was their essential role in the ongoing decision-making ability of the United States. They were responsible for trying to prevent the catastrophe. If they failed, and the bomb was activated, it would be up to them to decide how to respond. Who to hit back, and how hard.

"What are the maximum estimated casualties for this bomb? How many people will die? I want numbers, please."

"That very much depends on where the bomb goes off. If it explodes in a crowded place—say, Times Square—we're talking about a good couple thousand dead on the spot. Anyone within a radius of hundreds of yards of the bomb will die. Afterward, we'll have those wounded in the second wave: injuries, burns, radiation exposure...probably in the tens of thousands. The damage to the environment and the radiation that will contaminate the earth will prevent us from rehabilitating the area for years."

"And we still have no idea where the bomb is headed?"

"Not yet, sir. Let's hope that the Russians succeed in getting the information out of Potgorsky. Otherwise, our chances of stopping the bomb are very slim."

"How encouraging," the president said sarcastically. "What do we know about the Jewish professor? Who is he connected to in Russia? Who are his friends here? Where does he go and what does he do?"

Howard Simons hastened to answer. "We pulled his file and are busy compiling data right now. In the meantime, what we know is that he was born a non-Jew, to a family that was killed in a domestic accident when he was a child. The family of the Russian president took him in. The two grew up as friends, attended the same school, and more or less followed the same route, until Alex Kotorov turned to politics and Mikhail Potgorsky to the science of psychology. In time, he began to focus on research into anti-Semitism, and even founded an institute to fight anti-Semitism. President Kotorov always consulted with him and asked him to go into politics. Mikhail agreed, and advanced at the Kremlin until he quarreled with the Russian president over the subject of arms sales to Iran. As a punishment, he was sent to the embassy in Washington and lived here in America.

"The list of his friends and acquaintances is enormous, and it includes nearly every important politician in the United States. Wealthy people, and people of influence. The interesting thing is, the list of his close friends is very small: the billionaire Jeffrey Davis, the Israeli prime minister—who considers him a close personal friend as well as a friend of 'the whole Jewish nation'—British businessman and political activist Sir Dr. Harry Bonds, and just a few others. The common denominator among them all is that they're well-known, influential—and very Jewish."

"What are you trying to say?"

"I'm not saying anything. But the man really loves the Jewish people. He's chosen to join them and to do his utmost on their behalf. That's an angle that we can't ignore."

"What angle? That he's trying to set off a bomb in America that will kill thousands? If the bomb was in Iran I'd understand. But what's the connection here?"

"I don't know, Mr. President. I'm only stating the facts."

"Okay. Thank you. Let's talk about what we're doing to be ready, in the eventuality that the bomb does go off."

Matthew Klinger spoke up. "Emergency units from the NNSA division of the Department of Energy are the ones who take charge in a nuclear event. Their job is to determine the danger zone, enter the area in protective gear, establish a collection and triage center for the injured, and administer first decontamination and emergency first-aid for those in need of assistance. The National Guard or some other law-enforcement group—depending on the location—will be responsible for sealing off the area to civilian traffic. We want to prevent the curious and sensation seekers from entering the affected area.

"The National Weather Service will provide us with an estimate of the radiation spread, based on wind activity. Through these forecasts, we will know which sections to declare a closed military zone. The White House spokesperson will be responsible for the media, imposing strict censoring and deciding what may or may not be reported in the initial stage. The National Security Council, in this room, will determine, with your authorization, what must be done in the second stage, including whether and whom to attack, when, and how.

"Having learned our lesson from the Twin Tower bombing, we'll want to show you to the public as quickly as possible. You'll have to calm the nation, tell them that everything is under control, and show them—and the world—that America has a leader in these difficult hours."

"Thousands are going to perish in a nuclear blast, we have no idea who's behind the attack, and I'm supposed to tell them that everything's okay… Sounds wonderful."

"Uh...excuse me, Mr. President. If I may... I don't believe that thousands will die."

"Who are you? Who is this, Matthew?" The president didn't recognize the speaker. To the best of his knowledge, he'd never met the man.

"Professor Minkowitz, sir. A professor of physics at Washington University, and a world-class expert on the atom. I brought him here to help us understand what we're facing."

"Mr. President, one thing that hasn't been taken into account is the height of the explosion over the ground. The numbers that have been compiled here talk about an explosion at ideal height. For maximum effect, a one kiloton nuclear bomb should be detonated about two hundred meters above the ground. Every meter less than that lessens the radius of the blast.

"It would be almost impossible to smuggle such a bomb onto a plane. If we're talking about a suitcase bomb that is activated on the ground, the radius would be much smaller. In an optimal situation, we're looking at a circle with a diameter of two hundred meters of total destruction, six hundred meters of moderate destruction, and serious burns up to a kilometer away. I would cut that in half in our case, also taking into consideration the CIA's assessment that the accelerants being used, such as tritium, weaken over time. Perhaps a thousand will die if it goes off in Manhattan... On the other hand, the closer it is to the ground, the greater the contamination to the environment."

"A thousand is still a lot, professor," the president said. "But thank you for the explanation. Can the New York hospitals handle such an event?"

"The only emergency room set up to handle radiation sickness is in Tennessee, hours away by plane. The hospitals will do their best, but it's unclear how much they'll be able to help," Matthew replied.

"Then let's pray that they'll set off the bomb somewhere near Tennessee," the president said dryly. He stood up, and the others followed suit. "Go to work, gentlemen. Use every means at your disposal. We're not going to sit around and wait until the Russians decide to help us. I want results—and quickly!"

25

Jerusalem, 2011

THE MERCAZ CLAL BUILDING IN JERUSALEM IS ONE OF THE great failures in the city center. Its excellent location, with the *shuk* on one side and downtown on the other, should have turned the place into a bustling shopping mall. Instead, for some reason, it never took off. Some blamed it on the many stairs that made it difficult to go from store to store, while others blamed the failure on simple bad luck.

Either way, the place had never become the successful mall it was supposed to be. While it was still possible to find a few stores that earned a living for their owners, most of the building was populated with offices, including those of the government.

A faded sign on the building's top floor described the small corner office on the top floor as a place that offered "consultation and strategy." This vague name, which heralded a modest office manned by two clerks in a simple reception area, concealed a large hive of activity that emanated from the small space.

Into this office walked Ami Drori. The two clerks followed his entrance with a curious, severe stare. It was clearly not part of their job to smile politely at visitors.

The one on the left didn't wait long. "He's been waiting for you for the past hour. And he doesn't seem too happy about it…"

Ami threw him a dazzling smile. "He's never happy. Apparently, the coffee you fix him is too bitter… Why don't you try adding a little sugar?"

The clerk scowled, but Ami was unmoved. He went to the simple metal door behind the counter, knocked twice, opened it, and disappeared within. The clerks quickly glanced at the shuttered windows, ascertaining that no curious passerby could see inside.

The large room Ami entered was illuminated by numerous computer screens. No windows were open and the place was cooled by a quiet, sophisticated ventilation system.

Only one person sat in front of a large monitor, rapidly typing what appeared to be a random list of numbers. His back was to the door but he did not turn around to look at the newcomer.

"I don't like to be kept waiting, Ami!" he snapped, without slowing his typing.

"You didn't call me here to yell at me for being late, sir."

The man stopped suddenly, and his taut shoulders relaxed. "You're right. I wanted to yell at you about something else."

He pressed a few keys with stunning speed, and a short video clip appeared on the screen. Ami recognized Venice, the city from which he'd just returned. He also identified the video's subject.

"This has been airing for several hours now," the man said, still not looking at Ami. "Mazel tov—you're famous."

Ami looked at the shaky video, in which an amateur had captured the assassination of Jon Perrera. Starkly clear was the pistol spitting three bullets into the Italian. The videographer had attempted to follow Ami's departure from the scene, but the fear and screaming that had gripped the people nearby—including the man with the camera—had influenced the results. Numerous running tourists, powerful panic, and a trembling hand all made the video jerky and unfocused. The faces of several screaming people trying to flee concluded the film, which ended as suddenly as it had begun.

"What do you have to say about your behavior, Ami? There was no need to expose yourself that way."

The man turned around abruptly, his eyes probing Ami's. He was a stocky man in his 50's with broad shoulders and graying hair. His eyes radiated power and endless determination. Ami knew that the man seated before him was responsible for a significant number of Israel's daring operations outside her borders.

"An American boy, 15 or so," Ami began, "black New York Mets baseball cap; white T-shirt with 'Venice' printed on it, bought at a nearby stall; blue Crocs; and an iPhone he used to film his friends and then the kill. My face was not exposed, my cover worked, and the target was taken out. Don't I get some sort of accolade instead of a scolding? Whatever happened to the days when they loved me in this country?"

The man grinned. "They never loved you, Ami..." He stood up and shook Ami's hand. "Good job! A bit too noisy, but nice work."

"Oh, thanks so much! Just the accolade I was hoping for. Now, suppose you tell me what was so urgent that I had to rush home?"

The man invited Ami to take the chair beside him and look at some papers he thrust into his hand. Ami scanned the material for two minutes, but was still in the dark. "Well? What am I supposed to see here?"

"Nothing. That's the problem. There's nothing there."

"I don't understand..."

"Look. There's a lot of talk in the air about something big being cooked up in Russia. A lot of intangible hints pointing to some sort of security breach linked to Jewish interests. Right now, it's still a collection of half-rumors and unclear messages. But I have a bad feeling about this."

"Are we talking about the Russian government? The Russian Mafia? The Chechens? Who's it coming from?"

"That's the problem—I don't know. But I wouldn't have called you here if I didn't think it was serious. Three agents that I sent to sniff around have disappeared as though the earth has swallowed them up, and I still know no more than before. There's some sort of hidden threat over there, in Russia, and I don't have a clue what it is. I need you to get me more information."

"What do you want me to do? Go over to the Kremlin and ask the prime minister or the president? Ask them if they know about something that's threatening us and request their assistance?"

"Something like that…but without the Kremlin. I need you to bring me some sort of concrete information. Something that will explain these pieces of intelligence in a logical way."

"When do you need the answers?"

"As soon as possible. But you have all the time in the world. I don't want you back without information of some kind. Go to Russia and try to find something out without getting yourself killed. Do you think that's possible?"

"Like a walk in the park… just without the smiling children."

"Excellent! The flash drive has all the information you'll need. Contact with me will be made through the usual channels and at the usual intervals. Remember that we'll deny any connection with you if you're caught, so please try not to do anything foolish. Russia is not Venice. They have Siberia."

"I love you too, sir."

"Wonderful. Now get out of my sight."

———————

On the day after his attempt to speak to Jeffrey, Yisrael acted as though nothing had happened. His mother, watching him with worried eyes, was glad to see that he hadn't become downcast because of the situation. It pained her to see her children as orphans, without a father, and she'd promised herself not to let that fact sour their lives.

It wasn't easy being a widow. And it was far less easy when you have to support your family and don't want to ask anyone for help. She was happy that at least her children were behaving maturely and trying to help out as much as they could. There were still nights when she had to go into the girls' room to calm the heartbreaking sobs of a daughter who missed her father. Those difficult moments, when she had to be strong and struggle against her desire to join in the weeping, demanded an inner strength that she hadn't known she possessed.

For so many years, her husband had been home every day. She had never been alone. And now, so abruptly, it was all over. Suddenly, he was only a memory. Only her pillow was witness to the many tears she had spilled. To the rest of the world, she was even stronger than usual. Strong for the children.

Yisrael's return changed the picture slightly. How he'd grown up lately! He was no longer the small boy who had come home crying from kindergarten. He was a young man now, a young man who understood matters and noticed what was really happening. She hadn't intended to tell him about her financial situation so soon. She had wanted to wait a bit, until things became clearer. The realtor was supposed to get back to her any day now with a bid from the couple who had looked at the apartment. If they agreed to her price, she would sell to them.

The decision to move seemed like the right one to her. Though it would be hard to leave the house that held memories of her husband in every corner and every room, they really didn't need such a big apartment. A smaller place would better serve their needs, especially since Yisrael wasn't home most of the time.

Yisrael. How she had missed him. It had been so hard for her to give him up, now that his father was gone. She had had a powerful urge to keep her family as close as possible, to keep an eye on them and make sure they were safe. But she knew how important it was for him to return to yeshivah. He had been so close to the brink of disaster after that terrible time in his former yeshivah. They'd nearly lost him to the streets. And then he'd gone to that special yeshivah that had restored him to life. For his own good, she knew that she must not take him away from there. She understood that he must go on in life. His new status as an orphan must not impede his progress.

No one knew how hard it had been for her to insist that Yisrael go back when he pleaded to stay. She had hardened her voice and ordered him to get on the plane—as though she didn't want him to stay. In her heart, she yearned to keep him home; outwardly she had sent him off without a moment's hesitation. "You have to go back to yeshivah!" She reminded herself to call Rav Schwartz, to thank him for his special visit during the week of *shivah*. The world needed more good people like him.

Meanwhile, Yisrael looked wonderful. Though she could tell that it was hard for him to see his home without his father, she could also see that he had matured and grown much more serious since the painful funeral. He looked all right. He was not shattered as he had been after the episode in his former yeshivah.

Right now, he'd taken his sisters to the Biblical Zoo. They'd taken the number 33 bus from the Har Nof neighborhood and gone to spend the day gazing at the animals. How good it was to have him home! She would never have believed how much she would miss him.

Yisrael, for his part, was doing everything he could to make things easier for his mother. The idea for an outing to the zoo had been his own. She deserved a little respite from the girls. She worked so hard to make things easier for others until she had no time left for herself. He was well aware that things were no less difficult for his mother than they were for the rest of them; after all, she had lost her husband. Not even the strength she radiated could disguise the fact that she was an unfortunate widow with no source of income. But Yisrael knew that the last thing she wanted from him was worry. He mustn't show her how concerned he was over the situation, how he couldn't sleep at night for wondering how he could help her.

Outwardly, he put on a show of being happy to be home and as carefree as the girls. But what could he do? He was no longer a child. He understood the far-from-simple situation, and he *had* to do something about it.

The meager help he offered did not distract him from his primary purpose. He was going to talk to his uncle and explain to him that he'd better pay the money his mother had coming. He'd *force* him to do it!

If only he knew how…

The trip to the zoo lifted his spirits. The crowds of people, all determined to squeeze the most out of their vacation days, did his heart good. Though he felt a pang sometimes when he saw a complete family—father, mother, and happy children, the kind of family his own sisters would never have again—it was still nice to break free of routine for a while. After his long stay in Switzerland, he appreciated the fact that everyone around him spoke his language. Swiss German had not yet found its way into his heart.

They lingered in the zoo until closing time. The girls' enthusiasm at seeing the various beasts affected Yisrael as well. If his mother could see him now, she'd have been glad to see that the child within him was still alive and well. Though he tried to behave like a responsible adult, he was still young. Laughter, which had become a rare thing since his father's death, bubbled up in his throat when the monkeys raced after one another in a circle, much to the spectators' delight. When it came time to leave, they were tired but more contented than they had been in a long time. Only then did Yisrael remember that he had to daven Minchah. And not just daven, but serve as the *chazzan*.

Luckily for him, there was a *minyan* of yeshivah men forming near the entrance. The pitying glances he received when he asked to be *chazzan* because of his obligation as a mourner took some of the joy from the perfect day. The bus ride home was also not much fun, as there was no place to sit. But all in all, it had been a pleasant outing. The girls had enjoyed themselves immensely. It was good to be home.

Only later that night did the bad thoughts come rushing back. Maybe I shouldn't have gone to the zoo. Why did I ask Mommy for so much money? I could have taken them somewhere that didn't cost anything. Why didn't I think of that before? He found himself angrily dialing Jeffrey Davis' number.

Once again, he was politely rebuffed by the annoying secretary. He decided that he would not give up. What could they do to him? From now on, he would call every night, until she'd give up and pass the call on to her boss. For some reason, he'd made up his mind that all would be well once he'd spoken with his uncle.

The change came from the last place he expected. It was his fourth evening at home, and he decided to go to Sacher Park to play a little basketball. He felt a need to get out by himself for a while, without his sisters. He made his way there on foot, and the cool, crisp air did wonders for his mood.

His mood changed the instant he set foot on the court.

Out of all the people in the world, this was the last person Yisrael had expected to see here. This was not what he'd come for—to play basketball with his great enemy, Yossi Goldfarb.

His first instinct was to turn right around and go home. To get out of there before Yossi noticed that he'd come. But something inside him refused to let him go. Why should *he* leave? Let Yossi disappear! Was it he, Yisrael, who should be ashamed of himself? *He* hadn't done anything wrong! He was no longer the frightened young child he'd once been. If Yossi tried to start something, he'd show him a thing or two.

Yossi Goldfarb was absorbed in the game and didn't notice the newcomer. His team was leading by a significant number of points, and he was taking great pleasure in announcing it out loud. "Six-one! One more basket, and we're done!" He passed the ball to his teammate and ran forward to receive it back.

Meanwhile, on the side of the court, Yisrael was checking out the next team up to play.

"There are two of us," said an energetic, young, blond-haired boy. "You can join us, but we don't have a chance. They're the champs. We're wasting our time."

Yisrael smiled as though he had a secret. "No problem. The main thing is the game." At that moment, Yossi shot the winning basket. "All right!" he crowed. "Who's next in line to lose?"

His smile vanished the instant he saw Yisrael. Yisrael wasn't sure, but he thought he saw the color drain from Yossi's face. Yossi fell silent and stared at Yisrael in a way that caught the others' attention.

"What's wrong, Yossi?" asked a man in his 30's. He was a regular player here, and on Yossi's team today. "Do you know him?"

Yisrael was enjoying the scene. He hadn't known how much anger lurked inside him until this moment. "Not really," he said. "We've just played together before. Shall we begin?"

Yossi broke free of his shock, but he still appeared unfocused. Yisrael tossed him the ball forcefully. Yossi threw it at the basket, but missed by a wide margin. Yisrael's team would start the game.

"I'll guard the blond kid," Yossi's teammate said. "Koby will guard the kid in the blue shirt. And you," he pointed at Yossi, "guard your friend. You're about the same height."

Only now did Yisrael notice how much he'd grown in the past year and a half. When he'd been in yeshivah with Yossi, the other boy had been slightly taller than he; now he had the advantage by a centimeter or two. Another thing that had changed was that Yossi had been a strong and even violent kid, while Yisrael wouldn't so much as attack a fly. Now, after the training he'd undergone with Gilad, he had no doubt that, though it wouldn't be easy, he could subdue Yossi. The sense of power intoxicated him. He almost wished that Yossi would start up with him.

He received the ball at the three-point line and waited for Yossi to try to guard him. The moment he approached, Yisrael rose up easily and tossed the ball right into the basket. "Two-zero!" His teammates looked gratified.

"What's happening to you, Yossi? Don't give away those baskets!"

The other team's criticism was music to Yisrael's ears. His teammates began the next round and hastened to pass him the ball. Yossi made an effort, moving closer to him with arms spread at his sides. Yisrael dribbled rapidly, twisted away from Yossi in one fluid motion, and shot the ball at the basket—another easy point for his side.

"He's making a laughingstock of you," the man told Yossi. "Do you want to switch? Let me guard him?"

Yisrael knew how much this wounded Yossi's ego. "Shut up!" Yossi hissed. "I'm doing fine."

The problem was, he wasn't doing fine at all. Within a minute, Yisrael had added another two points, to a chorus of, "Five-nothing!"

The other team, which had played with such coordination as to beat team after team, shattered into tiny pieces when they found themselves lagging so far behind. The accusations were quick to follow. "You think you can guard him better than I can? Let's see!" Yossi was frustrated and annoyed.

Yisrael was happy when the man refused. "Okay, okay, go on guarding him. But I'll help you. I don't think the midget I'm guarding poses any kind of threat."

Yisrael watched all of this calmly. He now had two guards. Had this been an ordinary game, he would have passed the ball to the teammate who was free and let him do the work. But this was not an ordinary game. He had to show Yossi a thing or two. He caught the ball, dribbled slowly, and then burst suddenly between the two, swerved around them and threw the ball into the hoop.

Yossi reacted late. He thrust out his hand as the ball passed him, and accidentally smacked Yisrael's jaw.

"Basket and foul!" Yisrael's teammate cried gleefully.

But Yisrael wasn't happy. The fact that the ball had landed in the hoop despite the smack didn't pacify him. He whirled around to face Yossi and pushed him, hard. "What're you trying to do? Want to fight?"

To his surprise, Yossi didn't rise to the challenge. "Sorry," he said, despite the hard shove. "It was an accident."

"What's the matter with you?" The other players hurried up to separate Yisrael from Yossi. "Leave him alone! He didn't mean it!"

Yisrael caught himself. What was happening to him? What was this supposed to be? Was this what he had learned in yeshivah? To take revenge? He was ashamed of his loss of self-control. A believing Jew wasn't supposed to behave this way.

He breathed deeply and muttered an apology. He let someone else get the next basket and finish the game. They demolished Yossi's team, which hadn't managed to get even a single point. Yisrael's teammates rejoiced, but he wasn't enjoying the game anymore. Revenge wasn't as sweet as he'd pictured it.

"Wow! You're a great player!" the man on the losing team complimented him. "Have you ever thought about playing for a real team?"

Yisrael didn't answer. All the fire had gone out of him. He'd have felt much better if Yossi had responded in kind. If they'd fought it out and ended the story, once and for all. He'd never imagined that Yossi would step back. That he'd miss out on an opportunity to fight. That was not the Yossi he knew.

Meanwhile, a new team had organized itself to play against them.

"Sorry," Yisrael apologized. "I'm not playing anymore."

"What? Why not? You're an amazing player! We hardly did a thing!"

Yisrael didn't listen to the praise. He needed to think about what had just happened. He wanted to be alone with his thoughts and understand how he really felt about it all.

"Yisrael?" Yossi came closer, wearing an uncharacteristically meek expression. "Can I talk to you?"

Yisrael began walking away. "We have nothing to talk about."

Yossi didn't give up. He followed Yisrael, who was moving toward the broad green playing fields. "I've been wanting to talk to you for a long time."

"What can you possibly have to say? Huh? You destroyed my life! You stole money! You're a thief and a liar! What could you tell me that I don't already know? That you did it for *chesed*? Go tell it to the mashgiach!"

"I'm not in yeshivah anymore," Yossi surprised him by saying. "I left not long after…after you did."

Yisrael didn't look at him as he continued slowly across the grass. Though he was interested in why Yossi had left, it wasn't really relevant anymore. The kid was a creep, and that was that.

"The mashgiach caught me stealing money again," Yossi admitted in an almost inaudible voice. "He ambushed me and caught me red-handed."

Yisrael smiled to himself. Nice! At least now the mashgiach knew for sure that *he* hadn't been the thief.

"You should know that he believed in your innocence all along. He hated me, but he loved you. He was very broken up when you left the yeshivah."

"I left?" Yisrael finally spoke up. "As though I had a choice! You turned the whole place against me!"

"I know. And I'm sorry," Yossi said. "When my father heard

from the mashgiach, he forced me to meet with a psych— he got me some professional help. Today I know how spoiled and egotistical I was, and I'm asking you to forgive me."

"Forgive... What makes people think that they can say, 'Sorry' and all is forgotten? No, I don't forgive you! You hurt me in a way that can't be fixed. Because of you, I was kicked out of yeshivah! Because of you, I fought with my parents! Because of you, I was almost *mechallel Shabbos*! Because of you!" Yisrael was screaming now. A few youths seated on the grass not far away looked at them curiously, but Yisrael didn't care. He'd waited long enough to say this. He hated the boy who was following him and begging for his forgiveness. "No, I won't forgive you! Leave me alone!"

Yossi stood still and stopped following him. Then he started moving again, hurrying to catch up and block Yisrael's way.

"Get out of my sight, or I'll crush you!" Yisrael hissed angrily.

"Beat me up," Yossi said. "I deserve it."

Yisrael veered abruptly aside and continued walking, but Yossi ran to stand in front of him again. "Hit me!"

"This is not funny," Yisrael growled. "Move, or I'll break your nose!"

"Go ahead. Break it!"

"GET OUT OF MY WAY!" Yisrael was losing control again. "You're getting on my nerves!"

"I'm not moving. Hit me!"

Yisrael pulled his arm back, made a fist and sent it right at Yossi's face. Just millimeters before he made contact, he stopped his fist and left it hanging in midair. Yossi didn't move. His eyes had closed instinctively and he felt the rush of air from the fist on his face, but the blow itself failed to materialize. He opened his eyes and looked at Yisrael, who was breathing hard. "Why didn't you hit me?"

"I don't know," Yisrael answered honestly.

How he wanted to hit him! How often he'd imagined the moment he'd strike the face of his great enemy. But he couldn't do it. It wasn't right. After all, it was *Hakadosh Baruch Hu* who'd sent Yossi to make all that trouble. What purpose would be served by hitting the messenger?

"I want you to know that the thing that influenced me the most was when I heard that your father had died. I suddenly understood that what I'd done was no game. That someone real had suffered from what I'd done, and on top of all that he'd also lost his father. I really wanted to come be *menachem avel*, but I didn't think it would be smart."

Yisrael choked. It was a good thing Yossi hadn't come. That's all he'd have needed—salt on the wounds.

"I'm not in yeshivah anymore," Yossi added. "I'm helping my father with his business interests. I keep his appointment calendar and am learning the profession at the same time… And what about you? I heard you're abroad somewhere."

Yisrael didn't answer. He remembered what his American friend had said about Menachem Goldfarb's connection with his uncle. This was the chance he needed to reach his uncle.

And now, standing in the twilight of the holy city of Yerushalayim, he also remembered the words of his former rosh yeshivah, Rav Rubenstein, who had said that Yossi might be in a position to help him one day. Was he a *navi*? How had he known that one day he'd be standing here wondering if he should ask for Yossi's help?

"Look, I'm not asking you to forgive me for what I did," Yossi said after a long silence. "I know that I don't deserve to have you forgive me. But I do ask that you give me a chance to repair the past. Let me help you and your family a little. Like, if you need a reduction in your property tax, or something from the municipality, I have excellent contacts. Don't reject it out of hand. Ask your mother first. Sometimes these things can save a lot of money."

Yisrael was insulted by the offer. What was he, a beggar? He didn't need handouts.

But he swallowed his pride and didn't answer sharply. In truth, this actually would be a big help for his mother. What gave him the right to turn down an opportunity to ease her tax burden?

Yossi noticed his internal debate, and continued persuasively. "You know what? I'll call you at home tomorrow, and we'll talk. Okay? You'll come to see that I've changed. I'm not the same Yossi Goldfarb that I once was."

I'll believe it when I see it, Yisrael thought bitterly.

Yossi shook his limp hand with enthusiasm and walked away. But Yisrael remained where he was for a long time, trying to make sense of the millions of conflicting thoughts that were racing around inside his head.

26

YOSSI KEPT HIS WORD WITH ADMIRABLE EFFICIENCY. THE very next day, he came to Yisrael's house with a pile of papers for Mrs. Davis to sign. He promised her a discount of 70 or 80 percent on her property taxes within a few days' time—retroactive to the year before.

While Yisrael did not display any enthusiasm over the thousands of shekels in savings, the fact that he didn't throw Yossi out of the house was enough. He had decided not to forgive Yossi, but also not to fight with him. He'd give him a chance to try to atone in some measure for the past, even though Yisrael didn't really believe that was possible.

His mother, on the other hand, was very taken with the nice young man who'd saved her not only money, but also many hours and the endless procedures involved in any request for a discount. She didn't know that this was the boy who'd caused all the trouble for her son from the start—and Yisrael, for his part, didn't bother telling her. She thanked him, and marveled to Yisrael afterward over "*baalei chesed* who help people without getting anything in return."

Yisrael didn't want to admit it, but he was missing the company of boys his own age. Most of his yeshivah friends lived far away, and the friends who did live nearby had all turned in different directions. The tenuous connection of a childhood friendship no longer justified their spending time together. In this respect, Yossi fit the bill like a hand in a glove. After some effort, he managed to persuade Yisrael to join him in a game of basketball, and from there the road to spending a great deal of time together was a short one.

Yisrael tried, at first, to continue treating him with coldness and anger. He watched Yossi all the time, searching for the dark sides he knew so well. Though he found the same outbursts of anger that he remembered, Yossi always controlled them before he hurt someone. It was obvious that he was working very hard on himself. This didn't change the way Yisrael felt, but with time he found himself enjoying Yossi's company more and more. Yossi had connections everywhere and got a discount in almost any store he walked into. Everyone knew him and treated him—and his new/old friend Yisrael as well—with friendliness.

At the start, Yisrael had a hidden agenda in their friendship — to meet Yossi's father and ask him about his uncle. After a week of spending time together, when Yossi invited him to his home, Yisrael suddenly remembered that that had been his goal all along.

Yossi's father, Menachem Goldfarb, was as similar to his son as two drops of water. Both were a little taller than average, broad-shouldered and sturdy and at the same time very active and outgoing. If Yisrael had to paint a picture of a successful political activist, he'd have painted Menachem Goldfarb with his eyes closed.

Menachem shook hands and showed his teeth in a dazzling smile—the smile that was constantly displayed on the faces of politicians. He asked Yisrael questions and made him feel as though they were old friends. Yisrael couldn't help but be taken by Menachem Goldfarb's radiant personality, even as he sensed that this was also not a person he'd want to fight with. When something didn't please him, Menachem did not spare his tongue and could scold unmercifully. It was clear that his son had inherited his strong personality from his successful father, the prime minister's confidant.

Yisrael had conducted a small, private inquiry into the man, and discovered that Menachem Goldfarb, while not a member of the Knesset, was nevertheless involved in every stratum of Israeli politics in general, and *chareidi* politics in particular. On numerous occasions, he had served as a bridge between various parties, acquiring a reputation as a seasoned politician who knew how to find creative solutions and push them to a conclusion. Yisrael, who was always thinking about how to introduce the delicate subject of Jeffrey Davis, was surprised when Menachem asked him directly, "Tell me something, young man. They say you're from the United States. Do you happen to have any connection to Jeffrey Davis? I know it's a common name, but you said that your family is from New Jersey, and he's from there too. He's a good friend of mine. Have you heard of him?"

Yisrael nodded without speaking. Frantically, he tried to figure out how to present his case. Tell the truth? Lie? Reveal only part of the story?

"I believe we're related," he said at last. "Where do you know him from?"

"Where do I know him from? Oh...I've known him for years. We've helped pass a number of good laws that benefit Israel in the U.S. Congress. You could also say that he's the one who introduced me to the prime minister, who was then the Israeli ambassador to the United States. Every time I travel to America, I stay with him. That's what good friends we are. And you...? A cousin, you said?"

"Actually, I'm his nephew. My father was his brother..."

"What? Jeffrey has a brother? Why haven't I ever heard about a brother of his who lives in Israel?"

Yossi cleared his throat uncomfortably. His father didn't know that Yisrael was an orphan. But Yisrael ignored the comment, and said, "Because they quarreled. They can't stand each other."

"Really? What did they fight about? Money? Your father is no doubt very wealthy. What's his name? And why haven't I heard of him?"

"My father is dead. And no, he was not rich materially. In other ways, but not financially."

"I'm sorry...I didn't know. How long ago did he pass away?"

"A few months ago. He was killed in a traffic accident."

"*Oy vey*! Just a minute—Jeffrey didn't even come to the funeral? How can that be? I didn't hear from him that he had a brother who passed away!"

"He doesn't have anything to do with us. He's..." Tears welled up in Yisrael's eyes. "He's a terrible man!"

Menachem looked at him in silence. Yisrael wiped the corners of his eyes, ashamed of his weakness. What had happened to him? Was he a little kid? A girl?

"My mother was left without a shekel to her name. How could he do such a thing?"

Menachem did not reply at once. He considered what he had just heard. Was it true? The story suited Jeffrey, an egotist who thought only of himself and had made his way aggressively through the business and political worlds over a huge mound of corpses. If someone stood in his way, he was not afraid to use whatever means he had at his disposal to get rid of him. Many people had lost all their earthly possessions simply because they'd chosen to cross swords with Jeffrey Davis.

To tell the truth, the reason for their close friendship was the resemblance between them. He too had stepped on a great many toes on his way to his present success, though in much smaller measure and with a lot less money in the bank... But to leave his nieces and nephew like that, with nothing? As though it would hurt him to give up a million or two for his unfortunate relatives. He himself had seen Jeffrey spend much larger sums on some trivial outing or vacation, or a donation to some foundation. But when it came to his own family, he was stingy? It wasn't right.

"You know what?" he said, after thinking it over. "Wait right here." He took his cell phone from his pocket and punched in a long number from memory. Belatedly, Yisrael realized what was happening. He was amazed at the turn of events.

"Hey, Jeffrey, what's new? Do you have a minute? Great. Yes, yes, I'm coming at the end of the week. But that's not why I called. I have someone here who wants to talk to you." He handed the phone to Yisrael and motioned for his son to leave the room.

"Talk to him and tell me what he says," he whispered to Yisrael, and departed in Yossi's wake.

"Hello?"

"Yes? Who is this?"

"I... I... This is Yisrael. Yisrael Davis."

A thundering silence reached his ears from the other end of the line. Yisrael wasn't sure, but it seemed to him that the sound of breathing at the other end was heavier than before.

"You're the son of... Ram's son?"

Yisrael had never heard this nickname applied to his father before. It must be something he'd been called as a child. How had a name like Yerachmiel turned into "Ram"?

"Yes," he answered briefly.

"I'm sorry... I heard about what happened. How old are you, anyway?"

"Sixteen and a half."

"Wow, how time flies. You know, your father and I never got along. We disagreed about a lot of things."

"But how is my mother to blame for that? You stole all her money!"

"Hey! Watch it, boy! You sound just like your father! I haven't stolen money from anyone. Every cent I have, I made with my own blood and sweat. Your father is the one who tried to rob me, and he didn't deserve a dollar more than he got!"

Yisrael was taken aback. He shouldn't have attacked his uncle that way. However much he hated him, he should have addressed him respectfully. Otherwise he wouldn't accomplish a thing.

"Look, I don't know what happened between you and my father. I know...knew him well enough, and he never stole a shekel from anyone. But what does that have to do with my mother? She's a poor widow and was left without a penny. Is that fair?"

"Listen to me well, boy. Your father received far more than he deserved, and I have no intention of continuing to give him money after he's dead. If you need a donation, feel free to turn to my charitable foundation and I'll see to it that you get something. But you should be aware that by law, I don't owe you a thing."

Yisrael tried with all his might not to shoot back with a retort. *Hakadosh Baruch Hu* had been testing his trait of anger quite often lately... His hand tightened on the sophisticated cell phone until he nearly shattered it. He tried to think of how to respond to the cruel man at the other end. *Calm down!* He ordered himself. *Don't get mad!*

"Uncle Jeffrey, do I have any cousins?" he asked, abruptly changing the subject.

From the hesitation at the other side, he understood that he'd hit a nerve. "Um...what? Cousins? You mean, as in children? No...I'm not married. Why do you ask?"

"Nothing special. I just thought that if, after more than sixteen years, I finally have the privilege of speaking to my only uncle in the world, maybe it'll turn out that I have other relatives. Cousins or something. As you probably know, we have no relatives here in Israel—or anywhere else, for that matter. That is, apart from you."

"Look, boy..."

"Stop calling me boy! If you want to throw us out like dogs, you can at least do it politely! I don't know you, and you don't know me. If I'm talking to you respectfully, don't call me boy. Okay?"

"Okay, okay. Sorry... I didn't mean anything. You really *are* like your father. How sensitive! Look, I have nothing personal against you. On the contrary, you sound like a good kid. If you ever come to the States, drop in for a visit and we'll talk a little. But in the meantime, I don't have much to say to you. I'm sorry about your father, and wish you all the luck in the world. Okay? Now, where's Menachem? I'll teach him to spring surprises on me. Let me talk to him."

Yisrael didn't know if he was satisfied with the conversation or not. He hadn't really expected his uncle to apologize and promise to be the best uncle in the world from now on. Actually, he didn't know what he'd expected. He went out to look for Menachem Goldfarb, and handed him back his phone. "He wants to talk to you."

Yossi peeked in from another room and made a gesture that asked, "How'd it go?"

Yisrael shrugged. He didn't know what to say.

His mother would get along even without Uncle Jeffrey's money. He'd reached this conclusion after speaking at length with Yossi. The other driver's insurance would undoubtedly pay a respectable sum; it might take a little time, but it would happen. And the option of selling the apartment and moving into a small place seemed logical. But something had still driven him to have the conversation. He wasn't sure what it was.

Perhaps it was nothing more than the desire to get to know his only uncle. Maybe he wanted someone in his life that would remind him of his father? Or did he simply not want to be the only man in the Davis family? Anything was possible.

He didn't know what his next step would be. He would have to think about it, and daven that Hashem guide him in the right direction.

Menachem Goldfarb argued loudly with Jeffrey Davis, and suddenly disconnected. He seemed to have come to some sort of decision, but Yisrael didn't know what it was.

"Go home and pack a suitcase!" he ordered an astonished Yisrael. "I'm taking you to the States with me on Thursday. Don't worry— I'll talk to your mother. And, of course, I'll pay your fare. I'll show him what it means to ignore a nice nephew like you! From now on, you're under *my* protection."

Yisrael was bewildered. How had Menachem Goldfarb suddenly come to control his life? What did he mean, they were going to America together?

If he'd known the man better, he would not have asked that question. Menachem was known as a man of action who often decided to do something and only afterward thought about how to do it. If an idea popped into his head, anyone standing in his way had better look out. It was not for naught that the newspapers had dubbed him "the *chareidi* bulldozer."

Menachem continued issuing orders. "Yossi, take my credit card and go with Yisrael to buy whatever he needs for the trip. He'll have to be ready for a long flight."

Yisrael didn't like what he was hearing. He was not some charity case looking for a handout. "No, thanks," he said. "*Baruch Hashem*, I have everything I need. Can you please explain to me why I'm going to the States with you?"

"Because it's time your uncle stopped being so tightfisted and keeping all his money for himself. That's why! He said he has no objection to meeting you, so that is exactly what's going to happen. I'm going to dump you in his house—and let's see him deny you then! And if he does… *Oy va voy*… I'll show him what's what!"

Adrenalin pumped through Yisrael. He liked the idea. Although he didn't think that it was a smart move, and he didn't think it was the right thing to do right now, for some reason he very, very much wanted to do it anyway.

He was going to meet his rich uncle in America. He was going to stand up to him and demand an explanation. He was going to go head-to-head with a famous billionaire who had influence with the Israeli prime minister and the American president. It was going to be awesome.

Now, all he had to do was convince Mommy to let him go…

27

Long Island, New York, Summer 2012

MANY YEARS HAD PASSED SINCE THE LONG ISLAND TOWN of Brookville had been the place for raising horses. In the past, the town had supplied fine riding and carriage horses—things that had once been in high demand in New York. Today there remained only remnants of the past, in the private horse ranches belonging to some of the residents.

Over time, the town became a desirable place for people of higher-than-average incomes, eventually even winning first place in *Businessweek's* annual list of wealthy communities. An expensive school system, cultured surroundings, and large, spacious homes made Brookville much in demand. Some of the richest individuals in the United States had homes in this serene community, though few of them lived there year-round.

Jeffrey Davis was one of those who had built himself a house in Brookville. He had hired a noted architect to copy a castle that Jeffrey had admired on a visit to England. The architect labored for two years until he achieved the perfection that satisfied Jeffrey.

When they were done, the house became an attraction for architecture lovers, and even won a prize for its unique blending of contemporary style in the structure of an old English castle.

Jeffrey Davis intended to spend the weekend in his dream house in Brookville. He usually divided his time between the three places where he had homes: New York, Washington, D.C., and California. He recalled that a fool once asked him why he bothered with all those houses when he had so many hotels across the length and breadth of the United States—at any of which he could stay without paying a cent. Idiot. As though money was what he lacked. If he wanted, Jeffrey could have bought himself a house for every day of the year—and this fool was asking if he didn't mind spending the money. How limited people's thinking could be. Simply unbelievable.

This week, his Israeli friend was coming for a visit. Their friendship, which amazed most people, seemed very natural to Jeffrey. Both he and Menachem Goldfarb were men of ambition and vision who didn't allow anything to stand in their way. One might have expected this similarity to turn them into rivals, but the opposite had occurred. Instead of hating one another, they appreciated the traits they had in common and enjoyed arguing about every topic in the world.

There were those who might have labeled their relationship a quarrelsome one. But neither Jeffrey nor Menachem saw it that way. In their view, this was the only road to true friendship. The only hours that Jeffrey truly enjoyed were the ones filled with his endless arguments with Menachem. They were even more enjoyable than acquiring another company or a rival hotel. Jeffrey liked people who had the courage to stand up to him. Although usually such people paid a high price for attempting to go head-to-head with someone as ruthless as he was, he did enjoy them more than the yes-men who agreed with every word he said and never dared express an opposing view.

The phone call he had received that week had disturbed his peace. The young voice of his brother's son—his dead brother— had ruffled his equanimity. The boy's direct accusation still echoed in his ears. "But how is my mother to blame for that? You stole all her money!"

He'd stolen? He'd profited! Not a dollar was coming to his parasite of a brother, who had sat by while he worked like a dog. How dare that whippersnapper even imply that he deserved something? Without Jeffrey's work, the family empire would have crumbled to pieces. And that arrogant brother of his had dared behave as though the whole world belonged to him. Sitting in yeshivah and thinking that anyone who didn't learn as well as him was worth nothing... Let's see *him* remain religious in the dog-eat-dog world of business. He'd have been ripped to shreds by ruthless people who'd have pounced on his weaknesses.

Jeffrey, in contrast, had proven his own ruthlessness. It was no coincidence that he was where he was today. If only his brother had given him a bit of respect, everything would have been different. Instead, Yerachmiel had lorded it over him at every opportunity, calling him a failure and spineless. So Jeffrey had shown him who was a failure. He'd shown him what happened to a *yeshivah bachur* who thought he was the king of the world. If he thought that Hashem ran the world, then let him ask Him for money—not come asking for a portion of the mighty kingdom that Jeffrey had built with his own two hands.

But now his brother was gone, that schlemiel Yerachmiel. He'd been killed in a traffic accident. Though Jeffrey had been inclined to attend the funeral—he was his only brother, after all—in the end he had decided not to go. He wanted to bring to an end once and for all the complex relationship that they had shared and finally move on with his life. He didn't want to meet the widow or the orphans. They'd get along somehow. For his part, with his brother's death, a new chapter began, a chapter in which their history was over.

But now, that upstart Menachem had had the nerve to bring Yerachmiel's son to life. What was his name again? Yisrael? A boy in his teens who had dared pick up exactly where his father had left off, accusing him of stealing money from them. He'd show that Menachem.

Jeffrey decided to go out to the pool and start his morning with a few laps to calm himself down. He was a man who didn't waste much time on sleep. At 5:30 he was awake and ready to start his day.

The hot, humid air necessitated that he maintain a swimming pool for the summer months. The pool, which was custom-made, was half the size of an Olympic pool, no less.

He swam back and forth at a rapid clip, throwing his energy into his strokes in an effort to subdue his anger. Physical exertion always calmed him and helped him think clearly. After about ten laps, he was struck by a sudden realization. He stopped in midlap and paddled to the side of the pool, jaw hanging open. Impossible. Menachem couldn't do that. He wouldn't dare...But...he had. How had he not caught on earlier?

Menachem Goldfarb intended to land his insolent nephew here.

How had he not understood this before? He should have guessed, from the sudden way Menachem had ended the call, that he was planning something. He replayed their conversation in his mind, and realized that that was exactly what was happening. Menachem was on his way here with the crown prince, Yisrael Davis.

How could he get out of this now? He'd put Menachem in his place, but the problem still remained. What do to with the boy?

Then again, what was he supposed to do? Was it his fault the kid was coming? He didn't owe him a thing and didn't want anything from him. Let him hang around here for a day or two, and that would be that.

If his first instinct was to fly off to California and let the two of them arrive at an empty house, he dismissed the thought. He didn't run away from anyone. If the kid thought he could fight him, he could slug it out in court. Jeffrey retained a slew of lawyers, as little as an hour of whose time was far beyond Yisrael's ability to pay. If the boy tried to fight him, he'd encounter an old, cruel, and experienced fox. And if Menachem even dreamed of helping him, he'd quickly come to see that it wasn't worth his while to get involved in this kind of battle.

These thoughts, passing quickly through his mind, did nothing to calm his boiling blood. He kicked the water furiously and then hauled himself out of the pool. Until now, he'd been planning a few fun-filled days with his Israeli friend. But the plan had changed. It was going to be anything but fun.

He threw a thick white towel over his shoulders and reentered the house. He had to get ready. His guests were due in just a few hours.

28

THE FLIGHT TO AMERICA WAS NOT PARTICULARLY EXCIT-
ing. Yisrael, who already felt at home in Ben Gurion Airport,
was unmoved by either the glittering duty-free zone or by boarding
the plane. He was comfortable here. Though the plane was bigger
and the flight far longer than the one to Switzerland, everything
else was more or less the same.

As the child of American parents and a native-born American
himself, he had a U.S. passport and didn't require a visa.

The flight passed uneventfully, and before long they'd made
their way out of JFK. Yisrael was impressed by the sheer size of
everything in America, starting with the throngs of people and
ending with the buildings, but he didn't find himself admiring the
place the way he had expected to. In the end, it was just another
country, except that here they spoke a language he understood and
not some confusing Germanic tongue.

Menachem Goldfarb led the way like a seasoned traveler. It was
obvious that this was not his first time in New York. As they stepped
out into the heat of the big city, Yisrael was pleased to find that they

were not destined to suffer overmuch from the heat. On their exit from the airport—literally opposite the terminal doors—stood several stretch limos, the likes of which he'd never seen before, waiting for passengers. One of the drivers, a young man in uniform, stood beside a long, black limousine holding a sign saying "Mr. Goldfarb." Menachem walked toward the limousine and showed the driver the cart with their luggage. Menachem, a regular traveler, carried only a small overnight bag with the bare minimum he'd need for the trip. Yisrael, on the other hand, had been forced by his mother to drag along a huge suitcase filled with clothes and food to meet any possible disaster.

"Mommy, it's summer!" he'd protested when he saw her trying to stuff a coat into the suitcase. But he gave up when she insisted that you never knew what could happen. "Maybe you'll have to travel somewhere colder than New York. Someplace farther to the north and colder."

He couldn't let himself argue with her. He'd hardly managed to obtain her permission to go. Her "consent" had come only when she had realized that he was not prepared to accept no for an answer. She even got Rav Schwartz involved. He hadn't been happy about the plan, either. Yisrael worked long hours to get his rebbi not to veto the trip. Only after he promised to be in telephone contact with Rav Schwartz on a daily basis, to keep up his regular learning schedule, and, most importantly, not to separate himself from the religious activist who had taken him under his wing, did the rosh yeshivah wish him well—while warning him at the same time not to let himself be blinded by the materialism to which he was about to expose himself. "If you look closely, you'll be able to see that wealth is no guarantee of happiness. You can buy nearly everything with money, but not even a drop of satisfaction or real happiness."

Although Rav Schwartz would have been happy to forbid the trip altogether, he understood that, at this stage of his life, Yisrael would be incapable of accepting this in a healthy way. He would feel imprisoned and pitiable, and would stand in danger of losing everything he had gained in yeshivah. Yisrael had come a long way, but he was not permanently immunized. His desire to fly to America expressed a longing for freedom. Sometimes one had to know when to let go in order to hold onto something.

One more thing he discussed with Yisrael was the personal responsibility that every person bears for his behavior. "You're traveling with a person who is a respected Jew, but you alone are responsible for how you will behave in America. There are people who sometimes find leniencies when they're on vacation. You're not one of them. I hope you'll know how to hold onto your *emunah* and mitzvos even in places where that won't be easy, and even if it comes along with laughter and mockery."

Right now, Yisrael was trying to help the limousine driver load one of the heavy bags into the car—something that appeared to be unacceptable. "That's all right, sir. I can manage," the driver said with a false smile. He quickly opened the door for his passengers and returned to the rear to deal with the luggage alone.

Yisrael was impressed by the spacious interior. He could stretch out his long legs and not hit the seats in front of him. Thin curtains and a minibar completed the general resemblance to an elegant living room on wheels.

"Hi. My name is Tarif, and I'm your driver today." The driver, who had climbed inside and turned on the engine, smiled at them. He showed them how to close the tinted window separating him from them. "We have a ride of a little under an hour. Please make yourselves at home and unwind after your long trip."

Menachem thanked him, and closed the window. He had a great deal to say to Yisrael before they met his uncle. Although this visit had been his idea, carrying it out would call for care. Yisrael must not go head-to-head with Jeffrey. Who, more than he, knew how dangerous that could be? He wondered if Jeffrey had already guessed what he had done. Chances were he had. You could call Jeffrey a lot of things, but stupid wasn't one of them. He was no doubt already preparing for his nephew's arrival, and was surely not happy about it. It was time to plan their next steps. First of all, he had to prepare Yisrael for the encounter, and then figure out what they were trying to accomplish here.

He understood, from his son, that the Israeli Davis family had been left on their own, with no source of income at all. If there was one thing that was sure to be simple, it would be obtaining a respectable stipend for the bereaved family. A stipend that would help them get through this difficult time more easily. And if, on the way, it was possible to get them a small piece of the business... No. That would be impossible. Jeffrey guarded every sliver of his empire, however tiny, with endless zeal. He mustn't attempt that. A nice stipend would definitely suffice.

"We're going to your uncle's house on Long Island," he told Yisrael. "Well, actually, even the word 'house' is too small to describe the mansion he has there. It has very many rooms, and even more bathrooms. Don't ask me why, it's just part of the style... Anyway, at first I was supposed to fly directly to Washington. These days, I'm over my head coordinating the meeting between the prime minister and the president. The reason I'm going to Jeffrey first is to finalize some political plans that will bore you, so I won't go into detail.

"But from a scheduling point of view, just so you'll know what's ahead: Today is Thursday, 6:30 a.m., local time. If you didn't change your watch on the plane, this would be a good time to do it. From here we're going, as I said, to your uncle's house in Brookville, Long Island. We'll stay there tonight and talk a little, and then we'll go to New Jersey for Shabbos. You know, *Shabbos Kodesh* and your uncle don't exactly go together... We'll be staying with a family I know. On Sunday we'll return to your uncle's place, where we'll stay till Monday. On Monday we fly to Washington, and on Thursday we head back to Israel. Okay?"

Yisrael had absorbed the facts, but the truth was that tomorrow didn't really interest him. His entire being was focused on his upcoming meeting with his uncle. What would happen after that? He'd see. He smiled at his benefactor, and nodded.

Menachem continued, "Officially, you have no standing or program of your own in the next week. You're here as my assistant, and as such you'll have to listen to what I tell you. You know how to make coffee, right?" Without waiting for Yisrael's nod, he went on, "All you have to do is listen to me and no one else. I know that you're excited about meeting your American uncle, but take a tip from me: Don't build too much on it. We're going to cause him some unpleasantness. A lot of unpleasantness. Here he is, portraying himself as the savior of the weak around the world, a person who supports various organizations and charitable causes—and suddenly he's faced with a nephew who's not getting a cent. But trust me, he'll know how to get out of it. I just want to make him recognize you and your family, no more than that. If we achieve that minimum, we're okay."

Yisrael listened uncomfortably. He wanted to say that he wasn't doing this for the money—that he was no beggar. But then, why *was* he doing this? For fun? To go head-on against a man who considered all means kosher, a powerful man with influence worldwide? Better to step into a lions' den. The lions, at least, would not devour you if they weren't hungry…

Yisrael told himself that the reason was to make the uncle who'd caused his father so much pain finally admit his mistake. He felt a duty, as his father's only son and lawful heir, to restore the honor that had been stolen from Yerachmiel Davis. Maybe it had been easy to deceive his father, a nice, innocent man. But his son was a full-fledged Israeli who knew what was what.

Even to himself, he was not prepared to admit that the real reason for all of this was a feeling of guilt. He was angry at himself over the way he had treated his father in the period before the accident. He hadn't given his father enough respect, and he knew it. The memory of the big fight they had had after the theft floated back into his mind nearly every night. How Tatty had slapped him and how he, in turn, had run away from home. The many arguments they'd had, and Tatty's efforts to persuade him to get out of bed and take up life again, returned to him clearly in his dreams, along with a full measure of self-reproach. How had he dared speak that way to his father? And why, why, hadn't he told him, before he died, that he loved him in spite of everything?

Deep down, he knew that the real reason he was trying to get his uncle to change his mind was so that Tatty would forgive him. So that Tatty would see how important his honor was to his only son.

They rode the rest of the way in silence. Menachem was busy reading pages and pages written in English. Yisrael sat near him, daydreaming about the upcoming meeting. Before either of them realized it, the limousine driver lowered the automatic glass and announced, "We're here. Brookville."

Yisrael roused himself and looked out the window. Menachem, too, returned his papers to their folder and studied the passing scenery. They were moving along a long, narrow, two-lane road, marked with white and green lines and absent shoulders, which stretched through a dense forest. From time to time they glimpsed the roof of a house or a luxury car parked somewhere among the trees, behind a private driveway that was often guarded by a locked metal gate.

"You won't find a single shop or supermarket in the entire town," Menachem said. "Moreover, you won't find anyplace to park your car except in driveways—and don't even *think* about public transportation. If you don't have the address of someone who's willing to host you, there's nothing for you in Brookville. Those who live here are wealthy people looking for quiet and privacy. That's practically the only thing they lack."

"Just like in Sodom," Yisrael said.

Menachem chuckled. "You'll learn," he said. "Life is not black and white."

Yisrael swallowed his pride. This place certainly fit what he knew of his uncle. A rich man who liked his money more than anything else, and wasn't prepared to share it with anyone. Yes, Brookville suited him very well.

The limousine reached a huge metal gate, and the driver honked twice. Two seconds later, the automatic gate swung open and the vehicle slid inside to move slowly toward a mansion, the likes of which Yisrael had never imagined even in his dreams.

He stared at the house in disbelief. Was this a private home? Impossible! The acreage on which the mansion sprawled could have held any number of yeshivos.

The limousine swung into a gigantic clearing at the head of the long driveway. Ornate fountains sent jets of water to great heights. The heat that met them as the driver opened the doors was mitigated slightly by the colorful spray scattering in every direction. Yisrael stepped out of the limousine, his gaping eyes still riveted on the enormous house before him. Perhaps he'd read tales of such places, but he'd never imagined himself being a guest in one of them.

Huge, black marble pillars stretched several stories high, with an enormous wooden door, apparently weighing several tons, positioned between them. Dozens of windows punctuated the white walls, black on white. The roof seemed to consist entirely of turrets. A large central turret covered in shining black stone, and smaller ones on either side in black and white, gave the place the look of an ancient English castle. Lush green lawns surrounded the mansion, ending in a thick copse of trees that formed a natural concealment for a sophisticated electrified fence meant to keep out unwanted visitors.

While the driver removed their luggage, the great door moved silently on its hinges and a uniformed servant came out to greet them. He very much blended in with his surroundings. Yisrael nearly smiled when he heard the British accent.

"Good morning, Mr. Menachem!" the servant said, distorting the name through his inability to pronounce the Hebrew letter *ches*. "Mr. Davis is waiting for you in the family room." Completely ignoring Yisrael's presence, he gestured for Menachem to enter. Menachem Goldfarb grasped Yisrael's arm and pulled him along. The limousine driver loaded their suitcases onto a folding cart and rolled them into the house.

Yisrael felt like a child who had stepped into a fairytale. The sparkling chandeliers and heavy, expensive furniture seemed to belong to a different world. Old and new mingled, with automatic doors and computerized screens living side by side with rare paintings, hand-made Persian rugs, and specially imported oak furnishings. It was hard to believe that all of this belonged to one person, his uncle.

The servant led the way, and Yisrael was drawn along behind Menachem to a room of vast dimensions. The room, through which a minimal amount of furniture had been scattered in the best of taste to preserve the sense of space, could have held scores of people. Right now it was empty, but noisy. In the center of the room, a basketball game was in progress on a giant screen.

Hidden amplifiers carried the excited broadcasters' voices into the room, creating a sense that those present were watching the spectacle inside the basketball court itself. Facing the screen on a couch of black leather and fur sat Jeffrey Davis, watching the game.

The servant halted politely, and said, "Sir, your guest has arrived."

The gaze that had been fixed on the screen came alive. Jeffrey jumped up and, with a flexibility impressive in a man his age, strode over with a broad smile to shake Menachem's hand. The deafening noise of the game on the screen drowned the old friends' affectionate cries. Menachem embraced Jeffrey and clapped him on the shoulder. "Well, what do you say to my little surprise?"

"Surprise? What surprise?" Jeffrey feigned ignorance.

"Very funny, Jeffrey. Say hello to your nephew."

"My nephew? You mean, your assistant? Yes, I heard that you'd become so important that you need an assistant constantly at your side. Looks like a nice boy. But I don't know him."

Yisrael had no idea what he was supposed to do now. Jeffrey pressed a button on the remote control in his hand, and silence fell over the room as the game disappeared from the screen. Yisrael gaped as the huge screen began sinking slowly into the floor, until it was entirely swallowed up. This was the first time he had met his father's only brother, and instead of greeting him, he was looking at technology that he hadn't even known existed. Screens that popped up out of the floor and then disappeared again. Who would have believed it?

The silence that fell over the room was not pleasant for anyone. So this was his uncle's strategy—to deny Yisrael's existence even as he stood in the same room.

"I'm paying millions to a bunch of lazy athletes so that they'll play basketball. Millions! And what did I ask already, huh? That they win a few games and justify their inflated salaries. But—nothing! They just lost again to some inferior team. It's a disgrace."

Jeffrey's attempt to change the subject was obvious, and it was ugly. Menachem stared at him and tried to think of how best to go from here. He was well aware that Jeffrey had bought himself a basketball team and sunk a great deal of money into it. A big part of his decision to do so had been from a desire to brag that he had such a team in his possession. In general, he liked to invest in things that would make him and his wealth famous throughout the land. He was ambitious to have everyone envy him and try to copy him.

Now, like a little kid, he was waving his new toy around as he tried brazenly to ignore the fact that his nephew, the son of his deceased brother, had made his way here from Israel just to meet him.

Yisrael decided not to remain silent. He was not about to allow Jeffrey to treat him like air. "What do you know about basketball, Uncle? Maybe if you understood the game, you could build a normal team…"

Jeffrey didn't like what he was hearing. He gave Yisrael a penetrating look, snapped the remote shut, and came to stand right in front of him. He brought his face inches from the boy's.

Yisrael tried not to recoil. He would not let his uncle win! His body tensed as he strove mightily not to avert his eyes from his uncle's piercing ones. Menachem, standing to one side, could not help but notice the resemblance between the two. They were both of above-average height, with the advantage of a centimeter or two on Yisrael's side, thin but not scrawny, with a prominent nose, brown hair, and obstinate look.

They stood that way for a few long seconds, with neither of them willing to look away first. Menachem was forced to intervene.

"Enough, enough! What's wrong with you two? I've never heard of an uncle and nephew meeting for the first time and immediately starting to fight. Jeffrey, leave the boy alone. He's not his father. Yisrael, haven't you heard about showing respect to your elders?"

He moved toward them and placed his arms around both of their shoulders. "Listen, Jeffrey. I know it wasn't right of me to land him on you like this. But you know what? You also shouldn't start acting like a kid. I don't know exactly what happened between you and Yisrael's father, but I can tell you that from the little bit that I've come to know this boy, he's all right. Give him a chance, okay?"

"He doesn't leave your supervision the whole time he's here, and he's your complete responsibility. Understand?"

Menachem nodded. As far as he was concerned, it was a sign of progress that Jeffrey hadn't demanded that Yisrael be thrown out of his house.

"I'm not a child, and I'm not under anyone's supervision," Yisrael declared. Menachem hastened to shush him. The boy was going to ruin everything. This was not the way one dealt with Jeffrey Davis.

"Go unpack your things and have something to drink. Then we'll sit down and talk," Jeffrey told Menachem, turning away from Yisrael. "I'll be waiting for you in my office. You can let the boy play on a computer, or he can rest if he wants."

Yisrael didn't budge until Jeffrey left the room. His heart was thudding wildly and his mouth was dry. It hadn't been easy to stand up to his powerful uncle like that, but he felt as though he'd met a challenge of honor. This was the man who had stolen Tatty's money. He was supposed to hate him.

The servant appeared again from somewhere and led them upstairs. Yisrael was struck by the size of the room he was given, which was at least the size of his living room at home—if not larger. There was a well-appointed adjoining bathroom, a large screen in the bedroom, and a small one in the bathroom. Someone around here was obsessed with technology.

The bed in the center of the room was enormous, with five pillows scattered across it. He remembered how tired he was. Though he had dozed a bit on the long flight, the long trip from Yerushalayim to New York, along with the excitement and especially his recent confrontation with his uncle, had sapped him of his strength. He was happy to accept Menachem's suggestion that he rest for a few hours. He had nothing better to do anyway while the two men talked.

He kicked off his shoes and climbed into the soft, welcoming bed. It took him two minutes to grow accustomed to the size and to toss a few of the pillows off the bed. Immediately afterward, he sank into a deep sleep filled with frightening dreams about his uncle, Jeffrey Davis.

29

DINNER THAT NIGHT WAS AWESOME. AFTER MENACHEM vouched for the kashrus of the food, Yisrael allowed himself to indulge in the huge cuts of meat that were brought to the table. He had never seen steaks that big, and though he was skeptical about his ability to handle such a portion, he was surprised to find that he easily polished off the first steak and then reached for a second. The meat was soft as butter and wonderfully tasty. A special chef had been brought from an upscale kosher restaurant in Manhattan to prepare the meat in his own pots, in a special, kosher kitchen.

Although Jeff himself was not careful to observe the laws of kashrus, he took better care of his friend. Yisrael estimated that the meal they had eaten must have cost a minimum of several thousand dollars. A private chef, a special kitchen, plenty of meat. It would take time for him to grow used to this world, where money was unlimited.

The atmosphere too had improved remarkably since the last time they had met. While Jeffrey did not apologize for his earlier hostility, he was more pleasant now, and even addressed Yisrael several times in the course of the dinner-table conversation. Yisrael could only guess what the Israeli politician had said to Jeffrey; whatever it was, it had worked. There was no sign in his voice of his former animosity, and his plentiful smiles showed that he was enjoying his guests.

For his part, Yisrael unwound and joined the conversation. It was so easy to like Jeffrey that Yisrael found himself drawn into his uncle's jokes and amazing stories. He had to remind himself repeatedly that the man was a scoundrel. A thief. He mustn't like him.

Dessert was served when Yisrael thought he had no room left for as much as a seed. But the soft ice cream, filled chocolates, and other sweet confections were so tempting that he discovered that there was always room for more. He didn't remember the last time he had enjoyed a meal so much. Indeed, America had *olam hazeh* — and plenty of it.

"When are you leaving?" Jeffrey asked Menachem. "I imagine you'll be staying with your relatives in Jersey over Shabbos?"

"Unless you've become Shabbos-observant and forgot to tell me," Menachem laughed. Jeffrey joined in.

"Tomorrow morning, I'm hosting a basketball game," Jeffrey said, when the laughter had died down. "Will you still be here at ten?"

Menachem shook his head. "I promised Yisrael that I'd take him first thing in the morning. He has to say Kaddish, as you know, and he doesn't want to miss out on davening Shacharis with a *minyan*. We'll leave here, *b'ezras Hashem*, at around 7 in the morning. There's no way we could be back by 10, and also no reason. We'll return as planned on Sunday morning and take it from there."

"Your loss. I just thought that Yisrael wanted to teach me how to manage a basketball team. I thought it would be fun to make a basketball school for him."

"Ha, ha...I'd have shown you what it's all about!" Yisrael grinned.

"So show me. Stay here in the morning and then go for Shabbos. So what if you miss *minyan* just this once? I don't remember a halachah that says you have to travel miles for a *minyan*."

"Halachah? I didn't know you were also a *posek*…"

"There's a lot you don't know."

"I know that I could beat you at basketball."

"Let see you do it—tomorrow."

"That's enough," Menachem broke in. "Soon the two of you will be fighting like children. A person doesn't have to be a genetics expert to see that you're from the same family. You're both babies!"

Jeffrey and Yisrael burst out laughing. Indeed, there were a lot of similarities between them.

"What do you say, Yisrael?" Menachem asked. "It's your decision. Do we leave for *Shacharis* tomorrow, or just for Shabbos?"

Yisrael struggled with himself. He was in distant America. No one would know if he davened with a *minyan* or not. Not his mother, not his rebbi—no one. Besides, he'd attend *minyan* for Minchah and Maariv in any case. What difference did one *tefillah* make? He could play ball and show off in front of his uncle. And who knew? Maybe that would even lead to Mommy getting more money. She was a widow. It would be a mitzvah…

Yisrael was able to identify the *yetzer hara* disguising itself as a scholar. Nevertheless, it wasn't easy for him to say, "Um… We'll go to Shacharis. I don't want to miss…"

"You don't want to lose at basketball." Jeffrey didn't know how to value the sacrifice, which made things even more difficult for Yisrael. But he didn't change his mind. Better to be thought a coward by Jeffrey than to give up a *tefillah* in his father's merit. Tatty was undoubtedly sitting in the Heavenly Yeshivah and glowing with *nachas* from his courageous decision.

Despite this, all that evening and even when he got into bed that night after a long and fascinating conversation, he was still struggling mightily against his desire to give up the morning trip and stay to play ball. It wasn't until very late that night, or very early that morning, that he finally dropped off.

Jet lag, they called it. Yisrael discovered that it was no fun at all. When his alarm clock rang, it felt like only seconds since he'd fallen asleep. He looked at the clock in disbelief, and tried to think. Maybe the clock wasn't right, or perhaps it was set to Israeli time.

But Menachem, knocking on his door, made it clear that it was time to get up.

Yisrael's gritty eyes fought to stay open. When Menachem again offered the choice of staying and traveling later, it simply wasn't fair. How was he supposed to make a decision under these conditions? Yisrael didn't know where he got the strength to drag himself out of bed and climb into the waiting car. Small overnight bags with their Shabbos clothes were already inside. Yisrael was asleep again moments after getting into the limousine. He woke only when they stopped in front of a big shul and Menachem shook him.

"Wake up, Yisrael. We're here. Take only your tefillin; the driver will take the rest of our things. Come on, we'll arrange for you to be the *chazzan*."

Yisrael got out of the car, still half asleep. People glanced their way to see who had come to Shacharis in a limousine. Some of them recognized Menachem and came over to greet him with a hearty "*Shalom aleichem.*"

Yisrael found that things went far more smoothly when you had a skilled politician like Menachem at your side. Within minutes, he was put in charge of one of the *minyanim*. He struggled to lead the service in an American accent, but still pronounced the words of the *tefillah* in an Israeli accent so different from the others'.

The local Jewish congregation welcomed him warmly. Not only because of his companion, but also and mostly because a visitor from Eretz Yisrael was always received with love. How much more so when he was a young orphan… Yisrael very much enjoyed the Shabbos he spent in New Jersey, and was sorry when it was drawing to a close. He had needed that Shabbos sorely, to remind him that, apart from people who were absorbed only with themselves and their pleasures, America also boasted Torah-observant Jews who were doing their best to carry out their Creator's will, and not filling their time only with an insane race after material things.

It pained him that Shabbos went by so quickly. When Yisrael stepped up to be the *chazzan* for Maariv on Motza'ei Shabbos, he couldn't stop himself from feeling homesick. Shabbos in his parents' house… Well, actually, with his mother and sisters; Tatty was no longer there to make Kiddush and Havdalah. Now he was the one responsible for those things—at least, when he was home. When he wasn't, Mommy made Kiddush herself.

How had he done such a thing to her? To finally come home from yeshivah—and then run away to America? Poor Mommy and the girls, making another Shabbos on their own. Could that have been part of the reason he'd gone? To flee the suffocating sensation that overcame him when they sat down to a Shabbos *seudah* and Tatty's chair was empty? In truth, this Shabbos in New Jersey had been far more pleasant than another Shabbos at home. Another whole week when he didn't have to cope with his father's absence all over again.

They heard Havdalah in shul, and then Yisrael found himself left hanging as he waited for Menachem to finish chatting with his many acquaintances. Who knew how many important decisions were made in such conversations? One man needed help for his son who had gone off the *derech*, and asked Menachem to give him the name of a rabbi who was expert at dealing with such boys; another wanted to donate money to a certain yeshivah but had heard rumors of a falling-out among its senior staff and wanted an update on the situation. All sorts of important matters were discussed, while Yisrael stood by feeling abandoned and as if he didn't belong. He wasn't part of the world of Jewish activism, nor did he wish to be. More than once, the talk seemed to him to border on *lashon hara*. Or not even bordering, but the actual thing.

Finally, Menachem wound things up and parted from his friends. With a smile, he apologized to Yisrael and they headed for their hosts' home.

"Nice Shabbos, no?" Menachem asked.

"Very nice. Too bad it's over."

"Don't worry, things are going well. Your uncle has thawed a bit and it may be that I didn't bring you for nothing. You should know that there are a number of very important things that I'll have to deal with in the coming week. It would have been a lot easier if I hadn't brought you along, but I don't regret it. So far, you've been great!"

Yisrael blushed and hastened to change the subject. "What kind of things do you have to do this week?"

"Don't ask. It's going to be a crazy week. As I said on the way from the airport, I've been trying to arrange, by long distance, a very important meeting in Washington. We'll be returning to your uncle's house tomorrow morning; we still have a few loose ends to tie up. On Monday, we go to Washington, where we'll stay until we fly back home on Thursday.

"Now maybe it would be a good idea for me to tell you what's about to happen, so you won't be surprised. The Israeli prime minister comes to Washington on Tuesday. He's due to address the AIPRO convention on Wednesday, and then meet with the American president. If all goes as planned, the president himself will come to AIPRO, to deliver a speech on his policy regarding the State of Israel."

"I heard he's an anti-Semite. Is that true?"

Menachem smiled. "He's not a huge fan of Israel, that's true. But to say he's an anti-Semite is a bit exaggerated. Tell me—if you were the president of a nation like the United States, and one tiny country like Israel created more problems than Europe and Africa combined, wouldn't you want to get rid of her once and for all?

"Luckily for us, we have enormous political power here. AIPRO, the Israeli lobby, is the strongest and most influential in America. The Jewish vote has determined more than one election, and the president knows it. Therefore, he'll be forced to temper his personal opinions and support our basic demand: censuring Iran.

"I don't know if you've been following the news, but Israel's greatest existential threat today is a nuclear Iran. Our intelligence bureaus have discovered that Iran will have the nuclear bomb within a relatively short time. Israel can't allow that. What we're trying to do is make America feel that this is a red line from her point of view as well... But why am I going into such detail? All you have to know is that it'll be an interesting trip to Washington, and a chance to meet some world players."

Yisrael was silent. He had virtually no knowledge of politics, but even he knew how important such meetings were. The prime minister, the president of the United States, billionaires, and Congressmen—until today, these had been remote concepts for him. Now he was about to meet them all.

They reached their hosts' home and got ready for what remained of the evening. Shabbos ended so late that they would have to go to bed soon. They were due to leave for Jeffrey's mansion early the next afternoon. From then on, events would play out of their own accord.

But a phone call that Menachem received slightly changed the program. He asked the person at the other end to hold on, and turned to Yisrael.

"It's your uncle. He says that the game was postponed from Friday to tomorrow morning, and he wants to know if you'd like to participate. It makes no difference to me, of course, but he asked if you want to come."

Yisrael nodded quickly. He very much wanted to be there.

"Okay," Menachem said into the phone. "We'll come to you right after Shacharis. A little after 10, all right?"

He listened to the answer from the other end of the line, and then said good-bye.

"I don't know much about basketball," he told Yisrael when he'd hung up. "But from what I've heard, Jeffrey is a really good player. I would assume that his friends are good too. Remember that we have more important things to focus on than basketball. Even if they're better than we are at sports, that doesn't mean they're better people. Okay?"

Yisrael smiled to himself with ill-concealed pride. He wasn't afraid of anyone when it came to basketball, and certainly not Jeffrey.

A second later, he caught himself and regretted his pride. What Menachem had said was true. What was he so proud about, anyway? That he could play well? Let him overcome his *yetzer hara* once in a while—that was worth a whole lot more. *Then* he'd have something to be proud about.

These thoughts brought him back down to earth, but they did not entirely erase his excitement over the upcoming game. Tomorrow morning, he'd be playing one-on-one with his Uncle Jeffrey. He just *had* to win.

30

Y ISRAEL HAD GROWN USED TO THE LUXURY OF THE limousine that appeared whenever it was needed. The ride back to Brookville was much more pleasant than the outbound trip had been. This time, Yisrael had slept eight solid hours the night before, and after Shacharis and a hearty breakfast he was more than ready to face his uncle again.

Menachem spent the whole ride talking on the phone in a bewildering variety of languages, jotting down the occasional note to himself and barking orders at whoever was at the other end of the line. He had a great deal of work to do. He hadn't come here on vacation; he was charged with arranging a meeting with important consequences for the State of Israel. A meeting between the prime minister and the president of the United States.

There was a good reason the prime minister had chosen him to be his liaison in Washington. His well-known connections in Congress and other branches of government were valuable assets. These were connections he'd made through his friendship with the influential business tycoon Jeffrey Davis.

They arrived at the estate as planned, shortly after 10:30. This time the servant, whose name was Leonard, Yisrael had learned, was waiting for them at the door and welcomed them enthusiastically. "The office is at your disposal, Mr. Menachem," he said. "And I was told to show the basketball court to young Mr. Davis. Would you like to change in your room first? Mr. Davis told me to get clothes and sneakers for you. I hope you'll find something in your size. Call me when you're finished dressing, and I'll take you to the court, okay?"

Yisrael was amazed at how quickly they had arranged all of this. His amazement increased when he reached his room and saw boxes of new sneakers in sequential sizes. The servant had taken no chances; he'd bought an assortment of sizes to make sure that something would be suitable. Yisrael chose a pair in his size, 11½. They fit perfectly.

On the bed lay basketball uniforms belonging, apparently, to Jeffrey's team. Here too, Yisrael found one that fit him. Within a short time, he was ready to go.

The basketball court had been built specially for Jeffrey in a huge enclosure not far from the pool. As Yisrael followed Leonard, he tried to imagine how it must feel to be able to build yourself whatever your heart desired. A huge house, an indoor pool, an outdoor pool, a gym, and who knew what else. And all this for one person. You could have fit an entire neighborhood in this mansion with ease. And Jeffrey lived here all alone.

The familiar sounds of a dribbling basketball, running feet, and excited cries greeted Yisrael at the court's entrance. But nothing prepared him for the players racing over the court. Most of them were African-Americans, all of them were tall, and a few of them were giants. Jeffrey, holding the ball, stopped the game and welcomed his nephew. "Everyone, I want you to meet my nephew from Israel. He's come here to teach me how to play basketball."

Thunderous laughter echoed through the court. All the players approached Yisrael in a friendly fashion and greeted him with good humor. "Let's see if basketball runs in your family," one especially tall fellow quipped.

"Let me introduce you, Yisrael. This guy's name is Karim Abu

Rahim, the Nets' terrifying center—or former center, I should say. He's not as terrifying as he once was."

Yisrael smiled in confusion. In his opinion, the gigantic man would have been scary even if he were sitting in a wheelchair. Yisrael barely reached his chest.

"And this is Donald Sill," Jeffrey continued. "And Charles Bigge, and..." He continued introducing all the players, one by one, to Yisrael, who knew he wouldn't remember a single name. Apparently, all of Jeffrey's basketball buddies were professional players, either in the past or the present. This would definitely not be as easy as he'd thought.

Jeffrey divided up the teams again, and placed Yisrael in the opposing one. Yisrael had never worked so hard in a basketball game in his life. In fact, he'd never worked so hard, period. There was not as much as a second when he could rest or relax his concentration. The players all took the game very seriously, and they didn't stop for a minute. Defense, offense, and back again. Jeffrey showed himself a capable and talented player. Even more, he was a natural leader. There was no offense that didn't go through him, and he urged his teammates forward.

Yisrael did his best to play as well as possible. He had to show them what he was worth. This was the first time he'd set foot on a basketball court and realized that he was not the best player in the place. The athleticism, speed, and total coordination of the other players stunned him. He had to work very hard indeed not to lag behind.

"Listen, kid, you've got what it takes," Jeffrey praised Yisrael when the game ended with a close victory for his own team. "There's room for improvement, but you're a natural shooter. Don't you think so?" he asked Ron Hardaway.

Ron, a very fine shooter himself, agreed. "He still needs to learn a thing or two about teamwork, about how to elude a guard and things like that. But he knows how to shoot a hoop."

Yisrael was slightly insulted, but his uncle quickly placed a hand on his shoulder. "A compliment like that is worth millions, Yisrael. Ron is one of the best shooters in the history of the game. If he says you can shoot, that's a gigantic compliment."

"Come on, kid. Let's show them what you're made of," Ron suggested. The other players scattered to the sides to have a drink and towel away their perspiration. Personal towels and the room's air-conditioning system helped dispel some of the oppression of the New York summer heat. They sat down at the sidelines, laughing over every silly comment or joke. Ron stood underneath the hoop and passed the ball to Yisrael. "Throw!" he commanded.

Yisrael felt uncomfortable in front of all those curious eyes. His hands shook and he found it hard to focus. He threw the ball, which didn't even reach the rim—and landed right in Ron's hands.

"That's enough! Leave him alone!" Ron ordered the gleeful players. "Give him a chance. Anyone looking to make fun is invited to a personal contest with me."

"You don't get it, Ron!" Karim called, laughing. "He didn't even try to get a basket. He threw it right to you—alley-oop! That was a pass. You should've dunked the ball yourself!"

The other players held their middles as they dissolved in laughter. Yisrael's face burned. He was probably as red as a tomato. But why should he be surprised? It really had been a bad shot.

Ron stopped responding to the players' comments and turned to Yisrael. "Without thinking, I'll pass you the ball, and you throw it. Okay?"

Yisrael nodded, and immediately caught a fast throw from Ron. Without hesitating, he threw it and dropped the ball easily in the basket. The laughter quickly died down as Ron passed Yisrael ball after ball, sometimes to the right and sometimes to the left, and Yisrael swished it time after time. His misses were rare, and the laughter changed to shouts of admiration and encouragement from the discerning athletes.

"Hey, Jeffrey! Give me that kid and I'll make him a star!" someone yelled.

Ron came over to Yisrael and shook his hand warmly. "Like I said—you've got talent. Don't waste it. You play with some Israeli team or something? No? A pity. With a good coach and a little luck, you could be a big player."

"Save your breath, Ron," Jeffrey chuckled, as he also came over to shake his nephew's hand. "Yisrael's not planning to be a big athlete. He's studying to become a rabbi. Right, Yisrael?"

Yisrael didn't know what to say. He didn't know if he'd be a rabbi one day or not, but how to explain a yeshivah to these athletes? He chose not to contradict his uncle, merely saying, "I wish!"

"I have an idea for you, boy." Jeffrey silenced the others. "I'm prepared to take you under my wing. To pay for a personal trainer, your education, an apartment—in other words, everything you need—so that you can learn basketball. Afterward, I'll personally make sure you get a place in a professional league. You could make millions, and enjoy yourself on the way. Eh? What do you say?"

Deafening applause came from the sidelines, as the others expressed their enthusiasm for the idea. "Let me train him," said a player whose name Yisrael couldn't remember. "I'll turn him into a star!"

Yisrael hadn't expected this. There had been times when he'd dreamed of becoming a great basketball player, but never seriously. That is, not since he'd begun his stint in the Swiss yeshivah. But, right now, the yeshivah was so far away. And Rav Schwartz seemed far less persuasive. He could live the American dream here, surrounded by the kind of luxury that ordinary people never even imagined.

But what about Mommy? And the girls? And Tatty, *a"h*? How would they like it? And besides, was he really willing to give up a spiritual life for a bit of money? All right, a lot of money. But still, just money.

Jeffrey sensed his ambivalence, and grinned. "Okay, I know where you live. Get back to me when you're finished thinking." He turned around. "Do you guys see this? I offer him a once-in-a-lifetime deal, and he has to think about it!"

The other players laughed, and teased Yisrael. For his part, Yisrael enjoyed the attention. All these rich, famous men appreciated him. It was really flattering.

The laughter and good atmosphere lingered through the next game, in which Ron took care to set up special drills for Yisrael. Drills that gave him the second he needed to toss the ball in the hoop without letting his guard's long arm intercept the throw.

The games changed Jeffrey's attitude toward Yisrael. He found that he liked the boy, who often reminded him of himself. Menachem had been correct in saying that they were similar. Like him, Yisrael was stubborn and active—very different from his father, who'd been interested in nothing but his books. Yerachmiel had not possessed a drop of sports blood, and certainly not the slightest interest in business. His son was much more the thing.

Yisrael sensed this change in his uncle, but didn't know how to react to it. On the one hand, this was what he had wanted. On the other, why should he try to find favor in the eyes of the man who'd caused his father so much harm? He struggled with the conflicting feelings that roiled inside him.

He'd try to make order of his thoughts later. Right now, he was basking in the attention of the others.

A whole group of professional athletes who thought that he could have a future, if only he wanted it.

On Monday morning, Yisrael and Menachem rode the limousine to Shacharis. They would meet Jeffrey at the airport later in the day for the flight to Washington, D.C.

"We lost out on a helicopter ride," Menachem smiled. "Your uncle will be arriving at the airport later by helicopter. He hates long trips."

"Yes, but we get to daven with a *minyan*, something my uncle hasn't had the privilege of doing for years."

"Good point."

The time they spent in New Jersey was as pleasant as before. Several hours later, they parted from Menachem's relatives and rode to the airport. Yisrael was no newcomer to plane travel, but this was definitely the first time he'd be flying in a private plane.

"If you have to fly, this is the way to do it," Jeffrey declared, and leaned back in his seat.

The small Gulfstream was beautifully equipped. At the center of the aircraft was an area with a comfortable bed, if one were needed, and the seating section held six armchairs in pale gray leather.

Yisrael, used to the crowded conditions of commercial passenger planes, could certainly understand his uncle's declaration. Flying like this really was something else.

He decided to spend the flight time learning. One of the things he had promised the rosh yeshivah was a daily quota, decided ahead of time, of Gemara study that he must not skip, no matter what. These past few days he had neglected his obligations a bit, pulled away by his enthusiasm in the moment. The guilt he experienced had led him to decide to learn all through the flight, to make up for what he had missed.

He had chosen to take with him to America a copy of *Maseches Bava Metzia*, the tractate that his yeshivah would be learning in the coming *z'man* and the winter following it. Rav Schwartz had urged all the boys to try to learn as much material as possible in a superficial way—*bekiyus*—so that when the time came to look more deeply into the ideas they would have a broad sense of the material they had learned.

Menachem and Jeffrey sat together, talking. Yisrael sank into his studies, paying no attention to what they were saying. They, on the other hand, paused from time to time to look at the boy who refused to waste his time.

"*Nu*, what do you say about your nephew?" Menachem whispered.

"Listen, I have to admit that I'm glad you brought him. It's true that I had a big fight with his father. But seeing him like this reminds me what family means. There were moments in the middle of the night when I tried to remember what we even fought about. Believe it or not, I suddenly had a memory of a day in first grade, when some kid hit me. How I cried to my big brother and he forced the kid to apologize to me. I thought he was the greatest big brother in the world. How things have changed since then…"

Jeffrey fell silent for a moment, as the vivid memory from the past engulfed him. The gaze he fixed on Yisrael became blurred. Finally, he tore his eyes away and looked back at Menachem.

"Do you know, I cried when I heard he was dead. I'd always believed that we'd make up one day, that we'd put the past behind us and start fresh. And now, suddenly, that will never happen. He died without our working things out between us."

Menachem said nothing. He chose not to interrupt his friend. It was obvious that Jeffrey had been waiting for a long time to unburden himself of feelings he had carried around for many years. A great deal of time had passed since the quarrel that had ripped his family apart. Things probably looked very different today.

Jeffrey sat back and gazed at Yisrael again as he continued his train of thought. "How much he resembles him now. His father also used to wrinkle his brow like that when he learned. I always laughed at him, saying that he'd have a wrinkled forehead like our grandfather. That he'd be old by the time he was 20."

But Jeffrey did not allow himself to sink into his thoughts for too long. They had many other things to talk about. This week would be a decisive one for the State of Israel and its plan to attack Iran. Even if the attack brought about the desired result of destroying, or at least slowing, Iran's nuclear program, it was impossible to know what consequences it might bring in its wake. Anyone who saw the rapid changes that had been taking place in the Middle East in recent years knew that nothing was certain. It was impossible to predict the future in any real way. Saying for certain what the outcome would be was arrogant, if not downright stupid.

The United States' consent to such an attack was by no means guaranteed. The president was not war hungry. More and more, he was trumpeting a reduction of American involvement in world affairs. But Israel was not asking for his help in the attack; rather, it wanted assistance with the political fallout afterward. While the majority of Arab states would not be sorry to see the Iranians get a smack on the head—Iran harmed and threatened them too, in a variety of ways—they certainly didn't love the Israelis overmuch. The recriminations in the United Nations would be immediate, and Israel would need the backing of the United States in the Security Council. An Israeli attack unauthorized by the American president was too great a gamble, a gamble the prime minister was not prepared to take.

But the massive informational campaign in Congress and the powerful lobbying that would reach its climax this week were intended to elicit the president's silent consent to this course of action. Even his silence would be enough to give the prime minister the green light he needed.

Of course, Israel would have to pay something for that green light. That was the way politics worked. If you got something from the president of the United States, you owed him one. The prime minister would doubtless have to enter into intensive negotiations with the Palestinians, negotiations that his hawkish coalition would not like. But if an attack on Iran achieved its goal, the prime minister's enhanced political standing would bring him the consensus he needed. Public opinion would be on his side.

This very afternoon, a meeting had been scheduled between the two heads of state in the White House. The prime minister and the president would speak, in general terms, about what would be concluded in detail between their respective staffs later. The upcoming address to AIPRO would be critical. It would let all interested parties know whether or not the president had agreed to the Israeli position. In the next two days, the pressure would reach its peak. There would be two days of intensive politicking that, with Hashem's help, would bring about the desired results.

The Israeli delegation's first meeting was due to take place in a few hours' time, in Washington's Horizon Hotel. This upscale hotel—part of Jeffrey Davis' chain, of course—would be hosting the prime minister and his entourage and would serve as the venue for the vital conferences held in the upcoming days. Congressmen and other influential politicians would fill the five-star hotel. There they would be treated to an Israeli information campaign aimed at putting pressure on the White House.

Menachem, Jeffrey, and their Russian friend, Mikhail, had collaborated to plan this operation. Members of the Israeli delegation would work through them to avoid errors: Jeffrey, the wealthy owner who'd graciously host them all; Menachem, the politician who knew the Israeli side best and had the prime minister's trust; and Mikhail, the coordinating brain behind it all.

While most of their efforts had been directed at America, Mikhail had not forgotten that these days it was a good idea to operate on more than one front. It was impossible to move the Arab nations over to Israel's side, but many European nations—some of them also members of the Security Council—could be pressured.

Mikhail had sole responsibility for explaining things on the Russian front, though lately he'd sensed that his influence in the Kremlin was weakening. For the Europeans, he'd recruited all the political stars that supported Israel. After the attack, it would be a great deal more difficult to convince anyone in Europe of the mission's urgency.

The platform was united. A nuclear Iran was not just Israel's problem, but a worldwide problem. While Israel would be the primary victim of such an Iran, the rest of the free world would be under constant threat as well. If no one else was prepared to do the dirty work and demolish the Iranian reactors, Israel would do it, not only for her own security, but for the safety of every democratic nation, wherever it might be.

ISEMBARKING IN WASHINGTON WENT QUICKLY. AN expensive black car was waiting for them on the tarmac. They got off the plane and were on their way without delay. The day promised to be very busy. The game was beginning.

Although Yisrael had no part to play in the proceedings, he could sense the tension that gripped his two companions from the moment they landed in Washington.

"You're about to become part of a political game played out in the highest circles," Menachem said, thumping him on the back. "You have no idea how many journalists would do anything to be in your shoes right now. But let me make myself very clear: What you're going to see and hear is *not* for public knowledge. I'm taking you with me because I trust you. Don't let me down."

Yisrael nodded, not bothering to comment that politics didn't interest him at all. Let them do what they wanted; let them lie to each other's faces. He wasn't planning to join the fun.

Their first stop was a luxury residence surrounded by a spacious garden. Yisrael noticed cameras scanning the entrance and the tall stone fence that circled the property. Whoever lived here was very keen to protect his privacy. A huge and very pale guard at the door only confirmed his theory. The man's hair was completely white, despite the fact that he appeared to be only in his 30's.

The guard recognized them and was expecting them. Nevertheless, he did not let them in before checking with the master of the house.

"The visitors are here," he reported into a handheld radio, in a heavily Russian-accented English.

He listened to the response, and only then opened the door, ushering them in with a deferential gesture.

As they were entering, their host came to greet them. Yisrael was surprised to see a yarmulke on his head. Only then did he notice that there was also a mezuzah affixed to the doorpost.

"Hello, my friends. How are you?" He embraced and kissed Menachem and Jeffrey, and then saw Yisrael. "Menachem, have you brought your son with you? Is this the Yossi you've told me about?"

Menachem chuckled. "No, no. This is Jeffrey's nephew, who also happens to be a friend of my son's."

"Jeffrey's nephew? Jeffrey, I never knew you *had* a nephew. Wait a minute—why are we standing here in the doorway? Where is my *hachnassas orchim*? Come in! By the way, do you have a name, Jeffrey's nephew?"

"Yisrael." He shook the man's hand. There was something different about this man. His English was perfect, but there was a lingering hint of a Russian accent. And the way he'd pronounced the words *hachnassas orchim* had been a little strange, as if he didn't know how to say it with ease. That must be it. He must be a *baal teshuvah*, how special.

They entered a large living area, and their host hastened to serve them cold drinks. Yisrael accepted his with thanks, suddenly realizing how thirsty he was.

"I understand that the prime minister and the president are meeting right now?" their host asked Menachem.

"Yes. We're supposed to meet with him at the hotel after the meeting. I hope things can be worked out from the American's aspect. The chief of staff gave me a very hard time. It seems to me the president isn't looking forward to this week…"

Yisrael lost interest. He studied the room. It was large and comfortable, but it didn't look homey. It was too cold, more like a room in a museum. Not a place that gave you a sense of sheltering a family. On the walls were paintings by several artists. Yisrael was surprised to see, on the far wall, pictures from the Holocaust. He moved closer and gazed at a troubling photograph of four frightened children, peeking out of a destroyed building at a group of Nazi soldiers who were smiling in triumph.

His host noted his interest and hurried to his side. "Do you see the second boy from the left? He's the only one of the four who survived. He lives in Israel now, and he has about thirty grandchildren. I love this picture. It's a picture that offers hope."

"This is not the right time to start giving lectures, Mikhail," Jeffrey scolded. "We have things to wind up here. Let him look around on his own. We'll have to be moving on soon."

"All right, all right," sighed the man whose name Yisrael finally knew to be Mikhail. "Just one second."

He drew Yisrael to the opposite wall. "This wall is devoted to the Spanish Inquisition, and that other one displays artistic works from various periods in which the Jewish nation suffered. You can look at them and learn while we talk in my office. Just please don't touch anything, okay? These items are priceless. I've worked very hard on this collection."

Yisrael nodded. At least he'd have something to do while the men were talking. The three of them entered the adjoining room and shut the door behind them. Apparently there were things that he wasn't meant to hear. State secrets.

He wondered who that man was. On the one hand, he was a religious Jew, and on the other, he was clearly a top-level politician. If he weren't so important they would not have come to him directly from the airport.

He made a mental note to ask Menachem about the man when he returned. In the meantime, the paintings and photographs were really interesting. For a moment, he felt as if he were in Yad Vashem or some other museum of Jewish history. His host apparently had a deep interest in Jewish history.

He studied a huge and harrowing painting of people being burned. He pulled the name of the event from his memory: *auto-da-fé*—public burnings during the Spanish Inquisition. People who were deemed heretics by the Christian authorities were taken out to be burned in the central squares, as a deterrent to others.

The focal point of the painting was a man with a long, white beard in the center of a raised platform. Nearby stood three hooded figures in white robes, with holes to enable them to see. One of them was reading aloud from a long scroll—apparently, the bearded man's death sentence.

There was no question that the convicted man was a rabbi. While he wore no head covering, his wise eyes and long beard made this obvious. He stood erect, looking directly ahead as though he did not fear his approaching death. In the background burned a mighty fire, into which the man was due to be cast when the executioner finished reading. Yisrael shivered. What a horrifying thought. He wondered who the Jew was, and what had happened to him in the end. Had he really been killed?

As he continued gazing at the painting, he suddenly noticed a detail that had escaped him before: the crowd. All around the raised platform on which the Jew stood, a throng of bloodthirsty spectators watched. He could see the gleam of hatred in their eyes, and their anticipation at the prospect of seeing the accused man burnt at the stake. Grown-ups and children alike waved their fists at the Jewish martyr. Their loathing was so blatant, the murder in their eyes so powerful, that Yisrael felt a tremor of real fear. The painter had done a masterful job of portraying the harsh scene.

He moved on to the next painting—Cossacks, apparently. What wicked smiles, as though the suffering they were causing gave them tremendous pleasure. The same was true of the painting that came after that. Aha! That was what this collection was meant to portray. Each painting or photograph hanging on the wall showed the gentile happy to see the Jew suffering. Painting after painting. Picture after picture. They all shared a common denominator. He wondered why Mikhail had chosen to present this aspect over and over. The man was a real mystery. He must ask Menachem or Jeffrey about it.

The three were still in the adjoining room, talking animatedly. He could hear their excited voices through the door: "...a nuclear bomb... Iran... America... Israel." They really must be discussing important things. Like every Israeli, Yisrael was aware that the most serious threat against his country came from Iran. Now it looked as if the men in the next room might be deciding the fate of those Iranian reactors.

The time passed quickly as he made another round of the pictures. He had just begun to feel edgy when the men finally emerged from the room, looking exhausted.

"What's happening, Yisrael?" Jeffrey asked. "Hope you weren't too bored."

"Actually, I wasn't. I was interested in seeing all these pictures on the walls. Scary, but fascinating."

"Did you notice what you were seeing in all those pictures?" Mikhail challenged him with a superior smile.

"Mmm... I think so. You see the gentiles rejoicing over the Jews' suffering."

"Excellent!" Mikhail was impressed. "Indeed, one of the most striking things is how a human being can be so happy over the suffering of another creature—simply because he is a Jew. Good for you for noticing it. You have a sharp eye."

Menachem and Jeffrey enjoyed the praise being heaped on their young companion. Menachem was about to say something when Mikhail suddenly grew rigid.

"Hey! Did you go into my office?"

Yisrael was surprised. "What do you mean? Which office? I was here the whole time."

Mikhail strode quickly over to a nearby door that stood half-open. "This door was closed. Did you open it?"

"No!" Yisrael was confused. He hadn't gone anywhere near that door.

Mikhail pushed the door open and yelled, "The computer is on! Why did you turn on the computer?"

He whirled back around to face Yisrael, and grabbed his shirt. "What did you do with my computer? What were you looking for? Who are you?"

Jeffrey and Menachem stood by, stunned. What was going on here? Had Yisrael stolen something?

"The door was closed! My computer was turned off! This boy is a spy!" Red-faced, Mikhail tightened his grip on Yisrael's arm.

Yisrael didn't know what to say. What spy? What was going on?

"Are you sure the door was closed?" Jeffrey asked. "I thought so, too, but I'm not sure... Though I did wonder why we didn't go sit in your office, and went to the other room instead... Yisrael? What were you looking for in there?"

"I wasn't looking for anything! I didn't go near that room!"

Menachem tried to calm things down. "Mikhail, leave the boy alone. I know him, and he's no spy. This is some sort of mistake. Let go of him and let's try to figure out what happened."

Mikhail released Yisrael, though his expression was still enraged. Yisrael was truly frightened. There was something in Mikhail's face that held a real threat. He seemed to be laboring under enormous stress.

"Is anything missing?" Menachem asked Mikhail.

"I don't see anything. But that's not the issue. My computer holds secret and private things. Things that could cause problems for many politicians. State and military secrets."

"Yisrael. Did you touch the computer?"

"I didn't even go near it!"

The tension in the room was palpable. Jeffrey didn't know what to think. He really didn't know Yisrael at all. Was it possible? Could he be someone other than he claimed to be? Was he a spy?

Menachem tried to figure a way out of this situation. He believed in Yisrael's innocence. It was not possible that the boy was a thief. He had learned in yeshivah with Yossi and they'd had that whole episode over a theft... And apart from that, Menachem had checked out the boy's story, and it was true. His father had died, he attended a yeshivah in Switzerland, and he had come here to America only because he, Menachem, had pressured him to join him. There had to be an explanation for the open door.

"Let's ask the guard if he saw anything." The suggestion came from Jeffrey.

Mikhail went rapidly to the door, visibly shaken. He must have some very important material on that computer. He shouted in Russian to the giant seated outside. Yisrael didn't understand the gist of it, but he could make a stab at guessing what it was. The guard's answer was short and decisive: "*Nyet!*"

That was something that even Yisrael understood.

He couldn't believe this was happening to him again. Once again, he was suspected of doing something that he didn't do. Only compared to this incident, the episode with Yossi seemed like child's play. They weren't talking about 100 shekels here, but about classified political secrets. Information that could lead to turmoil.

"I still believe the boy," Menachem declared. Yisrael felt tears of relief fill his eyes. "I guarantee his innocence."

"I believe him, too, Mikhail," Jeffrey said. "You must have forgotten that the computer was on, and also that the door was ajar. Or else the door opened from the breeze or something. But I believe that it wasn't Yisrael who did it. From the little I've seen of him, he's a trustworthy boy."

Mikhail studied them. He returned to the computer, inspected the door, and reached a conclusion.

"Okay. Fine. If you believe him, then so do I. People sometimes forget things like that. Forgive me, Yisrael, for suspecting you. It's just that... I already told my friends that there's been someone following me lately. Apparently, someone in Russia doesn't like me very much. When dealing with Russians, one can't be careful enough. It was impossible for me not to be suspicious in such a situation. I'm sorry I shouted at you. Let's forget this incident and part as friends, okay?"

Yisrael was too bewildered to answer. One minute he was a spy; the next minute, nothing had happened. His heart was still beating too fast, though it was gradually slowing. The extreme changes in Mikhail's behavior made him suspicious, but when he walked them to their car amid profuse apologies, he decided to let it go. "Don't judge a person until you are in his place," our Sages advised. The man must be under excruciating pressure if he'd exploded like that. Later, in the car, he'd ask Menachem what the story was.

He did not have to wait long. The moment the car moved away, Menachem began to explain. "I'm sorry about what happened in there, Yisrael. But try to understand him. He claims that someone in Russia is trying to get him. To slander him, or worse. To harm him."

"But why would anyone want to do that? Who is he, anyway? And why would people want to hurt him?"

"The man you just met is Mikhail Potgorsky, the founder and chairman of the League for War on Anti-Semitism. He is a good Jew who was born a gentile in Russia, learned about the Jews, and researched the hatred against them. He reached the conclusion that Jews are hated because of their moral superiority over the gentiles, and it was this conclusion that led him to convert. He realized that Judaism is truth, so he decided to join us. There aren't many in our time who would make such great sacrifices for the truth. He's a special person who has helped and is helping many people in our nation and who is paying a heavy personal price for it.

"Until a few years ago, he was the closest confidant of the current president of Russia. That means that he could have been one of the most powerful men in Russia. But he ran into trouble with the president because of his opinion that Russia mustn't aid the Arabs.

"Also, taking Israel's side like that earned him a serious enemy. The rival's name is Vladimir Solosenko. He's Russia's prime minister, and an avowed Jew hater. If the decision were up to him, Mikhail would have been sent to Siberia long ago. Right now, Mikhail's status in Russia is unclear—somewhere between an asset and a liability. If they end up deciding that he's a liability, they'll want to get rid of him."

Now Yisrael understood everything. The poor guy. The stress he'd read in Mikhail's eyes had been clear. How was it possible to live like that when any minute could bring someone who wanted to kill you?

Menachem continued. "That was also what finally pushed him to convert to Judaism. He decided that he wanted to live and die like a Jew. He claims that if he really wants to help the Jewish nation, he must be an inseparable part of it. He is a man worthy of respect and admiration. Only a few people know how much he's contributed to the Jewish people."

"So that's the reason for all those pictures," Yisrael suddenly realized. "He's researching anti-Semitism. That explains everything. But I still don't understand what he said about people following him. Who's following him, and why? Have the Russians decided to kill him?"

"I don't know. Russia is a real mystery to anyone looking in from the outside. Matters are dealt with differently there than in Israel or America. Don't forget that they lived for many years under a communist regime whose influence has not yet been entirely eradicated. Someone over there doesn't like his sacrifice for Israel and is trying to rein him in. You have to understand that his actions run counter to traditional Russian ideology. The Russians are the Arab states' greatest friends and supporters. It's not because they love the Arabs but they wish to exert influence, equal to America. At the end of the day, everything boils down to self-interest."

The car swung onto the highway, moving in the direction of the hotel. Had its passengers looked behind them, they would have seen four black Jeeps with no official markings moving quickly into the street they had just left.

32

BARRY RADCLIFFE WAS PRESIDENT WALTERS' CHIEF OF staff. He had taken over at the White House when his predecessor left after suffering a massive heart attack. After three months on the job, Barry wondered why it was that *he* had not yet had a heart attack. It was a demanding and responsible position that came along with constant tension. The White House chief of staff was not only a secretary who organized the president's appointments. He did that too, but he also had to coordinate them all; know what each visitor needed, who he was, and what he wanted from the president; and then brief the chief executive before their arrival. He had to remember thousands of names and know the political views of each, whether the visitor was American or foreign.

The White House staff included spokespersons, secretaries, chefs, and maintenance workers, and someone had to be in charge of the whole kit and caboodle of them. That someone was Barry Radcliffe.

He approached the president, who was sitting with Matthew Klinger in a corner of the room. The bunker was extremely crowded.

There had been talk for years of expanding and renovating it but nothing had been done. The bunker's quasi-secret status had forestalled making upgrades.

"Excuse me, sir," Barry began. "Two things. First of all, the Israelis are angry and want to know why you didn't show up at the joint press conference. Second, I received a call from the *Washington Post*. They want to know the reason for raising our alert status. They're asking if this is linked to the Israelis and the meeting. What do I tell them?"

"Nothing yet. Play for time. Tell them you'll get back to them within the hour."

"And the Israelis?"

"Hm… I think it would be a good idea to give them something. Tell them there's been an unspecific warning. A threat that demands my attention. In my opinion, it would be preferable for the prime minister to fly home today. All we need is for him to be injured in a nuclear explosion."

"Do I tell them the nature of the threat?"

"Absolutely not. That would only play out to their benefit. I don't want any nonsense from them in the coming days. Don't forget that we ourselves have no concrete knowledge of what we're dealing with."

"Okay. I just wanted you to know that 80 percent of domestic flights have been canceled because of the threat. The air force has closed tactical areas to commercial flights, and our craft are flying over sensitive locations. The public has begun to notice that something's happening. We won't be able to hide this for long. We have to think about what to tell them before panic sets in."

"That's what I have you for, Barry. Think of something. I hope to have more information shortly."

"Yes, sir."

Barry returned to his phone to make the necessary calls. The president looked at his domestic intelligence chief. "I can't believe this has happened on my watch. On your watch! They're going to slaughter us over this."

"Yes, sir. But this is not the time to think about that. All of our resources are working on this matter, and I'm sure we'll have some answers in the coming minutes. Meanwhile, we're operating according to protocol. We're acting in close cooperation with all the intelligence agencies, the military heads are ready for any reaction, and the FBI is reviewing all of Mikhail Potgorsky's conversations and memos. They've confiscated the computer from his home and our experts are cracking it open right now. If he's the man behind the bomb, we'll know it soon."

"How is it possible? The man is so entrenched here. And without the backing of the Russian government? Am I the only one who thinks that something smells here?"

"We're looking into all possibilities, sir. All of them."

⁕⁕⁕

Horizon Hotel, Washington, D.C.

The ornate convention hall on the hotel's main floor could have been mistaken for an Israeli consulate. Israeli flags hung from the ceiling, side by side with the Stars and Stripes; tables laden with material in Hebrew and English had been set up near the entrance; and a large number of employees of the Israeli Foreign Ministry were crowded around the computers and were in charge of coordinating the event.

An update on the aftermath of the prime minister's meeting with the president caused a flurry of activity around the room. Contrary to the prearranged plan, the U.S. president had opted not to deliver a joint statement together with the prime minister. He had disappeared before the press conference began. Staff members had tried to elicit any information they could about the president's intentions with regard to Iran—in vain. Israeli officials had pulled all the strings they could think of and taken advantage of all their connections within the U.S. government, but all they'd received in return was a vague statement to the effect that the president was apparently not convinced that the time had come to attack.

Foreign Ministry workers began presenting facts about Iran's current air-defense system. The moment the Russian network became operational, the chances of a successful attack plummeted and the danger to Israeli pilots increased. Israel's argument against the proposed delay was this: If we wait any longer, we may lose our chance to succeed.

The Israeli prime minister's convoy was making its way back to the hotel. The prime minister was angry at the lackluster president. He felt that as a former lieutenant in the U.S. Army, Bob Walters should know that one mustn't miss out on an opportunity to carry out a mission or postpone it to some indeterminate time in the future. Instead of thanking him for not requesting practical assistance in attacking Iran—which would have posed no small headache for America—the president had put him off with some lame remarks about advancing negotiations with the Palestinians.

What did he want? Did he expect the prime minister to talk to the Palestinians and tell them to return to the negotiating table? He'd already offered everything he could, and the president knew it. His personal conclusion was that this preparatory trip had been a failure. He was annoyed with Menachem Goldfarb, who had said it would be all right. Nothing was all right. All the newspapers would discuss the meeting tomorrow and point out the fact that the president had refused to appear before the media with him.

The minute he left the White House, he picked up a phone to berate Menachem. Such poor preparatory work did not suit such a seasoned politician. Menachem tried to soothe him, promising explanations when they met at the hotel. *He'd better have some good ones,* the prime minister thought. Even a good explanation wouldn't satisfy him. The latest polls showed a significant drop among his supporters in Israel. Were an election to be held today, it was not at all certain that he would win. His options for rising in the polls again were down to two: either a successful round of negotiations with the Palestinians—who had no interest in that—or a successful attack on Iran, something that ought to be done without any reference to politics or elections.

The convoy weaved its way through Washington's congested streets. The passersby were used to sights like this. The American power center was a focal point for world leaders. While some were aware that the Israeli prime minister was in the country, there were so many more important things to hold their attention. Political matters, and especially foreign affairs, were not especially interesting to the average citizen. They were much more interested in the economic reforms that the president had promised, the state of the financial markets, and the weekly employment statistics. It was known that an incumbent president would never lose an election if the economic situation was rosy.

Five minutes later they reached the luxurious hotel. The prime minister went up to his room with orders that he not be disturbed until Menachem Goldfarb and Jeffrey Davis arrived. The few Israeli journalists who had flown over with them were gently shaken off. He had no answers for them.

"Mr. Prime Minister," shouted a reporter from a leading Israeli media outlet a moment before the elevator doors slid shut, "is it true that the president raised his voice in the course of your meeting?"

The prime minister turned—just in time to see the cameras pointed at him as he stood in the elevator. Not a muscle in his face moved. Not until the doors closed and the elevator began its ascent did he permit himself to expel his breath in anger. It was starting. At this very hour, Israel would be hearing reports about another sharp interchange with the president of the United States. As if he didn't already have enough troubles with the members of his coalition.

The three bodyguards crowded into the elevator with him were professionals. They did not speak, and they certainly did not ask any questions. Sometimes he would have preferred if they'd say something. Some encouragement would have been nice. Yes, even the prime minister needed a good word now and then—perhaps even more than other people did.

As the elevator doors slid open, the bodyguards carefully scanned the corridor, one of them holding the door in place while the others stepped outside. Only when they had ascertained that the security detail were the only ones waiting for the prime minister did the entourage continue on its way.

"Sir, Menachem Goldfarb has arrived at the hotel," said Yigal, the tallest of the three. "Shall I send him up?"

The prime minister sighed. He would have preferred to rest a little before the meeting. But this couldn't wait. They must do some damage control as soon as possible.

"Mr. Prime Minister, they would not make up such a thing."

Menachem was extremely insistent. The prime minister must leave Washington this very night. The news that had reached him from the White House pointed to a real threat of some kind in the area. A threat that worried the United States greatly.

"So you claim the president skipped the press conference because of an immediate threat?"

"That's what I was told, sir. And it's hard for me to believe that Barry was lying. Besides, I made a few calls and it seems that something big *is* happening. The alert level is at its maximum, and many commercial flights have been canceled. It won't be long before it'll be in the news. Meanwhile, I think we should listen to the U.S. administration's request and depart as soon as possible."

"How soon can we lift off?"

"The airplane crew is standing by. We can be in the air in half an hour."

"And you have no idea of the nature of the threat? Al-Qaeda? Planes, like last time?"

"I have no idea. But from the inquiries I've made, it seems that the American leadership is in a bunker beneath the White House. That means that the threat is very real, not something they fabricated."

"What time is it in Israel?"

Menachem looked at his watch. It was 7:30, local time. He added 7 hours. "It's 2:30 in the morning, sir. We'll arrive in the afternoon."

"So the newspapers have lost out." The prime minister grinned. "Another blow to the print media..." He heaved a sigh. "They'll say I fled like a coward, that the president threw me out and I ran away with my tail between my legs."

"We'll deal with them, sir. Right now, we have to move. The Americans are clearing an express lane for us to the airport."

"All we need is for this to turn out to be just a drill. I will personally strangle you if that happens, Menachem. It'll destroy my career in a minute."

Menachem sighed. The strangest thing about politics was the way it changed the priorities of even the most talented and idealistic leader. If, until then, a political leader thinks only about the good of the country and the public, the moment he is elected, the first thing that concerns him is his position. Will his actions help or hurt his chances to continue leading?

There was no question about it—the prime minister had to get out of here at once. There was some sort of threat. True, it would not be easy to explain all of this back home, but the meeting with the president had already taken place. What was left? The speech to AIPRO? That could wait for another time. Either way, most of the work would be done by the staff, not the prime minister. He had finished his job here.

As for himself, Menachem knew that he would stay on to see how to continue from here. It seemed the nation's leaders were busy with other things at the moment; nevertheless, he couldn't let slide the small accomplishments they had achieved so far. The impressive coalition in Congress that supported a military operation against Iran was worth a fortune. It was the result of an enormous amount of legwork that included every faction of the government. That mustn't be lost, even at the cost of exposure to some kind of danger.

On the other hand, he had a boy in his care. Yisrael went everywhere with him. How could he endanger him?

But Menachem was not one who frightened easily. Dispassionately, he analyzed the situation. He was not an important target. He was neither a cabinet minister nor a military officer. No terror organization would have any particular interest in harming him. He'd just have to take precautions and not go into crowded public areas or tall towers, places that stood the greatest risk for terror attacks. The chances of his getting hurt here were no greater than they were in Jerusalem.

The boy would remain with him. He wasn't sending him home on his own. There were still two and a half days before their flight, and nothing was going to happen. The boy would be a little bored by the long meetings and the endless phone calls, but there was no choice. That was life.

Tuesday morning

It was a long, fatiguing night for those in the presidential bunker. Most of them remained awake and directed their waning energy where needed. The president was finally prevailed upon to join his family in the small room in a corner of the bunker.

"We're going to need you fully alert during the day. If there is any progress overnight, we won't hesitate to wake you," the chief of staff urged the president. He himself was one of those lucky individuals who could function on very little sleep.

Morning dawned without any real change. Barry Radcliffe was updating the president when the FBI director hurried over to them.

"We've got something. The information coming from Mikhail Potgorsky's computer is starting to stream in. The agents who arrested him report that the data on the computer is protected by very advanced technology. They were forced to take the computer to our labs, where FBI experts have been working on them. In about two minutes, we'll have some interesting reading material."

"Good! What happened to the Russians? What do they say?"

"The CIA is in continuous contact with them. They're on their way back to Russia and have already begun the interrogation. We hope to hear from them in the next few minutes too."

"Any news from the borders?"

"No. Apart from a lot of questions and complaints about delays, we have nothing. But they're still on full alert. Every cargo hold and container is being checked. It involves a great deal of slow, hard work, but it's all under control."

The CIA operative approached at a run. "Sir! The Russians are transmitting an update."

The president straightened and quickly returned to the big table. Silence fell over the assembled group. Phones were put down as they clustered around the table to hear the news. The president saw the exhaustion in their eyes, and felt ashamed of his own fresh face.

"The Russians claim that Mikhail broke quickly. He said that he did provide the Iranians with an unregistered suitcase bomb, of the kind we spoke about earlier. Though at first he refused to say why he had done it, after some additional persuasion he said that the Iranians decided on their own to send the bomb to America, in spite of his personal wishes to the contrary."

"And we're supposed to believe that? That he gave it to them just because he felt like it, without knowing that it would be used against us?"

"At the moment, that's not the important thing for us. We can investigate his motives later. He claims that he doesn't know where the bomb was sent, but he guesses Washington, D.C."

"What is that guess based on? After all, he claims the bomb was sent against his will."

"I have no answer for that yet. But he maintains that the bomb will apparently be smuggled into this country across the border with Mexico."

The president and the others digested this news. There was a nuclear bomb. The threat was real. Now the only question was: could they stop it in time?

"How much do they believe him?"

The assistant director of the CIA thought for a moment before he answered. "They are fairly certain of the information's accuracy. For obvious reasons, they did not share with us the means they used to obtain that information, but the Russian agents are convinced he's telling the truth."

"Tell them that I want to know why he gave Iran the bomb. Who is he working for?"

"Uh, right now he's unconscious… When I asked, they said the minute he revives they'll resume the interrogation. They don't want to continue until they land in Russia and have medical assistance on hand should it be needed. Simply put, they don't want to kill him and lose the only lead we have right now."

Bob Walters stopped asking questions. He knew all about inter-rogation and torture. Many American soldiers who had ended up in Vietnamese prisons had undergone that horrific experience. The strongest man could crumble under the hand of an expert torturer. After several hours of torture, he'd beg them to kill him and release him from his suffering. If Mikhail had any secret information, the Russians would get it from him. Their expertise in this field had earned them a worldwide reputation.

Indeed, they'd acted cleverly. First, they had extracted the most critical information from him: there was a bomb, and it was on its way to Washington. The rest of the questions, about why and wherefore, could wait a bit. He almost felt sorry for the diplomat who had fallen into their hands. They'd met several times in the past, and the man had made a good impression on him.

Despite this, the president did not object to the questioning. There was an immediate threat posed to the United States. A threat capable of exacting thousands of victims. Sometimes one had to do everything possible to get the necessary information.

"What if it's a trick? What if he's trying to distract us and make us look in the wrong direction? Maybe the bomb will come by sea."

"That's a possibility too. But we can't ignore the information. Our state of readiness remains on high alert on all the borders, with a special emphasis on Mexico. The authorities there received our request and all available personnel have been sent to the border. If the bomb's there, we'll find it."

"What about satellite cover?"

"It's all under control, sir."

"It had better be. Meanwhile, alert the response teams to a pos-sible nuclear incident in Washington. Leave a minimal presence scattered throughout the other states. I want an enhanced force in New York, and the rest in Washington. If the bomb does go off, I want to be ready. We'll treat Washington as the first option, New York second, and pray that it doesn't happen in another state. If the bomb does end up somewhere else, I want us to be ready to send help there with all possible speed. Is that understood?"

"Yes, sir, Mr. President."

33

Tucson, Arizona

THE LIFE OF BUDDY JONES JR. WAS SUPPOSED TO BE DIFFER-
ent. He was born in Greasewood, Arizona. Greasewood was
a small town, population six hundred, and hard to find on a map.
His father, Buddy Jones, was killed in a barroom brawl one night.
His mother, a widow overnight, took out all of her frustrations on
her son.

By all indications, Buddy Jones Jr. should have been a classic
small-town loser, like so many of his undereducated friends who
worked at minimum-wage jobs and could barely make ends meet.
But he was made of sterner stuff. He completed high school with
reasonable grades and excelled in sports in general, and baseball
in particular. To his dismay, a neglected injury prevented him from
advancing in the field or winning any sort of sports scholarship to
a prestigious college. But that wasn't his big dream anyway. The
dream of his life was to serve in the Marines.

With his strength and abilities, he had no problem being accepted.
He was a natural soldier, obedient but stubborn, committed to

carrying out his missions. His chaotic childhood in miserable trailer parks had trained him to stand up to the most difficult conditions. He refused to be afraid of anyone, man or beast. His stint in the Marines was exceptionally successful, and when it was over, Buddy returned to his hometown, determined to get ahead in life.

As a child, he had enjoyed trapping snakes that slithered out of the nearby desert and into the trailer park. He was expert at catching them with his bare hands. Apart from a small bite he had suffered as a boy, no snake had ever gotten the best of him. It was natural, therefore, that he'd decide to try his luck as a snake trapper.

He was good at what he did, but quickly realized that this was no way to support a family. In the intervening years he had married and had become the father of three small children who viewed him as their hero and problem solver. He'd made up his mind that they would have a better childhood than he had had. But he couldn't do that with the small income he earned in his chosen profession.

Buddy Jones Jr. did not give up. Resolved to be better than his own drunken father had been, he joined the U.S. Border Patrol. Though the work was more demanding in terms of the hours he had to put in, at least it guaranteed a steady paycheck to feed his growing family.

Besides, Buddy Jr. was not looking for an easy life. He took his work seriously, and would spend long hours tracking and patrolling the lengthy border zone in Arizona. He wasn't like many of his colleagues, who did their jobs only because they had no choice. He showed up at the head office bright and early each morning, and rode out to inspect the fences even on the hottest summer days.

The unimaginable number of immigrants trying to sneak into the United States in the hope of a better life provided endless work for the members of the Border Patrol. Inspection tours near the borders sometimes brought a shower of stones hailing down upon them from the Mexican side. Drug dealers intent on smuggling in their goods posed a not-inconsiderable threat. Many of them were armed, and arrest attempts often degenerated into cruel gunfights.

The main problem in Buddy Jr.'s opinion was their inability to deter the illegal immigrants. He and his colleagues would catch them trying to cross the border, stop them, and send them back to Mexico. Most of those who were caught did not give up, but tried their luck again. He remembered in particular one Mexican youth whom he had caught three separate times in a single day.

The broad spectrum of people who wished to enter the United States was staggering. Most were their Mexican neighbors, but there were also Afghans, Syrians, and many South American citizens who tried their luck at getting through the diffuse border. Professional smugglers charged between 1,500 and $2,000 to help people across. Many people were glad to pay the price, in the hopes of finding their fortune in prosperous America.

The long fences, erected primarily in settled areas, slowed but did not halt the flow of illegal immigration. There were many who climbed the fences, but they were generally caught. Sophisticated cameras and other technological gadgetry hooked up near the fences made tracking these individuals easier. Those who more easily eluded capture were the ones who made the long and difficult trek through the deserts, far from human habitation. They took their lives in their hands as they set out on a journey that, more often than not, ended at the bottom of a precipice, or in dehydration and death from wandering. The insufferable desert heat, the snakes and other dangerous creatures that populated the area, along with the arduous contours of a land that featured steep cliffs and precipitous valleys, were believed to serve as a natural barrier between the United States and Mexico. But nothing stopped the immigrants. They kept on coming.

The many years he'd worked on the Border Patrol had softened Buddy Jr. a bit. If at first he'd treated any captured illegal with uncompromising firmness, with time he learned that life is not black and white. Many of these people had essayed this as a last resort. Some were forced to flee for their lives from organized crime and terror groups and sought safety in America. There were others who, when he returned them to the border, were going back to lives of pain and suffering. But these were calculations he could not permit himself. His job did not allow him to compromise.

The Border Patrol's primary objective was to prevent security threats against U.S. citizens. And so when Buddy Jr. stopped shipments of arms and drugs, he felt a sense of satisfaction, because he was helping to provide his children with a safer environment. Still, most of his day-to-day work involved catching downtrodden individuals and sending them back across the border.

Because much of his job entailed patrolling the border, he frequently worked alone. Buddy Jr. had made some friends among his colleagues, but he preferred to operate on his own. He spent long hours peering through his binoculars at the vast expanse of desert, astride his horse and searching the sand for footprints and other giveaways, or riding a Jeep along the length of the border.

With time, he became the area's expert in identifying a break-in. He could assess the illegal's age and weight by inspecting his footprints. His hobby of trapping snakes had taught him to notice the tiniest details. Through his binoculars, he could spot the smallest movement and know whether it had been made by a man or an animal. He was the paradigm of a true tracker and border detective. His territory boasted the highest capture statistics in the unit.

Tuesday was different than usual. It was clear that there had been some sort of early-warning signal, because the entire Border Patrol, without exception, had been summoned to work. The patrol numbered about 20,000 officers, with National Guardsmen filling in along the length of the border. Early that morning, all leaves were canceled, and even officers who had just completed their shifts were ordered to stay.

"What are we looking for?" someone asked at the daily briefing. Everyone wanted to know what the threat was. Not merely out of curiosity, but also—and especially—so that they might know what they were up against.

"Sorry, guys. I have no exact answers. The information I received indicated a lone individual preparing to cross the border with a bomb in a suitcase. What kind of bomb is unclear. Therefore, you are all to operate with great caution. I don't want any dead heroes today. If someone spots a threat, he calls for backup immediately. Do not approach in the usual way until help arrives. That order comes from as high up as it can get—the White House."

"Is this connected to the president's disappearance?"

"I don't know. But you can all take a guess on your own. Meanwhile, I want you to get to work immediately. Anyone making a mistake today will pay a high price. Understand?"

The officers scattered to carry out their orders, all the while trying to figure out what was going on. Buddy Jr. was about to leave with his partner when his superior officer asked him to wait.

"I need you here, Buddy. Raymond can go out with someone else today."

Buddy and his partner exchanged a surprised glance. Buddy stayed behind as the others left.

"It's not every day that I get a call from the White House," the captain said. "That means that I can't let anything get past me today. We've got to stop this terrorist. We've got to!"

"Yes, sir. But how am I supposed to do that from here?"

"I don't want you covering a territory like the others. I want something else from you. We seem to be dealing with a professional terrorist, someone who's passed this way at least once before. He's apparently very well equipped and funded by a terror organization.

"Okay…?"

"I want you to think like him. Tell me what you would do if you were him. I want you to go out into the field and try to think about how you would find a way to cross the border."

"If it were me, I wouldn't cross by day. I'd wait for nightfall. At night there are less men on patrol, the cameras are less effective, and our UAVs (unmanned aerial vehicles) can't do much. In short, I'd choose the night hours."

"You're right." The captain thought a moment, and then decided, "I can't give up our daytime surveillance. Who knows? He could decide to try it today anyway. But you… I want you to go home and go to bed. If the terrorist is not caught over the course of the day, I'll need you alert tonight. The other men will be bushed from the long day. But I have no choice; no one goes home before that terrorist is caught."

That was how it came about that, on the most critical day in the history of the Border Patrol, Buddy Jones Jr., the best man in the service, went home to go to sleep while all his colleagues spread out along the border.

———

Tuesday brought Menachem no news. Since his last conversation with the White House chief of staff, in which he was asked to send the Israeli prime minister home, no one had been answering his calls.

The media sensed a big story, and they were asking questions. Where had the president disappeared to? Was it true that the country's leadership was hiding in the White House bunker because of a terrorist threat? Whole articles were devoted to the canceled flights, the no-fly zone, and heightened security at the borders, but there was no concrete information. It was clear that there'd been some sort of alert, but of what kind, no one knew.

The White House issued a formal announcement on Tuesday morning, stating that the country was conducting a comprehensive drill to simulate a terrorist attack along the lines of September 11. The media didn't buy it.

"Impossible," said the news commentators and various security experts. "Impossible for there to be such a massive drill with no advance warning. Generally, the security forces would issue announcements to the media before carrying out a drill on this scale in order to prevent a panic. This must be a genuine threat. A threat they're not sharing with the public."

"WHERE IS THE PRESIDENT?" screamed the headline of Tuesday's *Washington Post*. The article that followed was two thousand words of speculation. The writer reminded his readers of the president's strange flight when the September 11 attacks were carried out, and listed the places where the president might find concealment in a time of danger. It was obvious that even this well-known commentator had no clue regarding answers to the questions he was posing.

The food chains reported a sharp rise in sales of bottled water and canned goods. The American public was bewildered. On the one hand, there seemed to be some sort of threat; on the other, maybe everything was fine after all. Perhaps within a few hours' time, it would turn out that nothing had happened. Sure, the main streets of the largest cities showed an enhanced police and security presence—but what did it mean? What was everyone supposed to be afraid of?

A radio commentator announced that many office workers who held jobs in skyscrapers had refused to come to work that day. A portion of them did come, but they left early when they heard about the possible threat. The memory of the thousands who had met their deaths in the Twin Towers was still too fresh to ignore. People chose to go home and feel safe, even if it meant cutting into their vacation days.

Menachem tried tapping all his contacts to learn more, but got nowhere. The oblique answer he received was that there was something important afoot right now, and he'd have to wait a day or two. He was forced to spend the unproductive hours with Jeffrey and Yisrael in the Horizon Hotel, repeatedly making guesses about what might be happening. Exactly the same thing that everyone else in the United States was doing that day.

One thing worried him. He'd been unable to get in touch with Mikhail. The man was not picking up his phone or answering any of his messages. Where had he disappeared to? Was he connected to the situation at the White House? Or had the Russian scenario actually played itself out, Heaven forbid? Had the Russians finally decided to get rid of him?

Jeffrey and Menachem decided that, should they continue to be unsuccessful at reaching him by that evening, they would pay another visit to his home. Even if he had nothing to do with what was happening, his contacts were among the best in Washington. He would surely know something they didn't.

For Menachem, Tuesday was a total failure. America was in a mess and Israel was in a bigger one, with its media wondering whether the prime minister was to blame for the chaos presently reigning in the United States. Was it possible that the prime minister had said something to the president that caused him to flee? This distressing question was being asked in Washington too. Had the Israeli shared with the president some information about an assassination attempt?

Menachem knew that this was nonsense. But there was a silver lining to all of this speculation: the media had forgotten the press conference that never took place. At least the prime minister's trip was not considered a monumental failure. On the contrary—the mystery only served to elevate the Israeli prime minister's stature. He appeared to have saved his American colleague.

But this didn't console Menachem. He was well aware that this was not the case. His gut feeling was that the situation was only going to become worse.

34

DIFFICULT MOMENTS WERE PART OF THE ROUTINE OF A president's life. Nevertheless, Bob Walters did not feel ready for the information that came flooding in.

The FBI was happy to be able to present some results at last. Howard Simons brought the findings directly to the president, making sure that no one else was within earshot. "We have the material from the Russian's hard drive. It looks like we're dealing with something big. Something huge. There are scores of names of American citizens involved in this thing. If the information is accurate, we'll have to institute a sweeping witch hunt."

Howard pressed a button on the computer, and a long list of names appeared on the screen.

"What is this? There are dozens of names here that I know!"

"Each one of them was in touch with Mikhail Potgorsky. Those at the top of the list also discussed with him a bomb that would be activated in the United States."

"So what? I was also in touch with him. That doesn't tell us anything," the president said. "I'd ask you to be very careful before you accuse someone of being involved in terrorist activity. The fact that we've overlooked the clues until now doesn't justify shooting in all directions."

Breathing hard, the president turned back to the list at the top of the screen: Joseph Steinberg, Speaker of the House—in the bunker with them right now. Billionaire Jeffrey Davis. The Israeli prime minister. Harry Bonds, the British Jewish peer. And on and on—the list was endless. The vast majority of the people on it were noted American citizens. Men of influence. Impossible. This couldn't be true. There must be some mistake.

"Just a minute! All the people on this list are Jewish, aren't they?"

"Yes, Mr. President. That's the way it looks at a glance."

"Well, there has to be a mistake. The computer must have amassed a list of Mikhail's friends. Everyone knows that he's always been very sympathetic to Israel and Jews. He was very active in the efforts to thwart the Iranian nuclear program."

"Yes, sir. You're right. We are certainly investigating all the possibilities. But I would not have shown this to you if I didn't think it possible that there's something here. Don't forget, there's a nuclear bomb making its way to us in total silence. A single person could not be behind such an operation—not even Mikhail Potgorsky. If he's had some sort of help, even from a portion of the people on this list, everything would become a lot clearer."

"Okay, okay, check out everything. But keep it absolutely to yourself. A list like this could end up being a global political bomb. It could turn out to be far more dangerous than our nuclear bomb. Give it top-secret classification. I don't want a single journalist to see it. Understand?"

Howard nodded. He didn't need the president to tell him to be careful. He'd worked in this field long enough to know that if even a small portion of this information turned out to be true, America would experience a major shake-up. Top-secret classification had already been imposed on the incriminating file. Very few people in the agency were authorized to work on the list.

"What else do you have for me?"

"No encouraging news, sir, except for the fact that I've got all my people out on the ground. We're checking every possible place inside the country's borders. Our nuclear sensors haven't picked up anything. We may be lucky, and the bomb has not yet reached American soil. If that's the case, our chances are much better. We're spread out along all the borders, with special emphasis on the one with Mexico. All personnel have been deployed. Satellites are scanning every foot of it. If he tries to cross the border, we'll catch him."

The president said nothing. He did not share Simons' optimism. Up to this point, not a single one of his agencies had produced results. Something very big was behind this bomb. Something big and frightening.

"What time is it, Howard?"

"It's 10:00 a.m., sir."

"I think it's time I tried to reassure the public. What do you think?"

"It's your call, Mr. President. But it seems to me it would not be advisable to leave the bunker at this time. I'm also not sure that you can risk it from a legal standpoint. America must not lose its president in an act of terror. That would be too harsh a blow."

"I don't need to leave this room, Howard. Barry says it would be a good idea to share the threat with the public. To urge people to take shelter and not go into crowded places. That would remove the element of surprise from the terrorist's plans. What's your opinion?"

"I think it'll cause a panic. It will only cause them to fall apart. From past experience, it's better to let them live in denial and not tell them about the threat."

"I tend to agree with you. I believe we can keep denying things and smoothing things over for another day. But I'm going to call a press conference for tomorrow morning, in the hope that we'll be able to tell them that everything is all right."

"Why don't we wait till tomorrow before deciding about involving the media?"

"Because we need to buy ourselves some time. If the people of the United States hear that they'll be getting an explanation tomorrow, they'll wait. People won't think that they're being lied to and having the truth kept from them."

"And what if we don't have any news, sir? What will you tell them then?"

"I have no idea, Howard. We'll have to pray that, by tomorrow, we'll have some results in the field. We can't hide here endlessly. Go get me some results, please. Give me good news for a change. And Howard?"

"Yes, Mr. President?"

"I'm dead serious about that list. It's a walking time bomb. Be more careful with that than with anything you've ever been in your life."

———

As far as Yisrael was concerned, Tuesday was a marvelous day. While his companions sat in the public rooms of the gorgeous hotel, awaiting developments, he proceeded to *shteig* in a way that he hadn't done in a long time.

During this summer break, he'd managed to review all the material he had learned in the previous *z'man*, and to start preparing the *sugyos* they'd be covering during Elul. The mere thought of the approaching *Yom Hadin* sent an electric current through him. Another year was drawing to a close. How much he'd been through in this long, difficult year... If only he'd known that Tatty would be taken from him, how he'd have prayed for the decree to be ripped up. How differently he'd have done so many things.

But what was done couldn't be undone. Now he had to think ahead to the coming year. He had to do everything in his power to continue on in the right direction, and bring *nachas* to his father in *Gan Eden*.

In his own mind, he'd begun to summarize his vacation. He shouldn't have been so stubborn about making this trip to America, and the challenges he'd faced here hadn't been simple ones. But it was impossible to expect perfection from himself. He was still young. In general, he had achieved what he had set out to do. He had formed a connection with his rich uncle. From now on, it didn't look as if he would have to worry about his mother. With Hashem's help, all would be well.

Al tivtechu b'nedivim. The verse popped suddenly into his head. Do not place your trust in philanthropists... Was that what he was doing? Placing his trust in a person of flesh and blood? Maybe a little. He'd have to think about this. In the meantime, he was trying to atone for his mistakes with the help of some long, deep learning.

One of the things he was most grateful to *Hakadosh Baruch Hu* for was the fact that when he learned seriously he truly found satisfaction. After some time spent in yeshivah, he knew that this was not something to be taken for granted. His friend, Gilad Gil, for example, had never really connected to his learning. He tried now and then, but he'd never discovered the satisfaction that Yisrael enjoyed.

Yisrael spent long hours poring over his Gemara that Tuesday. Jeffrey had arranged for him to use a small, quiet room as a study, and except for a short break to have lunch with the others, Yisrael hardly left it. How fortunate was the person who had Torah study! Downstairs was a group of men with nothing to do, and instead of undertaking some productive work they were passing the day in speculation and political talk. What would they get out of that? Nothing.

It was only as dinnertime approached that Yisrael decided he'd learned long enough for one day. He closed his *sefer* and joined the others in the sumptuous dining room.

"Look who's decided to leave his library—my dear nephew. What's the matter, Yisrael? Did you get tired of learning?"

"Heaven forbid!"

"Leave him alone, Jeffrey," someone chuckled, "or he'll end up turning you into a *baal teshuvah*!"

Menachem thumped Yisrael on the shoulder. "Yes, let him be. He's just jealous, Yisrael. We're all proud of your diligence."

Yisrael took their words matter-of-factly. He wasn't going to change anyone here. Everyone had a right to decide what he wanted. Let them be jealous...

"Have you heard anything from Mikhail?" Menachem addressed the question to Jeffrey in an effort to change the subject.

"No. It's as if he's vanished from the face of the earth. He was supposed to be here long ago."

"So maybe we really should visit him after dinner—just to make sure everything's okay. We have nothing better to do anyway."

"I'm not sure it would be a good idea to go outside, Menachem. You saw what's going on in the news."

"No one has a clue about what's going on. You've seen that for yourself. From a nuclear bomb to poisoned reservoirs—the bottom line is, no one knows anything. They're groping in the dark."

"Maybe. But it's certain that something's happening. Who knows better than you that the president's suddenly disappeared and can't be found? Maybe he was kidnaped."

"By aliens from outer space!" Menachem refused to take the situation seriously. The Americans took life too much to heart. So there'd been some sort of alert. In Israel, there were dozens each day.

But Jeffrey was not prepared to yield. "Look, I have no question in my mind that something very serious is going on. It might be the threat of war, or some threat or another from the Chinese or the Russians—but something's happening. My people in the news media are ready to swear that there's been some word about a nuclear bomb. They were even asked by the White House to take a soft line in their reporting of the news. Do you understand what that means? Intervention by the White House means it's serious. There's a real threat of a nuclear bomb here in America. This is not child's play."

"Okay. You're right. But what's the connection between that and a visit to Mikhail's house? I have to say that he worried me a little last time. It's not like him to be so stressed. Apparently, the threat against him is real. We have to make sure he's all right."

"I can send someone else to check on him."

"Coward! Do you think a nuclear bomb wouldn't flatten your hotel? Anyway, what could happen in a short trip? We'll check that he's okay and come back. We'll be right back here within an hour, tops."

Jeffrey stopped arguing. He didn't like the idea, but really, what could happen? He wasn't a lazy man and did not at all like the fact that an entire day's work had just gone to waste.

They finished their dinner and got ready to go out. Menachem asked Yisrael to stay in the hotel. After the long day he'd just put in, it would be good for him to rest a little.

Yisrael did not put up a fight. Despite the apology he'd received, he did not really care for Mikhail, who had attacked him for no reason. It would be better for them to go without him. Anyway, he was very tired. There were just two days left before his flight home, and five before the start of the new z'man. It would be a good idea to use as much time as he could for sleep.

35

JEFFREY OPTED FOR THE BMW JEEP FROM THE PARKING lot. He was filled with foreboding, and the fast, powerful vehicle afforded him a certain sense of security. The streets were relatively empty for this early-evening hour. Apparently, people had been taking seriously the veiled warnings that the various news outlets had been spouting. A press conference with the president had been promised for 10 o'clock the following morning. Jeffrey wondered what the president would have to say. How would he explain the past two days?

He steered the Jeep confidently through the deserted streets, and within a quarter of an hour they arrived at Mikhail's house. Jeffrey parked the Jeep at the curb and looked for the Russian's vehicle. The gray Lexus stood exactly where it had been when they had left, in the parking space next to the large building. Mikhail must be home. But why wasn't he answering his phone? Had something serious actually happened to him?

They exited the Jeep quietly and approached the gate. The guard booth was empty. The huge Russian who usually manned it was absent.

"What do you think, Menachem?" Jeffrey whispered. "This looks very suspicious. Where's the guard?"

"I don't know what to think. But it doesn't seem to me that it would be a good idea for us to go inside. What if they really did kill him and his body is in there? Or, even worse, what if 'they' are still there? Should we call the police?"

"And tell them what? That we're worried because our friend won't answer his phone? Be serious…"

Menachem tried to think of a better idea. Who could check out the house for them?

"It's okay," Jeffrey decided. "I have people who can handle this. Anyway, I'm not going in there. It's too dangerous."

Menachem nodded in agreement. There was no shame in being afraid. They had good reason to fear that something bad had happened to Mikhail. He had told them that Russians were following him and hunting him down. If there was any sort of danger, they'd be in no position to help. It would really be better to ask the police to handle this.

The two men were about to return quietly to the Jeep when they suddenly saw an array of guns pointed at them.

"FBI! Don't move! Put your hands where we can see them!"

They froze. The surprise and shock were numbing, to the point of making any reaction impossible. Menachem found it difficult even to carry out the simple order.

"I told you—hands up!" A rough hand in a black glove grabbed Menachem's hand and slapped it against the wall. A second later, the same hand forced Menachem around to face him. The gun that was pointed right between his eyes did not contribute to Menachem's ability to think. Everything had happened so fast that his brain was still trying to catch up.

Jeffrey, on the other hand, kept his wits about him. "We are innocent American citizens! Put down your guns!"

"Quiet!" The man standing behind him thrust Jeffrey up against the wall and began conducting a search. Menachem's captor did the same to him.

"Clean."

"This one too."

Menachem recovered. His mind began working at its normal speed, registering what had taken place. Something had definitely happened to Mikhail. That was the reason the place was swarming with FBI agents. Had Mikhail really been murdered? The possibility seemed suddenly all too real.

"Bring them inside." The voice belonged to a man standing in the doorway of the house, motioning to his agents. Jeffrey and Menachem put up no argument; the guns still pointed their way were extremely persuasive. Careful not to make a move that might be construed as a threat, they climbed the stairs and entered the house.

Menachem, who had steeled himself to see a corpse dripping with blood in the center of the room, was astonished at the appearance of the house he had visited just the day before. At least ten agents were busy taking the place apart. The plaster had been peeled from the walls, sofas and pillows had been ripped and emptied of their stuffing, and every tiny component in the house had been disassembled and inspected. It was obvious that they were looking for something.

"To the other room!" the same supervisor ordered, gesturing at the room in which they had spoken with Mikhail the day before. The room looked completely different today. The walls and ceiling had been stripped and the electrical wires were exposed and dangling. They were ordered to sit and not move.

Jeffrey was fed up. "What do you think you're doing?" he demanded. "The owner of this house is a senior Russian diplomat. This outrage will not pass in silence!"

"Jeffrey Davis. The man and the legend." The agent held Jeffrey's wallet, which had been taken from him. "So you're a friend of Mikhail's, eh?"

"Where is he? What did you do to him?"

"I'm the one asking the questions, not you."

"My friend, you don't want to start up with me. If you don't let us go this minute, I'll personally see to it that you're fired. You will be thrown out of the service, and not even the Washington police will hire you to walk the beat."

"With all due respect, sir, you'll have to wait before you fire me. You may be surprised to hear that I believe we've been looking for you at this very time."

"For me? What have I done? I want to see my lawyer!"

"All in good time. First, I want to ask you a few questions."

Menachem decided to intervene. His first shock had passed and he'd become his normal, energetic self. "With all due respect to you, sirs, I am not an American citizen. You have no legal right to detain me. Add the fact that I am here on a diplomatic mission from Israel, and you're really in trouble."

The agent was unmoved. He studied Menachem's passport. "Let's see… There's no diplomatic stamp here. As far as I see, you entered this country as a tourist."

"You can check it out in a minute! Though I'm not here officially as a diplomat, I was the one who organized the meetings between my prime minister and your president."

"I know," the agent said curtly. He turned to another agent, who was still standing with his weapon drawn. "Keep an eye on them. I have a few calls to make. I'll be back in a few minutes. Until then, they're not going anywhere. Got it?"

Despite his desire to join his friends, Buddy Jones Jr. did exactly what his supervisor had ordered. He called his wife, who worked in the local Walmart, and updated her on what was happening. The threat sounded pretty serious, so he wanted her to collect the kids right after school. No one was to go to their friends' homes or the park today. He wanted them all at home.

Buddy Jr. didn't remember the last time he'd been home at such an early hour. The clock stood at 11 o'clock when he walked in, and the silence that greeted him seemed odd. Usually, he entered the house to the shouts of three lively children. Even when he returned home from night duty, he still encountered his kids as they went off to school.

He went to the fridge and pulled out a cold Budweiser. How was he supposed to go to sleep now? He'd just woken up 5½ hours earlier… He tried to remember when his unit had last received such a dire alert. To the best of his memory, this was the first time. A lone terrorist with a suitcase… Was this another attempt at a terror strike against the United States, or a settling of accounts between warring criminal factions?

Simple logic told him that this was terrorism. The entire unit would not have been brought into play like this over a quarrel between rival crime gangs. There would certainly have been a heightened level of preparedness in such a case, but not this.

As a father, the thought scared him. If this was a terrorist attack, it could happen anywhere. Schools were a legitimate target for the animals who called themselves "freedom fighters." Maybe he shouldn't wait before bringing them home.

But what would he do with them all day? He had to sleep a little if he was supposed to stay awake all night. With the children at home, that would be impossible. But that was no reason to leave them in danger… In fact, his wife could also be in danger. A giant supermarket could serve just as well as a successful target, although it would not be as crowded at this hour as it would be in the evening.

He decided to wait a few more hours. It would not be right to change the routine of their lives because of every threat. That was no way to live. His colleagues were good at what they did, and the chances that someone would get past them in the current situation were next to nil. He'd wait a bit, try to sleep, and this afternoon he'd make sure that no one left the house.

He stretched out on his bed and tried to calm his fears about his family. To his surprise, he fell asleep within seconds. He woke up to the sound of his children's voices as they burst into the house and found, to their joy, that their father was home.

Within five seconds, all three of them had jumped onto his bed. The notion of sleeping on flew out the window. "Daddy! Let's do something together! Let's go to the park and play ball!"

Buddy Jr. smiled tiredly at his wife. Funny, he felt more tired now than when he had climbed into bed… He sent the kids to the backyard and told his wife what was going on. At 6 o'clock tonight he'd be going out to work. In the meantime, he didn't want anyone leaving the house or yard, and certainly not to go anyplace where there were crowds of people.

Later, they held a family picnic on the front lawn. Buddy loved his two sons and little daughter very much, and he enjoyed teaching them how to play baseball. The time passed pleasantly. After their early dinner, he kissed his children good-bye, parted from his wife as she began getting them ready for their baths, and went out to work.

"Look who woke up!" A group of tired border patrolmen were relaxing at command headquarters, their dusty shoes and perspiration-stained uniforms testifying to long hours of touring the dry desert under the searing sun.

"Who'd you bribe for this vacation?" a colleague by the name of Leroy asked. "Nothing I did helped me. Today's my wife's birthday, and they won't even let me go buy her a cake! I'll be in real hot water when I get home—and all because of that terrorist. And Buddy Jr. has the day off!"

"Leave it alone, Leroy. I'm sure your wife is calling up right now, to thank the terrorist for giving her some peace and quiet."

Their supervisor cut into the patrolmen's laughter. "Stop quarreling, children. You're on duty again in 10 minutes. Buddy, I want you in my office—now."

Leroy and his friends stood up. "Watch out. The boss is gonna punish you by making you clean the latrines."

Buddy made a face. He knew that his colleagues liked him. The teasing was not serious; they'd spent so many years together that kidding was just part of the routine. He followed his supervisor into the office.

"Close the door, Buddy."

Buddy did as he was told. His security clearance was no higher than that of his friends outside, and he wondered why he'd been chosen to hear classified information.

"The White House has been calling every half hour. I've never had such pressure in my life. From what I understand, they're fairly certain that our boy hasn't crossed the border yet, but they're convinced that he's planning to do so. We can't mess up here. Every hour that passes supports your theory that the crossing will happen at night. I need you to lead the operation."

"But sir, that's above my rank!"

"I know that. I will issue the orders, but I want you to arrange the forces where you think they're needed most. Between you and me, it's no secret that you're the best border patrolman in the unit. I'm going to give you the chance to serve in this, the most important case we've had in years. Succeed here, and you'll shoot right up to the top."

"Whatever you say, sir. I agree to organize this thing. But at the end of the day, I really work best in the field. It would be a waste to keep me here in the office while the other guys are outside."

"What do you suggest?"

"I'll help you choose the best places to position our men, but in the end I want to go out there myself. Let me wander around alone on Blackie, and I promise you to do my best."

Blackie was one of the patrol's horses. The unit had a full fleet of sturdy Jeeps, tractors, and other all-terrain vehicles, but they were of minimal use at night. In the decades that the unit had existed, more patrolmen had been killed in overturned vehicles than from any other danger that might await them. The crevices and fissures that dotted the area were death traps for an inexperienced or heedless driver.

Blackie, on the other hand, was a fantastic horse. He knew the territory nearly as well as Buddy Jr. did. His powerful legs never faltered, despite the challenges that the terrain threw his way. Buddy and he were a lethal pair that would not let any infiltrator pass them in silence.

36

THE BORDER BETWEEN THE UNITED STATES AND NEIGHBOR-
ing Mexico stretched over nearly 2,000 miles. The peaceful
relations between the two countries did not justify a huge force to
protect the border. But the problem of illegal immigrants swarming
into the western states had led the United States to try to contain
the stream. New security measures in the wake of 9/11 had also
contributed their share to firming up the line. Approximately
twenty thousand members of the Border Patrol, backed up by the
National Guard, were responsible for preventing illegal infiltration
into the country. They were responsible for maintaining the long
border passes between the United States and its two neighbors,
Mexico and Canada.

In terms of territory, the border with Canada was longer and
more porous, but the border with Mexico was the problematic one,
and it was here that most of the preventative forces were concentrated. Indeed, in the year 2011 only about 300,000 illegal immigrants slipped across the Mexican border, in contrast to the roughly
million and a half the year before. The numbers were still significant, but the government could live with them.

From a security standpoint, however, the border was no small headache. A lone, experienced terrorist could slip in without much trouble. Fences had been erected on the outskirts of the urban border areas—in San Diego, California, and El Paso, Texas—which had narrowed the passes and forced illegals to enter by way of the harsh desert. Yet with knowledge and the right equipment, one could still cross the border with relative ease.

That had been the choice of Ali Hamid, who planned to enter via the desert with his bomb. From his rich experience, this was the easiest way inside. For a soldier with his skills, stamina, and dedication to a mission, the arduous terrain posed no problem. In his childhood he'd walked longer distances than this.

He could have elected to enter through one of the country's airports, which he'd done twice before using false passports, but he chose instead to cross the desert on foot, because that was the best way to get by without having his suitcase checked through customs. The heat in the Arizona desert reached its peak in the summer, but a little hot weather didn't frighten him.

He reached Mexico without any real difficulty; he had a wad of cash that opened every door. No one asked too many questions about the suitcase he kept close to his side.

The stern instructions he'd been given about the suitcase convinced him that the Iranian president had not been candid with him. This was no ordinary bomb. With an ordinary bomb, they would not have warned him so strongly, or checked again and again to make sure he remembered the activation code.

"You'll have to arm the bomb first. And it's not a case of merely attaching two wires," explained the scientist, who'd reminded him of a teacher from his school days. "You have to enter the code, which will start an arming process that will take thirty seconds. My own invention. Only after that will you be able to press the button. Once you've pressed the button, you have another minute before the bomb is activated. A full minute to pray to Allah to accept your sacrifice."

So it wasn't an ordinary bomb. But what was it? A chemical bomb? Biological? He knew that his country had ambitions to achieve nuclear power, but he also knew that it was still a long way from acquiring the technology to build a mobile nuclear bomb. This clear understanding caused him to view such a possibility as illusory. But whatever it was, he was going to set off the bomb in the nerve center of the nation: in its capital, Washington, D.C.

He chose Tuesday night for the eighty-kilometer trek. At night, the journey would be triply difficult. In the deep darkness, it would not be hard to stumble over the edge of a precipice. Using a flashlight or lantern could lead to his immediate arrest. The many wild animals could also be troublesome.

But there were advantages to the darkness too. It provided cover from those annoying satellites, the oppressive heat, and the Border Patrol, which thinned out during the nighttime hours. He'd be on the other side by Wednesday morning and would make his way directly to Washington. He'd decided not to cross the border any earlier, in order to spend a bare minimum of time inside the United States.

He made the first part of the journey on an old, beat-up, but reliable dirt bike. Its headlights were concealed, for obvious reasons, but the night goggles he wore compensated nicely. He couldn't get up much speed in this fashion, but it was still a lot faster than making his way on foot. When the hilly, rock-strewn terrain made this method of travel unfeasible, he abandoned the bike and continued on foot. He hid the dirt bike under a large bush. It had done its job. Money had never been a problem for him. When Iran wanted something, it had the wherewithal to do it.

The heavy suitcase and the rest of the equipment in his knapsack slowed his progress. The extra poundage made the walk ten times harder than it had been on the previous occasion. Then, he'd entered the United States armed only with his beloved revolver. This time he was carrying some fifty kilograms worth of gear.

He checked his watch, which shone faintly in the dark: 2:30 in the morning. Two more hours of walking, and the border would be behind him. He set his jaw with characteristic firmness, and continued on without hesitation. His mission was clear, and nothing was going to stand in his way.

Ali Hamid walked without pause for three hours, stopping only when he was certain he was on the American side of the border. The pale light beginning to filter in from the east seemed to shine just for him, encouraging him to go on. It urged him to forget how heavy his feet had begun to feel, and how numb the perspiring hand clutching the suitcase was, and the weariness that was starting to overtake him. Soon, very soon, the painful trek would be over.

The noise of a helicopter's blades startled him. It had to be a patrol helicopter. Had they spotted him? He flung himself on the hard ground, and the suitcase he held received a hearty bang. Then he crawled as quickly as he could to a nearby thornbush, and froze. All of this took him just seconds to carry out. The helicopter was still out of visual range by the time he finished concealing himself. There was no way they'd seen him.

The helicopter came closer at a rapid clip and hovered over the area where he was hiding. Again and again it circled the spot. It refused to move on. They'd found him. But how was that possible? What had gone wrong with the plan? Someone had told them. Someone had leaked the Iranian president's secret plan. But who?

Ali Hamid had lived for years with the knowledge that he might one day be caught. He would have had to be stupid not to think about that possibility. The sound of Jeeps rolling in to secure the area told him that there was no way out now. This time it was really true. He was in their hands.

Even greater than the pain of what he might expect to find waiting for him in an enemy prison was the pain of having disappointed his president. His admired leader had counted on him to carry out his mission, and he had failed. What could ever erase the shame? His family would not be able to hold its head high. His honored father would become an object of scorn among his neighbors.

He looked at the suitcase in his hand, and made a snap decision. He would not let himself be captured without a fight. He'd die right here, as a *shahid*. The president of Iran would know that down to the final second he had not forfeited his mission.

He placed the suitcase on the ground and began inputting the long code he had memorized. The baying of dogs told him that the border police were coming closer. They were closing in on him. He breathed deeply, forcing himself to stay calm. He mustn't become confused. If he punched in the wrong code, the bomb would not explode.

"Come out of there with your hands in the air!" a voice shouted over a megaphone. "You are surrounded! Come out slowly and carefully, and everything's going to be okay. You have nowhere to run. Don't do anything stupid."

Though the patrolman shouted in English, Ali understood every word. The patrolman repeated his message in Spanish, and ended, "Come out now."

He placed his beloved gun on the ground and stroked it one last time. It could not help him now. There had been other operations when all had seemed lost and he'd managed to emerge safely. This time, it was over. With murderous slowness, the half minute needed to arm the bomb ticked past. The bomb was ready to be activated. All he had to do was press the button to trigger the explosion.

The patrolmen all around him were growing more and more nervous. Ali took a deep breath and pressed the button. In sixty seconds, the bomb would go off. It was done.

Now all he had to do was make them come closer.

He stood up very slowly, still holding the suitcase in a steady hand. He saw dozens of patrolmen surrounding him in a large circle, guns aimed directly at him.

"Throw down the suitcase!" the man with the megaphone cried. "Throw it *now*!"

Ali smiled. "Everything's okay!" he shouted back in perfect English. Then he began to mumble a hasty prayer.

"I told you to throw down the suitcase!" the patrolman screamed again in mounting stress.

Ali didn't move. Forty seconds. The story would end here. He was about to die, but he would take a number of these heretics with him. There was just one small difference: He was about to ascend to heaven as a *shahid*—while they'd be going straight down to the other place.

37

THE ATMOSPHERE IN THE PRESIDENTIAL BUNKER WAS GLUM. The previous day had been a hard one for a variety of reasons, the main one being the lack of progress in locating the bomb.

With each passing hour, it became more and more difficult to deny the threat. The first to call was a reporter from the *Washington Post* who asked about a nuclear bomb. After him came a steady stream of journalists and newscasters, all of them demanding clarification from the chief of staff regarding the president's removal to his secure bunker beneath the White House.

The day and a half they'd spent in the crowded space had soured all of those present. The stress level in the bunker, and the quantity of important figures imprisoned there, gave rise to quarrels and finger-pointing. Everyone blamed everyone else for the crisis that had caught them so much by surprise.

Bob Walters was tired. In a dark corner of his mind, he too was worried about his job, but as a man of principle he refused to attend to this egotistical concern. The primary thing—the only thing— that must concern him right now was finding that bomb. All of the United States' resources stood at his disposal: satellites and planes, helicopters and soldiers. And yet, they found themselves today in the same position they'd been in yesterday.

Each time the American superpower found itself caught flat-footed, it always came as a shock. It had begun with the surprise over not finding unconventional weapons in Saddam Hussein's possession; continued on through the long years when the U.S. Army, in the full glory of its strength, was unable to locate bin Laden; and now this. How was it possible that they were capable of broadcasting a live picture of a camel plodding through the Libyan desert, but they couldn't lay their hands on a lone terrorist supposedly making his way into the country from Mexico?

The other thing that disturbed the president was the news that kept streaming in with regard to the case of the Russian diplomat. The list he'd seen early that morning had been just the first salvo of a nightmare of international proportions. The number of people suspected of being involved in this terrorist action was growing. Even more worrying than the number of participants was their stature.

Earlier, the FBI had reported that two of the suspects had already been detained. It was early days for that, in his opinion, but the circumstances had warranted the arrest. The pair had been caught red-handed at the Russian's house.

Jeffrey Davis. Who would have believed it? The most influential billionaire on the American political scene—deeply involved in this deadly business up to his neck. Actually, it suited him. The man always exuded power and the desire to impose his views on others. He even treated the president as an equal.

But Walters was even more upset about Menachem Goldfarb's arrest. He was well aware of who Goldfarb was, and of the ramifications of this arrest. Menachem had been the man behind his meeting with the Israeli prime minister. Worst of all, it appeared that the prime minister was involved in this thing, too.

When he'd first heard of Goldfarb's arrest, he'd exploded. It had seemed to him that the FBI had moved too far, too fast. But the recording that the FBI played for him changed his mind. It held a clear discussion between Mikhail Potgorsky, Jeffrey Davis, and

Menachem Goldfarb about the consequences of a nuclear bomb set off in Washington. FBI agents had found the incriminating recording hidden in the Russian's house. It was dated yesterday.

From Mikhail's confiscated computer came very worrying data. E-mails depicting nuclear scenarios and estimated casualties had been sent to more than one address, betraying the fact that the attack had been planned down to the smallest detail. As the picture got filled in, it pointed to a plan to set off the bomb not far from the presidential convoy—preferably in a crowded area. There was now no doubt that Mikhail Potgorsky had been heavily involved in the plot. He'd planned an attack against the United States, a nuclear attack on Washington, D.C.

Armed with a special warrant issued by a federal judge, FBI agents swarmed through every one of Jeffrey Davis' homes, confiscating computers. Menachem Goldfarb's laptop computer was also found, and experts went through it all, down to the smallest entry. In addition, several other suspects had been put under 24-hour surveillance. Among them were senior senators and—most frightening of all—the Speaker of the House, who that very day was in the presidential bunker. This created a new problem, necessitating extreme caution when speaking in front of him. He might still be passing information out. Helping the terrorists.

Despite their suspicions, the FBI's directives were clear. No more arrests were to be carried out until more solid evidence was in their hands. The smallest error in identity could lead to destructive consequences. A nightmare of such proportions could lead to a world war.

Precisely because of this fear, the president made sure that the circle of those in the know was as limited as possible. He had to be careful not to the let the Speaker of the House sense that there was anything wrong. If it turned out that the Speaker really was involved, the element of surprise was essential. He mustn't have time to escape and wreak havoc. Meanwhile, this required the President to walk on eggshells, on the one hand, conducting a hunt and checking information, while on the other, concealing his darkest suspicions with many of the others who were with him in the bunker.

Mike Samuels, the director of the CIA, was due to arrive within the next few hours. The president needed him now. Samuels was a brilliant manipulator who was adept at handling complex situations. If other governments were involved in this plot, the response must come quickly. The United States must not reveal weakness. Her status as the world's sole superpower was already being constantly undermined. If he did not find a way to respond with strength and firmness, other nations would be encouraged to try to harm them as well.

The Russians, meanwhile, were sending updates. Mikhail was still being interrogated and information was being extracted from him bit by bit. All these bits, taken together, formed a clear and menacing picture. Influential Jews from a number of countries had united to harm the United States. The only thing that the Russians still lacked was a motive—but there was no doubt that it would come. Something had prompted Mikhail Potgorsky to direct a powerful attack against the United States. Some event, or some sort of ideology that had faithful adherents within America. The man's intentions were terrifyingly serious.

Despite all this dire news, the first priority remained finding the bomb. Once the terrorist had been captured and the bomb neutralized, that would be the time to deal with the no-less-explosive matter of a Jewish terrorist network. The problem was, there had been no real progress on that front so far. There seemed to be a consensus as to where the bomb would be coming from, but no exact timetable. It might already be too late. At any moment, the president might receive word of a nuclear explosion somewhere within his country's borders. The stress inherent in that knowledge was murderous.

The people in the bunker were doing their jobs. The heads of the various agencies were doing everything in their power to capture the terrorist, but his location was still a mystery. The security forces' failure to track him down was second only to the initial failure in realizing Mikhail Potgorsky's murderous intentions. Someone was going to pay for this. More than one someone…

Everyone in the bunker with the president was aware of this. All of them were trying desperately to escape blame. The trouble was, this attitude was leading to all sorts of quarrels and machinations, the last thing they needed right now.

Compounding their extended internment in the bunker was the lack of clarity as to when they would be released. For all they knew, they might have to spend weeks in there before the bomb was found. The president's men were working on a plan for this eventuality as well. A decision had been reached: If the situation continued through tomorrow afternoon, they would leave the bunker, though not the White House. A security zone would be maintained and pedestrians kept at a distance to ensure a maximum secure radius. This set of circumstances would remain in place until the bomb's location finally came to light. A bomb whose existence some of those in the bunker were beginning to doubt. After all, how was it possible that there was no additional intelligence to support its existence?

The long evening slid toward night. Most of the bunker's residents had been awake continuously for upward of thirty hours. At one o'clock in the morning, a final decision was made: they were going to bed. Only those personnel who were needed to continue the hunt would remain awake, while the agency heads went to sleep. They would require every drop of available energy for the day ahead, which promised to be no easier than the previous one had been. There was no reason for everyone to stay awake. If necessary, they could be woken in seconds.

It happened shortly before 5:30 in the morning. Bob Walters, who was the only one there to have slept on both nights, woke to the sound of a double knock on his bedroom door. Without bothering to get dressed, he stepped out into the situation room, careful not to wake his family. Matthew Klinger was standing there.

"What's going on?"

"There's been a possible ID at the border crossing," Matthew said. "An encounter in the Sonoran Desert in Arizona."

"Who do we have out there?"

"A fellow by the name of Buddy Jones Jr. His supervisor says Jones is the best tracker he's got. He reported a possible suspect. Jones is following him and has called for backup."

"What is their estimated arrival time?"

"Two minutes. We're talking about a large desert area. Their main concern is to prevent his entering the city. According to the report, they're just a few miles away from the highway, where the terrorist may be planning to meet a partner with a car. They're planning to surround him before he leaves the desert."

"Satellites?"

"We'll have a picture in half a minute. We've already established contact with the tracker, and the men who are moving in his direction have cameras. We'll be able to watch whatever happens in real time."

"Who's in charge in the field?"

"Randy Hayward, sir."

"Can I talk to him?"

"Of course, Mr. President." Matthew Klinger was eager to oblige. He pressed a button and spoke into the room: "Randy, this is Matthew Klinger, secretary of homeland security. Do you hear me?"

Loud static rose up from the microphone, followed by Randy's voice. "I hear you just fine, sir!"

"I have the president on the line. He wants to talk to you."

Everyone in the room swallowed a smile when they heard the tremor of excitement in Randy's voice as he replied in the affirmative.

"Hello, Randy. I understand that you have a lead?"

"Yes, Mr. President... We're pretty sure we've got something. The boy I've got out in the field is a real professional... If he says it's a terrorist, I believe him."

"How big a force do you have with you, Randy?"

"There's a helicopter due on the scene literally any second. On the ground, we have my boy, Buddy Jr., and we're on our way in full force. At least ten vehicles are closing in on the area. We'll be there in about sixty seconds."

"Leave the line open, please, and approach with caution. We mustn't lose him."

"Yes, sir! Thank you, sir!"

While they'd been speaking, the technicians had succeeded in hooking into the live feed. Those in the bunker were able to see the desert terrain whizzing past as the vehicle sped toward the infiltrator's position. The sun, which had just risen, painted the sand a stunning crimson. The scenery was breathtaking. Within seconds, three more cameras began streaming their own feeds from different vehicles. The satellite photos joined them, to provide a view from every possible angle. A shiver of excitement passed through the group as the satellite homed in on the potential terrorist. The large suitcase he carried was clearly visible.

Suddenly, he threw himself onto the ground. He'd apparently heard the oncoming helicopter. A moment later he was hidden beneath a desert bush.

Orders were issued, and the helicopter began to hover above the suspect. A moment later the Border Patrol vehicles arrived on the scene. Armed patrolmen jumped out with weapons drawn, forming a large circle around the suspect's position.

The tension in the bunker reached a new high. With four screens transmitting a live visual feed from the operation, they had the closest possible view of the scene. The operation's leader—apparently, Randy Hayward—picked up a megaphone and began shouting at the terrorist to give himself up.

"What if he decides to detonate the bomb?" someone in the room asked.

"Impossible. A bomb like that needs time to be armed. Right, Professor Minkowitz?"

"Correct! It would take half an hour, at least, for the material to become active."

They watched in tense silence as the man slowly crept out of his hiding place. "Throw down the suitcase!" Randy Hayward called. "Throw it down *now!*"

The terrorist didn't move. He did not release his grip on the suitcase. Instead, he smiled a strange smile and called back, "Everything's okay."

The watchers in the bunker stared at him. He did not appear to be under any great strain. Instead of putting down the suitcase and raising his hands in the air, he began mumbling rapidly to himself.

"Throw down the suitcase!" Randy yelled again.

Something in the terrorist's smile looked familiar to Bob Walters. He'd seen a smile like that once... A strange smile...

The memory came sharply into focus. He'd seen that smile in Vietnam. The President sprang up from his chair and screamed, "Get those men out of there immediately!" He turned to Matthew Klinger and added, "Right now!"

"But, sir, we have him! He's surrounded on all sides and can't do a thing!"

Bob Walters was not about to argue. He shot forward to the microphone and pressed the button. "Randy! This is the president! Take your men out of there this instant!"

The group in the bunker gaped at him in bewilderment. What was he doing? He could ruin the operation!

The screens showed confusion on the ground. Five precious seconds passed before Randy digested the order. "Retreat!" he shouted, and began to run back toward the Jeep, his rifle still pointed at the terrorist.

The patrolmen obeyed, but not fast enough. The helicopter was the only thing that managed to cover any distance in those seconds. The rest of the crew reached their vehicles, wondering what they were running from. Who were they afraid of?

"Get out of there!" the president yelled. "Now!"

From the video feed that was broadcast from the Border Patrol Jeeps, those in the bunker saw the ground begin to shake. The Jeeps' wheels raised a cloud of dust as they swiveled around and got ready to leave the area. The tension and the confusion in the room increased. What had the president seen that they had not? Why were the soldiers fleeing?

At precisely that moment, a second after the Jeeps began to move, all the cameras turned off at once and the picture was gone. The monitors that had been transmitting the live video feed all turned dark. The technician hastened to them, trying to find the source of the trouble.

"Randy! Answer me! Do you hear me?" Bob felt angry and frustrated. He pressed his hands down on the table, hard. "Randy!"

Deep silence reigned in the Situation Room.

"Randy, this is the president! *Answer me!*"

No answer came. The link with Randy Hayward and his men had been severed—forever.

38

Y ISRAEL DIDN'T WAIT FOR JEFFREY AND MENACHEM TO
return to the hotel. The long day had exhausted him, and he
elected to go to bed early for a change. About an hour and a half
after they'd gone off to visit Mikhail, he went to his room and got
into bed.

The beautiful room his uncle had put him in was especially luxurious. If, until now, he'd thought of a hotel room as just a place
with beds and an attached bathroom, now he knew better. The living room of his penthouse suite alone was the size of his mother's
apartment. A handsome, well-equipped kitchen branched off to
the left and a huge balcony with a stunning view of Washington
opened up on the right. Three steps led to the lower portion of the
suite—which held two large bedrooms with beds suited for Og, the
giant king of Bashan.

Yisrael didn't understand why he needed all this space. In his
mind, this was a real waste for a single boy. He could have shared
Menachem's suite and there still would have been room left over
for a *minyan* of men. But Jeffrey Davis didn't play the game that
way. In his world, every guest deserved his own room. A castle.

Yisrael slept very well that night. His room was well insulated, so he heard no voices coming from the neighboring rooms. He woke at 6:30, a little earlier than usual, and began getting ready to go out with Menachem.

Each morning that they'd spent in the hotel, he and Menachem would leave at 7:30 and drive to a nearby shul for Shacharis. Yisrael didn't expect today to be any different. He showered quickly and left his room feeling refreshed. He set off to find Menachem. It was time to go.

Three men with the letters FBI emblazoned on their shirts stopped him at Menachem's door. "This room is sealed. No one goes in."

Yisrael's heart skipped a beat. What was going on? Had something happened to Menachem? Had he been injured or something?

Not content with merely sending him away, the FBI agents asked him who he was and how he knew Menachem Goldfarb. Yisrael saw no reason to deny his friendship with Menachem—at which point they ordered him to join one of them for questioning.

Yisrael felt afraid and alone. He didn't know what these men wanted from him. What had he done? Even more disturbing, he had no one to ask. From the FBI men, he discovered that his uncle Jeffrey was also absent from the hotel. Who would help him if he found himself in trouble?

He rode down in the elevator with the armed FBI agent, who never took his eyes off him. Yisrael felt like some sort of criminal. He could see that the agent's hand was resting close to his gun, as though he expected the boy to try something.

Stress flooded Yisrael. He wished someone would explain what was going on! What had happened to Menachem and Jeffrey? And why was the hotel crawling with FBI agents? He even pinched himself surreptitiously, to make sure he was really awake. Not that he really thought this was a dream. It was all too real.

The agent brought him into a large conference room. As they walked, it became obvious that something serious had happened. Dozens of FBI agents filled the lobby and the hotel's public rooms. Several of them stood at the reception desk sorting a huge mound of papers. The reception clerk, who'd always been pleasant to Yisrael, looked distraught as he answered an agent's questions.

What was going on? Had something, *chas v'chalilah*, happened to Menachem and Jeffrey last night? Had they been hurt in an accident—or even worse?

Four tables stood grouped in the center of the big room. At each one sat an FBI agent, questioning a member of the hotel's staff. The agent accompanying Yisrael walked over to the table nearest them and whispered something in the interrogating agent's ear. The second man quickly looked Yisrael over, sent the security guard he'd been questioning on his way, and asked Yisrael to take his place.

"Did something happen to my uncle? Or to Menachem?"

"They're both fine, son. Don't worry. I understand that you are from Israel."

"Yes. I came here to visit my uncle."

"And what is your connection to Menachem Goldfarb?"

"Um… He's the father of a friend of mine… and he invited me… and…"

As always, when under pressure he forgot his English. The agent sensed this and offered him a drink of water. Yisrael took it with thanks, whispered the *berachah* and took a sip.

"How long have you known Menachem?"

"Only a few weeks. I told you, he's my friend's father. I was at their house not long ago."

"And why did he invite you to join him?"

"Because he knew that I was trying to reach my uncle… You see, I never really knew him. My father died a few months ago, and…"

Mark Kovak had been in this business for several decades. He was a seasoned interrogator who could spot a lie a mile off. He didn't need more than a few seconds to know that the boy was telling the truth. He was not connected to this affair. He was just in the wrong place at the wrong time.

Nevertheless, the information in his possession could be invaluable. Mark asked Yisrael to review all of his conversations with Menachem and his uncle—a vain exercise that led nowhere. These were not stupid men. They would not discuss the bomb in front of a boy who might blurt out critical information by mistake. It was only when Yisrael described the scene that had taken place in Mikhail's house that Mark became excited. He tried to squeeze out every last detail. What had Yisrael heard through the door? How had Mikhail exploded at him, and was he certain the door had been closed? Something in all of this seemed important to Mark, but he couldn't put his finger on the exact point.

Yisrael did his best to answer Mark's questions. He was an obedient boy and he assumed that there was a reason for the interrogation. It never occurred to him to consult a lawyer or anyone else; after all, he had nothing to hide. Not that he had anyone to consult with. His only acquaintances in Washington had disappeared and he had no idea where they were. Mark did not volunteer the information, saying only that they'd gotten into a bit of a mess.

After 20 minutes of questioning, Mark was finished with Yisrael. "You can go now," the agent said, returning Yisrael's passport. "Do you have anywhere to go? We'll be shutting down the hotel for a few days. Do you know anyone in the area, or shall we arrange something for you?"

Yisrael didn't know what to say. He didn't know a soul in Washington. On the other hand, he didn't want to find himself in a holding cell in the basement of the FBI building.

"I have to go pray now. I'll see if any of my friends are in the synagogue."

Mark nodded. "You can leave your things here and come back to collect them later. You're free to leave now."

Yisrael stood up and turned to go.

"Just a minute," Mark said. He took a business card from his pocket. "Take this, and call me if you need anything."

"Thank you."

Yisrael returned to his room for his tefillin bag. Why had this happened to him? Why did he always have to get involved in all sorts of problematic situations? What had he done to deserve it, time after time? First in yeshivah, then with his father, and now this. How was he supposed to manage in America all on his own? Who would help him get to the airport tomorrow to fly home? *And what had happened to Menachem and Uncle Jeffrey?*

Suddenly, he felt like a small, abandoned child. Though he was almost 17, tall and strong, he was still just a boy. What was he going to do now?

He left the room with the intention of going to shul and seeking help. This time, however, help came from an unexpected direction.

Chang Lu, the hotel's manager, was waiting for him at the door. In his 40's, the man looked twenty years younger. He ran the luxurious hotel efficiently, involving himself in even the most minute of details. Ever since Yisrael had arrived at the hotel with his uncle, Chang Lu had attended to his every need. Until now, Yisrael had assumed that the manager had done so merely to curry favor with his uncle. Now it seemed there was more to the man than that.

"Look, Yisrael," Lu said in heavily accented English. "Your uncle is in some sort of trouble. I don't know if it has to do with a bad business deal or something else, but it's clear to me that he's gotten himself into a mess. They don't send this many agents down just for tax evasion or an accident. We're looking at something much bigger. Anyway, it's hard for me to believe that they'll release him that quickly, and I know that you're here alone. I want to help you."

Yisrael shook his hand gratefully. It was true: he was completely lost and needed a helping hand.

"Your uncle is a very special man," Chang explained. "I'm the son of penniless Chinese immigrants who did not make it in America. Even when I was a child, I had to go out to work to help support our family. Your uncle hired me to help the cleaning crew, and continued promoting me over the years to what I am today. He recognized my devotion to the hotel and decided to invest in me. That's something that no other hotel owner would have done. To take a Chinese immigrant and help him like that... I owe him my life. And so, I will certainly help his nephew."

"I have to go pray in the synagogue now. The agent told me that I can leave my things here in the meantime, but the hotel will be shut down soon."

"True. It's going to be one big headache. But don't worry—if you need to, you can sleep at my house. I'll be busy most of the time trying to solve our problem here, but I'll be available for you until you get home. Okay?"

"Okay. Thank you!"

"Now, it might be a good idea for you to quickly pack up your things and we'll put your suitcase in my car. I'll drive you to the synagogue, and afterward I'll come get you. I don't think you should stay on here with everything that's going on. It could end up moving in unpleasant directions."

Yisrael did as Chang had suggested. The morning was rapidly passing and he wanted to get to shul before it got too late. A very few minutes later, they were following the bellboy who was carrying Yisrael's suitcase to the car.

Yisrael managed to come in time to join the second and last *minyan*. Luckily, he did not have to fight for the right to lead the service. He was the only one there with that obligation, and the adults were happy to hear his Israeli-accented rendition. One or two men came over to him afterward to offer a smiling, "*Shalom aleichem,*" but no one offered him help. How were they supposed to know that he was here all alone?

Chang was waiting for him outside. He'd used the time to arrange a cell phone for Yisrael, along with a bag of strictly kosher snacks, which Yisrael devoured. It was only 9:30 in the morning, but he felt as if it were already high noon. So much had happened to him that morning…

"Look, you can stay at my house if you like, but I think you'd be more comfortable in a different hotel. My parents are very nice people, but they're elderly Chinese and you'd have a hard time with them. I can get you a room in a hotel I know not far from here. That way, you'll be in a Jewish neighborhood with a synagogue, and you'll have your privacy. What do you say?"

"A hotel sounds great, but… I don't have the money to pay for it."

"Don't worry about money, my friend. I'll take care of that. The last thing your uncle lacks is money."

He turned at the next corner and pulled up in front of a large, impressive-looking hotel. Though the Horizon was bigger and more beautiful, this place looked more than adequate. Chang left the car in front of the door and gave the key to a boy standing there. Then he and Yisrael entered the lobby and approached the reception desk.

There was no doubt that Chang and the employees of this hotel were acquainted. They were eager to do his bidding. Within two minutes, Yisrael was checked in.

"Now we'll make one other stop, and then you can return to your room," Chang said. He pulled a checkbook from his pocket and scribbled something on it, then tore off the check and handed it to Yisrael.

Yisrael looked at him uncomprehendingly. The check bore the official Horizon Hotel logo and was made out in his name, "Yisrael Davis." No less strange was the sum written on it.

"Ten thousand dollars? What am I supposed to do with this?"

"Look, Yisrael, I'll be honest with you. If your uncle has really involved himself in something illegal, tax evasion or something like that, all of his bank accounts will be frozen within days. That means that it will be impossible to withdraw money from any of his accounts until matters are arranged. I know that he would not have wanted you to be stuck in America without a cent. I have no doubt that he will thank me for doing this."

"And what do I do with this check? I don't even have a bank account in Israel."

"You don't need a bank account to cash this check. There's a bank branch not far from here. Go there and ask for cash. They'll give it to you without any trouble."

"But what am I supposed to do with so much money? I don't need that much."

"You never know how much you'll need before your flight. Anyway, that's what Jeffrey would have done. He would not have given you any less. He was... is... a very generous man."

Yisrael stared at the check again. Ten thousand dollars was a lot of money. In all his life he'd never seen so much cash.

"Just do us all a favor and don't wave that money around, okay? Put it deep in your pocket before you leave the bank, and don't tell anyone that you have so much cash on you. There will always be people who'd be happy to relieve you of it."

Yisrael thanked him. He stuck the check in his wallet and left the hotel with Chang.

"I don't even need to take you there. See that bank? Yes, there— on that corner? That's it. Go to it now and then come straight back to the hotel. I have to take care of some things, but you can always reach me by phone. Okay?"

"Okay. And... thanks again. I don't know what I would have done..."

"Let it go, my friend. This is the least I owe your uncle."

Chang got into his car and drove away. Yisrael headed toward the bank. For some reason, his legs trembled as he passed the guard sitting at the entrance. He felt as though he were committing a crime. As though he were trying to steal money that didn't belong to him.

Inside the well-appointed branch were five tellers to serve the bank's customers. Four of them were busy with other people. The fifth was available.

Yisrael approached the teller hesitantly. The man had been typing something into his computer, but stopped and looked up at Yisrael with a broad smile.

"Good morning! How can I help you?"

"Um... hello. I want to cash a check..."

"That's fine. You'll have to stand in that line over there. This one is for investments. That teller will be happy to help you. Is the check yours?"

"Uh... yes. It was given to me as a gift..."

The teller's smile widened. "I meant, is the check from your bank account. I gather that it's not. Then whose check is it?"

"My uncle's."

"Okay. Can I see it, please?"

Nervously, Yisrael handed him the check. He had a feeling that this was not going to go smoothly. In the end, he'd be accused of stealing, and Jeffrey wouldn't be here to help him...

The teller's smile vanished when he saw the sum on the check. It wasn't every day that a boy walks into the bank and asks for $10,000 in cash. This was something that needed to be looked into.

"Is your uncle's name Chang Lu?"

"No... He works for my uncle, at the Horizon Hotel."

"Just a minute! Your uncle is—Jeffrey Davis? And you're his nephew?"

Yisrael nodded. The teller's manner changed abruptly. He stood up to shake Yisrael's hand. "Come with me," he said. "A nephew of Jeffrey Davis calls for special attention. Come to our VIP room, where you can have some refreshments while I take care of your request."

He led Yisrael into another room that opened up from the main one. Yisrael sensed the assessing gazes of the other customers. Uncle Jeffrey must have a lot of money here, if the bank's head investment manager was taking so much trouble over him.

They entered a handsome room paneled in dark wood. The investment manager offered Yisrael a black leather chair and sent the secretary to summon the bank's manager. Yisrael didn't like all the fuss being made over him. He'd have preferred to quietly cash the check and leave it at that. But he was afraid to ask. They might yet begin to suspect him.

The bank manager walked in and joined the investment manager. "Are you Mr. Davis?"

Yisrael confirmed this.

"Bill, you're taking care of this withdrawal?"

"Yes, I was just about to. Yisrael, I'm afraid I'll need some sort of ID... It's just routine. Do you have a passport or something?"

"Here's my passport!" Yisrael thanked Hashem that his passport was in his pocket. He'd nearly left it in the hotel, and only at the last minute decided to keep it with him. How was he supposed to know that the bank would ask to see it?

He handed it to Bill, who smiled again and left the room to handle the request.

Yisrael and the bank manager were left alone. The manager took a seat facing Yisrael and tried to engage him in conversation.

"Where do you live? Here in Washington?"

"No. Israel."

"Oh, wow! Isn't it scary there?"

This time, it was Yisrael's turn to smile. This wasn't the first time he'd met people who assumed that acts of terrorism occurred on a daily basis there.

"Actually, it's very nice there."

"Interesting. Maybe I'll go visit one day. Would your parents agree to host me? That is—your father *is* Jeffrey Davis' brother, isn't he?"

Yisrael couldn't help but notice the far-from-subtle interrogation. The man was checking out where he lived and who his parents were.

"My father was Jeffrey's brother. He died."

"I'm sorry... I didn't know."

"That's all right."

The conversation lagged, and the atmosphere in the room grew heavy. The bank manager studied his shoes uncomfortably, and then decided that it was up to him to keep things going.

"I understand that you're here to visit your uncle? I heard he's in the area."

"Yes." Yisrael answered briefly. He was getting tired of talking to this man, who wasn't being nice to him for any reason other than his uncle's money. He didn't owe the fellow anything.

Bill walked back into the room. He returned Yisrael's passport and added a thick envelope. "Ten thousand exactly."

Yisrael fought back an urge to count the money. For some reason, he thought they'd be insulted if he did. Instead, he stuck the envelope in his pants pocket and stood up to go.

"If you could just sign here before you leave, please. I need it for the transaction."

Yisrael took the expensive pen that was held out to him, and hesitated a moment. He'd long ago developed a signature in Hebrew, but he'd never signed his name in English before. Finally, he decided to simply write his name in block letters: YISRAEL DAVIS.

The branch manager shook his hand warmly and parted from him with expressions of goodwill. Bill walked him to the door.

"Shall I call a taxi or something?" he asked.

"No, that's all right. I'm staying nearby."

"Excellent. It's been a pleasure to meet you. If you need anything else, I'm here all day."

"Thank you very much," Yisrael said, and turned to go.

"Just be careful with that envelope," Bill whispered before Yisrael passed through the door. "There are people who'd be glad to lay their hands on that amount of cash."

Yisrael nodded, and stepped into the street. His hotel was only a minute's walk away, but with the envelope in his pocket it seemed much farther. All the way there, he kept glancing right and left, trying to pinpoint the suspicious face of a potential thief.

Recent events had matured him greatly. In his childhood, he'd lacked self-confidence, but that had gradually changed. He grew taller and bigger with each passing year, and the sports he'd played had strengthened both his body and his confidence. The difficult times he had experienced, at yeshivah and particularly with the death of his beloved father, had also lent a certain firmness to his character. He could have coped physically with most of the men he saw in the street, as long as they weren't armed.

Still, he was apprehensive until he finally reached his hotel. He was older now, but he still felt like a kid sometimes. There were moments when he was once again the awkward little boy he'd once been. This was a natural part of every boy's development, but for Yisrael it had seemingly happened overnight.

He went up to the reception clerk to ask for his room key—but the clerk, like everyone else in the lobby, was standing with dropped jaw, watching a news broadcast on the big screen.

Yisrael looked there too, to see what was going on. What was the clerk so absorbed in?

He recognized the figure of the president of the United States, standing and delivering a speech before the cameras. What was he saying that was so interesting?

Yisrael looked at the big clock on the lobby wall. It was 10:03 a.m. A little early for a presidential speech, wasn't it?

He tried again to snag the clerk's attention, but failed. Strange… What could the president be saying to transfix everyone in the place like that?

39

THE STUNNED SILENCE IN THE PRESIDENTIAL BUNKER WAS abruptly shattered. Matthew Klinger grabbed the phone and began ordering backup to the site of the incident. The FBI sent its reaction team to deal with the radioactive fallout and to seal the area. Each of the agency heads quickly worked to carry out his responsibilities.

The problem was—there was not all that much that could be done. None of the response teams could enter the contaminated zone without proper equipment. The life of a person exposed to radiation at such an early stage would end no less horribly than that of those who'd been caught in the blast itself. Before entering the area, both the radiation levels and the extent of its spread must be tested.

Meanwhile, the communications technician toiled to restore visual contact with the forces in the field. He tried again and again to hook up with the Border Patrol cameras—in vain.

"Leave it," the president ordered. "Give me the satellite!" Though that camera had gone dark with the rest, it had certainly not been damaged in the explosion. The satellite was orbiting above the earth, too far away to have been affected.

The technician did as ordered, and managed to bring up a picture on the big screen. All noise in the room instantly ceased as the horrifying picture appeared. A reddish-brown mushroom cloud hovered over the place where, just minutes before, the members of the U.S. Border Patrol had stood. It covered the entire area.

"We are entering a state of emergency!" the president announced. "I want this incident handled with maximum efficiency. Find out the wind direction and the affected area. Get me all the facts about that bomb, what kind it was and who made it. *And* the name of the terrorist who set it off. You have an hour to get back to me with details. I also want a list of casualties. Their names, and a list of their family members. I'm going to want to speak to them personally. Is all that understood?"

"Yes, Mr. President."

Everyone in the room scrambled to do his job at lightning speed. Right now, maximum efficiency was called for. At such moments of crisis there was no room for extraneous thoughts. It was time to act.

The president watched the frenetic activity for a moment, and then he reached a decision. The direct threat had passed. The American people needed their president now, fully functional.

"Gentlemen, I'm going upstairs," he announced. "In just a few hours, I'll have to stand before the American people and tell them what happened. I want to know who's responsible. Someone's going to pay for this!"

A feeling of failure filled those present. They'd had enough time and information to prevent what had happened—and they had failed. Each of them knew that the coming days would not be easy ones. The deployment of a nuclear weapon against the United States, on American soil. Such a scenario might appear in horror stories, not in reality. The president left the bunker with a firm stride, his staff following. This was going to be the most difficult hour in Bob Walters' career. The American people would want answers. Answers that he did not yet have.

The president passed his wife without saying a word. She knew better than to try to speak with him now. Though he was her husband and the father of her children, right now he was only the president of the United States.

"What do we say at the press conference?" Barry Radcliffe asked. "We have to prepare your speech."

"We tell them everything," the president shot back. "An event like this cannot be concealed. The American people deserve to know that their country has experienced a terrorist attack. The question is only—*who was the attacker?*"

"The FBI will speak to you about their findings in a few minutes, sir. There's no question that Iran was behind this. But this time, it seems that Iran was being used as the tool of someone a lot more sophisticated. Our intelligence points to the fact that they gave Iran the bomb so that it would be used against us. The reason? To force us to attack Iran in our turn. To make things easy for Israel. I think this really could be a Jewish initiative... but it's possible that Russia was the mastermind. What do you think, sir?"

"Right now, I'm open to all possibilities, Barry. I must say that the Israeli prime minister is certainly capable of such a ridiculous move. He'd do anything to persuade us to attack Iran."

Howard Simons and Matthew Klinger entered the Oval Office a moment later. The president sat in his chair and looked at them with weary eyes. "How did we miss this, boys? How?"

"We'll have to do some serious homework, sir. Right now, we don't have much to say."

Bob Walters heaved a sigh. How he'd aged since the first time he'd stepped into this room. From a young, energetic man who wanted to change the world, he had turned into an old, tired president who only wanted to end his watch in peace. Something that would not happen now...

"What did the investigation turn up?"

"Sir, it's exactly what we feared it was. We lifted the identical information from the computers of the Russian, Mikhail Potgorsky; from Menachem Goldfarb, the Israeli; and from Jeffrey Davis, the

American. They were all in written communication with each other. They planned the attack."

"How?"

"Mikhail has the right contacts in Russia. He took care of transferring the bomb to the Iranian president, knowing that the president would want to harm us."

"But what is *his* interest in all of this?"

"Very simple, sir. Simple and cold-blooded. Iran attacks us, we counterattack—and the Israelis can sit back while we do their dirty work for them."

"That's crazy."

"True, sir. But the facts speak for themselves. The entire plan, down to the last detail, was found on all of their computers."

"There's no chance that it was planted there?"

"Almost none, sir. For that to happen, you'd have to have direct access to the computers. Access, *and* information that's not available to everyone. No, this looks authentic."

"Who else is part of this?"

"It just gets more complicated, sir. There are two more individuals who were involved in the nitty-gritty of the plot, but at least five others who helped with money and planning the attack."

"Anyone I know?"

"Yes, sir. Joseph Steinberg is one of the two."

"Speaker of the House?"

"Yes. My people are searching his house right now."

"Do it quietly, please. Without noise or fanfare. Where is he now?"

"On his way to an interrogation room. It's unbelievable that he was in the Situation Room throughout all of this. He probably sat there hoping that we'd fail! I can't understand how such a patriotic American could work against us like that. He nearly became the president himself! What could cause a person like that to betray his country this way?"

"On the contrary—I'm not so surprised... He's an ambitious, egotistical man who would do anything to advance his aims. If he thought it would help him sit in my chair, he wouldn't hesitate for a minute."

"Yes, sir. But our problem gets even worse. The second man who was in on the secret is none other than the Israeli prime minister."

"What? The man sat opposite me just yesterday! Are you absolutely sure about that? A thing like this could be a catalyst for war."

"We checked again and again, sir. Transmissions that were recorded just minutes after your meeting with him reveal a bit more. The prime minister called Menachem Goldfarb and told him that, in his opinion, only a nuclear bomb in Washington would help."

"In those words?"

"The conversation was in Hebrew, so I can't say that I heard it personally. But our expert claims that was the gist of what he said. We're working on an exact translation right now."

"So what do you think? Who's initiative was this? His?"

"At this stage, we can't be sure, sir. It seems that Mikhail was the brains behind the operation, but there's still a lot of work to do. One thing seems unquestionable: the prime minister knew about it."

"Jews... Everyone involved in this thing is Jewish... What a traitorous people. I never would have guessed it."

"Sir. There's one more thing that we'll have to investigate here. Are we looking at only the tip of the iceberg? Is it possible that we have a situation in which the Jews are trying not only to force us to attack Iran, but more? Don't forget that they're talking about the Speaker of the House as the first Jewish U.S. president. We have to consider the possibility that they tried to cause you to leave the field clear for him..."

"What—some sort of plot to take control of America? Of the *world*?" The president seemed highly skeptical. Then again, right now he couldn't let himself feel sure about anything. Who knew? Could anyone have dreamed that they'd be insane enough to arrange a nuclear attack on the United States?

He thought about it again. Could other Jews be involved? Certainly they could. The question was only *who*.

"Just a minute! What's the name of the professor who was in the bunker with us? Was he by any chance a Jew? He was the one who kept claiming that there was no reason to worry about the bomb, wasn't he? Even at the last minute, he said there was no chance the bomb would go off so soon. Is it possible that he was involved? That he tried to cause us casualties?"

"We'll check it out, sir. Right now, nearly everyone is a suspect."

"Every Jew, you mean… And they're going to call us anti-Semitic for this."

"How much of this are you planning to reveal at the press conference?"

"Only the part about the explosion. We'll find the guilty parties in the coming days. Meanwhile, I want you to continue tying up loose ends. I want to know who initiated the whole thing, and I want concrete proof against each of the people you mentioned, before I start attacking. And Matthew?"

"Yes, sir?"

"Do us all a favor and keep all Jews away from this investigation. I have a feeling that they've planted spies everywhere. At this stage, I don't trust a single Jew. Not a single one!"

40

THE JAMES S. BRADY PRESS BRIEFING ROOM—NAMED AFTER President Ronald Reagan's press secretary, who was severely wounded in an assassination attempt against the president in 1981—was packed. Every single news network was there. In the digital era, news crossed the globe at the speed of light, and everyone already knew about the mysterious explosion in the Sonoran Desert. An explosion that had taken its toll in human lives. But beyond this, they were in the dark. The entire area had been sealed to traffic and admittance was forbidden. Many newspeople had attempted to discover whether there was any truth to the rumors of a nuclear bomb, but no official source had responded.

The White House chief of staff came into the room, ascended the steps to the podium, and began to explain the proceedings.

"The president will address the nation first. Please do not interrupt him with questions." The voices raised in protest from various corners of the room did not slow down the flow of his words. "After the president finishes his speech, you will be able to ask whatever you wish, though the responses will be limited. Your cooperation is appreciated."

He placed a pile of papers on the podium and stepped down from it. The White House spokesman approached him and they whispered together while everyone awaited the president's entrance.

A moment later, he walked in.

Everyone rose to their feet. The president made his way to the podium to the flashes of many cameras, as photographers sought to capture the picture that would appear in the next day's first editions.

Bob Walters stood facing the press. He skimmed the pages lying before him, lifted his eyes to the cameras, and began talking. The tense silence in the room was unbroken, except for the clicks of camera shutters that did not stop for a minute.

At the start of his political career, Bob had been a mediocre speaker. With the years, and continual practice, he'd improved greatly and learned how to shape his camera delivery. Nevertheless, he always needed a written text. He was not a spontaneous speaker who could face a crowd extemporaneously. His speechwriters would bring him draft after draft, until they hit on a text that satisfied him. Very few knew his secret: half an hour before an important address, he would go into a room by himself and practice what he was about to say, over and over.

He leveled a firm, decisive gaze at the camera and began to speak.

"Good morning, my fellow Americans. I know that this is not an ordinary hour for a presidential speech, but today is definitely not an ordinary day.

"These past two days, the news media has been asking a difficult question: Where is the president? Why won't he show himself to the public?

"The answer to that question is no less difficult.

"Ever since the founding of the United States of America, she has set herself up as a model and an example for the rest of the world. A paragon of freedom. A place where every person enjoys equal opportunity. A place where everyone can reach his or her potential, through mutual respect and cooperation.

"Our indisputable success indicates that we are moving in the right direction. We have become a nation that pursues justice; we are the conscience of the free world. We have reached a point where the entire world learns from us how democracy ought to work. My fellow Americans, you can be proud of yourselves!"

Bob ended on a raised note and let the words echo in his listeners' ears. That had been the introduction. Now came the hard part.

"In the nature of things, our success has displeased many who do not wish to see the good that dominates our world. Those whose ideologies impel them to violence and terror, who bring suffering on other people and who are incapable of rejoicing in another's good fortune. These people do everything in their power to damage the winds of democracy that are blowing through the world. They embrace the paths of fear and terror, in order to subdue the lives of free individuals everywhere.

"The United States has recognized these threats from their inception, and has always known how to stand up to the forces of evil. Our military complex is the most advanced in the world. Our brave soldiers are imbued with motivation and pride. And that's because they know they have a country worth fighting for. They have a good reason to want to defend America. Because America is not only our homeland. America is also our inspiration. She is our way of thinking and our way of life. Our truth!"

The president paused in his impassioned speech and grew sober before he continued. His voice was low and steady now, its cadences measured.

"In recent days, our security services uncovered an immediate threat against the United States of America. A large and real threat involving an attempt to attack us on our own beloved soil. A threat that called for our undivided attention.

"Indeed, in the past few days, hundreds and thousands of our security forces have not slept… Starting with the emergency Cabinet meeting in the White House and ending with soldiers in the field who did everything in their power to prevent the threat from materializing.

"I can now let you, the American people, know that we have succeeded. We have prevented those of evil intent from introducing their bomb into a civilian area where it would have killed many innocent citizens. We stopped the loathsome terrorist before he managed to carry out his mission, and we destroyed him. The citizens of the United States can breathe easy again. The threat against their lives has been removed.

"Unfortunately, today does not carry only happy news. As we celebrate the removal of the threat against our country, we must remember those who have given their lives to protect us. Those brave men who turned their nights into day, defending our borders against this kind of attempt. We will remember the twenty-seven border patrolmen who were killed today in the line of duty. Courageous men who, with their own bodies, stopped the attack against our citizens."

The president stopped again, and inclined his head. There were twenty-seven families who had just been informed of their loss. Immediately after his speech, he would personally call each one, or even meet with them face-to-face. It was not going to be easy...

"In this hour, we must join together proudly and support those bereaved families. Families that sent their loved ones out to protect us, so that we can live our lives in liberty and without fear. No one can restore to those families what was taken from them. But I promise you this." He leveled his eyes at the cameras. "I promise you that those who sent that bomb will pay dearly. We will avenge the deaths of our finest men at the hands of the cowards who sent this threat our way. Though we are a peaceful nation, we also know how to repay those who harm us. We know how to defend ourselves and to avenge our losses.

"Those who sent the bomb will live to regret their actions, and will pay with their lives—if it's the last thing we do. Justice will come to light and will show the world what happens to those who try to harm us."

The president studied his audience with hard, narrowed eyes. He had meant every word he had said. He would make those who had come up with this idea regret their intentions. But he needed a few more days. A few days for investigation, in order to be absolutely certain about who should pay the price for this criminal act.

The time for revenge would come. But right now, the dead must be buried—if there was anything left to put in the ground.

"First, we must mourn. We must cry over our loss before we go out to battle. Because the moral superiority of the United States derives from our recognition of the sacrifices that our soldiers make for us. From our grasping the sacred nature of the life of every one of our citizens.

"I declare this a day of national mourning. A day in which we remember those who were killed, and grant them the infinite respect they deserve. A day in which America will honor the hundreds and thousands of men and women who dedicate their lives to the defense of the United States of America, every hour of every day. In every place in the world. I ask you to join me in a moment of silence in memory of those who have fallen. A moment in which to thank those brave souls who protected us today, and to send a prayer up to G-d to give us the strength to stand up to our enemies with our heads held high, and the courage to defend ourselves against their relentless hatred. Thank you."

The president concluded his speech and bowed his head. The silence was total. Not even the photographers dared disturb the sanctity of the moment. Millions of viewers across the length and breadth of the United States bowed their heads too, and wondered who had died for them that day. The president's speech had sent a shudder through their hearts. The rumors were true! There had been a serious threat against the United States, a threat that had been diverted at the last moment. But no one understood, yet, what exactly had taken place. The president had not been clear.

The minute passed, and the White House spokesperson repeated his guidelines for questions from the press.

"Colin Maurer, you can ask the first question."

"Thank you." The veteran newspaperman stood and faced the president. "Mr. President, is it true that it was a nuclear bomb?"

"Yes."

A ripple passed through the room. The cameras began clicking again, and pens flew across pages.

"BBC, go ahead."

"Thank you, sir. Michael Flax, BBC. Do we know who was behind the attack? Was it al-Qaeda?"

"We have a fairly clear idea, but for understandable reasons we are not yet ready to talk about it. One thing I can tell you: the people responsible for this will pay."

"Samantha Brady, CNN. Mr. President, is it true that you were aboard Air Force One, the presidential plane, because of this threat?"

"As I said earlier, I was in the White House with my security council, personally supervising the operation. Next question?"

"Charles Lornes, *New York Times*. Am I correct in understanding that a nuclear bomb exploded on American soil this morning? Within our borders?"

"Correct."

"We're talking about a security breach of monumental proportions."

"This is not the time to point fingers, Charlie. Everything in its own good time… Are there any other questions?"

"Were all of those killed members of the Border Patrol?"

"Yes. And now, I must get back to work. Thank you all very much."

The president descended from the podium, ignoring the questions still being thrown at him from every side. The reporters followed him to the door, stopping only when he disappeared behind a wall of Secret Service men. Only then did they hasten to report excitedly to their viewers about what they'd all just heard.

On this day, for the first time in the history of the United States, she had been attacked on her own soil—with a nuclear bomb!

41

THE NEXT HOURS BROUGHT THE NAMES OF THOSE WHO
had been killed. The media aired their pictures and the details
of their lives, and preparations were set in motion for elaborate
funerals on Thursday morning. Bob Walters made a personal call
to nearly every family, promising to put in an appearance at the
funerals.

The sole ray of light in the whole tragic episode was the news that
the helicopter's pilot had survived the blast. He was the only one
who had managed to flee the core affected area, and he had been
hospitalized for radiation exposure. A media poll showed that popular support for the president had soared in the wake of the tragedy. American citizens felt that their leader had handled the crisis
in the best possible way. It would be a few weeks before complaints
and questions would arise about possible errors in judgment.

From a security perspective, the various agencies faced two primary tasks: At first, defining the scope of the contamination and
dealing with it, thereby putting an end to the first nuclear threat on
American soil. Only afterward would they concentrate on gathering information about those who had been behind the attack.

That information did not stop pouring in. Every additional computer that they confiscated provided fresh facts and proofs. The Russians continually updated them on Mikhail Potgorsky's interrogation. And the findings were distressing.

Within hours, it was proven beyond a doubt that Mikhail Potgorsky had been the brains behind the plan, Jeffrey Davis had been its principal funder, and Menachem Goldfarb was the man who had provided the ideological motive for the operation. This raised a question whose answer was not yet completely clear: the degree of the Israeli prime minister's involvement. Though there was no doubt that he had known something of the plan, there was no proof that he had personally authorized the attack. What did emerge clearly from the investigation was the fact that other highly influential Jews had been involved as well and had put their personal stamp of approval on the operation. One of the most well known of these was Harry Bonds, the Jew closest to the English royal family. A Jew who had been knighted by the queen herself, a signal honor in recognition of his service to England.

But what had led to this criminal banding together? How was it possible that Jews from such a broad spectrum of backgrounds had united to attack America, without a single breath of the plot having leaked out? The massive amount of incoming data left investigators stunned. How was it that nothing of this had been suspected until now? How could so many people have kept the secret without letting the smallest rumor slip?

The turnabout came when FBI investigators made the connection between Mikhail's research and the plot.

They found information that was known to all. The primary focus of his research—second only to his work on anti-Semitism—involved the document known as *The Protocols of the Elders of Zion*.

Mikhail had invested a great deal of energy in disproving *The Protocols*. He'd assembled a vast amount of material in the course of his research, and then presented his conclusions at length and in great detail: *The Protocols* were a miserable sham. He'd worked hard to condemn those who, through the centuries, had believed that this was an authentic document, and mocked their ignorance. In his research, he made a laughingstock of Henry Ford, Adolf Hitler, and the Arab states that believed in *The Protocols* to this very day.

In the clearest, most comprehensive fashion, he presented his arguments, one by one, and demonstrated how the document had evolved—beginning as a bad copy of an old German book by Russian youths in Paris, through the Russian czar's cynical use of them to incite his population, and up until its use in the formulation of German Chancellor Adolf Hitler's worldview.

All this research raised a question in the minds of the investigators. Why had Mikhail worked so hard to disprove the authenticity of *The Protocols*? Was it possible that there really was some sort of Jewish organization that plotted toward the goal of world domination? Some sect or secret club that passed from generation to generation and made very few mistakes? That could explain the rise of such a secret and well-funded organization today.

Or even if it hadn't been true until now, it might have inspired Mikhail—given him the idea of establishing a secret Jewish group of this kind...

The additional data that came to light only served to strengthen these suspicions. Jews were unquestionably influential. The frightening facts indicated how widely the influence of the Jews diverged from their numbers in relation to the world's general population.

Also, four of fifty state governors were Jews. Jewish names such as Einstein, Freud, Karl Marx, and others were known to everyone, and the number of Jews who'd won the Nobel Prize was disproportionate. They were doctors, scientists, lawyers, and judges. In other words, they wielded influence everywhere. Was it a mistake to think that there was no coincidence here? That they were distributed in this way because they were planning something big?

The fact that no less than 40 percent of the biggest contributors to presidential campaigns were Jews supported this theory. No wonder, in that case, that AIPRO, the Jewish lobby, was so powerful.

The president refused to accept this questionable theory. Though the ideas were definitely thought-provoking, he insisted on sticking to the facts. They were dealing with an organization that included a number of Jewish leaders, not all of them. As long as it was not proven otherwise, they were not to blame the Jewish people as a whole. There was no reason to point the finger of blame at every Jew.

His problem was that this whole organization spread far beyond the sphere of the United States. This was not a local problem that could be dealt with by placing a few suspects under arrest. The leader of another country had been implicated in a terror attack against America. That was tantamount to a declaration of war.

But Bob didn't want to rush. He was not one to go to war before his goals were defined. He was not about to flatten the State of Israel with a nuclear barrage. It was incumbent upon him to think very carefully about the results he wanted to achieve, and only afterward to plan the operation.

He spent the afternoon hours with his advisers and generals.

The chairman of the Joint Chiefs of Staff was the senior officer of the U.S. military arm. His job was to advise the president on military matters, and to coordinate action among the various branches of the military.

The U.S. Army was the main branch of the American military forces, being the largest and oldest branch of the armed forces and responsible for on-the-ground operations in various wars. The army had to work in full synchronization with the air force, the navy, and the Marines. Overseeing this coordination was Admiral Peter Taylor, chairman of the Joint Chiefs of Staff, principal military officer of all U.S. armed forces.

Under his authority were the vice chairman and the heads of the army, air force, navy, Marines, and National Guard. They generally convened in the offices of the Joint Chiefs at the Pentagon, but today they were gathered, at the president's request, in the White House. By law, the president was commander in chief and could issue orders, directly or through the secretary of defense, to his forces fighting in the field. However, presidents almost always operated through the Joint Chiefs of Staff.

Bob Walters had no intention of bypassing them, either. He had invited the senior officers here because he wanted their input. He wanted to ascertain the balance of power between the two countries, to hear a precise evaluation of Israel's forces, and what the chances were for success in a comprehensive war.

The Pentagon had devised numerous contingency plans for handling the most bizarre, worst-case scenarios. The best strategists that America had to offer had drawn up plans of action to address every emergency situation. A war with Russia or China, terrorist bombings, and terrorist takeovers. Oddly enough, nothing at all had been prepared to cover a war with Israel. The strategists had thought of everything, but not of a full-scale war against Israel. Why should they? The State of Israel stood staunch as the sole democracy in the heart of the Middle East, surrounded by hostile Muslim governments. There was no reason in the world to think about a situation that included a war with Israel. But reality trumped imagination every time, and it had now become a practical question. Was Israel capable of offering serious opposition to the world's superpower, or would she be conquered as easily as Iraq had been?

The generals engaged in animated discussion, thrashing out various strategies. They stopped only when the White House chief of staff received a phone call. Barry Radcliffe listened to what was being said at the other end, then hung up and broke into the conversation.

"CNN is broadcasting a feature on what happened," he said, activating the screen. A newscaster of serious mien was reading something from a paper. Barry raised the volume so that those in the room could hear:

"The last name on the list of those arrested is Jeffrey Davis, the Jewish tycoon who owns the News-Time media network as well as dozens of hotels throughout the United States.

"Davis, who appears regularly on the Forbes list of the 100 wealthiest people, was detained yesterday along with an Israeli, Menachem Goldfarb, and is undergoing interrogation by the FBI. In the early hours of this morning, FBI agents entered the hotels and homes he owns and confiscated equipment and computers in search of evidence.

"Surprisingly, the common denominator among the recent arrests is that all the detainees are Jews, Jews from various countries that, it is suspected, may have banded together to carry out this act of terror. The motive for this act is still unclear, but the detention of figures of such stature are a sign of the FBI's belief in the information it has relied on in making the arrests.

"In the wake of this stunning development, we will continue to update our viewers on the nuclear bomb that the president revealed has been detonated on American soil—Arizona desert. According to the President, the blast was an act of terror, but he has refused to name those who were behind it.

"We have credible information that claims a group of influential Jews from all over the world stand behind the nuclear terrorism. A powerful and varied group, as you'll see on your screen in just a moment… At this time, we are trying to obtain a response from the FBI and the White House. We will be back to update you with further developments. Stay tuned. This is Jim Rossini, CNN."

As Rossini stopped speaking, the promised list appeared on the screen. It contained the names of all those who'd been arrested, the positions they held, and their home countries.

> *Mikhail Potgorsky:* Senior Russian diplomat and a confidant of Russian President Alex Kotorov
>
> *Menachem Goldfarb:* Israeli diplomat who arranged the meeting between the Israeli prime minister and President Walters
>
> *Joseph Steinberg:* Speaker of the U.S. House of Representatives and the Democratic front-runner in the next presidential elections
>
> *Jeffrey Davis:* Business tycoon and owner of the News-Time media network

CNN paused for a station break, leaving those watching in the White House temporarily speechless.

"Where did they get that information?" the president demanded at last.

No one had an answer. The freedoms granted the media by U.S. law afforded the networks almost complete protection from the need to reveal their sources. It would be hard to discover where the leak had originated. And now, it didn't really matter all that much. The task at present was to deal with the news that had been shared with the public.

"We'll have to make a statement before matters mushroom out of control," the chairman of the Joint Chiefs of Staff observed, stating what they all knew.

"This has taken away the element of surprise in our investigation," fumed the FBI director. "Suspects who have not yet been detained will have a chance to get away."

"The prime suspects are already in our hands," the president said. "Now we'll just have to pick up the pace. At least the news about the Israeli prime minister's involvement hasn't leaked out yet—though that's probably only a matter of time.

"It looks to me as if we all agree about one thing that was said in this room. We must bring NATO into this. This can't become our personal war against Israel. I'd like to turn this into a global issue. For years, Israel has been operating in the world in a militant manner. They attack whoever, wherever, and whenever they deem it appropriate, and cause us more headaches than ten countries put together. It's time to put them in their place.

"Let's wind this up with three primary goals:

"First—putting the people involved on trial. If we manage to get enough proof, that would include the Israeli prime minister.

"Second—placing Israel's nuclear program under UN supervision. At a second stage, we'll demand its dissolution. There is no longer any justification for it. If they are capable of becoming involved in terror, they must not be allowed to have nuclear weapons.

"And, third—forcing an agreement with the Palestinians that takes them back to the '67 borders. This is the first time we have real justification to put an end to the conflict, once and for all. If we want peace in the Middle East, that's the only thing that will bring it about.

"The route to achieving these goals is through the U.N. We'll start working on a broad coalition against Israel. Based on past experience, that shouldn't be too difficult... We have to set in motion a process that will force them into a public revelation of their nuclear program, permit U.N. supervisors to visit their nuclear facilities, and limit the capacity of their reactors to the bare minimum.

"Now, I hope it won't come to this, but we have to prepare for the probability that they will refuse. In such an eventuality, we'll have to be ready for a military action that will force them to listen. It will be a lot easier to attack if Europe and the Middle East cooperate with us. The way things look now, Turkey, Egypt, and Jordan would be glad to help us in this matter... With a military threat on all her borders, Israel will have no choice but to capitulate.

"The second stage will be sending forces to the Middle East. We must be prepared for any and all scenarios. This will also help put pressure on Israel to submit to our demands, which will come through the U.N. Does anyone have anything to add?"

"Mr. President, I know the IDF well," said the commander of the US Army, General Martin Ford. "I spent time in Israel as coordinator of our forces. Actually, at this very moment there are American troops in Israel for joint exercises. Their army may not be large, but it's fast and it's flexible. If we send forces out there without a good plan, they're liable to strike first and cause us heavy losses. The strategy that drove them in the Six-Day War could help them again now. If we send aircraft carriers there, they'll launch a surprise attack—and they could succeed. Something like that could hurt us badly, especially in terms of our image.

"And another question: what do we do with our soldiers there? We have to get them out before we start attacking, to prevent the Israelis from using them as hostages."

"He's right," the secretary of defense agreed. "We also have plenty of civilians there. We can't attack before we bring them home."

"What about people with dual citizenship? And what about the American Jews? They'll also be a problem from our perspective," added the director of the FBI.

Silence fell on the room as those present pondered a solution. Barry Radcliffe's phone rang, shattering the quiet. He listened for a moment, and promised the caller that he'd get back to him in five minutes. The president didn't have to guess hard to figure out who it was.

"CNN?"

"Yes, sir. What do we tell them?"

Bob Walters hesitated. This was going to be the most difficult decision of his presidency. He would go down in the history books as the first president to demonstrate hostility to America's traditional ally.

But what other option did he have? This time, the Israelis had crossed a line. It was an act of terror, backed directly by Israel. An incident like this could not be allowed to pass without reaction. A harsher president might denounce the entire Jewish nation. The evidence he held was strong enough for him to make the accusations. History would sustain the claim. This was the first time they'd been caught red-handed. The cream of worldwide Jewry, involved in a gigantic terrorist plot... Who would have believed it?

"Confirm the information about the arrests, and tell them that we have a reasonable suspicion that foreign governments were involved in the episode. You can tell them that we plan to condemn them in the U.N., and that we're about to call a meeting of the Security Council to discuss our reaction."

Everyone in the room held his breath. What the president was doing here was irreversible. The minute this hit the media, it would be unstoppable.

"We need to urge all U.S. citizens to leave Iran and Israel in the coming days. I want to make sure there are enough flights for anyone who wishes to leave and return here by the end of the week. Also issue a travel advisory to those countries. And of course we'll have to withdraw our troops from there with all possible speed. But they don't have to be brought home. Just transfer them to a neighboring country—Egypt, perhaps. It's very possible that we'll need them soon, against Israel...

"What do you say, Mike? You were just there. Do you think it's possible to move our forces to Egypt?"

The CIA director didn't miss a beat. "Absolutely. The new regime needs our money in order to survive, and if we throw in the hatred of Israel that reigns in the streets of Cairo, they'll be glad to help us."

"So that's it? We're going to war?" Peter Taylor asked.

"No," the president asserted. "Not yet. First we'll act against Israel in the U.N. But if Israel refuses to meet our demands, we'll have no choice but to attack."

42

YISRAEL STAYED IN HIS ROOM ALL AFTERNOON. HE HAD gone there after the president's announcement of a terror attack, and hadn't left until it was time for Minchah. Because of this, he didn't hear the latest developments. The only thing he knew was that America had been attacked with a nuclear bomb. This was something that until now had been reserved for adventure books. And now, on his first visit to the United States, it had happened.

Earlier, he had spoken to his mother, who was in a panic. News of the nuclear bomb had reached Israel, and she literally wept when she heard that he was alive. The problem was, he couldn't provide much comfort. Jeffrey and Menachem had disappeared and he had no idea where to. He was alone in Washington, D.C. His return flight was not until tomorrow. Her only consolation was that there was someone looking out for him. She had never heard of Chang Lu, but now she thanked him from the bottom of her heart for helping her son.

Yisrael decided to stay close to the hotel until his flight. He didn't want to walk around outside carrying such a large sum of money, and he certainly didn't want to leave it behind in his room. Besides, what was there for him to do outside? He didn't know a soul.

He counted the hours until his flight and prayed they'd pass quickly. There were still a little more than 24 hours before he would be going home—a full day of this nightmare. He passed the time learning. That was the only way he could forget the situation he was in.

An hour before sunset, he decided to go out to shul. He thrust the wad of cash into his shirt, using tape to hold the wad close to his body. Yisrael went down to the lobby.

He didn't know if he was imagining it, but it seemed to him that everyone was looking at him oddly. As though they all knew his secret—the money taped to his chest.

Once in the street the looks continued. Yisrael wondered how that was possible. He looked down at himself; there was no way anyone could tell. So what was going on here? Why was everyone staring at him? Or was it all in his head?

"Hey, you! Jew boy! Get out of America!"

Yisrael whipped his head around. A black youth in torn jeans and a gold shirt with several chains was glaring at him from across the street. He'd seen Yisrael's yarmulke and was demanding that he leave America.

Yisrael walked faster. He'd heard that there was anti-Semitism in the States, but he'd never seen it here before. It was frightening.

He walked into the shul and found it in an unusual furor. Heated discussions were taking place on every side, and it didn't look as if anyone planned to start davening anytime soon. Yisrael listened to the snatches of talk, trying to figure out what all the commotion was about.

"Nuclear bomb...Jews...anti-Semitism..."

What was the connection between the bomb and anti-Semitism? And was the incident that had happened to him outside just now a part of it?

"Excuse me," he said to the man standing nearest to him. "When is Minchah? I have a *chiyuv*..."

The man turned to him in surprise. "What is an Israeli boy doing here? This is not a good time to visit America…"

"Why?" Yisrael asked. Had there been another bomb threat?

"You're asking why? The information that was released today is going to make life hard for all of us."

"What information?"

"Don't tell me you didn't hear. Jews were involved in the act of terror…"

"*Jews?*"

"Yes—some pretty well-known people too. We're facing a difficult time in this country."

The man resumed his conversation with his friend. Only the elderly *gabbai*, who recognized Yisrael, gestured for him to go up to the *bimah* and forced the others to stop talking and start davening.

Yisrael, like most of the others there, found it hard to concentrate on his *tefillah*. Was it really possible that Jews were involved in terror? What kind of Jew would do a thing like that? That was something that, until now, had been reserved for the Arabs.

He was due to leave tomorrow in any case, so he had nothing to worry about. But what about all the Jews who lived in America? They'd be swamped by a great wave of anti-Semitism. The only thing to do was daven… He remembered where he was, and struggled to push his troubling thoughts aside.

Yisrael stayed to learn between Minchah and Maariv. He ignored the renewed, animated discussions, which would help nobody. Strengthening his Torah study, on the other hand, could definitely be helpful.

When Maariv was over, he prepared to return to his hotel. Taking out his phone to change it back from silent mode, he was surprised to see twelve unanswered calls! He pressed the button and discovered that all the calls had come from the same number: Chang Lu's.

"Hey, Lu, were you looking for me? Has something happened?"

"Where are you?" Lu wanted to know. "I was going out of my mind with worry."

"I'm in shul. I was just about to go back to the hotel. Why? What happened?"

"Don't leave until I get there," Lu ordered. "I'll be with you in two minutes. Meanwhile, *don't go out*! Do you hear me?"

"Okay, okay." Yisrael was surprised. What could have happened to worry Lu like that? Was the money he'd given him illegal?

He had his answer the minute he got into the car. "Your uncle is in a much more complicated situation than I thought," Lu said. "They suspect him of being involved in the act of terror that took place today! From now on, you must not tell anyone that you're related to him. Understand?"

"What do you mean, 'involved'? Jeffrey knew about the bomb in advance?"

"I don't know exactly, but he's in real hot water. And not only him. I think we're headed for a hard time for your people—the Jews. People in the street are furious at all of you right now."

"But why should Jeffrey get involved in terror? He has everything! It doesn't make any sense."

"I don't know, but it's very serious. The FBI wouldn't have arrested him without hard proof."

Yisrael sank wordlessly into his seat. Things were becoming crazy. This whole thing felt like one big nightmare. Jeffrey—a terrorist?

"Just a second. What about Menachem Goldfarb, my uncle's friend?"

"He's involved too."

"Menachem too? That can't be."

"It's been in the news for a good few hours already. They're in very serious trouble..."

Yisrael tried to grasp it all. The people in whose company he'd spent the last few days had been arrested on suspicion of being terrorists. He tried to recall if he'd seen anything suspicious... But apart from the small incident at Mikhail's house, there'd been nothing.

Actually, what *had* they been discussing in that inner room while he stayed in the living room? He'd overheard snatches of what they'd said... And, yes, they'd said something about a nuclear bomb! He'd thought they were referring to the Iranian nuclear program. Not something that they were plotting... Was it possible?

Were they really engaged in terrorist activity?

Lu continued driving. He passed the hotel. "I've already collected your things from your room. You're not going back there. I don't want you to be alone at this time. First of all, you're a Jew—and, even worse, you're Jeffrey Davis' nephew. You're staying with me until your flight to Israel. Put this on your head."

He handed Yisrael a blue baseball cap. Yisrael put it on. In Switzerland too, he and his fellow yeshivah students been told not to stand out as Jews. A cap was not as revealing as a yarmulke. Right now, he mustn't stand out.

"The wave of arrests continued all afternoon. The FBI invaded the AIPRO offices, arrested a few senior people, and confiscated equipment. Exactly like they did in the hotel. This story is not anywhere near over. You have to get out of here as soon as possible. It won't be long before the media discovers you."

"My flight's tomorrow. What could happen already?"

"You're right. Nevertheless, I prefer that you not be alone. Sleep at my house this one night, and tomorrow I'll drive you to the airport."

They entered a quiet, upscale street. Lu parked near his house. An elderly Oriental woman was working in a flourishing garden. She looked up and smiled warmly in welcome.

Even in the darkness, Yisrael could see that the garden was especially lovely. Flowers in a wide assortment of colors edged the razor-sharp lawn, plants grew with precision and there were flower boxes on every window. There was no question that the elderly woman devoted many hours to this place.

She hugged Lu and greeted Yisrael with a long sentence in Chinese.

"She's happy that I brought you here. She is grateful to your uncle for helping me," Lu translated. "I'm sorry; my mother doesn't speak English."

They entered the house, with Lu's mother talking nonstop. In the living room, Lu's father, an elderly man with a small, pointed beard, sat on the sofa reading a book in Chinese. Lu came close and shouted something in his ear. The old man lifted his head slowly, measured Yisrael with his eyes, and then stood up with a hand outstretched in greeting.

"Welcome," he said in accented but correct English, pronouncing each syllable with great care. "A friend of Lu's is a friend of mine."

Yisrael thanked him for his hospitality, and followed Lu to the room that had been prepared for him. All the walls were painted red and gold, which provided an exotic look. The house was filled with the aroma of deep-fried and heavily spiced food—a smell that reminded Yisrael that he was hungry.

His room held a powerful scent that came from a different source. Lu sighed, put down the suitcase, and went over to extinguish the incense sticks that exuded smoke and fragrance. "I told her not to light them. I hope the scent won't bother you too much."

"It's okay," Yisrael reassured him. "I already owe you so much. I don't know how I would have managed on my own."

"Is the room all right?"

"The room's great!"

Lu smiled, and they returned to the living room. Lu's mother was busy setting the table for dinner. Steaming tureens emitting tantalizing smells were placed on the table. She gestured to her husband to abandon his book and take his place at the head.

Lu sat down too, and motioned for Yisrael to sit beside him. The round table was set for four. Beside three of the plates were a set of chopsticks; next to the fourth was a set of ordinary flatware.

"There's nothing like my mother's food," Lu said proudly, smiling at her. She returned his smile, though she didn't understand what he'd said. Yisrael didn't smile. He didn't know how to get out of this. How could he explain to them, without giving offense, that the food wasn't kosher?

The old Chinese woman loaded the aromatic stew onto their plates, her husband's first, then Yisrael's, and, lastly, Lu's. Yisrael saw a piece of some sort of meat on his plate and wondered what it was. Even if it was beef, it had not been ritually slaughtered. What was he going to do?

"Eat, eat. You'll need your strength for the flight tomorrow," Lu urged. He set an example, piling meat and rice onto his chopsticks and bringing them to his mouth with visible pleasure. "Ah!

Wonderful!"

"I'm not so hungry right now," Yisrael lied. Actually, he was very hungry, and the sight and smell of the food only added to his misery. But there was no way he was going to eat it. This was not even a case of *pikuach nefesh*.

"Taste it, and see how good it is," his host pressed. "You won't be able to stop eating."

Lu's father sat in his seat and watched what was happening. He was a very quiet, measured man. In contrast to his wife, he was well read and had learned much about Western culture. Life in the United States had given him a broad base of knowledge that he would not have received in Communist China. He knew about different cultures and nations, and he knew what was happening at his table right now.

"You need kosher food, right?" he asked Yisrael with a smile.

Yisrael was confused. It was strange to hear the word "kosher" spoken with a Chinese lilt. How did this man even know the concept?

"Ah!" Lu remembered, and smacked his forehead. There had been occasional guests at his hotel who'd had the same requirement. Very Orthodox people who received food from a kosher restaurant. Why hadn't he thought of that? Why, Menachem Goldfarb had been one of them. They'd had food brought to him from some restaurant in Baltimore. Not that he himself understood the difference…

"So you don't like Chinese food?"

"It's not that I don't like it. I'm just not permitted to eat it."

"Ah, so sorry. I didn't know you felt that way. I'll order kosher food at once, okay?"

"Thank you very much…but I'm not really that hungry," Yisrael protested feebly.

Lu waved a dismissive hand and left the room to order food for Yisrael.

"I understand that you're an Orthodox Jew?" the old man asked him. "I've never met one before, though I've read about them a little… You have a history no less lengthy than the Chinese. History is good. One of the problems of this generation is that they don't know history. They don't know where they're from, and why. That's why there's no respect for their elders!"

Yisrael nodded. Lu's mother smiled at him and asked something, gesturing at his plate. Her husband spared Yisrael the difficulty of answering by telling her something in their own tongue. Though visibly disappointed by what she heard, she whisked Yisrael's plate away with alacrity.

So Yisrael found himself spending the last evening before his flight home eating kosher *l'mehadrin* pizza in the company of an elderly and curious Chinese man who wanted to hear everything he could about Judaism.

43

THE PRIME MINISTER'S TROUBLES ONLY BEGAN WHEN HE landed in Israel. The journalists who had accompanied him on his trip joined those who had remained behind in Israel in a surprisingly united chorus that broadcast one message: the prime minister had failed.

The various news commentators competed in their descriptions of the contrast between the current situation and Israel's past friendship with America, and speculation about the prime minister's hasty flight home. One newspaper quoted a "senior source" as reporting a harsh verbal exchange in the course of the prime minister's meeting with the president. In fact, that had never happened. True, there had been some minor differences of opinion, but the dialogue had taken place in a relaxed and friendly atmosphere. Even if the U.S. president did not support an immediate attack on Iran, he had not dismissed the idea out of hand. With further effort, these areas would be resolved.

With the news of the nuclear attack, the tone of the articles changed sharply. The commentators outdid themselves in focusing on the stunning timing that lent color to the prime minister's claims. Iran had attacked the United States at the worst possible time—from Iran's point of view. After such an attack, the United States would have no choice but to authorize an attack on Iran—and would apparently not even ask Israel to carry it out. The Iranian president would soon feel the strong arm of America.

Within a short time, however, the prime minister began to sense that something negative had taken place. His repeated attempts to reach the American president failed. The man was simply not available. Though this was understandable in the first hours after the attack, when the media began reporting on the messages of support and encouragement that were issuing from the heads of various European governments, he realized that something had gone wrong. The president was avoiding him.

He called a hurried meeting of the heads of his intelligence bureaus, trying to squeeze out every bit of information they had about the attack on America. He heard nothing useful. A nuclear bomb—apparently made in Russia—had somehow reached Iran and been sent to America. The very scenario he'd been warning about had actually taken place.

The question was why didn't the president want to talk to him. Did he prefer not to hear "I told you so"? The prime minister would not be foolish enough to say that. All he wanted to tell President Walters was that he and the Jewish people shared in his pain and were prepared to offer whatever help might be needed. In just a few days' time, he would begin increasing the pressure for an attack on Iran.

The passing hours did not make the situation any better. Little by little, more information began trickling in. Important Jewish figures had been arrested on suspicion of being involved in terror. And not just any figures, but Jeffrey Davis and Menachem Goldfarb. The two men who, as far as he was concerned, had been most instrumental in planning his recent visit.

The minute the names were brought to his attention, the prime minister understood that the situation was far more complicated than he had realized. If the Americans had arrested them, something extremely problematic was taking place. To set in motion arrests of this magnitude, the United States had to have some firm and reliable evidence. An American billionaire and an Israeli politician; you didn't arrest men of that caliber unless you were very sure of your facts.

But what frightened him most of all was the fact that they hadn't even bothered to inform him of the arrests. International diplomacy prohibited the arrest of foreign citizens—let alone politicians—without prior notice to their governments. In this case, however, not only had he not been told of the arrests in advance, but they weren't even prepared to talk to him. Not with him, nor with any other Israeli. Something very bad had happened…

That "something" very quickly came to light. In the ensuing hours, the Americans wasted no time arresting other prominent American Jews. Taking things one step further, the United States issued a warning to its citizens to refrain from traveling to Israel. US citizens presently in Israel were urged to get on the first plane home. American news channels were filled with reports of a Jewish terrorist organization. Why, and who? That was still not clear.

Israel's security people were in an uproar. Plans were made and discarded, and hasty meetings convened in an effort to gauge the extent of the crisis. The trickle of information coming from America indicated that an accusation would be brought before the UN Security Council demanding condemnation of Israel for its involvement in the attack. Not a word was said about Iran, who was directly responsible for the act of terror. The blame was all on Israel—and Israel alone.

The prime minister demanded that his intelligence bureaus find the missing link. Without a doubt, the Americans had some information that he was lacking, information about someone on the Israeli side who had been involved in the attack. It might be a terrorist cell on the extreme right, or—worst-case scenario—someone from one of his own bureaus who thought too creatively. Either way, he had to find out who was to blame and hand him over to the Americans. A situation in which Israel's only friend on the Security Council demanded a condemnation of Israel was simply intolerable. He had to stop such a thing before it happened.

The problem was that there were no avenues of investigation open to him. All the suspects were in detention in America, and all of his contacts there had either disappeared or clammed up. Nearly all the information he had came from the news networks, which were having a field day with the story. Foolishly, the Israeli media had elected to join the party.

It wasn't until Thursday morning Israeli time that the picture became clearer. The dimensions of the arrests left no doubt. The American government suspected the existence of a large Jewish organization aimed at promoting terror. And that organization included personalities in Israel—including the prime minister himself.

The prime minister didn't hesitate. He immediately arranged air time, firmly declared his innocence, and agreed to answer all questions by any investigative committee that might be formed.

"It will turn out that Israel had no part in the attack. As a nation that suffers from terror more than any other, Israel knows the meaning of terror, and completely disclaims any connection to this act. All the signs lead to Iran, and that country must pay the price for choosing the path of terror. Israel has always, and will always stand with her American friends against every attempt to damage our mutual interests." He called upon the U.S. president to communicate with him to discuss the deepening crisis. No reply was forthcoming.

The Americans were taking the story much more seriously. Lines of anxious passengers crowded Ben Gurion Airport. The U.S. government recruited planes from international airline companies to bring its citizens home. A strange, warlike tension hovered over the State of Israel. The only question was: whom were they fighting?

It was only in the afternoon hours of Thursday in Israel—Thursday morning in Washington, D.C.—that the first official statement arrived from the United States. It was a copy of the demand for condemnation in the U.N., accompanied by a list of American demands of Israel:

1. Complete cooperation with the investigation into those suspected of involvement in the nuclear attack

2. Exposure of Israel's nuclear facilities to U.N. inspectors, and imposition of international law on Israel's nuclear arsenal

3. The start of immediate negotiations with the Palestinians on the return of the territories and the division into two states, based on the 1967 borders

In addition, Israel was told not to harm any American citizens living within her borders, and was strongly warned against rendering those citizens harsh treatment.

"The United States regards Israel's involvement in the attack as a despicable act of betrayal. After the ongoing assistance and support that Israel has received from the United States, Israel has damaged the friendship between our two countries with alarming acts of aggression.

"In the Six-Day War, we were silent while Israel attacked the *Liberty*, an American ship in which thirty-four of our soldiers were killed. And when we discovered an Israeli spy in our midst, we did not allow him to destroy the powerful bond between us. This time, however, Israel has overstepped its limit. If Iran must be condemned for her active role in this attack, Israel must be triply condemned for being the brains behind this criminal act.

"The United States has no doubt that, without Israel's initiative, this lowly act of terror would not have come about. Therefore, we reserve the right to react in the place and at the time that suits us."

There the message ended.

Thursday, United States

The people of the United States woke up on Thursday, the national day of mourning, to learn that they were practically in a state of war with Israel.

The official demand for condemnation of Israel appeared in the news media and took center stage in the world's headlines. Accusations were hurled at Israel from nearly every possible government, with the most bizarre coming from Iran herself, stating that she was "not at all surprised that, once again, the Zionist entity has been caught attempting to cause friction between Iran and her friends. Israel has always chosen the path of terror and fearmongering, and it is only to be expected that she would act against her allies. Israel is a nation that has chosen terror as a way of life, a nation that fabricated the Holocaust in order to permit her to do anything she wants."

Bob Walters flew to Arizona to participate in the official ceremony for the victims of the terrorist attack. The massive security surrounding him did not prevent him from paying a personal visit to each of the bereaved families. Despite the pleading of his security people, who were afraid of hotheads, he insisted on shaking the mourners' hands and bolstering their spirits at this difficult hour. He knew what it was to be bereaved and wanted to help however he could, even at risk to himself.

The cameras that accompanied him on the trip recorded every minute of the visit. Not an eye was dry when Bob spoke to Buddy Jones Jr.'s small children.

The three children clung to their mother, in sharp contrast to the other large, sprawling families. Buddy and his wife had had no other living relatives. The widow would be alone now to bear the burden of raising her children and keeping her home from falling apart. Even the most seasoned photographers shed a tear when little Maryanne gathered her courage and asked the president what her Daddy had done to get punished like that. And why wasn't he coming home?

Bob crouched down beside her and her siblings, so that he was eye to eye with them, and said that their father had been a hero. "A great many people owe him their lives," he declared.

The event was broadcast live in the United States and across the world. Buddy's story became famous, and long articles were written about him. In his death, he earned praise he'd never dreamed of when he was alive. It was praise that would, at least in small measure, ease his family's pain in the days and years ahead.

The president returned from Arizona determined to track down those responsible for the tragedy. The moment the information was made public, the race against time began. In an era when news was aired almost in real time, it was impossible to wait too long before acting. The American people felt betrayed. They wanted to punish someone for the murderous attack. The only question was: whom to punish? The fury and vengeful feelings sought an outlet. The people wanted someone to blame. And the many arrests provided ample material.

Astonishingly, Iran's role in the episode was minimized and nearly overlooked. Israel's role, on the other hand, never left the front page. As a wise person once said: "When a snake bites a person, that's not news. But when a person bites a snake—that's a headline."

The Jews of the United States, who had enjoyed decades of tranquility, were stunned to wake up to a new morning. A morning in which their colleagues regarded them with suspicion, asking themselves if their own friends were terrorists. Dozens of violent incidents of an anti-Semitic nature took place on the day that would be remembered as Dark Thursday—the day every Jew was transformed into a potential suspect.

For the first time in U.S. history, entire Jewish communities were afraid of what the future might hold. Though America's core value was freedom of religion and worship, that didn't stop the average gentile from hating the Jews. New York City, the place with the largest Jewish as well as Israeli population, also changed its stripes that day. If, until that morning, Jews had walked around with heads held high, now they preferred to blend into the crowd. Harsh confrontations were reported as spontaneous gatherings of angry youths attacked shuls and Jewish homes.

The police came out in full force to try to halt the violence, but an isolated incident in which a Jew under attack pulled out a gun and killed two young Islamic men ignited the streets. Thousands of Muslims, joined by groups of African-Americans and violent extremists, poured into the streets with a single goal: to expel the Jews from America.

The mayor of New York City tried in vain to mediate between the sides. He decided that, should the violence not be over by Sunday, he would call out the National Guard to restore order in the streets.

The city's economy suffered massive irreversible harm. In the wake of the violence, tourists fled and thousands of employees stayed home from work. It was clear that the situation could not be allowed to continue. The question was how to stop it.

The president himself was asked to step in, and he demanded an end to the violence. "We will deal firmly with anyone who takes the law into his own hands. It doesn't matter what nation or race he's from. We have the best law enforcement in the world, and only they will deal with those who break the law.

"I want to stress that we mustn't ever generalize. While a group of Jews has been implicated in this act of terror, that absolutely does not mean that *all* Jews are guilty. That was our attitude when Islamic terrorists toppled the Twin Towers, and that will be our attitude today. Anyone who attempts to act on his own is a criminal and a lawbreaker and will be treated as such. I demand an end to the acts of violence in New York and anywhere else in the United States. America knows how to protect herself, and she is going to do so. But we must be united in this trying time—not divided."

But not even these words succeeded in stemming the rising tide of violence. Impassioned young Jews joined together to protect their communities, leading to additional acts of violence. As the day wore on, the incidents spilled beyond the country's borders. Russia, France, England, and other locations throughout the world reported a steep rise in acts of anti-Semitism. Huge demonstrations took place in Arab countries, where the mobs called for the destruction of the State of Israel.

The U.N. Security Council, acting with uncharacteristic alacrity, met that same day to sharply condemn Israel. A weak denunciation was also included against Iran. A sweeping decision was made to join the United States in the demands that had been set down against Israel.

The State of Israel was under unprecedented international pressure. The speed of recent events prevented her from formulating a clear policy in response. Everything had happened so quickly that the Israeli prime minister was left reeling and helpless. Though it was in the middle of its summer break, the Knesset called an emergency meeting. Ministers and Knesset members rushed back to

Jerusalem from wherever they were vacationing with their families, and the State of Israel went into crisis mode.

The Israelis' first goal was to buy more time. They needed time in order to investigate the claims and study America's demands. The United States government sent over the investigative material and evidence that had been assembled against the suspects. Some of the evidence pointed an accusing finger at two senior Israeli ministers and the prime minister himself, who seemed to have known about the terrorist plot and did not do anything to stop it. The Americans demanded to see transcripts from meetings in which the suspects took part. In addition, they repeated their earlier demands: the dismantling of Israel's nuclear program, and intensive talks to reach a peace agreement based on the 1967 borders.

The Knesset forum was transformed into a mini-battlefield. Members of the opposition party called for an immediate dissolution of the government and the removal of the prime minister as a terror suspect. Legal advisers were called upon to check the law regarding such a scenario, leading to further chaos in the Knesset. Instead of the various factions uniting in the face of the immediate threat to Israel, the Knesset meeting only added to the rage and the chaos.

Anxious citizens descended on food outlets and bought out their inventories of canned goods and bottled water. The atmosphere of war, which had, until today, been limited to areas in the north and south, now reached every home in Israel. In Tel Aviv's Rabin Square, tens of thousands gathered on Thursday evening. They called for the ousting of the prime minister and for the government to accede to U.S. demands. "We don't want the bomb! We only want peace!" the demonstrators cried.

The U.S. ultimatum was clear. Israel had exactly one week to reply to its demands. By midnight on the following Thursday, Israel had to allow U.N. inspectors to visit the reactor at Dimona, send a negotiating team to Gaza, and supply the Americans with all the material they had requested.

If Israel refused, she would face an international coalition that would not hesitate to resort to force.

O N THURSDAY MORNING, YISRAEL WOKE EARLY. IT WAS
still dark outside. He was surprised to find the rest of the
household already awake.

"Good morning!" Lu greeted him cheerfully. "Did you sleep
well?"

"Totally fine," Yisrael replied. "But what about all of you? Why
are you all up?"

Lu chuckled, and explained the question to his mother. She
laughed too. Then Lu explained, "My parents have been starting
their day at 3 o'clock in the morning for the past fifty years. I too
have inherited from them a love of the early-morning hours. That's
when the air is clean, the streets are quiet, and one's head is clearest. There's nothing like starting the day early."

Yisrael nodded in appreciation. For him, getting up for davening was a daily battle—yet these people arose without effort. They
didn't even entertain the possibility of lingering in bed. A thought
to lend him strength…

He noticed that Lu's father did not join in the conversation. He
was standing at one side of the room on a small rug, eyes closed and

hands spread out in front of him. Lu saw Yisrael looking, and hastened to explain. "He's doing yoga. Every morning, we do exercises before we start the day. It focuses a person's energies properly."

Yisrael was astounded. The old man stood with eyes closed, in a state of intense concentration, his movements slow and exact. Yisrael knew nothing about yoga, but noticed that each move was carried out with extreme precision.

"What time is your flight today?" Lu's question startled him.

"At ten minutes to three, G-d willing."

"Very good. We'll spend a quiet morning here, and then I'll drive you to the airport at noon. Okay?"

"Thanks. Uh... I'd like to pray in the synagogue this morning."

"No problem. I'll take you there and back. Unfortunately, I don't have much to do today. The hotel is closed."

Yisrael got ready for shul and politely declined the offer of breakfast. He explained to his pleasant hosts that this time, the issue was not kashrut. He never ate before he had davened.

He left with Lu for the short drive to the shul, as the clear morning light chased away the darkness.

"Do you need a synagogue in order to pray?" Lu asked curiously. "Can't you pray at home?"

"I could," Yisrael tried to explain in brief, "but a synagogue is preferable, especially because it's preferable to pray along with other people."

Lu thought about this.

"And how many times a day do you need to pray?"

"Three. Morning, afternoon, and night."

"Interesting..."

They continued driving. Yisrael smiled to himself. In the past 24 hours he had answered more questions about his faith than in all the rest of his years put together.

"Stop!"

Yisrael's sudden cry startled Lu. Instinctively, he slammed on the brakes. "What's the matter?"

Yisrael didn't answer. He flung open his door and threw himself out of the car even before it came to a complete standstill. His feet flew over the asphalt and he reached the nearby street in seconds. There, he saw that what he had thought he'd seen was true. Three youths stood over a body sprawled on the ground, cursing and kicking at the helpless figure. Yisrael didn't stop to think. He jumped on the one closest to him and gave him a powerful shove. Before the second one could react, Yisrael aimed a kick at his stomach. And when the third turned around to see who was attacking them, Yisrael planted a quick, hard punch in the center of his face. In two seconds, all three were on the ground.

The first youth recovered rapidly. He pulled out a knife and waved it at Yisrael. The one who'd been punched still lay on the ground, clutching his bleeding nose, but the third was soon on his feet. The two circled Yisrael, prepared to attack.

At that moment, Lu appeared behind Yisrael.

"Yisrael, are you all right?"

Yisrael nodded without removing his eyes from the knife. His heart thudded powerfully in his chest, and his hands trembled. This was the first time he'd taken part in a real fight. Until now, it had been only practice. Here, it was real. One little mistake, and that knife would leave him scarred for life. And that was the best-case scenario…

The two youths looked at Yisrael and Lu and decided to beat a hasty retreat. Supporting their injured friend, they hurried off down the street. Lu crouched down beside the man lying on the ground.

"He's hurt pretty bad." He pulled a cell phone from his pocket and dialed 911.

Yisrael took in great gulps of air and willed his heart to stop pounding. Crouching beside Lu, he was startled to see that the injured man was familiar to him.

"Hey! That's the *shamash* from the shul."

Lu removed a tissue from his pocket and tried to stop the blood oozing from the *shamash's* head. "Help will be here soon," he said. The Jewish man breathed with difficulty. He did not open his eyes, but grunted as a sign that he'd heard.

Lu threw Yisrael an assessing glance. "That was very brave of you. I'm not sure I would have acted as you did."

Yisrael did not feel like a hero. Had he had any time to think, he wasn't sure he would have done it… He was shaken by the old man's condition. Why would anyone attack him so cruelly? It was hard to believe that he'd done anyone any harm.

"Yisrael, I think it would be a good idea for you to wait in the car," Lu said suddenly. "If the police find out that you were involved, they may make you miss your flight. They'll want to take your testimony and get a statement. That could take hours. Better that they don't know you were involved. I'll tell them that the attackers ran away when they saw me, and that's all."

Yisrael appreciated the fact that Lu had not stopped thinking clearly under pressure. He nodded and went off to find the car. He had just located it, parked nearby at the curb, when he heard the wail of a siren. A police car passed him and halted with a screech beside Lu.

Yisrael sat in the car and steadied his breathing. That had been scary. There had been murder in those hoodlums' eyes. What good luck that he hadn't had a chance to think about what he was doing. With some time to mull it over, he would probably not have dared to embroil himself with them.

A long quarter of an hour passed before Lu returned to the car. An ambulance had arrived shortly after the police and had taken the *shamash* to the hospital. Lu had given his contact information to the police. Yisrael checked his watch. It was hard to believe it was only 7:30 in the morning.

"Do you still want to go to the synagogue?"

"Sure. They probably started already."

He was mistaken. Huge, spray-painted swastikas on the front of the building had induced most of the worshipers to absent themselves. Three of them stood outside, taking pictures. They looked furious.

"America is not Germany," one of them cried angrily. "I can't believe we've come to this."

Yisrael quickly realized that there would be no *minyan* here this morning. As far as he knew, it was the only Orthodox shul in the area. After a brief exchange, he told them what had happened to the *shamash*. Then he went back home with Lu. How sad. This was the first time all year that he'd have to daven on his own.

Lu tried to cheer him up. While he agreed that things didn't look very good for the Jews right now, he was sure that it was just a passing phase. "We live in the greatest democracy in the world. Such behavior will not pass unpunished. The thugs will soon be chased off the streets."

Yisrael wanted to believe him, but the situation seemed hopeless. On the news, they heard about the violent disturbances in New York. If things were out of control there, where could a Jew feel safe?

In his room, he davened more fervently than he had in a long time. He prayed not only for himself, though he longed to return home safely, but also for the millions of Jews who lived in America. They would have to remain and face the violence that had erupted before his eyes. He prayed too for the health of the poor *shamash*, and tried not to think about what might have happened had he not intervened.

Fresh fruit for breakfast did not lift his spirits. He was counting the minutes until his flight home and they crawled, of course, with maddening slowness. A phone conversation with his mother did nothing to brighten his mood. She was very worried. Of course, she'd heard about what was going on in America, but that was only part of the story. A state of emergency had been declared throughout Israel. On the radio they were talking about a call-up of army reservists, and everyone was discussing the best way to cope with the situation. Most of the voices were calling for the prime minister's resignation and full compliance with the U.S. government's demands.

But there were others who were hungry for battle. "No one is going to tell us what to do," they declared. "Submitting like that would be tantamount to committing suicide. Without nuclear weapons, and at the old borders, we will not be able to defend ourselves."

At long last, the moment came for Yisrael to part from his hosts. He thanked Lu's parents for their gracious hospitality, loaded his baggage into Lu's car, and they drove through the crowded streets to the airport.

His flight's departure time was 2:50 p.m., leaving from BWI outside Baltimore. As there were no direct flights from Washington to Israel, he'd be flying back via New York. The plane was scheduled to land in New York at 4:30 p.m. and to continue to Israel after a 2½-hour stopover.

His good-bye to Lu was interesting. Though Yisrael owed him a great deal, it wasn't hard to part from the friendly Chinese man. He couldn't wait to get home. Lu, on the other hand, had tears in his eyes as he hugged Yisrael emotionally and wished him luck. Yisrael, who until now had always believed Asians to be stiff and unfeeling, felt extremely uncomfortable under the stares of the people around them. He thumped Lu's shoulder with halting thanks, promised to stay in touch, and moved onto the security line. From here on in, he was on his own.

Fortunately for him, airports all over the world function similarly. He had no undue difficulty finding the right gate, and within a short time was seated in the airplane, murmuring *Tefillas Haderech* and dreaming of home.

Eretz Yisrael—here I come!

45

SIR HARRY BONDS HAD MADE HIS FORTUNE IN THE EARLY 1990's. Born and raised in England, he had received his medical degree at Cambridge University, specializing in cardiology. Though his parents were Jewish, they had raised their children without any connection to Judaism or to the State of Israel. They had embraced the ideal that their children must be good Englishmen; Jewish roots might detract from that ideal. Harry worked hard at his studies and was a source of pride to his parents from a very young age.

It was his knowledge of computers and programming, however, that decreed that he play a much larger role in world history. Before he finished his degree, Harry Bonds filed a patent for a device that could detect heart arrhythmias and murmurs in newborn babies.

Even he never imagined how successful his patent would be. Within months, thousands of orders from hospitals throughout the world came streaming in. His device was far cheaper than any previous technology and drastically diminished the percentage of infants who were not diagnosed in time. In such cases, early detection is half the solution. Generally, these conditions can be treated—unless they are diagnosed too late. Harry solved that problem.

His dizzying success thrust him into the forefront of global science. He completed his medical degree shortly afterward, and while his friends were looking for jobs, numerous clinics and prestigious hospitals fought for the services of Dr. Harry Bonds. But he decided to move into the field of medical equipment, an area where he had a great deal to contribute. Indeed, in the coming years a number of his other inventions met with success—though none enjoyed the soaring triumph of his first patent.

All of England loved Harry, mostly because he didn't keep his wealth to himself. He opened medical centers to help the needy and provided scholarships for underprivileged medical students.

It was during this period that Dr. Bonds learned from the newspapers that he was a Jew. His curiosity was aroused, and eventually he evolved into an ardent supporter of the State of Israel and the Jewish nation as a whole. He visited Israel and donated medical equipment to hospitals in Jerusalem and Haifa. In time, he developed into an ambassador of goodwill in Great Britain.

When the queen of England deigned to knight him, his influence increased greatly. This honor was highly regarded throughout Great Britain. Few merited the title given to those who had made outstanding contributions to England and the world. With his newly minted title, Sir Dr. Harry Bonds became a political coordinator with vast influence on English-Israeli relations. His great popularity enabled many difficult deals to reach fruition. Usually, when Harry was involved, positive things happened.

When recent events exploded on the world stage Sir Harry was in Israel. He had been visiting Jerusalem to donate a cutting edge MRI scanner to Hadassah Ein Kerem. His many years of activism had brought him into contact with all the detainees, and he knew them personally. But when his own name was publicized on suspicion of his being involved in the terrorist bombing, not even his meteoric success was able to save him.

The government of England demanded that he turn himself in for questioning, though his many friends in Israel urged him to reject the demand. He managed to obtain a personal meeting with the Israeli prime minister, who found himself in the same unenviable position. Both had been named as guilty parties, and both denied any connection to the episode. The problem was that, from a legal standpoint, the State of Israel was obligated to give him up to England. He was an English citizen, not an Israeli one.

Subject to internal pressures, the prime minister agreed to take responsibility and told Sir Harry not to surrender. "Stay here with us. This is the Jewish homeland, and here is where both of our fates will be decided."

Israel's relations with England, already soured, worsened when the demand for extradition was rejected. England swiftly joined the U.S. in its demands and reiterated her legal right to Sir Harry Bonds.

Europe, as a whole, became hostile to Israel. Most of its nations had little love for the Israelis to begin with, and they saw in the present situation a golden opportunity to act out. Unfortunately, this attitude did not confine itself to the level of government. Hordes of Muslim agitators took to the streets of the European capitals where, for the first time, they were joined by local youth in their cry for Israel's extinction. Violent clashes became the norm, adding increased pressure on the governments to act against the Jewish state.

The next days were difficult ones for Jewish communities throughout the world. Despite the efforts of some police forces, dozens of attacks on Jews occurred daily. As in New York, there were violent clashes between young people, with the number of casualties rapidly escalating. In countries such as Greece and Spain, which were experiencing dire economic difficulties, the demonstrators began adding anti-Semitic slogans that blamed the Jews for their countries' situation. It was not hard to prove Jewish involvement in the financial crisis. The Jewish-owned Lehman Brothers, which had begun the financial downturn, stood as eternal proof of the Jews' guilt. Tens of thousands of idle street youths firmly believed that the Jews were to blame for their plight. Countries that boasted flourishing Jewish communities became places where Jews were afraid to walk the streets. It was hard to know how or when the situation would end.

The rage in the streets did not help the governments, either. In the present economic climate, each and every day that people didn't work was a tragedy. The heads of government, meeting at a European summit, called on Israel to accede to American demands with all possible speed. If Israel did not submit by midnight Thursday, the deadline for meeting the U.S. ultimatum, the nations would be forced to act, not only for ideological reasons but also for practical ones. After all, cynically they were well aware that there's nothing like war to boost the economy.

At that summit, the leaders also agreed to contribute troops as the Americans had requested. Should there be a war with Israel, it would not be a uniquely American operation, but a coordinated effort among many of the world's nations. The coalition that the United States had put together to attack Iraq would be dwarfed by the present one. There was hardly a single country that declined to join. The world was united in a single, rare consensus: it was time to put a stop to Israeli aggression. The time had come to put the Jews firmly in their place—once and for all.

The plane landed in New York at 4:30 in the afternoon, as scheduled. Yisrael followed the line of passengers who were continuing on to the next plane. This time, he would not be lingering in New York.

The moment he reached the central terminal, he noticed that something had changed since the week before. Scores of policemen were swarming all over the place, preventing any undue gathering of crowds. His queries about the gate to his connecting flight were met with hostile faces. But it was not until he reached the gate that he really grasped how complex the situation had become. Numerous passengers were shouting and shoving in the direction of the Israeli security desk.

To his apprehension, Yisrael saw that his own flight was particularly problematic. The heightened tension had led many Israelis to make the decision to return home. There were also American Jews who wanted to travel to Israel, either to escape the United States or to demonstrate their support for Israel. The result was a catastrophe with regard to flights to that country. People were fighting over every seat. Yisrael fervently hoped that his ticket was still valid.

What he didn't know, but the others did, was that there would be no additional flights to Israel in the coming week. As part of the severing of relations with Israel, the United States government had canceled all authorizations for the Israeli airline in America, effective midnight on Thursday. People had pulled every string they could think of in order to be on this one flight.

This was the tense situation into which Yisrael had just walked. The Israeli airline employees were doing their best to get the passengers lined up in an orderly fashion, but the shoving had quickly turned into a fracas that was spiraling out of control. The police, hurrying to help, were drawn into the fisticuffs with frustrated passengers waiting to board.

Clutching his passport, Yisrael tried to move to the head of the line, but the wave of humanity buffeted him to and fro. He did his best to protect himself from the flying fists. The police acted forcefully, arresting dozens of people, but this served to inflame rather than calm the crowd. People struggled against the police, leading to injuries on both sides. Reinforcements arrived, but it was already too late. The area had been transformed into a battleground, and the police began making mass arrests.

Yisrael attempted to talk to the two policemen who had him in their grip. He tried to explain that he had not been involved in the violence. He only wanted to return home in peace. But there was no one to talk to. No one was listening to a word he said. The police tugged his hands brutally behind him and snapped on a pair of handcuffs. His wrists ached from the pressure, but that wasn't what bothered him. He had to get free! He had to go home. A roar of anger burst from his throat, and he kicked out recklessly at the officers gripping his arm. With his hands still locked behind his back, Yisrael jumped back into the fray. He had to reach that airplane. He had to get out of here!

Shoves from the right and left made him dizzy, but he didn't let them deter him. He pushed forward, suffering the occasional blow that he could not deflect with his manacled arms, and forged onward. Jaw set, he advanced with determination. One meter, and then another. He would soon reach the desk...

Yisrael didn't see how it happened. The policemen had come up behind him. It wasn't hard for them to identify him in the crowd; after all, he was wearing handcuffs...

The officer he had kicked did not hesitate. He took out his baton and brought it down hard on Yisrael's head.

Yisrael collapsed onto the floor in a faint. He would not be flying home tonight.

46

H E WOKE UP IN A HOSPITAL BED. HIS HANDS WERE STILL IN
cuffs. A policeman sat beside the bed. When he noticed that
Yisrael was stirring, he summoned the doctor.

"Hello, young man," the doctor said. "Do you know why you're
here?"

Yisrael tried to make order of his thoughts. His head had begun
to broadcast sharp waves of pain, and he grimaced.

"Are you in pain?"

Yisrael nodded.

The doctor increased the dose on his IV, and the relief was immediate. As the sedation filled his veins, Yisrael felt relaxed but a little
foggy.

"I'm still in America, right?"

"Yes. You're in Mt. Sinai Hospital in New York. Do you know
why?"

Yisrael remembered. "Yes... There was a big mess at the airport...
Just a second! What time is it? I need to catch my flight home!"

The doctor smiled. "Today is Monday," he said. "You've been
asleep for a while."

Yisrael was stunned. *Monday?* He'd been unconscious for *four days?*

"The police are very angry at you," the doctor informed him. "They say you attacked an officer."

"That's not true! The officer attacked *me!* I was only trying to get on my flight!"

"All right. It doesn't really matter much anymore. Now that you've woken up, I think you'll get better very quickly. Within a couple of days, you'll be like new."

The policeman seated beside the bed moved closer. "You're in luck. They decided not to charge you. You did attack a police officer, but you had an airline ticket in your possession. You just have to sign a paper dismissing the charge, and you'll be free to go home."

"What kind of paper?"

"A statement saying that you won't bring charges against the NYPD here in New York."

Yisrael tried to think clearly. The pain in his head was still confusing him a little. "And why should I want to sign it?"

"Because, if you don't, we'll charge *you* with attacking a police officer."

Yisrael gave in. Weakly, he took the pen that was held out to him and tried to sign his name. His hand shook uncontrollably, and the pen fell from it twice.

"Don't worry," the doctor reassured him. "This is natural after such a long sleep. Your muscles are still a big groggy. Fortunately, you weren't unconscious too long and you won't be needing physiotherapy."

Yisrael managed to scribble something on the policeman's paper. The effort made him collapse against his pillows. The policeman wished him luck and turned to go. A minute later, Yisrael was sound asleep again.

He spent the next two days in the hospital, where he learned that the outside world had been rapidly changing. Israel was facing an existential threat, the Jews in America and worldwide no longer felt secure...and here he was, lying helpless in a strange hospital bed.

To his joy, he discovered that his money had not been lost. He'd been afraid that someone would have stolen the wad of cash he'd had on him, but was surprised to hear that the police had turned over the $10,000 on his admittance to the hospital, along with his passport.

His mother was nearly out of her mind with worry. She was at the point of hysteria. Her son had not returned home on his scheduled flight, and there were no longer any planes traveling to Israel. She had done everything she could to try to ascertain Yisrael's whereabouts, but the chaos in the United States had created many problems. Numerous people were seeking their relatives, not always successfully.

Four terror-filled days had passed in the Davis household before the phone rang. Yisrael reported that he was alive and well, but stuck in the hospital until Wednesday. At first, his mother didn't believe that he was really all right. If he was not injured, what was he doing in a hospital? To set her mind at ease, Yisrael was forced to describe the whole incident to her in detail.

"I want you to come home immediately! Do you hear me?"

"Yes, Mommy. Believe me, I also want to come home. But how am I supposed to do that?"

"Through Europe. There are some European countries that still allow flights to Israel."

"Switzerland too?"

"Yes, Switzerland has remained neutral, as always. Take a plane to Zurich, which you know so well, and continue on to Israel from there. Do you hear me?"

"Yes, Mommy. *B'ezras Hashem.*"

"But—just a minute. How will you pay for the flight?"

"That's okay, Mommy. I have a little money from Uncle Jeffrey. It'll be enough for a flight home."

"*Baruch Hashem.* I was worried. I don't have a credit card that you could use. Do you know how to order a ticket?"

"I'll manage. It'll be all right."

"I want to hear from you after you've bought the tickets, okay? I want to know exactly when you'll be coming home."

"Okay, Mommy. Please stop worrying. Everything's going to be okay."

"Here in Israel these days, we don't know how anything's going to turn out. The Jewish nation is in big trouble. Anyone who thinks that there could never be another Holocaust is mistaken."

"*Chas v'chalilah!*"

"Yes, *chas v'chalilah*. But I want you home as soon as possible. Be careful, Yisrael. We're waiting for you."

"*L'hitraot*, Mommy. And don't worry. Everything's going to be okay, *b'ezras Hashem*."

The sound of his mother's weeping did nothing to dispel his bad feeling.

The earliest flight he managed to book was scheduled to depart at 2:35 a.m. on Thursday morning. His luggage was waiting for him at the hospital's reception desk when he was released Wednesday afternoon, but Yisrael had no idea where to go. He was afraid to seek out the Jewish neighborhoods, which as evidenced in the news had become miniature battlefields. Therefore, he decided to stay in the hospital one more night, until his flight home. He no longer had a bed there. He sat on his suitcase near the emergency room, and waited for the hours to pass.

A steady stream of wounded people continued to flow through the hospital doors. Though the National Guard had been called in, violent incidents were still occurring on a daily basis. New York City had changed beyond all recognition. New Yorkers were prohibited from leaving their homes at night, and any gathering of people required a special license. Yisrael sat huddled in his corner, detached from what was going on around him. All he wanted was to get peacefully through the remaining hours until his flight.

Despite his resolution not to look at anyone, it was impossible for Yisrael not to notice the two men who appeared in the ER early in the evening. They stood out from the other unfortunates waiting there because they were well-dressed and quite huge. If Yisrael had to guess, he would have said they were a pair of thugs from the criminal underworld. Everything about the pair radiated strength. But they did nothing but sit quietly on a bench at one side of the room all evening. By the look of their faces, Yisrael surmised that they were Russians. As an Israeli, he'd learned to distinguish between various nationalities, though he wasn't absolutely certain.

His flight was scheduled for 2:35 a.m., but Yisrael decided to get to the airport early. He would make sure to reach the terminal no less than four hours before his scheduled departure. He had already learned, the hard way, that anything could happen before one actually boarded the plane. He had managed to book a seat on a flight from JFK to Zurich, and from there to Israel. Luckily, the Swiss still had no quarrel with the Israelis.

He already knew the regular flight schedule from Zurich to Tel Aviv. Each day there were El Al planes that lifted off at noon and again at slightly before 9 in the evening. A Swissair flight was due to depart Zurich at 10:45 p.m. That was his flight. The last one of the day.

Yisrael, of course, preferred Zurich over any other place in the world. He knew the city and he was familiar with its airport. He could get around there. He could have flown from New York to Zurich in several possible ways: a direct flight on Swissair that took approximately seven hours, or a flight on another European airline, with a stop in that country. Yisrael preferred the nonstop flight. He had already suffered enough from flights with stopovers. But the only available seat to be had on the direct flight was for the next day, Friday. Reluctantly, he had bought a ticket from Air Berlin instead, for a flight that would take much longer and pass through Germany.

This time, the airport was far calmer than the last time he had been there. Though there was still a heightened police presence, Yisrael saw no unusual crowds. He gave in his luggage and passed through security without a hitch. There was still plenty of time left before liftoff.

According to his calculations he would land in Berlin at about 4:00 p.m. and continue on from there to Zurich. He had learned that flights from Germany to Israel had also been canceled, so his destination remained the Swiss airport.

Switzerland, a country that clung fiercely to its neutrality, had maintained its flights to Israel until further notice. At worst, if he was unable to find an immediate flight home, he could always take a taxi to his yeshivah, or go to the rosh yeshivah's house and stay there overnight. *B'ezras Hashem*, he would get a seat on the Friday morning flight and arrive home before Shabbos.

It was his good fortune that he knew Zurich so well. In America he had known no one, but he had friends in Zurich. Even if he had to stay for Shabbos, he would be all right. Right now, though, he just wanted to pass the time until his flight.

Suddenly a cluster of Orthodox Jews caught his eye on a nearby monitor. Yisrael moved closer to the screen, which was broadcasting news in English. The newscaster explained to his audience that a huge prayer rally was taking place at the Western Wall. "Over half a million people have gathered this morning at the Western Wall plaza in order to pray," said the professional voice, while the pictures continued to play over the screen. "The ultimatum that the nations of the free world have given Israel is about to expire, but a decision has yet to be announced. The Israeli prime minister has refused to grant an interview, and the Knesset is divided.

"Some members are calling for submission to the demands and giving up Israel's nuclear program, while others reject these demands out of hand. Meanwhile, the prime minister has managed to hold his coalition together remarkably well. No-confidence votes have been rejected, and representatives of the Ministry of Foreign Affairs have been doing everything in their power to delay the deadline—so far, without success.

"The feeling in the street is calm but tense," the newscaster continued, as the camera panned back to him, standing on the walls of the Old City. "People are armed, and army reservists have been called up. It is possible that war-weary Israel is facing her last battle. I have yet to meet an Israeli who is feeling optimistic. They don't believe that this is a war they can win. The vast majority believe that the prime minister will have to give in. And giving in means that Israel will lose its protection against its neighbors in the region. That, at least, is the way the Israelis see it.

"Tune in later this afternoon, when we will join the daily session at the Knesset. Right now, let's hope that the prayers of all those in this holy place are effective, and that no more blood will be spilled in a region that has already seen much violence. This is Jay Silberman, reporting live from Jerusalem."

The screen flipped to a talk show hosting a professor of literature. The topic was still the State of Israel. Yisrael, who until now had been immersed in his personal troubles, suddenly became aware of the momentous story developing around him. The Jewish people were in danger.

The things he had just seen and heard were all too real. The State of Israel stood on the brink of war, and he was doing his level best to get there...

"What do you think about the situation?" asked a heavyset fellow watching the program with him. "Is there going to be a war?"

"I don't know," Yisrael said. "I hope not."

"Why not? Let's show them, once and for all," the man declared. "Those Jews are really everywhere. They're trying to take over the world. It's time we put them in their place!"

Yisrael tensed. If this man only knew that he too was a Jew... His baseball cap and fluent English had caused the man to size him up as an average American youth. It was incredible how even the simple man in the street was infected by anti-Semitism.

"Did you know that they're to blame for the Twin Towers tragedy?" the heavyset fellow continued. "The Israeli Mossad arranged for those planes to be hijacked. They also recruited the terrorists, who thought they were getting their orders from bin Laden himself. And you know why? So that America would invade Iraq. So that America would do their dirty work for them. That's how the Israelis operate."

Yisrael had heard enough. He moved away from the vociferous man and went to buy a bottle of water. This was the reason he was going to Israel. Though war might await him there, at least he would be among brothers. Among people who didn't desire his death.

His plane lifted off as scheduled. By 2:45 a.m. they were in the air, and Yisrael promptly sank into a restorative sleep. The time in the hospital had not been very restful. He made up for it now.

This was the first time Yisrael spent an entire flight lost in sleep. He woke only as they started their descent, to hear the stewardess asking him if his seat belt was buckled. The landing in Berlin passed uneventfully. Yisrael moved alongside the stream of passengers making their way to their connecting flights. He had about an hour and a half to his flight.

Suddenly, he saw them. Near the restroom door, Yisrael spotted two familiar human gorillas. At the most unexpected time and place, he saw, to his trepidation, the same two Russians from the previous night in the emergency room. They too were waiting for the next plane.

What were they doing here? How had they gotten here? Had they been on the plane with him the entire time? What did they want? Yisrael couldn't believe that this was nothing but coincidence. Too many things had been happening lately. There had to be a connection.

Just a minute. Could they know about the money he was carrying? Maybe they knew that he was walking around with about $9,000 in cash. Were they thieves?

He rejected the idea. For a mere $9,000 they would not have invested in airline tickets. They would have robbed him before he boarded the plane.

Then what *did* they want? Was this linked to his encounter with those policemen in New York? But that case had been closed... Just a second. These were Russians. This must have something to do with the trouble Jeffrey and his friends were in. Mikhail was a Russian! Were the Russians who had been pursuing Mikhail now after *him*?

But what could they want from him? Did they think he was involved? He didn't even know what, exactly, his uncle had done. Did they believe he was a part of it?

Yisrael wandered around the big terminal, peeking over his shoulder from time to time to see if the Russians were behind him. And he saw that, though they tried to maintain a safe distance, the pair always made sure to keep him in their line of sight.

What was he supposed to do now? Run away? How? If he left the airport now, there was no place for him to go. He'd never been in Berlin. He didn't even know if there was a Jewish community there.

His eyes searched for a Jewish-looking face in the crowd of passengers milling around the huge room. Nothing. He was surrounded by Muslims, Indians, and people of other nationalities, but he saw not a single Jew. He'd have to manage on his own.

Yisrael decided that he had no choice. He must continue on to Switzerland. There, at least, he had a chance of getting away. Here, he'd only get lost. He was banking on the fact that if his pursuers wanted to hurt him, they wouldn't do so in a place this public and monitored by security cameras. The security people would catch them in a matter of seconds. The pair would undoubtedly wait until they landed in Switzerland and reached some side street where they would be unobserved. And that would play out to his benefit. Zurich was a place he knew.

He boarded the plane and noted that the two men boarded it as well. They sat behind him in the craft's rearmost row. Had the situation been different, Yisrael would have laughed at the sight of the two overgrown figures struggling to find room for their knees. But this was no laughing matter. Those gorillas were after *him*.

On this flight, he didn't close his eyes. His brain worked feverishly, trying to analyze recent events. The first thing that occurred to him was that the two were making no attempt to hide. They were not trying to conceal the fact that they were following him. Why? He had no answer.

The second thing he tried to unravel was his uncle's story. From what he had grasped from the FBI interrogator and the news broadcasts he'd seen, his uncle had been involved in terrorism. The reason for this astonishing fact had been supplied by Lu: Jeffrey, it seemed, was one of a group of influential Jews—including Mikhail Potgorsky and Menachem Goldfarb—who had planned to force America to attack Iran.

Their plan had been simple. They would make sure that the Iranians attacked the United States with a nuclear bomb. That would leave the U.S. president with no choice but to strike back at Iran.

The genius of the plan was frightening. Was this really the way things worked in the world? Did sophisticated plots like this take place all the time? After all, if it hadn't been discovered, the plan would have worked. The Americans were obligated to fight back. The problem was that the plot *had* been exposed. But—how? What had failed in their planning? Who had leaked the secret?

Yisrael tried to solve the riddle. What had gone wrong? And now another thought occurred to him—one that raised an even more puzzling question. If Menachem was so heavily involved in this plot, why had he chosen to take Yisrael to America with him? To meet his uncle? That was hard to believe... The man had far more important things on his mind. Things like planning a nuclear attack... And he decided to bring along a boy who could only complicate matters? Impossible. Or was he just the cover story? Who knew?

But suppose they were *not* guilty? Perhaps the whole plot had been fabricated? Maybe Uncle Jeffrey and his friends were innocent. That would explain why Menachem had not hesitated to bring him.

Then why did the FBI think they were guilty? They would not have arrested such prominent men for nothing. They must have had a good reason. Proof. Evidence that would change the face of the world until it was unrecognizable.

From the news, he had learned of the ultimatum Israel had been given. They had until midnight tonight to submit to the American coalition's demands, or they'd find themselves in very hot water. It must be so scary to be in Israel right now... He tried not to think about Mommy and the girls waiting for him at home. They were alone, with no relatives to look out for them. They were probably terrified. He must get home tonight.

All at once, for the first time, another thought entered his mind: Most likely, it would be impossible to get back to Israel after tonight. Switzerland, from what he understood, was not a member of the war coalition, but even she would not continue flights to Israel if war broke out. This was his last chance.

But would he succeed in getting a seat on the plane? He was due to land in Zurich at 7:30 p.m., and the last flight to Israel would lift off at 10:45. He'd have over a three-hour wait. If he missed his flight, the only way he'd be able to reach Israel would be if the ultimatum were extended. Though Switzerland was not at war with Israel, she would surely not continue sending planes to a country that was embroiled in war. Only if Israel won some time would he be able to board the first flight tomorrow morning and manage to get home before Shabbos.

And then there was his other little problem. What was he supposed to do about the two gorillas seated behind him? How could he get rid of them? He had no doubt that they would act against him at the first opportunity. He would not be able to walk freely around the terminal in Zurich's airport. If they believed he was about to flee to Israel, it was very possible that they would harm him even there. It was essential that he get away from them. That had to be his first priority. *Pikuach nefesh.*

He tried to formulate a plan for escaping from the pair. He knew the Zurich airport like the back of his hand. It would be the perfect place to disappear. From there, he'd quickly travel to the rosh yeshivah's house. The rosh yeshivah would know how to help him. He probably knew someone in Switzerland who was also planning to take the last flight to Israel, and everything would turn out all right. He'd get back to the airport in time, *b'ezras Hashem.*

The flight from Berlin to Zurich was brief. The pilot thanked the passengers and ordered his crew to prepare for landing. It was time.

Yisrael walked from the plane into the familiar terminal. He checked his watch. 7:20. The time difference was confusing. How many hours had he been traveling so far? Eleven? He reminded himself that Israel was an hour ahead of Zurich. If it was 7:20 here, then it was 8:20 at home. When it was 11:00 p.m. here, Israel's time to comply with the ultimatum would run out.

Yisrael did not have to turn around to sense the two Russians following him. They maintained a shorter distance than before, so that Yisrael was able to see their reflection in every passing shop window.

He pretended not to see them, studying the various displays with feigned interest. His plan had to be perfectly timed. He had to make them think that all was well.

Yisrael glanced again at his watch. One minute left. It was too soon. He set his knapsack down on the floor, trying to decide whether to enter the nearby restroom. His shadows also stopped a short distance behind. This was the moment Yisrael had been waiting for. He grabbed his knapsack, threw it over his shoulder and began racing toward the closest stairs. People stared at him in astonishment, and the two Russians hesitated. Yisrael bounded rapidly down the stairs and into the airport's Skymetro.

Meanwhile, his followers had recovered and began racing down the stairs as well. But they were too late. The train door slowly closed and the train began moving—with Yisrael inside.

The two men reached the door and pounded on it, to no avail. The train was moving. Other passengers arriving on the scene explained to the Russians that they must wait a few minutes for the next train.

Yisrael slipped into a seat. That had been close. They'd nearly managed to get inside. And now, they knew that he knew. They knew that he was running from them. He must get out of here with all possible speed.

What luck that he'd thought of this plan! One of the things he and his friends had always enjoyed doing in the airport was riding this train, which connected the landing strips to the central terminal. Swiss punctuality had played in his favor today. This train went to and fro among the terminals with the precision of an atomic clock. The ploy had gained him a few minutes over the Russians. He had to use them to make good his escape.

To his good fortune, there were no long lines at passport control. A sleepy clerk stamped his passport without asking questions. Next came the luggage carousel. Yisrael decided to give up his suitcase. He didn't have a minute to waste.

He continued rapidly to the customs counter. A moment later, he was filling his lungs with Swiss night air. Yisrael looked at his watch. It was a quarter to eight. He'd better hurry…

He approached a new-looking BMW taxi parked at the terminal entrance, and slipped inside.

"Bradschenkestrasse," he said. That was the only street name he could remember just then. From there, he'd figure something out.

The driver nodded his head and started driving. Instinctively, Yisrael turned his head to see if the Russians were behind him. Nothing. The terminal doors remained closed. He leaned back on his seat and tried to steady his breathing. What a miracle. He'd managed to get away.

The familiar streets passed quickly. The loss of his suitcase would serve as atonement for his sins. Right now he had to reach the rosh yeshivah's house. After that, things would work themselves out.

47

Washington, D.C.

THE PRESIDENT SAT IN THE OVAL OFFICE, SURROUNDED BY bodyguards. A pointed warning about a possible Mossad attempt to harm the chief executive had led to heightened security. His senior Cabinet members and intelligence directors were in the room as well. The countdown was on.

Communication with Israel had reached a dead end. The Israelis had dug in their heels, claiming that American demands posed a threat to their existence. A number of compromise positions had been offered by Israel; the common denominator was a refusal to dismantle her nuclear program.

Top activists had been working around the clock in an effort to get the Americans to withdraw their ultimatum. Although AIPRO had been dealt a mortal blow, with its leaders behind bars, some senators had tried to help the Israelis. Most political figures had hastened to disassociate themselves from Israel, claiming that a red line had been crossed, but those few who still clung to their fierce loyalty tried with all their might to extend the deadline.

The president was firm. He could not waver. This business had to end here and now. In the final analysis, he knew that the conflict would not end in a military confrontation. The Israelis were too responsible to act in such a heedless fashion. They would be forced to accede to his demands, and they knew it. The question was only how long they would manage to drag this thing out. Bob Walters was determined to end it as quickly as possible.

The rage in America and throughout the world had not escaped his notice. The anti-Semitic outbursts across the globe had not benefited anyone. They were reminiscent of a darker age. An age that he did not wish to see return. The sooner this was wrapped up, the better. The moment the Israelis submitted and gave up their nuclear bomb, the way out of this tangle would be quick. Jerusalem would be divided, Israel would achieve peace, and Jews from all over the world would head there—especially after the latest anti-Semitic demonstrations.

A small Jewish state without nuclear aspirations or nearby enemies—that was the president's dream, and he was about to make it come true. All he needed to do was withstand this last pressure. Just a few more hours, and the ultimatum would reach its deadline. His intelligence sources claimed that Israel was aware that she had no options. At precisely midnight Israeli time, the Israeli prime minister would announce his acceptance of all the demands.

The president waited impatiently. This would be his finest hour. But in the meantime, he had to be prepared for anything. He had to ensure that his military preparedness was up to par, just in case matters deteriorated quickly.

The broad coalition he'd put together had opened the door to a wide range of possibilities. To Israel's east, the Jordanian Army stood ready, under the Jordanian commander-in-chief and in coordination with the head of the coalition forces. The Egyptians had advanced their troops to the Sinai Peninsula and were ready to act in the south if needed. The Europeans had increased their local military presence, and numerous warships patrolled the Mediterranean.

As for the United States, she had sent five aircraft carriers to the region—two to the Mediterranean and three making their way up from the south, from the Indian Ocean and the Red Sea. The planes and firepower on those great carriers would be the spearhead in any air battles with the Israeli Air Force. In addition, the area was swarming with ten American nuclear submarines, whose job was to locate and deal with the four Israeli submarines. They would also assist the war effort by sending long-range missiles to various strategic points in Israel. The warships carried both attack missiles and antimissile missiles, for use in the event of an Israeli offensive.

Israel was surrounded. She didn't stand a chance.

Projections spoke of thousands of casualties on both sides. War with Israel would not be easy, but ultimate victory was guaranteed. Israel would be committing suicide if she attacked the coalition forces. The only thing that made the coalition commanders lose sleep was the possibility that Israel might opt to attack with nuclear weapons. That would drag the entire region into a dizzying and painful round of nuclear retaliation. Israel would be erased from the map. She might manage to inflict some damage first, but the end result would be her own destruction. Total decimation of the state for many years to come.

That scenario did not appear to be serious. However, for the president and his subordinates, the possibility existed. It was an option that must be prepared for. In a direct broadcast earlier that morning, Bob Walters had forcefully urged the Israeli prime minister to submit to his demands—for his good, and for the good of his people.

The FBI was also very busy. The violent confrontations throughout the country had been subdued with difficulty—and then a new and frightening menace had reared its head. Jewish youths had begun assembling. They claimed that the United States had gone out on a crusade against Jews, so they had to defend themselves and it was feared that this would escalate into home-grown terror attacks.

Orders had been issued to deal firmly with these hotheads. Matters could not be permitted to spiral out of control. Those youths could leave America with no choice other than to expel all

Jews from its boundaries—as had happened in darker regimes. Who would ever have believed things would come to this?

―――――――

Israel, Thursday afternoon

Certain members of the Israeli Security Cabinet were meeting in advance of the ultimatum deadline. Their grim faces said it all. They had no choice. The prime minister, seated at the head of the table, put his hands on a written draft, and pushed it to the center of the table.

"This will be our statement. At exactly 12 o'clock, I will make a public speech announcing our submission. I will appeal to the free world to forgo the dismantling of our nuclear program and will pledge to reach a comprehensive agreement with the Palestinians. But, bottom line, this is not in our hands. They are serious. They want to take away our ability to protect ourselves.

"The saddest thing about all of this is that I have no idea how it happened. The terrorist organization that was exposed in the United States did not emerge from here. You have my word on that. It appears that the three men accused of plotting this thing— Mikhail, Jeffrey, and Menachem—acted on their own initiative. I have no idea what they were thinking, how they hoped to operate without being found out. But the upshot is that they dragged us into a mess we never dreamed possible. We've been branded as a terrorist nation, so all means against us are now justified.

"As you know, without the nuclear bomb, the balance of power will shift to our detriment. It's hard to believe that the United States will act so firmly against Iran as well—Iran, which really is planning to achieve nuclear power. Our security people will have to work out new strategies, not only because of the lack of nuclear weapons but also—and primarily—because of the new borders that will be forced upon us.

"To the best of my understanding, the situation will be untenable. Terrorist penetration and missiles aimed at the heart of Jerusalem and Tel Aviv will become our new reality. The State of Israel will be vulnerable. But we survived the Holocaust, and we will survive this, too.

"In addition, I will have to tender my resignation tonight. The Americans want my head. They claim that I am involved, and that I must give myself up to be tried. I've already spoken to top-flight lawyers in Israel and abroad, and they are prepared to represent me—successfully, I hope…

"In the next few hours, I ask each of you to continue in every way you can to try to delay this decree. Every additional hour is to our benefit. Hope is not yet lost for finding some honorable way out—a way that will satisfy the Americans and rescue the State of Israel.

"For now, all I can say is that it has been an honor to lead you, and I will never forget the trust you placed in me up until the last minute. I had hoped that I would be able to stay on as Israel's leader, but I know that even though I cannot, you will continue on in my footsteps and ensure that all is well. The nation of Israel will continue to be strong and united.

"Thank you very much. And…may the Almighty watch over and bless His people."

The president of Iran was taken no less by surprise than the rest of the world by the swiftly moving developments. But he was not one to let an opportunity slip through his fingers. From the beginning he had recognized his good fortune. The Americans should have been furious with him. Ready to blast him… Instead, suspicion had fallen on Israel. He had more luck than he deserved.

His intelligence people had been working furiously since the explosion in Arizona. Something had gone wrong. Someone had learned that Ali Hamid had been sent to the United States. Somehow, the Americans had learned about the Iranian terrorist. Worst of all, they'd managed to stop him from reaching Washington. Though Ali had succeeded in detonating the bomb, the explosion had taken place in a desert region, with a miserable toll of a few dozen casualties. This was not what the president had hoped to achieve with this rare nuclear weapon.

But then the wave of arrests began, and suddenly the cards were all in his favor. For some reason, the Americans were convinced that the Israelis were behind the episode. It had been his idea from start to finish. Even the Russians, who had supplied him with the nuclear device, had done so with a different goal in mind.

But why should he care? Let them blame Israel. The Americans were about to make life easier for him. They would separate Israel from its nuclear power. In just a few years' time, he would be the only strong one in the neighborhood. The only one in the Middle East with nuclear capability.

Right now, all he had to do was keep from making any mistakes. He mustn't cause the worldwide coalition to turn against him instead of Israel. In a speech that had been broadcast across the globe, he had been quoted as saying that there would be no need for him to have a nuclear bomb now. "If the Zionist enemy lacks such power, why should we need it? After all, the Iranians are a peaceful people. We have only worked to protect ourselves from Zionist aggression. An aggression that the world has finally discovered for itself..."

The president had not stopped with just words. He'd announced his permission for U.N. inspectors to visit "all of Iran's nuclear facilities." They would see that Iran's reactors were built for peaceful purposes only. Of course, as was his way, he would make sure that they didn't see everything. There were places he would not allow them to go—though on the surface he would show himself sincerely ready to cooperate.

The Iranian president had offered to join the coalition against Israel, but his offer had been declined. The Americans would not go that far. Behind the scenes, he'd ordered the forces that heeled to his command—Hamas, Hezbollah, and the other local terrorist groups—to lay low until the battle began. Nothing must happen to make the coalition back away from attacking Israel. Who knew better than he how a terror attack could change minds in the West...

Later, when the Western armies finally decided to act, *that* would be the moment for his soldiers to show their strength. Missiles would rain down simultaneously from Gaza and Southern Lebanon onto the central cities of Israel. Cities that had escaped attack until now for fear of harsh reprisals—cities like Tel Aviv—would come under fierce fire. The Iron Dome would not be able to turn back the barrage of missiles, and casualties would be high.

It was unbelievable how, in an instant, the international pressure that the Jews had activated against *his* nuclear power had boomeranged right back at them and *their* nuclear capability.

48

THE TAXI RIDE PASSED QUICKLY AND UNEVENTFULLY. YISRAEL thanked the driver and paid him in dollars. The driver was not happy about the foreign currency, but a hefty tip appeased him.

Yisrael got out on the familiar street and consulted his watch. It was almost time to return to the airport. But first he had to see the rosh yeshivah, the only one who might be able to help him tonight.

Hoisting his knapsack onto his shoulder, he began walking. Something in the familiar street looked strange to him. Long seconds passed before he realized that it was emptier than usual. Though Swiss streets are relatively quiet in general, tonight they seemed deserted. Almost like a ghost town. A few cars passed from time to time, breaking the silence, but apart from him there were no pedestrians.

Yisrael turned into the rosh yeshivah's block. It was a thriving Jewish street. Here too, all was desolate.

The deep silence shook his confidence. Something had happened. Something not good had occurred in this familiar place. He reached the rosh yeshivah's house and discovered that the low gate at the garden entrance had been torn from its place.

Yisrael stepped cautiously inside, went up to the front door, and knocked. Nothing happened.

He tried knocking again, this time more strongly. But apart from the muffled echo that reached him from the deserted street, there was no reaction at all.

He set down his knapsack and tried to analyze the situation. Something had undoubtedly happened. The question was what. And, even more important, what was he going to do now?

Go back to the airport and cope with those thugs? They could kill him with ease. They had not followed him thousands of kilometers for nothing. On the other hand, he also couldn't remain here. First of all, he'd left his suitcase and all his things behind—and the rosh yeshivah wasn't home. Who would he stay with?

He decided to try his luck at a different house. Nearby lived one of the married kollel men from the yeshivah. Even if he couldn't host him, perhaps he could at least tell him where the rosh yeshivah was.

He knocked on the door, but the response was the same. No one opened the door. The place was deserted.

A noise from the window of the house next door caught his attention. Someone was looking out at him. Yisrael lifted his eyes, but the moment the stranger saw him he shut the window and disappeared from view. So there were people here. But why were they hiding in their homes?

Only now did Yisrael notice something different about the door in front of him. Until today, a mezuzah had been nailed on the doorpost of every Jewish home. Now the mezuzah was gone. This house, like the rosh yeshivah's, had no mezuzahs! They'd been removed.

Yisrael decided to try the yeshivah building. This was his last recourse. If he found no one there that he knew, he'd have to return to the airport and cope on his own.

He walked at the edge of the street, trying not to stand out in the dead streets. Had anti-Semitism reared its ugly head here as well?

Had local Jews, Heaven forbid, been harmed? Where were they all? Why were they hiding?

The frightening answer became apparent on the next block. A group of youths with shaven heads were rampaging there, scrawling Nazi swastikas on the walls and laughing uproariously.

Yisrael froze before they saw him. He knew these gangs from before. Until now, however, he'd only glimpsed them late at night in the train station, where they'd congregate every night. This was the first time he was actually seeing them in action. Scrawling graffiti and wreaking havoc.

He decided to bypass them. Only one street separated him from the yeshivah. He knew the area well enough to find an alternate route. Very quietly, he moved behind the destructive group and passed them, until he reached the building he remembered so well.

This was the first time he had ever seen the yeshivah so dark and empty. Yisrael did not have to go in to know that there was no one inside. But he decided to enter anyway. Just for a minute.

Like most of the buildings in the area, the yeshivah was locked with a combination code. Anyone who knew the code could enter easily without using a key. He hit the right buttons—one, eight, one eight—twice *chai*—and walked into the yeshivah.

He turned on the light in the entryway and discovered that nothing had changed. The familiar benches, the bookcases overflowing with *sifrei kodesh*, were all exactly as he remembered them. It was an unpleasant feeling. The total silence grated on his nerves, which were already stretched thin.

He decided to go up to his room. He'd just make sure that everything was in its place, and leave. It was growing late; he had to get back to the airport.

His room was exactly the same as he remembered it. Yisrael opened his closet and withdrew two chocolate bars that he'd left there. He'd buy new ones during the next *z'man*… He had hardly eaten a thing all day. No kosher meals had been offered on the plane, and he had been living on the sweets that his mother had sent with him. The problem was that the rest of his goodies were in his luggage—which was gone.

He unwrapped one candy bar and put the other in his knapsack. The chocolate perked up his spirits a bit. He felt more prepared to go back and cope with those Russians. He would not make life easy for them. Switzerland was his home turf!

The sound of raucous laughter outside changed his plans. Yisrael peeked through the window and saw with alarm that the group of young thugs was approaching the building. He hastened to the front door—too late. They were already on the other side, pounding on it and cursing all Jews.

Yisrael looked out through the peephole. There were eight of them. Far too many for him to tackle alone. Though they appeared drunk, they could still overpower him easily.

He recoiled. He could only imagine what they'd do to him if he were to fall into their hands. He'd be lucky if they left him alive.

The pounding on the door intensified. He began to wonder how long the door would last under the barrage. He had to find another way out.

He raced to the kitchen, trying not to bump into anything on the way. The only light came from the entryway. He was afraid to turn on any other lights, lest the hooligans outside notice. The kitchen was on street level, and its large window would permit a quiet exit. Who would have believed that the same window that he and his friends had used to break in for some *cholent* one Friday night would one day serve as his escape route out of the building? Under different circumstances, Yisrael would have smiled at the memory, which had infuriated the rebbetzin. Right now, he was too busy trying to save his life.

The problem was that after that episode, the yeshivah administration had replaced the window. Instead of a window that slid open sideways, they'd installed one that opened only halfway up. Yisrael realized to his horror that his body would not fit through. His only recourse was to break the window. But that would make noise and alert the shaven-headed thugs.

He returned to the central room. He had to find another way out. The pounding on the door had become very forceful. It sounded as though they were battering it with the aid of some heavy object.

Indeed, when he peeked out an adjacent window, he saw that they had uprooted a bench from its place in the yeshivah courtyard and were using it as a battering ram.

"Hey!" someone yelled. One of the thugs had glimpsed Yisrael peeking out and was calling it to his companions' attention. Yisrael quickly withdrew. The pounding stopped. From the little Swiss-German that Yisrael understood, he could hear one of them telling his friends what he'd seen. Bloodthirsty calls emerged from their drunken throats, and they redoubled their efforts to break down the door.

The hinges, he saw to his horror, were beginning to come loose. A few more minutes of this, and they'd be inside!

He ran over to the door and began piling tables and benches against it. That would delay them a little. He felt like a hunted animal who had no way out and was just waiting for the moment when it would be devoured.

Once, as a boy in *cheder*, he and his class had been taken on a year's-end trip to Masada. To this day, Yisrael still remembered the guide's description of how those trapped on the citadel had seen the siege tightening around them and the Romans' siege engines coming closer, day by day. He'd tried to imagine how they must have felt. To know that in just a few days' time, the enemy would gain entry to slaughter them. Now he knew exactly how they'd felt. And it wasn't a pleasant feeling at all.

Panic began to overtake him. He sprinted from window to window, looking for a way out—in vain. With no other option, he grabbed a metal chair and decided to use it on the kitchen window. He'd jump out and run away as fast as he could. With Hashem's help, by the time they got wind of him he'd be a safe distance away.

Yisrael forced himself to stop and get a grip on his fear. The many difficult experiences he'd been through that year had taught him to control his behavior.

"Calm down!" he ordered himself. "You have to think clearly."

He took long, deep breaths, and managed to slightly relax his tense body. Okay. *Think...* The only way out was through the window. The problem was that the sound of shattering glass would

bring the gang running immediately. He must distract them first…
Cause them to look the other way.

The battering at the front door was even steadier now. The hinges
were already out of their sockets, the door remaining in place only
because of the furniture he'd piled up in front of it. Anytime now,
they'd be inside… Yisrael quickly went up one floor, to the window he'd opened a few minutes before. He looked down. The eight
were directly below him, gripping the bench and battering at the
door. Yisrael didn't hesitate. He picked up the chair in his hands
and threw it into the crowd of skinheads.

The chair did its job well. It struck one of them right on the
crown. The youth slid to the ground, unconscious, blood trickling
from his forehead.

If Yisrael had hoped to buy himself some time, he was disappointed. The hooligans spotted him and began hurling whatever
came to hand in his direction. Yisrael withdrew rapidly as a large
rock passed just centimeters from his ear.

The skinheads, it seemed, had chosen to ignore their wounded
comrade. They dragged him aside and renewed their frenzied
attack on the door, while one of them kept an eye on the upper window. Yisrael hastened back downstairs to the kitchen. Luckily, they
hadn't gone all around the building and noticed this window. This
would have been the easiest way inside. Or—in his case—outside.

He had no choice now. Two more minutes, and they'd be upon
him. He must act quickly. Now that their attention was fixed on
the upper story, where they thought he was hiding, perhaps he'd
gained a little precious time.

Yisrael had dragged a blanket along with him. He placed it near
the window. The minute the glass broke, he'd have only seconds to
act. He'd throw the blanket over the shards to spare himself a painful passage. Then he'd climb rapidly onto the counter and jump out
to the street. The gap between himself and his pursuers would be
miniscule. It would take them about five seconds, at a run, to cover
the distance from the front door to the kitchen window. Five critical
seconds. If anything went wrong—a bad landing, or a scratch from
the broken glass—they'd be on him before he could escape.

Yisrael looked at the front door one last time. It was already open a crack, and one of the hooligans' hands appeared, trying to push the blockading furniture aside. Yisrael muttered a hasty *perek* of *Tehillim*—a quiet prayer to his Creator. *Don't let me fall into those hands. Don't let me turn into another item in the news...*

He lifted the chair. He had only one chance to get this right. The noise would alert them and expose his escape attempt. This had to work the first time. He smashed the glass with all his might, and the large window shattered into smithereens. Yisrael clambered onto the counter, kicking aside shards of glass, and placed the blanket over the gaping hole.

A terrifying silence fell over the crowd at the front door. The hooligans paused for an instant in their work, trying to figure out where the sound of breaking glass had come from. Yisrael didn't wait. He climbed through the window and shot out onto the street.

It was a bit higher than he'd thought, and his landing was not smooth. As he rolled on the ground, a sharp pain rose from his left ankle. Yisrael didn't let that stop him. There was no time now. He had to get up.

He scrambled to his feet and was glad to see that the pain wasn't too bad. He'd been injured worse at basketball. It was probably just a slightly twisted ankle. His hand, however, was bleeding heavily. He'd apparently cut it on a piece of jagged glass. But that wouldn't kill him. That job was reserved for the skinheads that had just appeared at the corner of the building.

Yisrael began running for all he was worth in the opposite direction. He had to put distance between himself and the gang. Luckily for him, he was a good runner. With a little help from Above, he'd get away.

The crack of gunshots gave him pause. Someone had a gun! And was using it!

Yisrael slowed down and glanced over his shoulder, trying to gauge the new danger. He was surprised to see that the hooligans were just as startled as he was. One of them fell to the ground, and the others scattered to the four winds with cries of terror. Someone was shooting at them! Someone was trying to help him!

Yisrael decided not to stop. It was impossible to know exactly what was happening back there. The smartest thing he could do now was make good his escape. He had to get away from this area. In just a minute, he'd reach the Limmat River, in the center of the city. It would be easier to escape from there.

At that exact moment, a black Jeep appeared at the end of the street. The tinted windows were down, and a steady hand was holding a gun and firing repeatedly. In total shock, Yisrael recognized one of his Russian pursuers. He'd been the one who had shot at the hooligans! Stunned, Yisrael stopped running. What was this about? Were they on *his* side? Was it possible that the Russians were actually trying to protect him?

The painful answer came sooner than expected. The hand holding the gun aimed it at him, and pulled the trigger.

The Jeep barreled rapidly toward him as the Russian fired again and again. Yisrael jumped off the sidewalk and dove down to the riverbank. He could hear the bullets whistling above his head. This time, his fall was even more painful than before. His left foot was hurt for the second time in minutes, and the pain returned, sharper now.

He forced himself to get up. On the other side of the river he saw a young couple hurrying away; aside from them the area was deserted. Only the Russians and the skinheads—two different groups, both intent on harming him.

Yisrael raced away. Behind him, he heard the doors of the Jeep slam as the Russians emerged. They hurried down to the riverbank after him. Yisrael didn't stop. He must keep moving. These people were terribly serious.

He bit his lips and tried to ignore the sharp pain in his ankle. Perspiration beaded on his forehead and his heart beat wildly in his chest. But he had to go on. At least the skinheads seemed to have given up the chase. That was some small comfort.

Despite his efforts, his injured foot was slowing him down. He could hear the Russians closing in on him from behind. For such big men, they ran pretty well. He could hear their labored breathing. They would not be able to go on like this for long. But he too would have to stop soon. The pain in his ankle grew more intense with every step he took.

He decided to climb back up to the street. His chances of finding concealment were greater there. The bullets whizzing past him helped him ignore his aching foot. He leaped up the stairs two at a time and returned to the street. The Russians were right on his heels.

He had to think of something to do. How to get out of this? He couldn't run much longer. Fortunately, though traffic was sparse, there were some vehicles moving on this street. One of them was a taxi. It stopped in response to Yisrael's extended hand. He jumped inside and gasped, *"Flughafen!* The airport!"

He looked behind him as the taxi started moving frustratingly slowly. He saw his pursuers reach the street, breathing hard. The problem was that they saw *him,* too. The hunt was not over.

The cab driver was too polite to ask questions. Curiosity made him try to guess why a boy, panting as though he'd just run a marathon, had stopped his taxi and asked to be taken to the airport as though he had a flight to catch in five minutes—when he didn't even have a suitcase. Perhaps his family was waiting for him there. He didn't see the Russians, and didn't know that Yisrael was fleeing from some threat.

They moved out of the Russians' range of vision, but Yisrael knew the pair would not give up. They had not made such an effort to follow him only to become discouraged now. He tried to figure out how they'd managed to track him down. After all, he'd escaped them at the airport. They had to have specific information about him. They must know which yeshivah in Zurich he attended. But how? Who was it that was trying to hurt him? Why should anyone invest so much energy to get him? What had he done?

They passed the train station, and Yisrael began to calm down. Maybe, despite everything, they'd decided to quit. Maybe they wouldn't catch up with him. He'd be at the airport in about 10 minutes' time. He looked at his watch. 10:05. He could still board his flight at the last minute…

At precisely that moment, the taxi was bumped from behind.

The driver yelled in fury when the black Jeep rammed into his cab again. Yisrael was stunned to find his Russian pursuers trying to overturn the taxi he was riding in. No, they had definitely not given up.

The driver was at a loss. With no other choice, he pressed on the gas and veered sharply left, trying to avoid another blow.

"No!" Yisrael screamed, when he saw that they were turning aside instead of continuing straight. "I have to get to the airport!"

The driver understood English. "Are you crazy?" he yelled back. It had been years since he'd been under such pressure. "They're trying to kill us!"

With a screech of its tires, the Jeep followed the taxi. It was clear that the gorillas were not about to give up the chase.

The cab driver continued driving wildly as he tried to think of a way out of this situation. He was an experienced driver and knew the roads well, but this was the first time he'd been pursued like this. His passenger, apparently, was involved in some sort of criminal altercation. But what did he have to do with any of that? He drove on and made another quick left. Now they were on a two-lane bridge that crossed the river—traveling in the opposite direction from the airport.

The Jeep closed in again and slammed into the taxi's left side, hard. The two vehicles were moving side by side now. Yisrael could see the Russians clearly. How had they found him again? What did they want from him? Another powerful blow to the taxi's left side nearly sent it flying into the river.

Pressing the pedal to the floor, the driver managed to inch forward. He turned suddenly into Limmatplatz Street and earned a few precious seconds when the Jeep missed the turnoff and was forced to go around. The driver pulled up in front of a hotel and shot out of the cab. His passenger could take care of himself. He wanted nothing to do with this madness.

Yisrael hurried out of the car after him. He didn't know how to drive, and certainly not well enough to shake off those Russians. But he had no other way to escape. There were no vehicles moving down the dark street. Knowing the Swiss as he did, he was aware that no one would get involved, even if they saw a young boy running for his life.

He limped as quickly as he could down the street. He was at the northern end of the city now. The airport was situated a few kilometers further north. But he'd never make it in time. Not with the Russians after him.

His hunters closed in rapidly, forcing him to run between the houses. The Russians leaped from their Jeep and continued pursuing him on foot. Yisrael didn't slow down. Immediately behind the next set of houses, Zurich's residential section ended. Only metal train tracks passed here. He decided to continue on down to the tracks. The darkness would be his friend. It would hide him from the enemy's eyes. With a little luck, he could follow the tracks back into the city.

He crossed the street just as the Russians appeared behind the houses. One of them shot randomly in his direction, but Yisrael was too far ahead for the bullet to pose any real danger. He quickened his pace. It was imperative that he lose them.

The Russians darted into the street, but their energy was beginning to flag. They didn't notice the speeding sports car that showed suddenly at the edge of the upscale street. One of the Russians was hit broadside. The other sent a burst of gunfire at the car, which did not stop. The Russian reported the incident on the communication device in his hand. A quick order arrived from the person at the other end: Do not stop. Continue the hunt. Someone else would take care of the injured man.

The Russian, noticing Yisrael's limp, knew that it was just a matter of time now. Another minute or two, and he'd catch up with the kid. This had been meant to be a much easier mission. A mission that had become complicated only because they had been banned from killing him in America. His boss had insisted: Not on U.S. soil. He wanted to be present in person.

The Russian continued the chase, updating the boy's exact location periodically on his device as he ran. With today's technology, even that was unnecessary. The GPS he carried transmitted the youth's precise location at any given moment. That was also how they'd tracked him down after he'd given them the slip. Back in America, they'd planted a tiny GPS transmitter in the boy's clothing. That transmitter sent a signal to the device he was now holding in his hand. Theoretically, he didn't even have to run after the boy. He could follow him at his leisure and catch him the minute he stopped moving. But he couldn't take any chances. This was a mission that must not fail. The boss himself was supervising it directly.

He continued racing after Yisrael, who was growing steadily weaker. They left the populated area and reached the railroad tracks. So this was the kid's brilliant plan: to hide in the industrial area in the dark... Too bad that little transmitter was about to destroy all his plans.

The Russian paused for a moment to check Yisrael's location on his device. The boy was right on the tracks now, about a hundred meters ahead and moving slowly westward. Apparently, he was crawling on the ground in an effort to conceal himself. Idiot! In the kid's place, he'd be running to reach the train station. It would be far easier to hide there. The Russian smiled to himself as he made a slight detour to the right—and popped up at the exact spot where Yisrael was crawling.

"Hands up!" he ordered in halting English.

Yisrael froze in place. The order had taken him by surprise. He hadn't expected the Russian to get ahead of him.

But he had no choice. He'd lost. The Russians had caught him. He raised his hands in submission and tried to stand. His swollen ankle refused to obey and he collapsed back onto the ground. The Russian reported into his device. A chillingly familiar voice answered him in Russian from the other end.

Yisrael was in shock. It couldn't be. That could not be the person he thought it was. It was probably the Russian accent that had thrown him off...

"What do you want with me?" he asked the thug who'd trapped him. "What did I do? And who are you, anyway?"

The Russian didn't bother to answer. He executed a quick search of Yisrael, and found the money taped to his chest. This was not what he'd been looking for. He'd been searching for weapons, but money was good, too… He thrust the wad of cash into his jacket pocket, his gun trained on Yisrael the entire time.

One minute later, the black Jeep drew up alongside them. The beam of its powerful headlights blinded Yisrael. He threw an arm up to cover his eyes, but a barked order from the Russian compelled him to lower it. Two figures stepped out of the Jeep and approached them. Yisrael tried to see who they were, but the bright light made it hard for him to focus. Heavy footsteps sounded on the gravel. Heavy and menacing.

As the two men came closer, one of them blocked the beam of the headlights with his body. Yisrael narrowed his eyes in disbelief. Yes! It *was* him! He recognized Mikhail even in the dark. And the man with him was the albino guard who had sat at the entrance of Mikhail's home.

The guard stood in front of the Jeep. He, too, was gripping a drawn gun. The Russian who had caught Yisrael joined him. Mikhail took a step forward.

"Hello, Yisrael," he said in Russian-accented Hebrew. "How are you?"

Yisrael stared at him, stunned. What was *he* doing here? From what he'd been given to understand, Mikhail was supposed to be in a Russian prison! How had he managed to escape?

"Surprised to see me?" Mikhail continued with a broad smile. He switched to English, which was easier for him. "The truth is, this was not exactly in my plan. But what can one do? I was forced to tie up this loose end."

"What are you talking about?" Yisrael finally found his tongue. "What loose end? And why are your people trying to kill me?"

"You really don't know? Interesting… I gambled on the fact that you were a real problem. I never thought it had happened by chance."

"What had happened? What do you want from me? Who *are* you?"

"You're not exactly in a position to ask questions. I'm the one doing the asking, understand?"

The thugs tightened their grip on their weapons. For some

reason, the boss was taking his time. That wasn't healthy. Any time now, the local police would be showing up. It was time to finish this thing once and for all.

"What did you do to my computer?" Mikhail demanded.

"I told you. I didn't touch it!"

"Listen, my friend. I am going to kill you, here and now. If you tell me why you touched the computer, I will do it painlessly."

"But I don't know what you want from me! I didn't touch any computers! And anyway, the FBI took it away. So what difference does it make if I saw something? They've already seen everything."

Mikhail smiled. The kid really didn't know. He was able to read people easily, and this boy was no different. He truly had no idea what was going on. Strange—he'd attached such significance to the episode, and now it turned out that it had been nothing but an innocent mistake. How absurd…

"The FBI saw only what I wanted them to see," Mikhail said proudly. He appeared visibly calmer. The knowledge that Yisrael had not done anything to his computer had relieved him.

"What you are seeing now is the climax of a great plan. One of the most brilliant plans there has ever been, if I do say so myself. What a pity you will not be around to see the end…" He chuckled, and signaled to the men behind him. They moved slightly forward and aimed.

"Just a minute!" Yisrael screamed. "At least tell me what the plan is. I have a right to know why you're going to kill me."

With another gesture, Mikhail stopped his men. Disappointed, they lowered their guns.

The Russian henchmen were anxious to leave this area. Dozens, if not hundreds, of trains passed this way each day. Though traffic was much sparser at this time of night, there was still a chance they'd be seen.

Mikhail glanced at his watch and said, "You are right. In any case, we have a few minutes, so why shouldn't I share my genius with you? These apes don't know how to appreciate anything but power. A yeshivah boy like yourself will be able to appreciate the brilliance of my plan." With another glance at his watch, he continued. "It is now 10 minutes to 11. Which means that, in Israel, the ultimatum will expire at midnight—exactly 10 minutes from now. I have no doubt that the Israelis will be forced to capitulate. Tonight will see the start of a new era in the Middle East. An era that I, personally, created!"

"I don't understand," Yisrael said. "How are you connected to the ultimatum?"

"How am I connected?" Mikhail laughed. "I am the only one who is connected! No one else... Let me explain what I mean. Have you ever heard of President Kotorov?"

"The president of Russia?"

"Yes. Good. Alex Kotorov thinks of me as a brother. We've known each other nearly all of our lives. But what he does not know is that it was all part of my plan. All of it!"

"What plan?"

"To erase you people from the map! To destroy the Jewish nation once and for all!"

"But why? What have we ever done to you? You even converted to Judaism."

Mikhail laughed again, with real enjoyment. "I am as much a Jew as you are an African. Don't you get it? It was all part of the plan."

"You decided to become a Jew so that no one would suspect you?"

"Nice. That is the Jewish head everyone talks about... Congratulations! But it is a lot more complicated than that, my friend. Don't you see? I studied the history of your people better than anyone else. There is no Jew in the world who knows Jewish history as I do. And you know what I discovered? That it is really not easy to get rid of you people. You are like leeches. You attach yourselves to a body and refuse to let go. That is what you did to Pharaoh, and to Haman the Agagite, and that is what you did to Hitler. Each of them tried to destroy you, each in his own way, and in the end you always survive. Exactly like a cancer. I decided to be cleverer. Dozens of years of research went into my plan. The first plan in history that is bound to succeed."

Yisrael realized he must get him to keep talking—to buy time. It was obvious that Mikhail was happy to finally share his secret with somebody.

"What's so brilliant about your plan?" Yisrael challenged. "So the world thinks you're a Jew. So what?"

"Fool!" Mikhail shouted. "You don't understand. I checked carefully, and found that those who did the greatest damage to the Jewish nation were always the ones who came from within. With your self-hatred, you people always manage to quarrel among yourselves. Anyone who tries to harm the Jews loses in the end—but the Jews' talent for self-destruction does the job best of all. And then I discovered *The Protocols*, and it all became clear. The plan just flowed. Simple genius."

"*The Protocols of the Elders of Zion*?"

"Yes. They gave me the inspiration I was looking for. Do you know who wrote them?"

Yisrael shook his head.

"How would you know? No one knows. Everyone thinks that agents of the czar were responsible for the successful fraud. But I found the source. A talented young Moldovan fellow who started the whole story."

"But what do *The Protocols* have to do with what's happening here? What's the connection?"

Mikhail laughed out loud. "What's the connection? *The Protocols* gave me the idea. If I want to get the Jews in trouble, I have to do what those who wrote *The Protocols* tried to do: force the Jews to write the accusation against themselves. That was the libel that worked best of all over the course of history. And you know why? Because it touches on some true points."

"So you're saying that my uncle was not really a terrorist?"

"Ha, ha! That man loves himself so much that he does not have a thought to spare for anything else. Neither he nor any of the other Jews were involved in the explosion. It was all part of my plan."

"How did you manage to make it happen?" Yisrael asked in astonishment.

"Just as I said. The minute they believed that I was a Jew like

them, they trusted me implicitly. They gave me access to everything I wanted. They let me shape policy."

"And...?"

"And that is just what I did. Understand? Alex Kotorov got a
good brainwashing from me. He believes that the Jews really want
to dominate the world. That fool would never have made it to the
presidency without me. I raised him up with my own two hands—
and, in exchange, he gave me a free hand to act. I gave the Iranians
a nuclear weapon, knowing full well that their president would not
be able to resist the temptation. I had no doubt that he would send
it straight to America. I can read that ape like an open book. Then
all I had to do was tie in the Jews.

"What did I do? I made sure there was plenty of worldwide
Jewish pressure on America over Iran. There is your motive. Then
I made sure to plant incriminating material in my Jewish friends'
computers...and the rest is history. It worked like a dream. The
Jews have been implicated in terrorist activity, and they are going
to pay through the nose."

"But you'll never wipe out all the Jews that way. Only a few will
die. You just said that Israel will give in and there won't be a war."

"Those are the words of a small-minded person," Mikhail
snapped. "Is that all you have learned from the Gemara? Don't you
understand that this is just the beginning of a long road? From past
experience, I learned that it is impossible to destroy the Jews with
a single blow. What I have started will take generations. The Jews
have been branded as plotters, sly creatures who aim for world
dominion. Until today, anyone who claimed such a thing was
labeled an anti-Semite. Now its truth has been proven. Because of
me, the Jews will be forever depicted as an evil and despicable race.
That will serve as justification for the persecution of Jews the world
over—even in this high-tech generation."

"But the Jewish state will still exist."

"It's only a matter of time before it will be destroyed. With inde-
fensible borders and no nuclear bomb, the State of Israel will not
last even ten years. The beauty in all of this is that no country in
the world will want to take you in. You have seen for yourself what

the locals think of you. Even here in Switzerland there were violent outbursts that sent all the Jews scurrying. And the phenomenon will only grow stronger—until no Jew will ever be safe again, anywhere in the world."

A freight train was approaching in the distance. One of the thugs hastily turned off the Jeep's headlights. The train chugged past, making the ground shake. From inside the train it was impossible to see Mikhail and his men. The darkness was too deep.

When the train was out of sight, the lights came on again.

Yisrael thought about what he had just heard. "You're worse than Hitler."

Mikhail laughed again. "I don't know if I am worse—but I am certainly smarter. I did not have to conquer a single country to get what I wanted…"

"Just a minute. Everyone thinks that you're also a Jew. You'll end up suffering from your own plan."

"You really don't get it, do you? How do you think I got out of jail? It was all planned. The Russians insisted on taking me, ostensibly for interrogation. The Americans had no choice. I boarded a plane for home and was immediately released. Understand? Alex and I pretended to be on bad terms so that the plan would work. People are certain that I am languishing in a Russian prison right now. But in a few days, I will undergo some plastic surgery, and the world will hear that I died in prison. No one will shed a tear for the Jew who was part of a worldwide terror organization. Simple but beautiful, don't you agree?"

Yisrael absorbed what he had heard. It was truly clever. Mikhail had pretended to be a Jew, and thus incriminated the entire Jewish nation. *But what made him hate Jews so much?* he wondered. *What did we ever do to him?*

49

THE PRIME MINISTER SAT AT HIS DESK FOR THE LAST TIME. AT his side a large Israeli flag was draped, and facing him was a video camera mounted on a tripod, ready to record his final speech.

"Two minutes," signaled the cameraman. "When the red light goes on, you'll be on the air and can start talking."

He nodded. This speech would unquestionably be the most important and most difficult of his life. He'd tried everything in the past few hours, both pleading and threats, but nothing had helped. The Americans, with the full support of most of the world, had decided to take this matter to the bitter end. To the point where he was forced to announce Israel's surrender to America's dictates.

His personal fate frightened him less. He knew how the legal system worked, and understood that it would be years before his fate was sealed. As a former soldier, he'd seen death more than once. That was not what frightened him. But he was all too aware of the significance of these demands on Israel.

Who better than he knew how threatened his tiny country was?

How many acts of terror had been prevented because Israel's enemies thought twice before daring to act? Now all that was about
to come to an end. Israel's strength was about to receive a mortal
blow, a blow from which she would never recover. Her enemies'
fear of Israel would disappear, and with it her citizens' security.
And all this was taking place on his watch... He would be forever
remembered as the prime minister who had lost everything.

"One minute."

The prime minister straightened his tie and scanned the pages in
his hand. Only a miracle could save him now. He fixed a level gaze
directly on the camera lens. He must project pride, pride and honor,
as befit the leader of a proud and honorable people. Though he was
about to deliver a speech of submission, that did not mean that he
had abandoned his self-respect. The Jewish nation had experienced
innumerable sufferings and had always known how to rise from
the ashes.

Mikhail glanced at his watch. One minute to 11. It was time to
end this story once and for all. He motioned to his gorillas—who
sprang forward, ready to shoot.

"Just a second! Mikhail! Don't you have an ounce of pity? Don't
you care that millions of Jewish children will die? What have we
ever done to you?" Yisrael was crying in earnest now. He had
accepted the fact that he was about to die. There was no way out.
He would never see tomorrow. But the knowledge that the situation throughout the world was only going to get worse made him
weep uncontrollably. His own death would be only the first in a
long line of suffering.

What would become of his mother? And his little sisters, Bracha
and Tamar? Who would protect them through the terrible times to
come? Terror attacks, wars, every kind of affliction—was that what
they would see in their lifetimes? What kind of world was that to
live in?

Yisrael threw himself at his captor's feet and pleaded for mercy.
But Mikhail only laughed.

"Mercy? Do you think I care about some Jewish children dying?" He laughed again, cruelly, and said, "Allow me to let you in on a secret that no one else knows. When I was a boy—about ten years old—I spent a night at a friend's house. Alex Kotorov. What no one knows is that in the middle of the night, I sneaked out ever so quietly, and ran all the way home. Everyone in the house was asleep at that late hour: my father, my mother, and my brothers. No one knew that it was *I* who tipped the candle over onto the curtain. I burned down the whole house. I killed them all! I murdered my family in cold blood. So do you really think I'd care about a few Jewish children? Think again."

He turned around and began striding toward his Jeep. "Go ahead," he ordered his men.

They lifted their guns in synchronization. Instinctively, Yisrael closed his eyes. In a storm of emotion, he began to scream, "*Shema Yisrael!*" He was going to die as a Jew.

What happened next occurred so fast that Yisrael didn't have time to absorb it. Two quick shots rang out. Yisrael was surprised to find that he wasn't hurt. He opened his eyes and began feeling his head, searching for a stream of blood. Instead, he saw both Russians collapsing onto the ground with a thud. Their guns flew out of their hands as their dying eyes registered surprise. A figure emerged from the shadows. It shot forward and grabbed Mikhail around the neck.

"Are you all right, Yisrael?" The man spoke fluent Hebrew. "Are you hurt?"

In shock, Yisrael didn't answer. Who was this man? What was he doing here?

The newcomer shoved Mikhail onto the Jeep's hood and patted him down. When he'd made sure that there were no weapons, he quickly bent over to check the fallen men, who were dead.

"You're coming back to Israel with me," he told Mikhail. "There are some people there who will be very happy to hear your story."

"You're from Israel?" Yisrael asked.

Ami Drori nodded. "Everything's okay, Yisrael. From now on, everything is going to be all right."

But Mikhail had other plans. With a sudden lunge, he grabbed one of the guns that had landed on the ground. Ami was taken by surprise. Mikhail lifted the weapon and aimed it at him.

Acting instinctively in self-defense, Ami shot him twice in rapid succession.

The bullets sent Mikhail staggering back, fatally wounded. But it seemed as if Ami was the wounded one. With a cry, he sprang over to the dying man. He needed him alive! Mikhail must not die. He was their only proof.

But it was too late. There was a death rattle, and then Mikhail was no longer among the living. The bullets had penetrated vital organs. Nothing could have saved him, and Mikhail had known it.

Yisrael was taken aback to see Mikhail smiling, even in death. As though he was glad that his plan had worked after all. He might not be alive to see it succeed, but succeed it undoubtedly would. Because the final proof had died along with him...

The president of the United States sat with his closest advisers. Local time was 5 in the afternoon, but the critical hour was in Israel, where it was midnight. This was the moment when the Israeli prime minister would deliver his speech, submitting to the ultimatum.

Bob Walters had won, but there was no joy in this triumph. Nothing would ever be the same again. Scores of Jews in key positions would be forced to give up their jobs, and less qualified people would take their places. The social fabric had changed. Order had begun to be restored to the streets of the United States. The firm treatment doled out to rioters on both sides had markedly decreased the incidence of violence. It would take more time before the present wave was fully over, but nothing would ever be the way it had been before. The world had changed forever.

The president was glad that at least the Israelis were not trying to commit suicide. Though it was still too soon to know exactly what the prime minister would say in his speech, the essence was clear. They could not go to war. They were ready to submit unconditionally.

News channels across the globe had been following developments closely. Every single station was ready to air the Israeli prime minister's speech. Even the Arabic-language Al Jazeera would be broadcasting the speech live. In the meantime, the news commentators were debating the exact nature of Israel's reply.

Walters wasn't overly excited when the CNN commentator declared that the president had won this battle with a "knock-out punch." He did not feel like a victor. The road was still very long before justice was done.

The countdown continued. At exactly midnight, the prime minister's face appeared on screen. The president was surprised by the changes he saw in his Israeli colleague. He could have sworn that when the two leaders had met two weeks earlier, the prime minister's hair was much darker. Streaks of white had suddenly appeared, giving him a much older appearance.

But the prime minister did not look defeated. On the contrary: he stared confidently into the camera. Bob shivered. The man had courage. He would not have wanted to meet him on the battlefield.

"Citizens of the State of Israel," the prime minister began. "As citizens of the Jewish state, you know what it means to be accused of crimes that you never committed. The Jewish people have always served as a scapegoat for various ludicrous claims. Starting with the Black Death, and ending with war crimes in Gaza.

"As you all know, I am being accused—*we* are being accused—of crimes that do not become our nation. They say we dealt in terror. The same terror that we have suffered from so much ourselves. If it hadn't been so sad, we might have laughed at the absurdity of such a claim. How is it possible that we, who are constantly fighting terror, would encourage it ourselves? It is unthinkable. But our energetic denials have not helped us.

"And this evening, this evening I am forced to stand before you and say that I have no good news for you today. I have no promises for a rosy future. Only a prayer to the Creator of the world to come to our aid…"

50

AMI DRORI SAT ON THE GROUND AND PUT HIS HEAD IN HIS hands. This was a catastrophe on a global scale. How could he have let it happen? This had been the only way to put a halt to the worldwide calamity. And now—Mikhail was dead!

"What time is it?" Yisrael asked urgently.

Ami lifted his head, uncomprehending. What difference did it make? Nothing could stop Israel's submission to the ultimatum.

"I asked what time it is," Yisrael insisted.

Ami lifted his hand and replied, "It's 11:01. A minute after midnight in Israel."

"Do you see that?" Yisrael indicated a spot on the far side of the tracks. Ami followed the pointing finger with his eyes, and was surprised to see a camera mounted on a pillar. He leaped to his feet. "What is that?" he cried.

"That camera transmits a live feed every ten minutes," Yisrael explained. "Now it will start transmitting what happened here up until a minute ago."

Ami needed no further explanations. He pulled a device from his pocket and pressed a button. Ami Drori was more excited than he'd ever been. "Give me the director," he yelled into the device. "Immediately."

A second passed, and then Ami shouted again. "Sir, I'm standing at a railway track in the center of Zurich—not far from the main train station. You have to find a camera that transmits from here. You have to use it to break into the prime minister's speech!"

Ami listened again. 'Yes, exactly! That's the place! Now you have to interrupt the broadcast... Don't ask me that now! Just trust me! This is the proof you wanted. And don't forget to make a copy. You know that I'm serious."

He listened another second and then ended the conversation. "Good. I'll get back to you in ten minutes."

Police sirens began to shatter the silence somewhere in the distance. Ami moved among the sprawled bodies, collecting evidence. "Come on," he told Yisrael. "We've got to get out of here."

Yisrael tried to put his weight on his injured foot, but it refused to obey him. The swollen ankle had reached worrisome proportions. Ami checked the injury and said, "This isn't too bad. Within a week or two it'll be just like new."

Before Yisrael could realize what was happening, Ami lifted him up and threw him over his shoulder. The man's strength was amazing. Hastily, Ami left the place as the sirens came closer and closer.

They walked for two minutes, until they reached the road where a familiar sports car was parked.

Yisrael understood. "You're the one who ran over the Russian," he said. But there were a great many more explanations that he still wanted.

Ami placed him gently into the passenger seat, then got into the car and drove. He looked very thoughtful.

"That idea about the camera was brilliant," he told Yisrael.

Yisrael didn't answer. He had heard enough about brilliant ideas for one night. In truth, it was only when he'd reached the train tracks that he'd recalled the cameras that Shmulie Kahan had showed him around the time that they were learning *Hilchos Shabbos* in yeshivah. It felt as if that had happened many years earlier. Hard to believe less than a year had actually passed since then.

He remembered how Shmulie had insisted that they walk all the
way out there to see the cameras he'd spoken about, even though
Yisrael hadn't wanted to go... It had all been prepared from Above.
Unbelievable that the Russian had stopped him right there. Without
that, they'd be left without a shred of proof.

"Let's turn on the news," Ami said. He was being careful not to
drive above the legal speed limit. "Let's hear what our prime minister has to say."

Alex Kotorov was watching the Israeli prime minister's speech
in the company of his friend, Vladimir Solosenko. This was their
finest hour. Both of them despised Jews in general, and the Israeli
prime minister in particular.

Developments in the Middle East were playing out in their favor.
The world's attention had been diverted from Iran to Israel. Arab
oil was flowing copiously to Russia, and Russian arms were making the return journey. Everyone was happy.

They filled their goblets with excellent wine as the prime minister's image appeared on the screen in front of them. Their intelligence bureau had guaranteed an Israeli submission. All that was
left now was to look after Russia's interests in all of this.

The Israeli prime minister's words were simultaneously translated into Russian for those listeners who did not speak Hebrew.
Alex and Vladimir laughed when the prime minister's question
was translated: *"How is it possible that we, who are constantly fighting terror, would encourage it ourselves? It is unthinkable."*

"That's the way it goes, my friend," Vladimir told the image on
the screen with a broad smile. "Our world is not always fair..."

The broadcast continued undisturbed, and the words of the
Israeli prime minister continued in translation: *"This evening I am
forced to stand before you and say that I have no good news for you
today. I have no promises for a rosy future. Only a prayer to the
Creator of the world to come to our aid..."*

"Hey! What's that?"

Alex shot up in a panic. The image of the prime minister had suddenly become blurred, and another familiar face appeared on the screen in his stead. Though it was dark all around and the picture had been filmed at a distance, it was still possible to clearly make out the features of Mikhail Potgorsky.

"Hey!" Vladimir was on his feet too. "Isn't that your Jewish friend? I thought we had him in custody?"

"Sssh..." Alex was very pale. What was Mikhail doing there? They'd agreed that Mikhail would remain in hiding until he'd had plastic surgery to alter his looks. How had he suddenly ended up in Israel?

The video feed began exactly as Mikhail was talking about him: *"How am I connected?" Mikhail laughed.* He was talking to someone who looked beaten down and in pain. *"I am the only one who is connected! No one else... Let me explain what I mean. Have you ever heard of President Kotorov?"*

"The president of Russia?"

"Yes. Good. Alex Kotorov thinks of me as a brother. We've known each other nearly all of our lives. But what he does not know is that it was all part of my plan. All of it!"

Alex turned even paler. His friend had betrayed him. This was going to be painful.

"Mr. President," Vladimir Solosenko faced him squarely. "Are you a part of this?"

"Quiet!" Alex ordered. "I have to hear what he says."

Mikhail appeared to be amused at something again. *"I am as much a Jew as you are an African. Don't you get it? It was all part of the plan!"*

"You decided to become a Jew so that no one would suspect you?"

"Nice! That's the Jewish head everyone talks about... Congratulations! But it is a lot more complicated than that, my friend. Don't you see? I studied the history of your people better than anyone else. There is no Jew in the world who knows Jewish history as I do. And you know what I discovered? That it is really not easy to get rid of you people. You are like leeches. You attach yourselves to a body and refuse to let go. That is what you did to Pharaoh, and to Haman the Agagite, and that is what you did to Hitler. Each of them tried to destroy you, each in his own way, and in

the end you always survive. Exactly like a cancer. I decided to be cleverer. Dozens of years of research went into my plan. The first plan in history that is bound to succeed."

Vladimir had found the opportunity he'd been waiting for. "Mr. President, you were working with that criminal? You planned this together? We're going to talk about this, you and I."

He stormed out of the room. He must act quickly now. He must turn this situation to his advantage. He picked up a phone and reached his closest confidant. "Are you recording this? I need you to record it and figure out what's going on—as quickly as you can. I think we've got Alex around the neck. He's gotten himself into something serious."

Alex Kotorov did not even notice Vladimir's departure. He stood mesmerized before the screen, where his lifelong friend was busy laying out his endless plots.

"And that is just what I did!" Mikhail continued explaining to the shadowy figure. *"Understand? Alex Kotorov got a good brainwashing from me. He believes that the Jews really want to dominate the world. That fool would never have made it to the presidency without me. I raised him up with my own two hands—and, in exchange, he gave me a free hand to act. I gave the Iranians a nuclear weapon, knowing full well that their president would not be able to resist the temptation. I had no doubt that he would send it straight to America. I can read that ape like an open book. Then all I had to do was tie in the Jews.*

"What did I do? I made sure there was plenty of worldwide Jewish pressure on America over Iran. There is your motive. Then I made sure to plant incriminating material on my Jewish friends' computers…and the rest is history. It worked like a dream. The Jews have been implicated in terrorist activity, and they're going to pay through the nose."

The telephone in his office rang. Without thinking, Alex picked up the receiver. He was still listening to Mikhail, who had just been revealed as the greatest traitor in history. Alex's wife was on the line.

"You have to stop this!" she screamed. "He's going to drag you down. I always told you that he'd get you in trouble."

Alex hung up without a word. It was too late. There was nothing he could do to stop this. He stood and watched the full video of Mikhail's gloating rant. And then, for the first time in many years, he gave free reign to his emotions.

Alex Kotorov sat in his office and cried like a little boy. A boy who has just found out that his best friend in the world has betrayed him.

51

THE ISRAELI PRIME MINISTER WAS AS SURPRISED AS EVERY-
one else. Three minutes after he launched his speech, the cameraman cut him off. "Someone has taken over the air waves. We've
stopped broadcasting your speech. They're showing something else."

The prime minister watched Mikhail Potgorsky along with the
rest of the world. "Who's airing that?" he demanded. His personal
phone rang, and he received a quick explanation for what had
occurred.

"Where did you get that from?" he asked the caller excitedly.
He didn't believe in miracles—but he'd never seen a miracle like
this in his life. Mikhail's video was detailed and to the point. As he
outlined his plans, he incidentally cleared the names of the other
suspects.

The next call came from the president of the United States himself. Bob Walters had hastened to call and let him know that he was
canceling the ultimatum "until further notice." The prime minister
thanked him warmly and promised his full cooperation.

"We'll have to study the new material before we make final decisions," the president concluded. He had to carefully analyze all the

recent events. The confusion that had been sowed for him and his intelligence people frightened him.

Throngs of excited Israelis poured into the streets. The insane tension of the past few days dissipated in an instant. The media networks hurriedly reported the removal of the ultimatum, and the joy in the street knew no bounds. People hugged one another with emotion. Strangers shook hands, and the Kosel plaza filled spontaneously with thousands of worshipers who'd come to say thank you. No one would sleep that night.

The prime minister had his hands full. He quickly put together a committee to draw up a letter of understanding to be given to the coalition forces present inside the borders of Israel. He sent a strongly worded message to the United States and its allies demanding that they remove their aircraft carriers from Israeli waters. He made a similar demand regarding the warships, and insisted that the soldiers stationed in neighboring countries retreat.

Israel's military readiness would remain on full alert in the coming days, until the last of the coalition forces left the region. Though the immediate danger seemed to have passed, missiles could still be aimed at Israel from Gaza or Lebanon. Missiles of frustration over this latest development.

And there was something else he needed to do. Although it was something that would be difficult to accomplish, nevertheless he had to try. If it were up to him, he would have focused the entire military buildup in the region against Iran. He'd sent a formal request to the United States, but knew that the answer would come back negative. For some reason, when it came to Iran the world was slow to react.

But everything in its own good time. Dealing with Iran would have to wait a bit. Right now he had to tend to the aftereffects of recent events. The media had already labeled them, "The Protocols of America." Of America, Russia, and the rest of the world. The anti-Semitic outbursts in cities across the globe had surprised many. They had exposed a racism assumed to belong to an older world. Just when it seemed to have become extinct, it had shown itself to be alive and well, stirring beneath the surface.

He had once heard this fact from Mikhail himself. It had been just a few years before, when they had met in Washington. The Russian had outlined his theory of anti-Semitism to him then: "Every nation needs to have a feeling of superiority. Even the most advanced generation needs to feel that it is special. This feeling is achieved through trampling on a power inferior to it—in most cases, the Jews."

The man had known what he was talking about. You could say a lot of things about Mikhail, but it was impossible to say that he was stupid. He was the smartest man the prime minister had ever met. A true genius. And now, a dead genius.

The recent riots in Europe had led to a huge wave of *aliyah*. While the situation was so dangerous, thousands of Jews had taken advantage of the Law of Return. Now that the threat had been removed, the prime minister expected another wave. Many Jews who had learned firsthand about their neighbors' hatred for them would decide to leave their countries and move to Eretz Yisrael. And the government of Israel had to be ready to absorb them all.

For the first time all evening, the prime minister smiled. If all his problems were like these, he'd be one happy man.

52

AMI HUNG UP HIS PHONE AND SMILED AT YISRAEL. "THIS IS the first time in my life that I ever heard him laugh."

"Who?" Yisrael asked. "And how did he manage to get Mikhail onto the news?"

"Don't ask such hard questions," Ami said humorously. "Let's just say that a lot of people owe that man their lives. He's one of the best intelligence heads in the world."

"So what does this mean? What's happening in Israel right now?"

"What's happening is that you're going to be very famous, my friend. I imagine that the prime minister will want to meet you, and the president—and every media personality in the world. Your story is worth millions."

"Are you telling me that this thing was broadcast live all over the world?"

"Exactly. Because of you, the threat was removed from the State of Israel."

"But I don't understand one thing. How did you know to come

to the train tracks? How were you able to get here just in time to save me? Were you following me?"

"You'll be surprised to hear it, but this isn't the first time we've met."

"I don't understand." Yisrael couldn't recall ever seeing Ami before.

"Well, remember your visit to Mikhail's home in Washington? When he suspected you of being a spy?"

"Of course. But how do *you* know about that?"

"I was inside the house. I was standing just meters away from you. By the way, I can beg your pardon now for getting you in trouble…"

"*You*? You're the one who hacked into the computer? How come I didn't see you? I was in the room the whole time!"

"That's my specialty," Ami smiled. "The truth is, I thought I'd failed then. But it turns out that that's what finally brought about a good ending."

"Can you please explain what you're talking about?"

"No problem." Ami guided the vehicle toward a gigantic hangar. "But first, we've got to catch a flight home." He honked twice and the big gate opened.

"We're at the airport," he said. "Now I have to ask you a favor."

"Whatever you want."

"Good. The plane that's waiting for us is a new medical transport belonging to a private airline. A doctor and a nurse are waiting for us on it. Officially, you were injured in a traffic accident and we're flying you to Israel to continue treatment. Though the doctor and nurse know the truth, we'll have to officially carry you aboard on a stretcher. Let's see how well you can act. Try to look as if you've been injured."

Yisrael grinned. "What do you mean, 'as if'? My ankle is really hurting."

The boarding took place without any problem and a short time later they were in the air. The doctor and nurse sat on the far side of the plane, ignoring the passengers. Yisrael demanded Ami's promised explanation.

Ami leaned back comfortably in his seat. "This is the way to fly." At that moment, he reminded Yisrael of Jeffrey. He wondered where his uncle was now…

"So, it's like this," Ami said. "I began to shadow Mikhail a few months ago. We had information that something was happening in Russia, but we had no idea what it was.

"My first clue was when an Iranian scientist was snatched by the Russians. That was strange. Why would the Russians want to kidnap him? If anyone had an interest in that, it would be the Israelis or the Americans. Why would Russia want to harm a scientist from Iran? Sure enough, his bullet-riddled body was found in a pond a few days later.

"The interesting thing is that just hours after the kidnaping, a senior Russian general had paid a visit to the president of Iran. At the time, we thought he was trying to get something out of the Iranian, but we didn't know what. Luckily for us, the general made his first mistake. When he left the president's office, he made a phone call to someone high up in Russian circles. You can guess who."

"Mikhail?"

"Yes. But it was very odd. According to our information, Mikhail had lost his influence in the Kremlin. We, along with the rest of the world, believed that Mikhail had been sent to America in order to keep him away from Russia. So why was he involved in important decisions in Iran? That was Mikhail's mistake. The first clue.

"From that point, I began digging into him, and a few other question marks popped up. But there was nothing incriminating. The man was pure as driven snow. Even the increased security around his home was justified. After all, he presumably had enemies in Russia.

"The evening you visited him, I'd managed to penetrate the house through a breach in the security system. I saw you looking at some pictures on the wall. You were very absorbed."

Yisrael smiled in confusion. He didn't think such a thing was possible—for someone to have passed that close to him without his noticing a thing.

"Anyway, I entered the adjoining room and turned on the computer. The problem was that your friends ended their conversation at that exact moment. I was forced to leave the room in a hurry. You have no idea how angry I was at myself. I hadn't even had a chance to erase the evidence of my presence. An amateurish job... But it ended up being useful. From Mikhail's furious reaction, I learned that he was definitely hiding something.

"Unfortunately, I had no time to do anything about it. The minute you and your friends left the house, Mikhail turned on the computer and conducted a quick search. He discovered that no material was missing, and quickly erased something from the computer. He was a real professional. He knew how to erase data with no possibility of restoring it. A minute later, FBI agents burst into the place and I had to disappear. I thought then that I'd lost my only chance.

"And then, suddenly, two days ago, word reached me that Mikhail was in Switzerland. I was stunned. This was the proof I'd been looking for. If Mikhail was not locked up in a Russian prison, then he *had* to be involved. I flew here as fast as I could—and this evening, the circle closed. It turned out that his suspicion that you'd hacked into his computer had caused him to do the only stupid thing he'd ever done in his life. Had he stayed in Russia, nothing would have come to light. But he was a perfectionist, and you were a question mark for him.

"He didn't know what your part was in the story—where you'd come from, and what you'd managed to find on his computer. Therefore, he decided to come here personally and make sure you were taken out of the picture. To be sure that there was no dangling thread leading back to him. The rest, you already know."

Yisrael leaned back in his seat. It was a shocking story. A story in which he, through no desire of his own, had become a central player.

He spent the rest of the flight in a brooding silence. His life had been in real danger, and he had been saved. He had nearly been the one who had ended up lying on the ground by the tracks, instead of Mikhail. The thought was chilling. But what he needed to do now was to figure out when he had behaved appropriately and when he hadn't. He had to learn to improve his behavior—because who, more than he, knew how suddenly life could come to an end?

Yisrael reached a clear resolve: When all of this was over, he would return to his learning with renewed fervor. Jeffrey could propose whatever he wanted—money, fame, or even basketball—but he was going back to yeshivah. With money or without it, that was what he was going to do.

In the meantime, Ami was busy. A special phone on the plane allowed him to arrange everything. The prime minister wanted to meet Yisrael in person, and Ami could not refuse.

It was 5:30 a.m. when they landed on a remote airstrip at Ben Gurion Airport. The sun had begun to lighten the sky in the east as Yisrael walked across the hot asphalt on shaky legs. The doctor had bandaged his injured ankle on the plane, and Yisrael was now able to walk on that foot. It still hurt, but the doctor had promised that that would pass.

An official car waited for them near the plane. Ami helped Yisrael climb in.

"I have a surprise for you in the terminal," he said with a conspiratorial wink. Yisrael knew enough not to ask what the secret was. Ami would never tell him.

They reached the central terminal, where a waiting guard opened the car door for Yisrael. Ami got out after him and motioned for him to follow the guard.

They reached a security door. The guard grasped the knob and opened it wide.

Yisrael walked inside—and was instantly blinded by the flashing of camera bulbs. Dozens of journalists and the merely curious stood in a room behind a red ribbon, pointing at him in excitement.

"That's him!" someone shouted, and the entire crowd burst into applause.

Yisrael stood still in confusion. He didn't know what to do. Suddenly, he heard a familiar voice. "Yisrael!"

He looked swiftly around, and saw his mother running toward him, Bracha and Tamar, his sisters, racing along with her. A second later he was engulfed in hugs. Tears began pouring from his eyes.

The applause grew louder, and many of those present wiped away tears of emotion as well.

The four of them stood that way for a long moment, until a sudden silence fell over the crowd.

Wiping his eyes, Yisrael looked up to see what had happened. A door opened on the far side of the room. Then, flanked by two guards, came the famous figure of the prime minister. He strode across to Yisrael with a hand outstretched, and shook the boy's hand warmly. Cameras clicked vigorously as Yisrael tried to smile through his tears.

"I've heard a great deal about you," the prime minister told Yisrael, though his words were actually directed at the throng of reporters. "Millions of Jews owe you their thanks for the courage you showed—and I am among them."

Yisrael had never felt so uncomfortable in his life. He was naturally shy, and this glare of publicity was not at all to his liking. He turned bright red and tried to retreat a step. "It's not me you should be grateful to," he told the prime minister. "It's Hashem. I didn't do a thing."

The prime minister smiled. "And he's modest, on top of everything else," he told the crowd with a laugh. "A boy after my own heart. I invite you all to continue the celebration at the Knesset in Jerusalem. Additional events will take place throughout the country. And you, my friend"—he turned to Yisrael—"will be my personal guest."

Yisrael didn't answer. He was too busy trying to find Ami in the merry throng. The guard by the door came over and handed him a familiar-looking suitcase. "The man you came with asked me to give this to you."

Yisrael smiled. It was impossible. But in his short acquaintance with Ami, he'd learned that anything can be possible. The mystery man was probably already on his next mission. Risking his life again to protect the ordinary citizens of his country. But who knew? Maybe one day they'd meet again. And then Ami might agree to tell him how on earth he'd managed to get Yisrael's suitcase, which had been left behind in Switzerland.

Deep inside, though, Yisrael knew that this had been their last meeting. Ami had returned to the shadows where he operated, leaving the spotlight to someone else. Someone who had actually been a full partner in the successful outcome. Only, Yisrael had no desire for this kind of fame. He just wanted to go home and be with his mother and sisters. How worried he had been about them! Another resolution he had made on the plane had been to do everything in his power to help them. He wanted them to have no more worries. After all, he was the only man in the family now.

He would happily have given the prime minister's party a miss. He was thinking about asking the prime minister if that were possible, when the man was handed a phone by one of his men. He listened for a minute, smiled, and walked back to Yisrael. "There's someone here who wants to speak to you."

Curious, Yisrael put the phone to his ear. Who could it be?

From the other end of the line came a broken voice. Jeffrey Davis. "Yisrael? Is that you?"

"Yes," Yisrael replied emotionally. It sounded as though his uncle had been through a rough time. In his voice there was no trace of the arrogance that had once typified him.

Jeffrey was crying like a child. "I just wanted to tell you one thing... I'm sorry...so sorry...for what I did to your father. And... thank you. Thank you for saving my life. I owe you."

Yisrael struggled to keep his voice steady. He didn't want the spectators to see him cry again.

"That's all right, Uncle Jeffrey," he said, trying to smile. "I'm sure that Tatty forgives you. And you don't owe me a thing. After all, that's what family is for."